"FAST-PACED . . .

Gracefully written . . . [with] one of the most believable journalist-protagonists in American fiction . . . Brinkley mixes fact and fiction creatively and convincingly."

Kansas City Star

"Joel Brinkley's first novel, THE CIRCUS MASTER'S MISSION, is a wow! The novel is as current as tomorrow."

The Richmond News Leader

"Fast moving . . . The climactic confrontation between Nicaragua and the United States is exciting, plausible reading."

San Antonio Express News

"Brinkley has written the best kind of thriller: a cautionary tale that rings so true readers start to wonder whether it might be so."

The Patriot Ledger (Quincy, MA)

"IMPRESSIVE."
The Kirkus Reviews

"THE CIRCUS MASTER'S MISSION takes readers from the inner sanctums of Washington politics to the jungles of the Nicaraguan mountains."
Erie Times-News

"Brinkley brings to his first novel an admirable eye for crystalline detail and a keen ear for a journalist's persistence. . . . Brinkley whips up a plot that is fleshed out by characters similar to personalities very much in the news. . . . Readers of political fiction will hope Brinkley can produce more of this caliber and soon."
Library Journal

"Posits, with convincing attention to detail, circumstances that could lead to full-fledged combat with Nicaragua . . . What gives his story its edge is insight into the workings of government—the squabbles, the denials, the carefully planned leaks—that can't be faked."
Publishers Weekly

The Circus Master's Mission

Joel Brinkley

FAWCETT CREST • NEW YORK

A Fawcett Crest Book
Published by Ballantine Books
Copyright © 1989 by Joel Brinkley
Map copyright © 1989 by Anita Karl and Jim Kemp

Library of Congress Catalog Card Number: 88-43367

ISBN 0-449-21906-2

This edition published by arrangement with Random House, Inc.

Manufactured in the United States of America

First Ballantine Books Edition: November 1990

For my mother,
whose courage has been an example to us all

This is a work of fiction. With the obvious exception of a few world leaders and historical figures mentioned by name, none of the characters in this narrative are based on any real persons, living or dead. However, the characters carry out their fictional actions in the political and social environment of the real world. Historical references are in all cases accurate. Except in a few cases where license is taken, the United States government functions in this novel just as it does in real life. In addition, descriptions of notable government actions that have never occurred are based on actual proposals or contingency plans.

"We want to talk to the circus masters, not to the clowns."

Sandinista leader Daniel Ortega Saavedra, dismissing an
American proposal for direct negotiations with the contras

N
BELIZE
GUATEMALA
EL SALVADOR
Palmerola
Air Force
Base
Comayagu
TEGUCIGALPA
Cholute
Cholute
Gap
Radar Facility
Tank Traps
Inter-American Highway
UNITED STATES
MEXICO
CUBA
Area of Map
Pacific
Ocean
Kms.
0
75
0
Miles

CHAPTER ONE

MANAGUA, NICARAGUA, AUGUST 6

SLIPPING INTO MANAGUA WITHOUT BEING NOTICED wasn't easy for Major Paz. First there was the matter of appearance. Nicaragua didn't have many orange-haired mulattoes.

Paz grew up on the Caribbean Coast, where most of the people are descendants of Indians or slaves. His mother was black. But Paz's paternal grandfather, he liked to brag, had been a United States Marine, part of the occupation force in the 1930s, and Paz's every feature seemed to be a fighting compromise between the two. He was so light-skinned he could almost pass for white, except that his face was covered with large freckles that were almost brown splotches. He had a short-cropped Afro, but it was the color of teakwood. His eyes—well, who could tell what was under those Ray Ban aviator sunglasses he always wore. Before the revolution they were standard uniform for National Guard officers. But Major Paz still wore them with pride.

All of that made sneaking into town difficult enough. But appearance wasn't the biggest problem. Major Paz was notorious. Until the revolution he'd been in the Guardia's Office of National Security, one of General Somoza's storm troopers. The OSN had been charged with rounding up suspected Sandinista sympathizers, pulling them screaming from their homes in the middle of the night. That had been Major Paz's job. Then, in the revolution's final days, the OSN tortured them to death. Electric shock. Progressive amputation. Water hoses up the ass. That had been Paz's job too, and from it he had earned his Guardia nom de guerre. *Paz*, or peace. The eternal kind.

Now, more than a decade later, the name seemed just as appropriate. If he had a first name, nobody knew it. To his fellow contras he was just Paz.

The Sandinistas knew that name quite well. Even now Paz was on the government's list of most-wanted enemies of the state. If he was caught, the comandantes would probably execute him, even though in theory capital punishment was no longer allowed. But that was the least of his problems. Managua was teeming with relatives of the OSN's victims, and few of them had forgotten the mulatto major. So if Paz was noticed, he probably wouldn't survive long enough to face arrest.

Paz had no trouble getting from his camp in Honduras down through Jinotega province to Matagalpa. This was rugged, mountainous terrain, difficult to patrol, impossible to secure. Long ago the Sandinistas had ceded it to the contras. Just outside the little town of Esquipulas, he stood waiting at the rendezvous point for his ride to Managua. To Paz the oppressive hundred-degree August heat felt like a warm, welcoming embrace from his homeland. When the impossibly high humidity turned to a thunderous rain, Paz, standing at attention behind a tree, turned his wet face up to the sky.

Just before midnight a battered Toyota pickup screeched to a stop, and without a word or signal to the driver Paz crawled into the bed, under the tarp, and lay on top of some coffee-bean sacks. The city was only two hours away. The major carried a small canvas kit bag holding his favorite AR-15 automatic rifle, disassembled—it was the civilian equivalent of an M-16—along with his proud new possession: a U.S. Army–issue Beretta pistol, the 9-millimeter automatic handgun that had replaced the Colt .45 a few years ago. Many American soldiers and veterans still refused to accept the Italian-designed pistol. But as soon as the Army adopted it, Paz had ordered one and given his Colt away.

Lying under the tarp, he slipped the Beretta out of his bag, rubbed the barrel, and sniffed at the grease. Then he patted the bayonet knife strapped to his leg. One of his men was bringing the explosives. For this mission, that's all they would need.

Paz's driver, an old farmer with a son in the force, didn't intend to stop on the bumpy ride into town, and at first it seemed as if the trip might pass without incident. Sandinista checkpoints usually weren't manned at night. But just outside Tipitapa, on the shores of Lake Managua, the pickup pulled to a stop six feet short of the metal strip of tire-killer spikes that soldiers had laid across the road to make a checkpoint.

"Out, old man," Paz heard a soldier snarl. "What are you doing on the road at this hour?"

"Coffee beans, taking in my coffee," the old man answered, but Paz was sure his faltering voice would give everything away.

"Coffee, old man? You sure? Maybe you have contraband back there? Maybe something good you'd like to share? Huh? Let us see."

As he heard them moving back toward him, Paz was already unsheathing his knife and releasing the safety on his Beretta. It sounded like just two soldiers, but he couldn't be sure.

"Let us see, let us see," the same voice said. Paz squeezed down between two fat coffee sacks, poised, muscles tensed, pistol pointed toward the voices. The tarp was fastened down with snaps; they could tear it off in one stroke.

The town probably wasn't far off, and he didn't want to have to shoot. If these were just two soldiers caught by surprise, maybe he could kill them with his knife. But just then something ripped through the canvas right beside his ear and slammed into a coffee sack. Paz pushed away as far as he could, pressing against the other bag. A rifle bayonet had torn into the bag; even in the dark Paz knew what it was. The soldier pulled it along, cutting a bigger opening, inches from Paz's face.

The soldier pulled the bayonet out and in an instant Paz saw a hand thrust through the opening. It was so close he could have bit it. The soldier grabbed some coffee beans and pulled his hand out.

"Coffee," he spat. "Just coffee." Paz heard the beans scattering across the road.

"Get out of here, old man."

"Yes, yes" was all the driver said as he leapt back into his truck and started off with a jolt.

The tension eased, and after a while Paz could tell he was in the city. In the quiet of early morning, engine noises bounced off buildings crowding the street. And a few minutes later the fetid odors of overused cooking oil, bad meat, congealed blood, and human waste told him he was in the barrio, Ciudad Sandino.

As soon as the truck stopped, the driver's door opened quietly, and the old man lifted the tarp just enough to point Paz toward a tar-paper shack a few feet away. Paz peered through his Ray

Bans at the dirt street and cardboard shacks. It was after two
A.M. and the place was dead quiet, so he leapt from the truck
and without looking back at the driver hurried through the door.

Inside, María Artolía, cowering, stared at Paz as he moved
into the room. She was young, maybe twenty-two, married to
the comandante of another contra unit, and she stayed in Managua partly to provide occasional intelligence. Still, she was frozen, like a fawn ready to bolt, at the sight of Major Paz. Looking
at her short, full figure, large brown eyes, and moist, dark lips,
he was aroused. But he had no time for that.

He barked only one word—"Food!"—and she raced over to
light the little butane stove. Paz whipped the bayonet knife out
of his leg sheath, and wielding it threateningly, he quickly in-
spected her three-room shack.

The front room was a black-market store of sorts. A few light
bulbs, some two-liter jars of cooking oil, even some half-rolls of
toilet paper, were arranged on rough pine shelves along one wall.
The Sandinistas tolerated the black market, though theoretically
it was illegal. Shortages were so severe that they had no choice,
unless they wanted their people to starve.

Behind the main chamber was María's room and another tiny
bedroom, where two children, a boy and girl, probably two and
three years old, slept on a foam mat. Paz lifted their mattress
with his toe, spilling the babies on top of each other, and then
let the pad drop again. They whimpered briefly but quickly settled back to sleep.

In María's room he opened drawers, picking blouses and un-
derclothing out with the point of his knife and dropping them
to the floor. Then he pulled the few pieces of stick furniture away
from the wall and looked behind them. Back in the main room
he pointed to her room with his knife and declared, "I will stay
there." She nodded without turning around, and continued frantically stirring a small pot of beans. It was only for twenty-four
hours. Then Paz returned to her room, laid his knife and pistol,
cocked, on the table behind the door, and sat cross-legged on
the bed. Right away he started assembling his automatic rifle,
inspecting each piece with extra care before laying the oily parts
on her sheets.

Major Paz was not a politician. He was a soldier, always had
been, proud to follow every order without question or thought.
But even he knew how important this operation was to the strug-
gle.

The Communists had been in Managua more than a dozen years now, and every day their army grew stronger. Every day the contras' task grew larger. But if this mission succeeded, the fight would rise to a new level. Paz was determined to make the Americans know they had been right to pick him, even though some on the contra Directorate had wanted to send their own man, Comandante Venganza.

Major Paz had got the job because he had a benefactor: Rafael Mendoza, the one man not even the Directorate could ignore. Mendoza was the Central Intelligence Agency's station chief in Honduras. He was also senior control officer for the contras, and soon after coming to Honduras early this year he had picked Paz and the Pena de Muerte commandos as his own personal squad. When Rafael Mendoza had a special mission, it went to Major Paz and his men.

Paz knew why he'd been picked. He was one-quarter American, after all. One-quarter United States Marine—a living symbol of America's strong commitment to Nicaragua, he liked to think.

Paz's grandfather, a Marine corporal, first came to Nicaragua in 1925, part of an occupation force sent initially to quell civil disturbances. But a year later Secretary of State Frank Kellogg warned the U.S. Senate that "Soviet bolshevism" was creeping down from revolutionary Mexico and threatened to sweep through the region. So the Marines should stay to protect Nicaragua from communism.

They did stay, until a Nicaraguan general, Augusto Sandino, organized a guerrilla force that so harassed the Marines, killing a few of them, that they were withdrawn, finally, in 1933. By then Paz's grandfather had impregnated an Indian woman who'd been hanging around camp.

Before the Marines left, they created and trained the National Guard, the military/police force that Paz would later join. The Americans named a loyal general, Anastasio Somoza García, as the Guardia's commander, and as one of his first acts he ordered the assassination of General Sandino. What Somoza didn't know was that he had created a martyr who could come back to plague his progeny—and the United States.

With the Guardia behind them, the Somoza family grabbed control of Nicaragua and ruled it with a heavy, greedy hand for forty-six years, all the while remaining ever loyal to the American government, their protector and provider. Three different Somozas held on to power until the Sandinista rebels, who took their name from General Sandino, threw out the last of them, General Anastasio Somoza Debayle.

Toward the end, Somoza had taken a liking to Paz—the major had handled some of the general's dirtiest jobs. And in 1979 General Somoza had promised to call a few people in Washington, pull a few strings, so Paz could attend Marine officers' general staff training school at Camp Lejeune, North Carolina. Somoza, after all, was a West Point graduate. Paz had been convinced that once he was with the Marines, the Americans would let him stay. It's where he knew he belonged.

That had been Paz's dream, but the Sandinista Communists had taken it away from him; 1979 was the year they drove Somoza into exile. So instead of going to Camp Lejeune, Paz, like many of his Guardia compadres, moved to Honduras and became a contra—paid and equipped by the United States, once again, to fight the Communists.

Even today, Paz kept a 1979 pocket calendar in his wallet. On the back was a color picture of General Somoza in full uniform, five stars on each shoulder, a chrome-plated steel-pot helmet cradled under his arm.

And now Paz was back in Managua for the first time since the revolution, on one of the most important missions of the war. Some of the other contras had returned home for a while, under the temporary amnesty programs that had come with one or another of the failed peace plans over the last few years. But not Paz; he knew there could be no absolution for him.

There weren't any peace plans in the works now. In fact, every month the Sandinistas seemed to grow more belligerent. Last month some of their thugs had beat up the archbishop. That had been in all the papers. And in a few weeks, the United States Congress was due to vote one more time on whether aid for the contras would be renewed. It was vote number fourteen, and this time there seemed little doubt that the contras would get more money. Still, as before every past vote, Washington and the Directorate wanted to carry out a high-profile operation to impress Congress. But not even the directors knew the extra task Rafael Mendoza had given Paz and his men. If he succeeded, the whole tenor of the war would change.

When the AR-15 was assembled, Paz snapped the bolt in place, and the sound brought a gasp from María in the main room. She was afraid of him, and that was good. In fact, for this mission María and her house were just right. The neighborhood

Sandinista Defense Committee captain was accustomed to seeing people come and go from her black-market store all day long, Paz knew. That was useful for her intelligence mission. It was also good for Paz.

The other Pena de Muerte, or "Death Penalty," commandos were supposed to be slipping into Managua by ones and twos. The nine selected for this mission all had family or friends in neighborhoods and barrios scattered around town. Only Paz had been assigned a place. Other than his men, he had no friends or family, here or anywhere else.

The commandos weren't supposed to go out except at night, to avoid the risk of running into someone who knew them to be contras. But before tomorrow night they were to check in with their platoon leaders, either in person or using friends as messengers. And then one by one the platoon leaders would come by María's place to see Paz. It was all arranged.

Still sitting cross-legged on her bed, Paz ate the bowl of beans María brought him. Then, loaded pistol in hand, he stretched out to sleep. Without a word María curled up with her babies in the other room.

In the morning the barrio was crowded with noise even before the roosters had finished crowing. Paz was up right away. He ripped away a corner of the fluttering plastic sheet that served as a bedroom window and relieved himself through the opening; a hot breeze from outside caressed him. A moment later María brought him a plate of fried banana slices and pork sausage—quite a treat in Managua these days. They spoke not a word, and Paz didn't leave the room.

Very early, jabbering women started coming by. Most wanted cooking oil, heavily rationed by the government. Paz listened to the chatter, trying to stare through the green plastic shower curtain that served as the bedroom door; big-eyed fish swam back and forth in regular rows, bubbles rising from their mouths.

One woman was saying she'd heard the government would be selling dollars today at the currency exchange over by the Intercontinental Hotel. The line at the *casa de cambio*, she said, was already two hundred people long.

A girl who sounded not much over fifteen brought her squawking baby with her. The mother was whimpering too. It sounded like the tail end of a long night of tears. Her husband had just been picked up for the draft.

So it went through the morning. Then just after eleven A.M.— Paz kept checking his green-strapped Army watch—he heard a nervous-sounding young man say to María: "I am looking for a friend of peace." A clumsy code question, Paz thought, and he didn't recognize the voice. He leapt up and, grabbing his knife from the table, pressed himself against the cardboard wall beside the door. He saw María's little hand brush open the green curtain, and in a moment a teenage boy stepped tentatively in. Instantly Paz grabbed him around the chest and laid the knife against his neck, drawing a little blood. In the doorway, María gulped and backed from the room.

"Comandante, Comandante," the boy sputtered. "I come with word from Coyote!" Paz loosened his grip but kept his knife at the boy's throat.

"Proof," Paz demanded, voice hard, and the boy pulled a small paper out of his pants pocket. It was a white sheet with Paz's unreadable signature scrawled at the bottom. He'd given one to each of his platoon leaders, telling them to use only these for sending confirmation messages if they could not come in person.

This message was brief: "All the packages arrived." Coyote had spent a lot of time in Tegucigalpa watching American cable TV. Paz let the boy go, and he darted to the door.

"Wait," Paz commanded, and the boy froze, looking back at Paz, mouth open, one foot already out the door. Paz reached into his pocket and gave the boy a dollar. He broke into a broad smile and bowed his head, saying, *"Gracias, gracias, gracias."*

A little later, Balita came by. "Little bullet" was Paz's youngest platoon leader, not quite twenty years old. He came from León and was Paz's favorite. Among the contras, Balita was a legend—the child-fighter, everybody had called him for years.

He was only seven or eight years old when the revolution came. Both his parents were killed when General Somoza bombed León. Balita's brother, a Guardia officer, fled to Honduras just after the revolution, taking Balita with him. It seemed as if he hadn't been long out of diapers then. But he was wearing a uniform, firing weapons, before he was ten years old.

Balita was uneducated, ingenuous, but intensely loyal, motivated by fear. As a platoon commander he imitated Paz in every way. In battle he was ferocious—mostly, it seemed, because he was afraid of what would happen if he failed. Tiny, easily excited, he certainly did not look the part of a fierce guerrilla leader. But in battle his fear of rebuke turned him into an extraordinary fighter. Under fire, Balita's eyes would dart over at Paz, who would stare back, his expression as usual grim and unreadable.

But Balita would see a rebuke, and he would leap into the battle, shooting and killing.

Paz loved no one, never had since he joined the Guardia when he was fifteen, hoping in the military to escape the ridicule heaped on him since birth because of his unusual appearance. But in his own way he was fond of Balita. He thought of Balita as the son he knew he'd never have. Balita seemed to feel the same way about Paz. The major had even promised to take Balita with him when he finally went to the United States, to Camp Lejeune. They talked about it sometimes, and Balita often fantasized about their secret pact. They would become proud Americans, United States Marines. Paz would be the commander, Balita his lieutenant. That was the boy's life goal.

"Comandante," Balita said now, all nervous energy, shifting his weight from foot to foot as if dancing in place. One hand held the green shower curtain in a tight-fisted grip. "All my squad is here but one. Pitufo has not appeared."

"Maybe he will come yet," Paz said in a soft tone and with a twitch of the mouth that only someone who knew Paz well would recognize as a smile. All the men knew their rendezvous points, so even if Pitufo was unable to check in during the day, he might still appear.

"Now go look after your men," Paz said. His back to Balita, he straightened his bayonet and Beretta on the shelf beside the door, making sure both butts pointed out. Then he sat cross-legged on María's bed mat again. Balita scrambled off.

A little later, Tigrillo sent a messenger carrying the little note Paz had given them. By late afternoon, only El Muerte had failed to check in.

Then at four in the afternoon, as Paz sat immobile on the bed, he heard someone walk into the main room without a word, and María let out a small gasp. Paz crept over to the doorway and around the edge of the shower curtain saw a Sandinista officer in standard olive green Army fatigues, black lace-up boots, and a green "baseball cap." A single cloth bar was sewed to each wrinkled epaulet.

The lieutenant had an AK-47 automatic rifle slung at ease over his shoulder—it was Czech-made, Paz could tell from the shape of the wooden butt—and the officer whispered to María as he handed her a piece of paper. Paz snatched his Beretta from the table, but when he looked back the officer was leaving, a black-market light bulb in his hand.

María hurried into the bedroom and gave Paz the paper, say-

ing, "He said to tell the comandante that he is a friend of El
Muerte." On the paper, one of Paz's signed slips, El Muerte had
written, "All is well. The officer is a friend." But Paz wasn't so
sure. He snapped up his AR-15, shoved a clip into place, and
left the bedroom for the first time since he had arrived. Rifle in
hand, a round in the chamber, he backed against the front door
frame and gave a darting glance outside, looking left and right.
But everything looked normal. Several children kicked a rusty
can up and down in the dirt. Across the street a fat woman held
her nose as she dumped a bowl of dark liquid into the open ditch
that served as the sewer. A rooster strutted past the door. Paz
slipped back into the bedroom but kept his rifle loaded.

Later, at about seven-thirty, dusk was falling and the temperature was beginning to drop. Through the fluttering plastic-sheet
window Paz heard the clanking of pots and pans. After he'd
eaten another bowl of beans, Paz called to María.

"Water," he ordered when she came into the room. "I want
to bathe." She left the house right away and five minutes later
returned with a bowl of water and a cloth. Paz was naked except
for his Ray Bans and sat with his legs still crossed under him,
his arms folded over his chest. María gave a quick embarrassed
look, set down the bowl, and started backing out of the room.

"No," Paz snarled. "You will wash me." María stood for a
minute, not sure what to do. But Paz lifted the dripping cloth
from the bowl and held it out to her, stiff-armed, so she took
it and began to wash his back. She passed the cloth gingerly, as
if his skin were hot to the touch. Paz didn't move except to uncross his arms, holding them straight out in front of him, fists
clenched, as María washed his chest. Neither of them said a
word. Paz sat frozen, his Ray Bans pointed straight ahead, when
reluctantly she bathed his crotch. His tiny penis did not react
in the slightest as she swiped the cloth over it once and then
moved quickly on. With that the worst part over, María was
calmer as she washed his legs.

All of a sudden they both heard the front door open and close.

"María," a man called out softly from the front room. Immediately she dropped the cloth and held a finger to her lips.

"CDS," she whispered, then scurried from the room. CDS—
Sandinista Defense Committee. That meant the visitor was the
party block captain, Interior Minister Zelaya's security enforcer
and informer. Under a system modeled after Cuba's, every urban
block had one; he dispensed ration cards and decided who would

be drafted and who spared, giving him extraordinary power. It was also his job to know everything that went on.

Paz had known all along that the CDS captain would be his greatest danger. He picked up his knife from the table and once again pressed himself flat against the wall beside the door—except this time he was stark naked.

"Ronaldo," María said in the main room, surprise in her voice. "I didn't expect you tonight. What about your meeting?"

"Later. It's later," Ronaldo said. "You know I always have time for you."

Paz peered around the curtain as Ronaldo, a large, smooth-skinned man with slicked-back hair and a threatening grin, glanced around the room. María stood away from him, arms crossed. Over in the corner her babies were playing and giggling together on the dirt floor.

"Looks like you had a good day today," he said, gesturing toward the shelves. "Did you make a lot of money?"

"Yes, Ronaldo. You can have whatever you want." She took the top off a jar and held out a wad of fifty-cordoba bills. Paz recognized the denomination from the bills' purple color, although from fifteen feet away, he couldn't quite make out the etching of Comandante Carlos Fonseca, martyred hero of the revolution, bespectacled, somber, and determined, on the top bill's face. The Guardia had killed Fonseca, though Paz had not been involved. That was one of his great regrets. But with inflation, the fifty-cordoba bill was virtually worthless now. That, Paz thought, is justice.

"No, María, you know I do not want your money," Ronaldo was saying as he gripped her wrist with one hand and the wad of bills with the other. He took the money and put it back in the jar, then wrapped his arms around her.

"No, no," she whimpered. "Please, Ronaldo, no. Not tonight." But he smiled, undeterred, and pulled her to him, his white *guayabera* pressing against her breasts. María's hands were tight fists on his shoulders as he drew her close for a long kiss.

"Please, no," she sputtered.

"Come, María, we haven't much time," Ronaldo said, arms still wrapped around her as he pushed her along in front of him toward the bedroom. When María's back brushed against the curtain, Paz tensed, his knife poised directly in front of his nose, the tip almost touching his orange Afro.

"No!" María insisted, her voice firm as she pulled away at last and moved to the other side of the room.

"Why not?" he asked. "What is wrong?" Ronaldo sounded more baffled than angry.

"It is not the time. I am unclean."

"María, you know I do not care about that."

"But I care. It's not right. I won't."

Ronaldo didn't say anything, and María opened the front door. He looked at her, pensive for a moment, and started for the door. Paz relaxed a bit. But then, all determination, Ronaldo slammed the door, seized María's wrist, and started pulling her to the bedroom.

"If you are unclean down there," he said, his voice hard now, "then there are other things we can do. I let you run your little market without any trouble. I give you extra ration cards so you have things to sell. I don't ask much in return."

María struggled, but Ronaldo overpowered her with little difficulty and even started unbuttoning his shirt. He pushed the curtain aside, yanked hard on María's arm, and shoved her through the door before him. Catching her balance, María wheeled around and stepped back several feet into the room without even glancing at Paz against the wall. Then she seemed to relax, shoulders slumping as if she were giving in at last. Smiling, Ronaldo made directly for her, arms outstretched.

The instant Ronaldo crossed the threshold, Paz jumped behind him and wrapped his left arm around the man's chest. And while Ronaldo's hands scrabbled at the arm tight around his midsection, Paz's right hand whipped up with a flash of steel and sliced deep into Ronaldo's throat, slitting it quite literally from ear to ear. Ronaldo's scream came out as a desperate gargle and he slumped to the floor, head flopping, dark blood spurting out of the long gash, the little spouts growing smaller and smaller until finally Ronaldo's heart stopped beating. María stared at the body, fists to her mouth, and started to cry.

"Get a sheet. Wrap him up," Paz commanded.

"He's CDS. He's CDS. What am I to do?" María cried as she turned to look at Paz, standing there naked with a bloody knife in his hand. He had a full erection.

María gagged. But after a minute she managed to tear the sheet off her bed. Grimacing, she threw it over the body, pulling her hands back tight against her chest and stepping away even before the sheet had settled over the bloody corpse. Shaking his head, Paz rolled the body in the sheet, then wiped his knife blade clean on Ronaldo's pants leg sticking out the end.

"We will take the Communist with us," he said. "Now leave me. I must get ready." With no hesitation she ran from the room.

Paz kicked the body into a corner. Then he pulled his all-black U.S. Special Forces clothing from his kit bag. After washing the blood from his arms, he got dressed. He'd never worn a turtle-neck before his training and still didn't like the feel of the cloth rolled up against his chin. But if this is what the American fight-ers wore, it must be okay, and it would make him difficult to see in the dark. Still, the clothing was too hot. The Americans never knew how to dress for the tropics. Maybe when he got to Camp Lejeune he would tell them.

He rubbed black and green camouflage paint from small tins over his cheeks and then covered his orange hair with a black cotton stocking cap. Paz's Beretta was stuck in his belt; ammuni-tion pouches hung beside it. He picked up his AR-15 by the double-purpose handle and sight on top and stepped into the main room. It was almost time to leave.

María sat huddled on the floor in a corner, holding her squirming babies to her chest. She was crying.

"They will kill me. They will kill my babies when they learn."

Paz shook his head and said, "We will take the Communist's body with us." He rooted around in his bag and held out a twenty-dollar bill. She shook her head, saying, "They will kill me if they find that." Paz walked over and stuck the bill in the jar with the cordobas. She didn't protest, and Paz returned to the bedroom.

They didn't speak again as Paz waited, standing at attention, behind the bedroom curtain, with rifle and kit bag in hand. At eight-fifty, right on time, someone knocked at the door. Paz heard María get up, sniffling, and open the door. A man said, "Hello, María. Supplies."

"Hello, Alfonse," she said, her voice still quaky.

Paz peeked out. The man was carrying two 3-liter glass jars of cooking oil over to the shelves. Through the open door, Paz saw a van parked right up against the entrance. The engine was running, and inside he saw several of his fighters, dressed as he was, huddled in the dark against the van's far wall. When Paz stepped into the main room, the civilian did a double take but quickly glanced away. Without a word Paz waved two of the fighters into the room, and they jumped through the door. The van was parked so close that it was unlikely anyone outside could see.

"In the room," Paz whispered, pointing behind him. "Get the dead Communist and put him in the truck." Without a word, the two fighters hauled the corpse out, but as they came into the main room carrying the sagging body wrapped in a heavily bloodied sheet, Alfonse sucked in his breath and dropped a jar of oil with a splattering crash. María started crying again.

"Watch the floor," Paz commanded, pointing at the spilled oil. The guerrillas stepped carefully, and Paz followed them into the truck. They sat there a moment looking back at Alfonse, who stood frozen in the middle of the room, his left hand hanging out in front of him as if it still held the jar of oil.

"Come—*now*!" Paz hissed, and Alfonse jumped through the door. Expressionless, Paz looked at María. She stared back, her eyes round with fear as she closed the front door.

Their mission tonight was simple, at least as far as the Directorate knew. The objective was the Los Mártires electrical substation, the switching center for power to downtown Managua. It was just the sort of target the bureaucrats in Washington liked to assign—an undefended civilian installation. This was a mission at which even a squad of deaf-mutes could succeed. The Directorate—the contras' political and military leaders—issued the orders, and often they even believed the plans were their own. But in truth the "generals" worked out of cubbyhole offices in Langley, Virginia, and they always came up with plans like this one: Attack an undefended station so there is little chance of trouble, and then get out fast. Even after all these years—even after hundreds of millions had been spent on training and weaponry, both legally and under the table—the CIA still had little faith in its small guerrilla army.

But with Rafael Mendoza as their control officer, the missions were not turning out to be as bland as originally conceived. Mendoza worked for the CIA, but he had grander ambitions than the agency knew.

It was dark by the time they'd picked up the last of the fighters. The van was packed tight with Paz and nine of his men. A couple of miles east of town they pulled into the parking lot behind an auto parts store, out of business for lack of parts. They went over the plan one last time, and everyone checked his weapons, snapping clips into place. They opened the side door, rolled Ronaldo's body into a ditch, and then Paz nodded to the driver. With a start he pulled back onto the highway.

Half a mile farther east, toward the airport, they turned onto a dirt road, and after a hundred yards or so it looked as if they were in the countryside. Scrub pines and garbage piles lined the road.

Soon they saw a field of electrical towers up ahead. Cables fed into and out of an incongruous-looking brick building of vaguely colonial American design. It could have been an interstate rest stop in Virginia, and no wonder. The switching station had been built twenty-five years ago by the U.S. Agency for International Development.

The van stopped fifty yards up the road, and Paz leaned forward, studying the scene. Two cars were parked in the parking lot. No one else seemed to be around. Maybe the place was guarded during the day, but the Sandinistas were almost invariably lackadaisical about posting guards or manning weaponry after nightfall. Again Paz nodded, and the van pulled to a stop beside the building. Immediately all the fighters piled out, guns pointed ahead. As planned, four men swept around the sides of the building. They poked their heads carefully around the corners, stuck their rifles into bushes and peeked for a moment into a window. Satisfied, they returned to the front, nodded at Paz, and with the major in the lead, seven of them poured through the door.

In all of Nicaragua at that moment, no man could have been more startled than Marco Alvarado, a frail old man late in his sixties with just a wisp of white hair. He was Nicaragua's foremost electrical engineer. His two assistants, scrawny boys working here only because they were too sickly for the army, sat with their mouths open, hands in the air.

The low hum of generators filled the room. The three sat before a dated control board lined with rows of heavy black ceramic knobs and banks of oversized needle gauges. The room's scarred and dirty white plaster walls were bare except for one large electric grid-chart and several generations of handprints. The view out the back window was of electric towers and switches sweeping off into the distance, toward the city.

Alvarado and the boys clearly didn't know what to expect from these seven fierce-looking men dressed in black from head to toe who were pointing automatic rifles at their faces. One of the assistants was so scared he began to shiver. A wet stain spread across his crotch. A couple of commandos lowered their rifles and snickered.

"What do you want?" Alvarado asked, his eyes barely visible behind thick bifocals.

"All of you," El Muerte ordered, "away from the controls, over by the wall." As they got up, fighters shoved them over to the back and down on the cement floor.

"Are you the contras?" one of the assistants asked, looking up in wonder at the commando standing over him. The fighter smiled back.

Coyote unfolded a paper on the floor. It was a schematic diagram of the control panel, showing all the knobs and gauges on top and the connections underneath.

"Agency for International Development/U.S. Army Corp of Engineers," the legend said. Coyote kept turning the chart this way and that, looking up at the control panel and then back down at the sheet, trying to get his bearings.

"I don't know," he said at last. Someone had drawn a big red X on the schematic, showing the critical spot they were to destroy to set off a chain reaction that would turn out the lights. The idea was to keep the explosion small so it wouldn't make too much noise, and they had been shown how to break off just enough plastique to do the job. But with all seven of them standing over the plans, heads turned sideways, hands on their chins, nobody could tell which end was which.

"Must have changed it since these plans," Coyote said.

Finally Paz said, "Just blow the whole thing."

"No, you can't!" Alvarado shouted, standing up and waving his arms. A fighter shoved him back to the floor, knocking off his glasses. Obviously blinded without them, Alvarado was groping on the floor when Paz walked over and said, "Old man, you are serving the Sandinista Communists. You do not deserve to live. But we are the Democratic Resistance, and we have special plans for you." Then slowly Paz crushed the wire-rim glasses under his boot, grinding them into the rough cement floor. The old man moaned and sagged back against the wall.

"El Muerte, set the charge," Paz commanded. Since they had decided against "surgical" application of the C-4, El Muerte stuck the entire wad of plastique under the center of the console.

"Jesus, Mary," one of Alvarado's assistant's muttered.

One of the fighters ran out to the van and brought in a spool of wire. El Muerte attached the end to a blasting cap and stuck it into the plastique. Then, backing up, he rolled the wire out the door.

"Balita, take the old man to the van," Paz said. "Coyote, finish the work in here. The rest, let's go."

Balita pulled a red bandanna from his pocket and gagged the old man, tied his hands behind his back with a piece of wire, then pushed him through the door. Outside Balita shoved him face down on the floor of the van. The rest of the fighters followed, leaving only Coyote with the two assistants, who looked up at him in terror.

Everyone piled into the van, stepping all over the old man, and Tigrillo began driving at a crawl, trailing the wire along as they went. After a minute Coyote emerged with the two assistants at gunpoint, then fired a short burst into the air, sending the boys away on a tear, running and tripping in the dark as they fled into the woods. Coyote trotted over and jumped into the van, now about fifty yards away.

El Muerte clipped the wire from the spool, then connected one end to a dry-cell battery that had been under the front seat. He grinned at Paz who nodded back, and with a look of fierce concentration El Muerte touched the second wire to its post.

The explosion poured straight up through the roof and then seemed to settle back down, blowing out the building's sides too. Finally the station collapsed in a pile, and a second later bricks started landing all around the van. Several smashed into the roof, and inside everyone covered their heads.

When the bricks stopped falling, those who could looked out the window. Sparks were flying across the small field of cables; wires wiped up and down, electric bolts arced. The fighters whooped and cheered. One stuck his M-16 out the window and fired a burst into the air. On the floor Alvarado sobbed.

"Go!" Paz commanded, and Tigrillo floored the pedal, spewing dirt and gravel as they sped off the way they had come. After they'd turned right onto the highway, several of them pointed gleefully at the dark stores, homes, and streetlamps.

In the back, El Muerte held Alvarado by his wisp of hair, pulling his head up and looking him in the eye. Grimacing in pain, the old man looked back unfocused, blind without his glasses.

"Old man, we have turned out all the lights," El Muerte sneered. "And now you are going to make us famous." As he let go of Alvarado's hair, several strands stayed in his hand, and the old man's chin hit the floor with a thump.

Blowing up the substation had been the CIA's idea, of course. Since the beginning of the war, tacticians had argued that the contras could not succeed unless they moved into the cities. Military actions up in the Highlands were fine, but everybody who mattered was in Managua. So finally, after more than a dozen years of ever-changing tactics and sputtering support, the CIA had sent down this order for the first major raid in the capital. The president and Congress now wanted to see some results, but the bureaucrats who really ran the program were leery. If the contras grew too ambitious and screwed up, as they had so often in the past, their control officers in Washington knew they would get the blame.

So the theory for this raid was straightforward: Turn out the lights and demonstrate that the Sandinistas cannot control even their own capital—standard guerrilla warfare doctrine. The plan had been almost moronically simple too: Blow up the station and run. No, the intelligence bureaucrats in Washington didn't have much faith in their guerrilla army. But that wasn't true of Rafael Mendoza, their new handler on the ground.

When Mendoza arrived in Honduras early in the year, Paz and his men had been nothing special in the contra hierarchy, just one of the many commando squads. In fact the Pena de Muertes had been among the least favored. Everybody knew Paz's past.

Before Mendoza, a Cuban émigré, all the CIA handlers had been swaggering gringos, blue-eyed Washington bureaucrats more often than not. They kept telling the Directorate to use only the comandantes who were former Sandinistas, saying they were "more viable politically." And because of that advice, Comandante Venganza, the contras' highest-level defector—he used to be a lieutenant in the Sandinista Popular Army—had become the star. Meanwhile, former officers of General Somoza's Guardia, like Major Paz (their enemies called them Somocistas), were shunned. Sometimes the Guardia officers would sit around at night drinking and cursing the CIA for rewarding the former Communists while penalizing the people who had been fighting for democracy all along.

Then Mendoza arrived, and at first many of the fighters shook their heads. The new chief was a little man, maybe five feet four. He was about fifty years old, balding, and his natural expression when relaxed was a childlike innocent grin.

"What have the Norte Americanos given us now?" Tigrillo had muttered, shaking his head, the first day Mendoza had walked through camp, grinning and waving. But as they quickly learned, Mendoza proved the maxim that appearances can be deceiving.

The new man hadn't been in country a month when he called Paz to the command hut he used while in camp and, leaning back in his desk chair, smiled, saying, "I know all about you, Major Paz."

Paz had been standing at attention then, looking through his Ray Bans at a spot on the wall over Mendoza's head. Watching him just then, no one could have read his rising rage. One more North American who doesn't like the Guardia.

But the next thing Mendoza said was "We are going to do great things together, you and me." And before Paz knew what had happened, he and his Pena de Muertes had become the golden children, to the Directorate's obvious dismay. Mendoza set them up in their own private area about ten miles down the road—Cascabeles, Camp Rattlesnake. And a couple of months later they were sent to Florida for six weeks of secret training at an Army Special Forces base.

Although he believed his U.S. Marine blood was a factor, Paz had sometimes wondered why Mendoza picked him and his men. But one day in the main camp, Tigrillo overheard two other comandantes discussing the very same question.

"So I asked Mendoza: Why Paz? Why'd you pick him?" one of them was saying. "I told Mendoza, we've been on more penetration raids than the Pena de Muertes have. And you know what he says? Paz, he says, follows every order, no questions asked, no matter what the orders are."

That was Paz's reputation, and it was true. When Tigrillo repeated what he'd heard, the major swelled with pride.

Just a couple of weeks before this mission, Mendoza had come out to Camp Cascabeles for a talk. It was Paz's first political discussion with his new boss, though "discussion" was probably the wrong word. Paz didn't debate things with his superiors. He nodded and said, "Yes, sir."

They'd been sitting on the floor in Paz's new command hut, a tiny plywood number on stilts his men had built, using the lumber Mendoza sent over. Paz had never had a command hut before. He had no furniture.

"We'll send over some chairs," Mendoza had offered first thing. Then he told Paz: "One thing I've learned is that Latin revolutionaries like you and me don't win on the battlefield. We win in the hearts of our countrymen. That was true in my country for Castro and the Communists. And it will be true for the democratic fighters here in Nicaragua."

Paz nodded but rolled his eyes behind the Ray Bans; he'd heard that line before. CIA officers had been floating it for years. The white men who'd been down here before kept telling the contras to stop and talk to campesinos they saw while traveling through the countryside.

"Tell them about democracy and freedom," they insisted.

"Sure, sure," the fighters would answer, grimacing as the CIA men turned their backs. But Mendoza had a different idea.

"How'd the Sandinistas win the last revolution?" he'd asked, sitting with Paz on the floor of his hut, still heavy with the smell of fresh plywood. "They won with daring raids, that's how. Like Edén Pastora's raid on the National Palace in 1978."

Paz remembered that well enough. Never had General Somoza been so angry. Never had the Guardia looked so bad.

Edén Pastora—Comandante Zero, he called himself then—had sneaked into Managua, stormed into the palace with two dozen of his men, and taken the Nicaraguan Congress hostage for three days. They demanded freedom for Sandinista political prisoners, plus half a million dollars in ransom, plus safe passage to the airport. President Somoza did as Pastora asked. He had no choice. And to Somoza's dismay, thousands of Managuans cheered Comandante Zero as he rode out of town. Overnight he was a folk hero, and the Somoza government never recovered. It fell the next year.

"Wouldn't you like to do that back to the Sandinista Communists?" Mendoza asked.

"Yes, sir," Paz said, and a careful listener could have discerned a hint of emotion in his voice.

But Mendoza's immediate superiors weren't keen on this idea, or any other, for that matter. Their abiding rule seemed to be: Keep the program going. But don't fuck up.

The program was run by the contra RIG, the "Restricted Interagency Group," a special committee with one representative each from the State Department, the Defense Department, and the CIA. Each member of the RIG knew full well that over the last decade many a promising government career had been ended by overzealous pursuit of the contras' cause. Now nobody wanted to take a chance. They only wanted to get through their terms on the RIG without getting hurt. So without even hesitating they rejected every idea Mendoza proposed.

Mendoza didn't tell Paz all of that. "They don't think you can

do it" was all he said. "But let's you and me prove them wrong.
We'll start small."

And so Paz and his men were bumping up the Inter-American
Highway. Marco Alvarado, Nicaragua's foremost electrical engineer, was bound and gagged on the floor in the back. Actually,
Alvarado was just about the nation's only electrical engineer. He
was the one man who knew how Managua's power grid worked,
and without him the Sandinistas were in trouble—especially now
that the Los Mártires station was gone.

As they drove along, the fighters changed back into civilian
clothes, and then one by one Tigrillo dropped them off at designated spots, where they picked up rides or started the long walk
north.

Once, they saw a troop transport truck coming toward them,
undoubtedly full of Sandinista soldiers under the green canvas
cover. Tigrillo jerked the wheel to the right, sending everyone
in the back slamming against the wall. He turned onto a plowed
field and lurched along, bouncing everyone around in the back.
Alvarado was face down on the floor and groaned in short bursts
with every bump. After a minute Tigrillo pulled back onto a road
and turned around to grin at them.

Ten minutes later they had dropped everyone off; only Paz,
Balita, Tigrillo, and the old man were left. Up ahead was a market—the sign said MERCADO CASTILLO—and they pulled around
back. The place was closed, but an old Plymouth Fury sat in
the lot.

"Carlos came through for us," Tigrillo said, jubilant when his
headlights fell on the car. Carlos, the brother of a fighter in
Honduras, was trading his old car for this van, which a supporter
in Managua had donated. In case the van had been spotted, Paz
and his men now had a car they could drive deep into the countryside, where they'd have to get out for the walk across the frontier.

"We're home free!" Tigrillo said.

They pulled out of sight behind the store and Tigrillo turned
off the engine.

"Turn on the inside lights," Paz ordered before any of them
moved to get out of the van, and a weak overhead lamp came
on. Paz turned around in his seat and looked at the old man,
still face down on the floor. He wasn't making any noise now.

"Turn him over," Paz said to Balita. "Untie him. Take off the
gag." Balita unbound Alvarado, flipped him over, and leaned

him up against the van's back wall. The old man gagged, sucked in his breath, and opened his eyes slowly.

"Señor Alvarado, we are taking you with us to Honduras," Paz announced. His voice now held a leering threatening air, a tone he hadn't been able to use much since his Guardia days. But the man didn't answer.

"You are our hostage. To get you back, the Sandinista Communists are going to have to release some of our brothers. It will be in all the papers. You will be famous."

Still the old man was quiet. Paz jumped out of his seat, moved into the back, and squatted in front of him. Alvarado's eyes seemed unfocused. His breath came in short gasps. To Paz his skin looked clammy, kind of yellow. Maybe it was the light.

"Señor Alvarado, you say nothing. You do not believe me?" Still Alvarado did not speak. "Well, there is more. In addition, after our brothers are released you are going to defect. You are going to join the Democratic Resistance and tell the world all about the Sandinista Communists."

With that Alvarado's breath grew raspy, his head fell back against the wall.

"What, still you do not believe me?" Paz asked.

The major moved closer and put his face up to Alvarado's so the old man could see him, bad eyes or not. Alvarado's breathing grew even more erratic. He was trying to swallow but was having trouble.

"Well, believe me, old man," Paz said. With that he reached up, ripped off his black stocking cap, and moved even closer, pulling on the old man's hair so they were nose to nose.

Slowly, enunciating each word, Paz said, "Believe me, old man, because I am Paz. Major of the Guardia."

Alvarado sucked in his breath as he looked up to Paz's orange hair. He moaned, and then his eyes seemed to roll back in his head. His hands clawed at his chest, and his breath came out as a desperate gargle.

"My pills, my pills," he choked. His hand tore at his shirt pocket.

"Major, Major, I think it is his heart," Balita cried out. Alvarado had slumped to the floor, still grabbing at his pocket. Balita pulled the man's hands away and took a small brown glass bottle out of the pocket. He tore off the top, and then pried the old man's mouth open, fingers slipping on Alvarado's clammy skin. Balita tried to shake a pill or two onto his tongue, but suddenly about twenty nitroglycerin tablets poured out of the bottle.

Balita stuck his little hand into the old man's mouth, frantically trying to retrieve the pills.

Moaning, Alvarado jerked a couple of times. Then he let out a long sigh as his body relaxed. In a moment he was quiet and still.

Balita stared at the body for a full thirty seconds, his eyes wide, mouth open. The other two looked on, stunned. Paz's ears buzzed with panic.

"Major, Major, I . . ." Balita was near tears. He couldn't finish the sentence.

Wearily, Paz whispered, "Leave the old man here. Let's go home."

They dumped the body, got into the Plymouth, and pulled back onto the road. Worry gnawed at Paz. He'd failed Mendoza's first assignment. Would the little Cuban pick another squad for his next one? Paz couldn't be sure, though of one thing the major was certain. Already he knew Mendoza well enough to see that, unlike his predecessors, he was committed. Despite this failure, without a doubt he would try again.

CHAPTER
TWO

MANAGUA, NICARAGUA, AUGUST 8

F INISHING HIS MORNING LAPS, COLONEL ERIC GUSTAF-
son pulled himself out of the water and stretched out on
the slate walk, still wet from the morning rain, and
whipped through seventy-five pushups without the slightest
strain. Then he sat at the edge of the pool, his back to the haci-
enda, and faced the lush green of his carefully landscaped yard—
date palms, plantains, and ficus trees stretching back toward an
electrified fence.

The sun was just up, so only the first blush of the day's scorch-
ing heat had swept across the lawn. After a moment the colonel
raised his right arm over his head and waved it a couple of times,
seemingly at nothing in particular. Right away a screen door behind him slammed, and a tiny woman carrying a wicker tray came
trotting toward the pool.

Through the corner of his eye Gustafson could see the tray
being set on the concrete beside him, and he heard the woman's
nervous voice: *"Señor, señor. Buenos días, señor."* But the colonel continued wiping the water from his face and smoothing
back his short blond hair as she bowed at his back several times
and then scurried off toward the kitchen. The screen door
slammed again before Gustafson finally turned and took a few
gulps from the mug of heavy black Nicaraguan coffee. He
downed a plain doughnut in three bites, then stretched out for

another thirty or so pushups, cut short with a lithe leap to his feet when it started to sprinkle again. The rainy season still had a few weeks to go.

Draping a towel over his neck, he strode into the house, where the gardener, pruning more palms in the large open-air front hall, put down his shears and turned to him, nodding with a sycophantic smile. But the colonel was so tall, six feet four, and walked with his chin pumped up so high that it often appeared he could not see the little Latin people around him—an image the colonel made no effort to dispel.

In the master bedroom he dressed quietly. It wasn't yet seven, and his wife still slept. He had pulled on his blue jeans and a light green Izod sport shirt when Jeannie called to him in a thick, sleepy voice.

"Eric, you going to be okay?"

He sat on the edge of the bed and rubbed her back through the sheet. "Yeah, sweetie. I'll do just fine. Thanks. Now go back to sleep."

He pulled on white Reebok tennis shoes, bent to kiss her on the cheek, and left without another word. In the circular drive, he climbed into his motorpool-issue Ford LTD.

Gustafson indulged himself a moment, as he did on occasion, bending to look through the windshield at the large white stucco edifice with plaster pillars and vaulting many-paned windows that was his home. He smiled. At almost no other embassy in the world would a military attaché live in such grand style. But in the years before the Sandinista revolution the United States had kept a large contingent of senior embassy officers in Managua, and as was the custom in inexpensive Latin American countries, they lived in grand homes like this one, built at the turn of the century for an American banana baron. Ever since the revolution the Sandinistas had been trying to wrest the haciendas away, saying they belonged to the people; actually, party members liked the homes for themselves. The U.S. embassy had fought to keep them, and as the diplomatic staff was gradually reduced, the haciendas went to progressively less senior officers, like Gustafson.

Some billet for a Marine grunt, Gustafson thought.

Since it was still early Saturday morning, hardly any cars were on the road to town, a result of gas shortages as much as of the time of day. Gustafson passed a Toyota and a Fiat, both of them belching noxious black exhaust. Auto maintenance was not high on the priority list here.

Even more than ten years of tension and a full United States trade boycott had failed to eliminate the heavy Yanqui flavor of Managua. American chain stores still lined the streets, but now most of them sold goods from Cuba or Bulgaria.

When he got into the city Gustafson saw to his delight that the traffic lights were still out. After thirty-six hours the Sandinistas still hadn't been able to turn the power back on. He smiled to himself, proud of his own small role in the operation.

Part of his job today was to find out if Major Paz's raid had worked the way his good friend Rafael Mendoza had planned. The results would settle months of friendly debate. If the raid was a success, then Mendoza had won and the two of them would push the CIA man's tactic for unseating the Sandinistas as far as it would go. But if it turned out that the raid was a failure . . . well then the colonel planned to make the case that it was time to start moving on *his* strategy for taking out the Marxist bastards.

Gustafson stopped in front of the embassy's high steel gate until the security officer inside pulled the lever opening it. Grinding, the gate slid slowly to the right, and the colonel pulled up to the vehicle barrier, a three-foot steel wall set into the pavement, raised and lowered from the guardhouse. The barriers had been installed in embassies around the world after the truck bombings in Lebanon many years earlier; there'd been no truck bomb attacks against any American installations, defended or undefended, in a decade. But embassy security officers worldwide still made protection against truck bombs their first priority, even in countries that had no heavy trucks.

Gustafson got out of the car, leaned against a rail, and watched, arms folded, as two Nicaraguan security employees began a desultory search for bombs. One poked a mirror on a long pole under the car—the idea was to see if any bombs were tucked under the chassis—but the Nicaraguan didn't look into the mirror. He just waved it back and forth, as if the mirror itself were an antidote. The other guard opened the LTD's doors and pointed a flashlight inside, though it was a bright day. When he stuck it into the well-lit glove compartment, closed the door, and waved Gustafson back to the car, the colonel snorted and grimaced. As usual, they hadn't looked in the trunk.

He parked in the side lot, almost empty. The embassy's emergency generators were still humming away over to the right.

In the bare lobby inside the front door, the Nicaraguan receptionist nodded at him with her curious, unreadable smile. American policy was to hire nationals for low-level embassy jobs, even in hostile countries. It was too expensive to send American cooks, janitors, and service workers to 257 embassies, missions, consulates, and interest sections around the world. But the hidden price for employing nationals was that in places like this almost anyone hired was presumed to be an intelligence agent. The Nicaraguans were kept out of secure areas, but it was Gustafson's view that just by sitting at the desk, just by seeing who came and went, the receptionist could gather valuable intelligence for the Sandinistas.

The Marine guard saluted as he buzzed Gustafson through the security door and into a narrow cluttered hall. The plasterboard in some places was held up with packing tape. The grand old United States Embassy building had been destroyed in the great earthquake of 1972 that also ravaged most of Managua, killing twelve thousand people and leaving more than a quarter million others without homes; this temporary prefab Butler building, as it was called, had been thrown up quickly and was supposed to be used for only a couple of years; it had been there now for about twenty. It seemed to be held together by Band-Aids and Wrigley's Spearmint. Everybody called it the cardboard embassy. It had the feel of a mobile home, which in essence it was. But relations between the United States and Nicaragua had been so unsettled these last years that it had not been possible to replace the building; any decision to build a new embassy would have been taken as a significant statement about future intentions.

The building was almost deserted—hardly anyone worked on Saturday, especially this early in the morning. But one of Gustafson's deputies, Major Rosen, sat with his feet up on his desk, reading reports. Gustafson stopped at Rosen's door.

"Hi, Eric," Rosen said looking up. "Time for the mood-of-Managua again?"

"Yeah. One more feel of the pathetic little pulse." He pointed to the small pile of cables and other documents that had arrived in the overnight diplomatic pouch from the States. "Anything interesting come in?"

"Naw, just the usual. Think they're gonna get the power back on today?"

"Not unless they can do it with flashlight batteries. Takes a while to get the Cuban repairmen in."

"Did the contras really do it?" Rosen asked.

Gustafson put his hand to his heart and with a tone of mock

indignation asked, "Bill, why would you ask me, just a lowly military attaché? All I know is what I read in the papers."

"Yeah, yeah." Rosen shook his head and turned back to his work.

Gustafson sat behind the desk in his own fluorescent-lit office. The fake-walnut walls were bare except for a contour map of Nicaragua, festooned with colored pins to mark Sandinista military facilities. A red-and-black party flag of the FSLN—the Sandinista National Liberation Front—hung on the back of the door like a souvenir of war.

Looking through his own photocopies of the day's papers, Colonel Gustafson found the weekly intelligence report from INR, the State Department's bureau for intelligence and research. It came on Saturdays and often included useful background material for his job. This one confirmed what had been rumored for the last several weeks: New intelligence showed that the Soviet Union had decided to take advantage of the landing rights for military aircraft that Nicaragua had offered last year. Though the Soviet Union had said nothing about it publicly, the United States had noticed additional technicians and advisors filtering into Managua, joining the several hundred Soviets who'd been in Nicaragua for years.

It was this change—this typical Sandinista blunder, as Gustafson and many others viewed it—that had saved the contras yet again. They'd struggled along in near-dormancy for several years with only "nonlethal, humanitarian" subsistence funding from the United States Congress. Though Congress hadn't been able to muster the votes to keep the contras in arms, the congressmen also hadn't found the nerve to abandon them after all these years. That had been just fine with the new president, who'd come into office an ambivalent opponent of contra aid. But as a pragmatic moderate on this issue and most others, the new president was willing to accept the humanitarian-assistance compromise rather than endure the infighting that had plagued previous administrations. The contras had been able to scratch up a little military assistance from other countries, but their forces withered. And as they did, the Sandinistas grew more and more belligerent. Arrogant. Their newly pugnacious attitude coincided with the rise to power of Miguel Zelaya.

Minister Zelaya was tall and pencil-thin. A widow's peak seemed to be reaching down for his nose. He walked with a pronounced limp that was said to be left over from years of torture in one of General Somoza's prisons. To Zelaya it was a badge of honor. Zelaya was a Sandinista ideologue who had been interior minister for years; in that job he had set out to quash the few vestiges of democracy remaining in Nicaragua. He'd been forced to move slowly at first, held back by moderates on the Directorate, but after some years the job of foreign minister opened up, and Zelaya was appointed to this position too. So the architect of Sandinista repression now controlled the nation's foreign policy as well, and under Zelaya's steady hand the Sandinistas slithered out of the first Central America peace plan. Then last year Zelaya, on his own, openly bludgeoned a second one into pulp. After that, his influence had grown exponentially, and he managed to overpower his opponents on the Directorate. With no one to restrain him, he stepped up Nicaragua's march to totalitarianism.

As foreign minister, Zelaya had also become the nation's unofficial spokesman. He'd gone to school up at Loyola University, in Los Angeles, and knew English better than anyone else. He spoke it not with an accent but with a curled-lip nasal sneer that seemed perfectly suited to his bony face and beady eyes. The Sandinista Directorate loved the image he projected, and he was frequently interviewed on American television, where he showed a penchant for overwrought bellicosity. Asked once what he thought of the second Central America peace plan, he told CNN with a characteristic smirk, "The imperialist circus masters are telling us: Drop dead, or we'll shoot you."

In the State Department, Minister Zelaya quickly became the single greatest obstacle to moderation in the policy toward the Sandinistas. The Sandinista "threat" began to seem genuine even to the American public, now that it was personified by a bile-mouthed, satanic-looking character like Miguel Zelaya.

All of this, everyone around him could see, angered the new president of the United States and began to soften his views of the contras. But when Nicaraguan president Daniel Ortega made the landing-rights announcement a year ago in a bellicose speech on July 19, the anniversary of the Sandinista revolution, both the president and the Congress turned molten. It seemed to confirm the hard-liners' worst fears—Nicaragua really was turning into a Soviet beachhead on the American mainland.

Full military aid for the contras was reapproved with almost no debate. At the same time, the president warned both Nicaragua and the Soviet Union that if the privilege of landing and refueling aircraft turned into the right to establish actual military bases—well, he wouldn't say exactly *what* manner of drastic action he would take. . . .

How ironic, the commentators wrote as all this was going on. This president had come into office riding the overwrought rhetoric and contra scandals of previous administrations, so who'd have guessed that he'd be drawn in too? On the other hand, as several smug newspaper pundits pointed out, years ago Ronald Reagan had been elected largely because Jimmy Carter had become mired in Iran. Who would ever have predicted that Reagan's presidency would come close to collapse because he had become mired in Iran himself? All any of this proved was that foreign policy dilemmas didn't come and go in neat four- or eight-year intervals. As one senior member of the Reagan administration remarked shortly after he'd resigned, fed up, "In Washington no problem ever gets solved."

The new president's threat and the renewed U.S. military aid failed to moderate the Sandinistas at all. The day after the president's televised speech from the Oval Office, Minister Zelaya announced that two U.S. diplomats were being expelled. "We caught the imperialist rats red-pawed in the act of spying," he declared. The two had been seen standing beside a public road in Managua, watching as a military convoy rolled past.

The American resolve did seem to affect the Soviet Union— at least at first. For a long time the Soviet military declined Nicaragua's offer to allow Soviet military planes the right to land at bases for maintenance and refueling. But after a while they couldn't resist. Landing rights in Nicaragua gave the Soviet Union the ability to fly high-altitude surveillance missions off the American West Coast, something that had not been possible from its bases in Cuba. And besides, after the warmer moments of the glasnost era, Soviet-American relations were well into one of their periodic pendulum swings toward the other, chilly, extreme.

Pondering all this as he read the report, Colonel Gustafson was thinking: Now the president's really going to get steamed. Now we're really gonna roll! He was grinning as he slapped his desk top and flipped the report into a basket on his way out the door.

"Have fun, cowboy," Major Rosen shouted after him as he marched down the hall. "Don't get in too much trouble this time."

Outside the embassy, protesters were already walking back and forth on South Highway, in front of the fence. Mothers of

Heroes and Martyrs, they called themselves. For years and years they'd been marching almost every day; all of them were said to have had sons who were killed fighting the contras. But Gustafson figured they were really agents reporting for Minister Zelaya.

Looking straight ahead, Gustafson walked right through the line of tiny women, rudely brushing aside any who happened to be in his path, and set off down Salvador Allende Pass toward the Roberto Huembles market, one of his favorite reporting spots. It would be mobbed this early in the morning. By noon the vendors would have run out of their East German light bulbs, Cuban beans, and Bulgarian powdered soap.

It was almost eight-thirty now, and the August heat was already oppressive; when it wasn't raining the moisture seemed to hang in the air, ready to surrender and fall. Three blocks away he stopped at a street vendor's battered plywood shed. A DRINK COCA-COLA sign was still tacked to the side, even though Coke hadn't been easily available here for years. Sitting on a stool squinting out at him was a grizzled-looking man probably in his mid-sixties—old for Nicaragua, where most men didn't live much past fifty. He was new at this corner, and Gustafson could see it was not a promising location. In front of him was an open field that had been a bustling downtown block before the earthquake. Now the shed overlooked some tall grass and rubble, including one free-standing brick chimney half covered with vines. General Somoza had carried out earthquake reconstruction with bulldozers. He'd plowed most of the rubble flat while pocketing the reconstruction money. Even today most of Managua was open fields like this one; longtime residents still gave street directions by referring to the schools, hospitals, and department stores that stood before the devastation.

The old man must have gotten in trouble someplace else or he wouldn't be trying to make a living here. Most of the shelves along his shed's back wall were bare. He had a few packs of Chiclets and other American candies that weren't such big sellers at home but had become popular in the Third World. Some Cuban cigarettes and Venezuelan cheese-and-cracker packets. That was about it.

"Orange drink," Gustafson said in his heavily accented Texas Spanish. The man reached under the counter and handed Gustafson a clear plastic sack filled with bright orange liquid. Gustafson grimaced when he saw the unnatural color. Cuban. But he gave the man a wad of cordobas anyway. Nicaragua couldn't afford cups, cans, bottles, or boxes these days, so soft drinks were "bottled" in these sacks. Gustafson loved taking new embassy employees out for a look around Managua and to get "a local soft drink." Handed one of the bags, most of them would be too embarrassed to ask how it worked. So they'd untie the knot at the top, only to find it wasn't so much a bag as a plastic sheet. As Gustafson watched, laughing to himself, they'd stand there hapless as the sticky drink poured through their fingers all over their shoes.

Ducking his head, Gustafson stood in the shade of the shed's small overhang and turned his drink bag upside down. He bit a small hole in the sack, spit the plastic fleck into the street, and sucked a few squirts of the sickly liquid. Then he turned to the old man.

"How's business doing?"

The man gave a noncommittal shrug that seemed to say it didn't really matter. Another Nicaraguan whose expectations were low.

"Trouble with the government?"

The man didn't look at him. "Always. All governments." His voice was a monotone. Gustafson settled back against the stand. This old man showed promise.

"You got a family?"

The man smiled, showing the wide gaps between his brown-edged teeth. "Three sons, two alive, and one daughter. Eight grandchildren."

"Hey, you must be very proud."

The old man nodded.

"Grandsons in the army?"

"Two fighting up north. Roberto, my second oldest, killed last Easter up in Matagalpa. They picked up my youngest last month."

Gustafson smiled to himself and took another squirt of orange drink. "Picked up" was the euphemism for forced recruiting, a brutal practice that had helped set Gustafson's career on an unusual path, leading him here today.

Only a few weeks after he'd arrived, more than two years ago, Gustafson had been walking downtown when across the street a Sandinista Popular Army troop truck pulled up in front of a bus stop. Half a dozen young men waiting for the bus started to scatter, but soldiers leapt out of the truck and quickly surrounded them, automatic rifles raised. A small cluster of people gathering on the opposite corner watched, horrified, as the soldiers herded the young men toward the back of the truck. A sergeant had grabbed the young men one by one, tied their thumbs together with string, and pushed them up into the truck bed.

Beside Gustafson a middle-aged woman started to cry. Mystified, he bent down to her and, using the little Spanish he knew then, asked, "What's this all about?"

"The military," she said, choking. "The draft."

"That's the way they draft people here?" Gustafson muttered to himself, staring back across the street.

"They picked up my son in April," she said, tears beginning to drip down her cheeks. "He was waiting for the bus to go to work. He died in Jinotega last month. The Sandinista *piricuacos*," she hissed, spitting the last word as she turned and hurried off. Literally the word meant something like "beggar dogs," but here it was a bitter epithet, an unusually harsh phrase for a woman to use.

New to the city, Gustafson had been fascinated by the strength of her animosity. It seemed to confirm what he wanted to believe, that the Nicaraguan people hated the Sandinistas, and when he got back to the embassy that day he made some notes. A few days later he'd been sure to mention the incident in his monthly military report to Washington. And to his surprise, a few weeks later he got a cable back from the Defense Intelligence Agency.

"Interesting observation on the draft situation," wrote the deputy director for foreign intelligence research. "If you pick up more intel on those lines, please provide." So from then on, Gustafson had gone out of his way to get just that kind of material, though it was unusual work for a military attaché.

In most embassies, the attachés acted as liaison with the host country's military. Theoretically that was true in Nicaragua too, but needless to say the Nicaraguan military didn't have much interest in discussing things with the United States Marines. They'd already occupied Nicaragua four times in the last century.

In a place like Italy or Greece, the military attaché's job might be to gauge the readiness and esprit de corps of the army, assessing what help it might give the United States and NATO in time of war. But the United States armed forces could foresee only one possible form of interaction with the Nicaraguan military. And so Gustafson's job was straightforward. He had to assess how easy it would be for the United States to invade Nicaragua, if it ever decided to do so. That was simple enough. Early on he'd looked over Nicaragua's military and concluded that taking out the Sandinistas would be a breeze—"like falling off a fucking log," he liked to say.

His military assessments were all he was required to put in his monthly reports. But ever since that first note on forced recruiting, Gustafson had taken it upon himself to add an extra element. He knew that winning a military victory would be only half the battle here. Washington would never commit troops to Nicaragua unless it was certain the conquerors would be welcome—a new necessity in this the age of televised wars. So Gustafson wanted Washington to know how the populace would react if U.S. troops dropped in, whether they'd be welcomed or caught in a hornet's nest—another Vietnam.

Once a month he prowled around the cities and talked to people he saw in markets, schools, stores, and on the streets, people like this old man in the vendor's shed. His Spanish was getting better. And now he found that people talked to him easily, appreciated that a blond-haired gringo was at least trying to speak their language. They liked Americans, strangely enough, although sometimes they cursed the government. And from all they had told him, Gustafson had concluded that ordinary Nicaraguans would welcome American "liberators."

"The ordinary Nicaraguan will not take any part in the defense of the Sandinista regime," he'd written in his first annual report, the one that caught the eye of the Defense Intelligence Agency's chief. "Most of them would stand aside and let us do our job, happy to be freed of Communist control." The report also predicted that many Sandinista soldiers would defect.

"Young boys kidnapped from Chinandega with their thumbs tied together are not going to die for the Sandinista regime," he wrote and he quickly dispatched the theory that Nicaragua would become "another Vietnam."

True, he wrote, after an invasion "the Sandinistas and their few sympathizers would flee to the hills, from whence they fought during their own revolution. But, because the government has so alienated the peasants in the war zones, the Sandinistas would find a rather hostile reception in the Highlands. The mountains are now contra country."

The week after that report went to Washington, the ambassador called him across the hall to his office and looked up with a wholly undiplomatic glower.

"I'm not exactly sure why," he said, "but your boss loved it." Gustafson got dirty looks, too, from the embassy's CIA station chief, who probably thought the colonel was stepping over into agency turf. But that was fine with Gustafson; to him, the embassy's CIA station was a bunch of cowardly careerists anyway.

The next thing the colonel knew, he was aboard an Aeronica flight to Miami and then on to Washington, where twenty-four hours later he was at Defense Intelligence Agency headquarters, standing at ease in the general's office, elaborating on his report, recalling interviews from memory and offering colorful anecdotal asides. The general and his aides had smiled and nodded at each other as Gustafson talked.

With earnest frowns they'd told him: We have no plans to invade, mind you, but it's good to know firsthand what might happen if that should ever change.

Over the next two days Gustafson had been shipped all over town. He talked to friendly members of the House and Senate, even to the president's national security advisor. All of them had congratulated him and said his information was especially valuable. Oddly, no one from the State Department, Defense, or the CIA was at any of the briefings. But when he'd finished talking to the national security advisor at the White House, General Dayton had clapped Gustafson on the back and told him the president wanted a briefing too. As everyone knew, the president was a late convert to the contra cause, but the general had assured Gustafson, "He's with us now. We'll call you back for a talk with him."

Gustafson returned to Managua convinced that, sooner or later, Washington would do the only sensible thing. They'd send in the Marines.

The White House never called back. In fact, for the last year or so Gustafson had seemed to be sending his work into a void. He'd send his reports up and get no response. Not a word. The truth, he figured, was that once his reports had been circulated outside the Defense Intelligence Agency, the ass-covering bureaucrats in the other agencies had begun stuffing them in their burn bags.

Washington wasn't going to send in the Marines. But the colonel kept trying.

"Be nice if this war got over, wouldn't it," he said to the old man, who was brushing flies from his face.

"If it wasn't war, it would be something," the man answered. "Always is."

"What do you think about the Sandinistas, are they doing the best they can for you and your family?"

He shrugged again. "Nobody does any good here."

"Think the contras can win?"

"Contras can never win, no, never." At that he was vehement. "The government is too strong. They have tanks and helicopters from Russia."

"What if the contras got help?"

The old man looked up at Gustafson. "The Yanquis?"

Gustafson nodded.

"Yanquis will never come in here. Not again. Not after Vietnam." That seemed to be the conventional wisdom here.

"What if they did?"

The old man peered at Gustafson, apparently trying to figure out what this tall gringo was up to.

"The Yanquis? If they come, lots of people are going to die. I know. My grandfather, he fought with General Sandino. I think the North Americans should leave us alone."

Gustafson sucked on his drink and looked at the man for a moment.

"But are you happy with your life now? Look at what you've got to sell here. Almost nothing." He swept his hand toward the bare shelves. "You think the Sandinistas can ever provide enough for you and your family?"

The old man shrugged again, but this line of questions seemed to interest him. He poked his head out of the shack, peered left and right, then sat back down.

After a long moment the man looked up. "I don't want the Yanquis here. But maybe we'll get some money and things from North America. Cigarettes and candy. Maybe we'll get food and more things to sell. You think we'll get Coca-Cola again?" he asked, looking at the colonel.

"Oh sure," Gustafson said with a wave. "Coca-Cola and a whole lot more."

They were both quiet for a minute. The old man was thinking.

"Maybe I could fix my car. I got a seventy-four Pontiac, you know," he said with a gap-toothed smile. "Maybe I could go to Miami, visit my brother before I die, maybe . . ." A pause. "If the Yanquis come again and don't bother my family, maybe I wouldn't get in the way."

Gustafson grinned, patted him hard on the shoulder. It's always the same, he thought. All of them hate these Marxist bastards, and goddamnit, it's about time we did something about it. So now Gustafson asked the most important questions.

"You got your electricity back on yet?" The old man shook his head.

"What do you think happened? Think the contras did it?" That's what *Barricada*, the Sandinista party newspaper, had said yesterday afternoon.

The old man looked at him. "They say everything is the contras," he asserted, standing up now. "They take our water away and say it is the contras." Water service in Managua was cut off two days every week.

"Why would the counterrevolutionaries take our water? You know what I think? I think Minister Zelaya's selling our water to Cuba to pay for all the guns and tanks. Cuba's an island, you know. They need water."

Gustafson smiled. He took another sip from his drink and said, "What do you think really happened with the electricity? Heard anything?"

"We were talking yesterday, me and my friend Fernando. I think the government doesn't know how to make the electricity work. I think they broke it, and now they say it is the contras." He gave a sharp nod and sat back down. Gustafson reached over and patted him on the back again.

"Maybe you're right, old man," he said. Beaming now, he slapped another wad of cordobas on the counter. The old man let the money sit there as Gustafson walked off; then he stuck the bills inside his shirt.

A couple of hours later the colonel was jubilant. All morning he'd been talking with people milling around the Huembles market, and hardly anyone thought the contras were the ones who'd turned out the lights. Most of them wrote it off to Sandinista incompetence. So in Managua, at least, the contras weren't getting any benefit from this. The raid would not begin accelerating the contra war, as Mendoza had planned. Mendoza's strategy wasn't working. Now it was the colonel's turn.

As he talked to vendors and their customers, young Interior Ministry soldiers, AKs slung over their shoulders, leaned against the walls. Zelaya's Interior Ministry troops were responsible for domestic enforcement. These soldiers were eyeing the girls and occasionally glanced at Gustafson without special interest. But he glared back at them, thinking: Maybe soon you Marxist bastards are finally gonna get what you deserve.

By noon the stalls began running out of merchandise, and the women started folding up their stands. Gustafson was talking to a pretty young girl who'd driven down from Achuapa with a load of rag quilts, learning from her about shortages and general dissatisfaction up there. He dropped a thank-you wad of cordobas on top of the quilts and was walking off. She didn't touch the money and glanced nervously back at the soldier just behind her, then shouted after Gustafson, "Señor, señor. Your quilt!"

When he turned, she was waving a quilt at him, though he hadn't bought one. He smiled, waved back at her, and walked on. But a moment later he heard her screech, and when he looked the girl was scuffling with the soldier. He had her by the arm and was dragging her toward a building fifty yards away. "I have done nothing," she was crying. "Nothing, nothing!"

Gustafson didn't hesitate. He turned and marched back toward them, crossing the short distance in just a few seconds. He walked right past them, then stepped directly in front of the soldier, crossed his arms over his chest, and commanded: "Leave that girl alone, soldier. She's done nothing wrong." The soldier stopped, startled, and looked up at the colonel, who was standing almost on top of his feet. The soldier was just a boy, maybe eighteen. The colonel, at least a foot taller and twenty years older, scowled down at him. The boy froze for a moment, scared. But then he stiffened, rose to his full height of five feet three, and said, "Get out of the way. This is government business."

All activity in the plaza stopped; everyone turned to watch. A couple of the other soldiers stood up straight and put hands on their weapons.

Gustafson didn't move. He spread his legs, hands on his hips, elbows out, and ordered in his toughest military voice, pausing a full second between each word: "Let—her—go. *Now!*"

The soldier suddenly let go of the girl's arm, and she fell to the ground, scrabbling through the dirt to get a few feet away. The boy stepped back and reached to unsling the AK-47 from his left shoulder. Still Gustafson didn't move as the soldier pulled the automatic rifle into his right hand, snapping the safety off, and began to lower it toward Gustafson's chest. Then suddenly the colonel reached out his right hand and with all his force slapped at the rifle. With a loud crack it spit a single round into the sky and then flew out of the soldier's hand, clattering into the dirt six feet away. All around the plaza the other soldiers scrambled to attention and raised rifles to their shoulders. The boy stood, startled and scared, looking up at Gustafson with his mouth open. He was starting to step backward, cowering, when

Gustafson suddenly raised his fist and slugged him full force in the face. The little soldier crumpled to the ground, out cold. In a second, blood was seeping from his nose.

No one moved for a moment. Then Gustafson stepped over to the girl, reached down, and asked, "You all right?"

"Get away from me, leave me alone," she hissed as she slid a few more feet away. But then Gustafson looked up, and five little soldiers surrounded him, AKs raised and pointed at his face. The boy lay senseless in the dirt behind them. Gustafson stood all the way up and raised his hands in front of him, palms up—more a shrug than a surrender.

Two hours later he was leaning against the wall of a moldy, windowless jail cell, one foot flat against the damp stone behind him, arms folded across his chest, when Major Chamorro came back for him. The major unlocked the cell door and looked at him without expression for a moment, before turning back toward the exit. Without a word, Gustafson followed. He knew the drill. He'd been here before.

"How many times, Eric, how many times," Kiernan, the embassy's deputy chief of mission, whispered when Gustafson walked up to him in the foyer, coming so close that he almost stepped on Kiernan's toes.

"This time they're going to kick you out for sure," Kiernan said, stepping back.

"No way," Gustafson said. "We have an understanding."

Outside, blinking in the sun, Kiernan whined, "I'm going to have to report this one, Eric. I have no choice."

"Fine with me. But the Sandis aren't going to say anything, I can tell you that."

"What do you mean they aren't going to say anything? A United States Marine beats up one of their soldiers? Sends him to the military hospital with a broken nose? They're not going to say anything about that? You're crazy!"

"Lemme tell you, I laid it out to my old buddy Chamorro, how this Sandi soldier was dragging a young girl away at gunpoint to beat her up and rape her just because she'd been caught talking to a gringo. How one single, solitary United States Marine, dressed in civvies, unarmed, disarmed one of the Sandi army's finest and laid him out flat with one hand while trying to protect a Nic national, a pretty little girl just in from the country. That's how I'd tell the story to the papers when I got back to the States. No, they're not going to say a word."

"Eric," Kiernan whimpered, shaking his head as they climbed into the car. But driving back to the embassy he didn't say another word. *He won't report*, Gustafson thought.

Back at the embassy, Gustafson closed his office door and called the U.S. embassy in Honduras right away, using the secure telephone. In a little computer under the desk top, his conversation was translated into scrambled bursts that were then buried in a wash of white noise. The matching phone at the other end removed just the right amount of white noise and then reassembled the speech. Anyone listening on the line heard only electronic shrieking.

"Hey, Raf, how's it going?" he asked.

"Well enough, Eric," Mendoza said. But he didn't sound his normal, cheery self.

"You don't sound so good, old buddy," Gustafson said. "You okay? Wouldn't want anything wrong with you now. You and I have important work to do, pal."

Mendoza's voice was warm but weary. "I'm okay, my friend."

They were unlikely friends, this tall swaggering Texas bully and Mendoza, the tiny Cuban CIA agent whose normal expression was a silly grin. But the first time they met, almost a year ago at a regional diplomats' meeting in Miami, they realized they had a common interest. While most people in the American government seemed content to sit on their hands and let the contras muddle along for another ten years rather than make any hard choices, Gustafson and Mendoza both wanted to find a way to "take the Sandinista bastards out," as Gustafson liked to put it. Their motivations were as different as their intended approaches.

Gustafson looked on the Sandinistas as little better than cockroaches who deserved only to be squashed. That's why, if it were up to him, he'd send in a couple of Marine amphibious brigades and the 82nd Airborne. No more half steps and political compromises—just solve the problem, once and for all.

Mendoza was virulently anti-Communist, like most Cuban emigrés, and he certainly wouldn't object if the United States decided to invade Nicaragua. But Mendoza was also a Bay of Pigs veteran, and now he was passionately dedicated to making sure that the United States did not desert another Latin guerrilla force in the breach. His preferred solution was to use the contras more effectively, let them drive the Sandinistas out.

After they'd talked awhile that first evening, sitting in a vinyl booth at the back of Miami's Omni Hotel bar, they discovered that they'd run up against similar brick walls. Washington had stopped reading Gustafson's reports. And as for Mendoza, the contra RIG up in Washington had rebuffed every one of his proposals for more effective use of the contras.

Mendoza and Gustafson were convinced they knew what was best for Nicaragua. Unlike those ass-covering bureaucrats up in Washington, they were here, on the ground. They managed to get together every month or so in Managua, Tegucigalpa, or Miami and liked to debate tactics and strategy, each trying to convince the other that his approach was best. In the end the debate may have been academic. Gustafson blustered and swaggered, but he'd never been able to explain how he would dial up an invasion, though once with an enigmatic smile Mendoza had told him, "If it ever comes to that, there might be a way."

For now, though, they had decided they needed to give themselves some independence, some personal power, so they wouldn't be wholly reliant on those spineless office boys up in Washington. To that end, they'd recruited Major Paz and his men and set them up to carry out Mendoza's and Gustafson's own more ambitious operations, such as this "enhanced" electrical substation raid. Mendoza would run them from Honduras; Gustafson would provide intelligence from Managua and promote any successes in his monthly reports.

So now, over the phone, Mendoza asked Gustafson, "What did you learn on your walk today. Did our plan succeed?"

"Honest, ol' buddy," Gustafson said, "I wish it wasn't so, but it just didn't work out." On the other end Mendoza listened quietly as Gustafson told him about the interviews, how nobody believed the contras had really been behind the raid.

Then the colonel asked Mendoza, "So what about the electrical engineer, Alvarado? Was he there? Did Paz get him?" Gustafson's contribution to the plan had been to watch Alvarado over a week's time and learn that he spent Thursday evenings at the Los Mártires station.

"He was there," Mendoza said, his voice soft now. "And Paz got him. But the old man had a bad heart. He died before they could get him up to camp."

"Hey, I'm sorry, pal."

"I'm afraid Washington found out, too," Mendoza added. "Basham called here this morning."

George Basham was a sour intelligence bureaucrat and Mendoza's immediate supervisor in Washington. On the phone a couple of hours earlier, he had shouted at Mendoza, "What the fuck are your greaseballs doing down there, kidnapping that engineer? This better not have been your idea, Mendoza!"

Now Mendoza told Gustafson, "I said I didn't know anything about it."

But with that the colonel slapped his desk top and sat up straight in his chair. His words came fast now. "So Basham's on top of you, meaning now we can't try this kind of operation again, right?"

Mendoza started to answer, but Gustafson cut him off. "Listen, Raf, some of Zelaya's boys picked me up again this morning. I'm fed up. It's time we went after these pissant Marxist soms-uh-bitches, struttin' around down here, spittin' on our boots. I've really had it with these—" He caught himself. Gustafson was about to say "these tacos" but remembered who he was talking to. "We gave your way a try. It didn't work. Now it's my turn."

But Mendoza's voice picked up. "Don't be so fast, my friend. This operation was just a start. We learned some things. And I also have information from Washington that we may have a new window of opportunity opening up for us. I got word that the president is about to put a new man on the contra RIG."

"So what?" Gustafson spat back. "It's just gonna be another good-for-nothing, sit-on-your-hands bureaucrat. What's that mean? It means nothing."

"Don't be so quick to judge," Mendoza interrupted. "I got a line on him from somebody at Langley who looked up his file for me. His name's Ascher, from State. He doesn't know he's been picked yet, but this fellow has a very interesting history. It looks like he's ambitious, willing to take chances."

"So?" Gustafson wasn't sure what Mendoza was getting at.

"So, he's had no involvement with the program before. If he hasn't already made up his mind, maybe he can be influenced. We've gone a long way toward setting up independent capabilities for ourselves down here. What we need now is someone to carry our water for us up in Washington." Then in a voice shorn of inflection, Mendoza said simply, "I think this may be somebody we can work with."

That remark rang in Gustafson's ears. He remembered the last time he'd heard Mendoza use the line, early in the year.

A Honduran major general, the sort who was all Latin bravado and gold-trimmed epaulets, tried to shake down the CIA, threatening to kick the contras out of the country. General Salinas could have done it, too. It wasn't really clear who ran Honduras, the civilian leadership or the military.

Rafael Mendoza had been the general's target because he was relatively new to Honduras and had the highly deceptive appearance of an easy mark. Mendoza played along at first, while he sent one of his Honduran operatives out to learn what he could about "the general's interests," Mendoza's euphemistic phrase for the general's exploitable weaknesses—drugs, money, women, little boys. It turned out Salinas had a particular fondness for busty blond American women. And, not surprising, he got off by roughing them up.

Well, without skipping a beat, Mendoza brought a stunning blond hooker down from Miami and set up what the agency calls a "honey trap." She pretended to be a free-lance journalist writing about the "power of the Honduran armed forces," and she seduced the general—actually she just gave in to him—in a CIA safehouse-apartment that was monitored through the wall.

He began beating her after they'd been together a couple of times. As instructed, she pretended to love it, so he beat her some more, harder. Less than a week later he beat her to death, splattering blood all over the headboard. And when the agent monitoring the apartment called to tell Mendoza, legend had it, he responded, "All the better."

Mendoza didn't have to mention the tapes or the photos. The general knew. Mendoza disposed of the hooker's body. The general moved to Guatemala.

At the time, Gustafson hadn't been sure how he felt about Mendoza's tactics. He knew what he would have done—held a .45 to the little general's head and told him: "You fuck with me, buddy, and you'll be deader than you ever dreamed, faster than you ever thought it could happen." But in his own way Mendoza sure got the job done, Gustafson thought. God, he was a ruthless son-of-a-bitch. Looking at him—small, balding, and that ever-present happy grin—who'd have guessed?

So now Mendoza was saying, "We've got another chance. Be patient, my friend. I think this man Ascher is somebody we can work with. I'm going to send somebody at State over to find out what his interests are."

Poor son-of-a-bitch, Gustafson thought.

CHAPTER THREE

THE WHITE HOUSE, WASHINGTON, AUGUST 8

Late Friday morning Terry Ascher took a cab over to the Northwest Gate. His State Department photopass hung from his neck on one of those ubiquitous silverball chains that everyone in the bureaucracy had to wear. Only Cabinet members and others who were unmistakably recognizable could get in and out of their offices without their passes flopping about over their forty-dollar neckties. Washington's response to terrorism.

Washingtonians liked to say the capital had the nation's worst climate—gray, snowy winters and summers so humid that vain men changed their shirts three times a day. Today was no exception. The hum of crickets filled the air even downtown; workers drifted lazily through the day, each moment outdoors sapping their energy and resolve. But Ascher looked to be a man of great purpose as he pushed his pass up to the tinted bulletproof window at the gatehouse.

He wore a dark blue suit with soft, slight pinstripes. Seven or eight of them, more or less identical, hung in his closet. They were the staple of his daily uniform. Some were wool, some linen, for Washington's wildly disparate seasons. The jackets had cuff buttons that could be unfastened to no known end, three inside pockets plus a half-inch fountain-pen slot, white silk sleeve linings, and a single vent; no cuffs on the pants. Ascher couldn't conceive of wearing the same suit two days in a row but switched among these almost identical versions more or less at random. It was a paradox he seldom chose to ponder.

He wore a bleached white shirt, a red silk tie, and slim black wingtips polished, as always, to an unblemished sheen. Ascher's was the uniform of Washington's near-powerful. The men really on top didn't seem to care about what they wore. He kept his black curly hair short enough to be respectable, he figured, but just long enough to show a little dash. He was slim, dark, nice-looking, he knew. The sunlamp helped. And today he wanted to play every asset.

He'd never expected to be here. But two days earlier, Arthur Kutler, his boss at the State Department, had thrown a question at him that landed with the force of a cinderblock.

"You want to go to the White House?"

Ascher had tried to show no reaction. For a foreign service officer, that question held such a range of possibilities, from fascinating to frightening, that it was best to betray nothing before knowing all the facts.

"Doing what?" he'd asked.

"Working with the contras."

He had jolted forward. "Art, come on. You're kidding. The contras?"

"Terry, the president asked for you."

"What do you mean, the president asked for me? The president has never even heard of me. And who'd want to get involved with the contras after all this time? Art, what's this really about?"

Kutler leaned forward, elbows on his cluttered desk, sleeves rolled up two turns. "You know they're having trouble with the program. The president and Congress are behind it, within limits. But under this new funding law, the doves in Congress insisted that the daily administration of the program had to come from career people, not political appointees from State, Defense, and the agency. Well, nobody wants to take a risk, so the whole program's stagnant. The president wants it moving forward again before the reelection campaign gets started.

"The White House wants its own man to administer it. You'd fill a new position, White House representative, and you'd run the office. You'd be the coordinator, administrator. The congressional leaders have agreed to the change, and nobody thinks you'd have any trouble getting congressional confirmation.

You'll be the one who can finally make some good out of this thing."

Ascher said nothing.

"It's a White House appointment, Terry. It'll be good for you." His voice now held a slightly imploring air, unusual for him. "If you do this well, it can only help you. It's the White House, and I'll bet you can get a good post coming out of this."

Not likely, Ascher thought as he looked at the floor, his head a jumble of conflicting thoughts.

"Why me for this job?" he asked without looking up.

"You've compiled quite a record over here as someone who can get things done. I recommended you. But they already knew of you. That Bahamas treaty got a lot of people's attention." In fact, *The Washington Post* had written a story about it. "It was a hell of a feat, and maybe they think you can do the same thing with the contras." Then, shaking his head, Kutler said, "You know, I still can't figure out how you did it."

With that remark, Ascher felt a chill.

He'd been in a U.S. Army Blackhawk helicopter flying west over the Caribbean toward Bimini. Strapped into the web seat next to him was the Bahamian attorney general, the Right Honourable Mr. Wilcox, who was, Ascher thought, treating him with the deference that was due the deputy assistant secretary of state for the Caribbean, the senior State Department officer for this little part of the world. The attorney general kept smiling at him with the strained grin of a proud man who knew he still had to please.

Ascher was supposed to meet the prime minister that evening to make one more pitch for the Mutual Legal Assistance Treaty. The Justice Department kept saying it was an indispensable weapon in the drug war, but the Bahamians kept stalling. They wouldn't sign.

Critics said the Bahamian government was balking because the prime minister and his men were corrupt, in bed with the drug lords. Probably because of that, early in the morning the attorney general had called Ascher in his suite at the Cable Beach Hotel. The Royal Bahamian Defence Force had just spotted a target, a ship loaded with marijuana, steaming north toward Bimini. Would the assistant secretary like to watch Bahamian law enforcement in action? Ascher knew what they were up to. They had no intention of signing the treaty. So this afternoon they wanted to put on a show to make him think they were serious about drug enforcement anyway.

The helicopter's wide side door was swung open, and a Bahamian police officer dressed in a bright-buttoned uniform mimicking a British bobby's pointed a deck-mounted machine gun at the blue coral reef passing fast underneath. Three other Bahamian policemen sat beside them.

Mr. Wilcox leaned over and in the lilting tones of a black Bahamian said, "The treaty isn't everything, you know." Ascher didn't answer. For him at that moment it might not have been everything. But it was undeniably important.

Mutual Legal Assistance Treaty was a cunning name for an agreement that would give American officers unfettered rights to rifle through secret bank accounts of suspected drug traffickers and tax cheats. There really wasn't anything mutual about it; the Bahamas had little interest in going through American bank accounts. And like every one of the countries the United States had approached with these treaties, the Bahamas wasn't interested. Accepting the treaty meant, in essence, agreeing to cripple the country's offshore banking industry by piercing the absolute confidentiality that made it so popular. Ascher knew that. But for two years he and others had pounded and pleaded with such persistence that the treaty had taken on political importance far beyond its actual worth. Ascher just had to get it signed if he hoped ever to be promoted out of this job.

He'd been in the Caribbean bureau two years and had done well enough. He was the only son of a career foreign service officer, Wallace Ascher. Though Wallace had retired, he was still remembered with respect in the department, and so Ascher believed expectations of him were high. He knew full well, and his father in his own subtle yet brutal way had reminded him, that his was not a high-profile post. The Caribbean. It could be worse. He could be over at Oceans and International Environment. Still, at forty-one he was young to be a deputy assistant. Arthur Kutler, Ascher's immediate supervisor and the full assistant secretary in charge of American policy toward all of Latin America and the Caribbean, was in his early fifties. Nonetheless, it galled Ascher that while Kutler often testified on Capitol Hill and got on TV, Ascher was invited to speak at travel agents' conventions.

As had been true in his previous postings, he was dogged at his work, forever afraid someone would find something he hadn't done. And when he visited these little Caribbean countries, the presidents and prime ministers greeted him with dignity and awe that bordered on fear. He liked that. People he met from the outside assumed he must be a State Department favorite. Why else would he be assigned to work in the Caribbean, where many of them chose to spend the two or three weeks a year when they could go anywhere they wanted? Actually, the United States had few important strategic interests here: tourism, immigration, economic development, drug trafficking. But the one real career-booster, the Communist Threat, had been eliminated with the Grenada invasion years earlier. Jamaica seemed on the verge of heading too far left now and then. But the secretary of state wasn't about to call senior staff meetings to discuss the Jamaican threat.

From this position, if he was lucky, maybe he'd get an ambassadorial posting to some place like Barbados. Nice spots like Jamaica that occasionally got into the newspapers almost always went to political appointees—the campaign chairman from Michigan, people like that. When he let himself think about it, really, this job was a mire. The treaty, that was one way to get out.

The helicopter pilot, an American Army lieutenant, leaned back and shouted, "Target dead ahead." These U.S. Army Blackhawks and crews were on semipermanent station here to help the Bahamians chase the dozens of drug traffickers who passed through the islands every day on their way to the United States.

The helicopter banked right, and out the left door Ascher spotted a large freighter, two hundred feet at least, half a mile away. The pilot pulled around the stern until they could read the ship's name. *Espíritu.* Cartagena, Colombia.

Close up now they could see brown bales of marijuana, scores of them, lying all over the deck. They'd come at just the right moment, after the bales had been hauled up on deck to be unloaded. More than a dozen high-speed cigarette boats nestled along both port and starboard. Their crews were catching marijuana bales being lobbed to them over the side; they looked like piglets feeding from a sow.

"Call the Bahamian Defence Force base," Mr. Wilcox shouted to the radio man.

"Call the U.S. Coast Guard," said Ascher. The Coast Guard patrolled the Bahamas almost as if it were U.S. territory.

"Coast Guard Cutter *Bear* in vicinity, sir," the radioman

yelled back to Ascher. "ETA, two to three minutes. Cutter *Harriet Lane* close behind."

The traffickers ignored the helicopter. But when the Coast Guard cutter *Bear* came roaring at them, bow high, forward 50-caliber machine gun spitting warning bursts into the water all around them, most of the cigarette boats took off at high speed toward Miami, fifty-five miles away. The *Bear* peeled away after them, though she was hopelessly slow for the chase. But one fully loaded speedboat headed in the other direction, toward Cat Cay, one of the Bimini islands.

"Let's get that boat heading to the island," Ascher shouted, and the Blackhawk took off in hot pursuit.

In just over a minute Ascher could see ahead of them a beach crowded with Bahamians, watching the vessels charging at them from both sea and air.

The cigarette boat slowed only a little before it plowed right up the sand, finally stopping after it had sailed twenty yards up from the surf. The Blackhawk roared past and set down behind all the people. As they touched down the pilot switched on the public address speaker and pulled the microphone from the ceiling.

"This is the United States Army and the Royal Bahamian Defence Force. You people on the boat are under arrest. The rest of you on the beach, please step away."

"Oh, no," the attorney general moaned. "That was a mistake."

The cigarette boat was fifty feet away, and the crowd moved toward it from both sides.

"Keep away," the pilot shouted through the PA, but the Bahamians broke into a run. Dozens of them grabbed at the marijuana bales, ripping them into pieces and carrying the marijuana off. The boat crew was gone.

"Bloody fools," Mr. Wilcox said, and as he spoke something clunked against the side of the Blackhawk.

"Shit," said the pilot, and when Ascher looked out the door, the crowd was rushing at the copter, hurling stones, empty bottles, shoes—anything they could find. The Blackhawk was being pummeled by Bahamians shouting, "Get away, Americans!" Ascher glared at the policemen seated across from him.

"Aren't you going to do anything?" None of them moved.

Then they heard a gunshot, and a spot of light appeared in the copter body just over the attorney general's head.

"Get us out of here," Ascher shouted, and the copter lifted off in a rush.

Ascher had read of incidents like this but never expected to find himself caught in one. At Government House that evening he didn't offer even the hint of a smile. The prime minister, usually arrogant and sneering, was embarrassed and apologetic, and so Ascher got an idea. He improvised.

"Mr. Prime Minister," he said as soon as he sat down, "this afternoon's events were most distressing not just to me but to the entire United States government." Actually he hadn't told anyone yet, but judging by the prime minister's expression, he didn't know that.

"In light of what happened, if you do not sign the Mutual Legal Assistance Treaty before I leave Nassau tomorrow at noon, the United States will have no choice but to conclude that the Bahamas is not serious about drug trafficking. If the Bahamas is not serious, then the State Department will have no choice but to place the Bahamas on our official list of major drug-trafficking nations, under the Drug Enforcement, Education, and Control Act." There was no question that the Bahamians were familiar with the new law. Their embassy in Washington had asked Ascher's office for a copy. The prime minister sat forward in his chair, all attention.

"Once you're on that list, as you know, trade sanctions and other penalties are automatically put into place." Ascher didn't even have to mention the worst sanction, the inevitable publicity and resulting drop in tourism, lifeblood of the islands.

That was all he had to say. The prime minister looked startled. The attorney general sat mum. The next morning the treaty was signed.

To this day, Ascher was sure, the prime minister hadn't figured out that the Bahamas wasn't really eligible for the major-drug-traffickers list, treaty or no. Under regulations written just a few weeks before the trip, only drug-producing nations, not transit countries like the Bahamas, were in jeopardy. And to this day, Ascher knew, the State Department still hadn't figured out that he had won the treaty by using an unusual diplomatic tool. Extortion.

But Ascher didn't think of it that way. This episode and others that preceded it were just "pushing the edge of the envelope," he liked to think. Ascher's way of making a name for himself.

And it had worked. In the department the treaty was still regarded as a wondrous feat. And now it had brought a job offer from the White House.

As he left Kutler's office at State that afternoon, at first he wasn't sure he wanted to pursue the job. The contras. They'd been in the field more than a dozen years without making even a dent in the Sandinistas' stranglehold on Nicaragua, despite several hundred million dollars in legal and illegal U.S. aid. When President Reagan left office, everyone was sure the program would die a well-deserved death. Even now, years later—with the president and Congress finally in agreement and opinion polls showing that a bare majority of the American public also supported the program—Ascher doubted that the contras could ever make a real difference. Congress had approved new military aid last year, but with the old and familiar restriction that the money couldn't be used to overthrow the Nicaraguan government. And just to be sure, the House of Representatives had placed administration of the program in the hands of the do-nothing Restricted Interagency Group. As if that weren't enough, they insisted that RIG members be subject to congressional approval. That, of course, ensured that no firebrands, ideologues, or even people with uncommon ambition would have a hand in running the program.

Under these restrictions, Ascher knew, the contras could never win a military victory, even with lavish funding. And as long as they remained simply a harassment force, weren't they actually propelling the Sandinistas to even greater belligerence?

To Ascher by now all this was an old, old debate. Impossible to settle, wearying to ponder. He was a contra supporter, of sorts. His office was a part of the Latin America bureau, the contra program's home in the State Department. Hardly a week went by when he hadn't found himself at the cafeteria with colleagues from adjacent offices debating contra strategy. Actually that usually meant figuring out how to dupe Congress for aid one more time. Ascher seldom participated in any meaningful way; he would sit there feeling grateful to be over in the Caribbean.

But at other times he wanted part of the action. The contras were the highest-visibility program in the bureau, maybe in the whole department. Sometimes Ascher believed the other deputy assistants must be sneering at him behind his back. A Harvard graduate, son of a respected career officer, stuck over here in this sunny backwater.

Boy would they be surprised when they saw his picture in *The Washington Post*—a new special assistant to the president.

Maybe it was worth the risk. Maybe the contras would come through yet. The White House. This time, at last, his father would have to be impressed.

At the Northwest Gatehouse, the uniformed Secret Service guard leaned forward and squinted to read his name, then checked a computer printout list and picked up the phone to ask for clearance.

The door buzzed, and he walked through the guardhouse metal detector, then out onto the wide drive leading to the West Wing, the low building one hundred yards ahead. It looked innocuous, an add-on that might just be the garage where they kept the president's bullet-proof limousines. Actually the Oval Office was in there, along with the offices of all the senior staff. Teddy Roosevelt had it built when he was president.

Off to Ascher's left the main building, the residence, gleamed white. Curtains in all the windows perfectly arrayed. High shrubs, flawlessly shaped. The lawn neatly trimmed.

Several network television cameras sat on tripods halfway up the walk, as they usually did, aluminum equipment cases scattered carelessly on the lawn. One reporter was doing a stand-up, holding a microphone and talking into the camera. Probably CNN, Ascher thought. On the air all the time. Ascher could see his mouth move but couldn't hear his words. The reporter stood so the White House residence was with him in the camera's frame, just over his left shoulder. Even under a full-noon sun, a technician pointed a spotlight at the reporter from atop a pole. His smooth face glowed.

Walking on, Ascher felt pretty good. Confident. He smiled. He'd taken a Valium just before coming over. Cracked a little yellow five-milligram pill in two and put the other half back in the small envelope he kept hidden under the stationery in his middle desk drawer. Valium helped him. It took the anxious edge off the nervous energy that drove him and gave him the gift of calm confidence. Ascher was careful not to take more than a normal dose and never—well, seldom—two pills in a day. He was not a big drug user. Never had been, not even in college. At times, though, he needed it. And it had been proven safe. After all, years earlier former presidential aide Robert McFarlane had tried to kill himself with Valium. He'd failed. So over the last few years Ascher had hidden those little envelopes of pills almost everywhere he might be: in the car, at the office, in his travel kit. It felt good to know they were near in case something came up.

At the entrance, the Marine sergeant in dress blues offered a brief nod and held open one of the double doors. Ascher stepped into the West Lobby and over to the receptionist, who was speaking softly into the phone. He looked down at the young woman's pretty auburn hair, and when she didn't look up right away he leaned forward, sniffing discreetly to see if he could smell her creme rinse. Strawberry-jasmine. He stretched to his full height—six feet, his driver's license said, but really it was five ten and a half. After a moment she lifted her gaze, and Ascher smiled, looking directly into her eyes, his sunlamp tan glowing, his large green eyes open wide for full effect. But none of it was working on this pretty secretary. She gave back a gracious but obligatory smile and waited for him to speak. Already today a dozen of these Washington men had stood there smiling down at her.

"Hi. I'm Terrence Ascher, here to see Mr. Christopher."

"Yes, Mr. Ascher," she said, looking down at a list Ascher couldn't see. "Mr. Christopher is expecting you. If you'll just have a seat, someone will be out to escort you."

He sat on a peach-colored Queen Anne sofa and looked around. He'd been here a time or two before but examined the place with new interest. The West Lobby was a long room with doors in three walls and seating clusters at either end. A very old Simon Willard wall clock ticked away over his head. Eastman Johnson's rendition of *Washington Crossing the Delaware* hung to his right.

At the room's other end, a two-star Army general and his lieutenant-colonel aide were whispering to each other, hunched over a document inside an open Samsonite briefcase sitting on a butler's table. As the general perorated, the colonel grunted and nodded unswerving agreement. Probably preparing to pitch someone to spend more money on something that wouldn't work, Ascher thought.

Through the door in the far wall came a woman so large that Ascher must have looked startled when she walked up to him. Three hundred and fifty pounds, he guessed. She looked at him with an I-don't-care-about-nothing-or-nobody expression, her defense against a lifetime of reproachful looks from strangers.

"Mr. Ascher? I'm Greta Harkin, Mr. Christopher's assistant. Would you follow me, please?"

He stepped behind the swishing mass of flesh through a couple of doors and down a carpeted hall carefully lit with recessed lights. A Frederic Remington bronze of a cowboy on a horse sat atop a credenza. On the walls hung eighteenth- and nineteenth-century oil portraits of American political figures, some of them easily recognizable, some of them not.

They turned a corner and walked past the Oval Office. The door was open, a maroon theater rope across the opening. The president was out of town, on vacation in Arizona, and on a day like this dozens of people on private tours were brought down this hall for a peek inside. A telephone with what looked like a hundred lines sat on a table just outside the door. The defense-alert phone. Ascher glanced inside the office as they walked past. It looked smaller than he'd imagined, probably because the newspaper and magazine photos he'd seen over the years all were taken with wide-angle lenses. He'd have liked to stop and look but didn't want to seem too interested. Greta lumbered on, not even turning her head, and they passed a couple of other offices, with secretaries at desks just inside the doors. They turned into a room on the left, and Greta waved him to a chair, then settled into her own seat with a heavy sigh. The chair groaned. A light on her telephone console was lit. When it went out Greta pressed a button, and Ascher heard a buzzer in the office behind him.

Out of his office bounded Christopher, a pixieish man in his early fifties with curly hair, prematurely silver-white, and an effervescent smile.

"Terry, Terry, how are you. Come on in, come in." As they shook hands, Christopher gently propelled him into the office with his other hand on Ascher's back, a gesture not of haste but of informality. Ascher had met Christopher a couple of times before at receptions around town. He always reminded Ascher of his dentist.

Christopher bustled. Always in motion, always smiling, he was the classic aide-de-camp to the powerful—an "aw, shucks" kind of guy up front, a ruthless manipulator behind the scenes. He'd worked for George Van Nostrand, the White House chief of staff, for nearly thirty years, in and out of government; Christopher was an indispensable Van Nostrand appendage. And here in the White House, he had grown to be an unusually powerful player.

"Sit down, sit down," Christopher said, motioning toward a plush couch. Ascher sat with a whoosh. This was the first down-filled sofa he'd seen in a government office.

"We'll have lunch in a minute," Christopher said. A small dining table on wheels sat in the middle of the office, with a perfect white linen cloth and two place settings. Ascher had seen this done once before, in the under secretary of state's office. He tried to glance quickly around the office, noting details—fresh flowers in a cut-glass vase, polished brass fixtures, original works of American art—but saw Christopher watching him and quickly returned his attention to the conversation.

"First," Christopher said, "tell me what you're doing these days over there in the Caribbean. I'll bet your friends give you a hard time about a plush job like that. But we've got some real tough issues down there, don't we?"

"Yes, sir, we do," Ascher said, playing along.

"Please, call me Rich," Christopher said with a backhand wave. "Tell me, Terry, just what are we going to do about the drug smuggling down there? You know the president is very concerned about that."

Ascher couldn't believe the president of the United States had spent even fifteen seconds thinking about the Caribbean drug-smuggling problem.

"Terry, you've done a hell of a job over there," Christopher was saying. "That Bahamas treaty was a real coup. And that's one of the things that caused us to think you'd be good for this new job we're going to have over here helping us manage the program to aid the Nicaraguan resistance."

"Well, I'm certainly flattered to be considered," Ascher said.

"This isn't meant as flattery. We're just being pragmatic. Look, I don't want to play games with you. You're a bright guy, and I want to put everything right up front. We've looked over a lot of people, and we think you've got just the right background and qualifications."

Ascher said nothing.

"For one thing, you know the place. You spent most of your youth in Latin America with your father."

Not strictly true. He'd lived with his parents at his father's first Latin American post, when he was ambassador to Venezuela. But when Ascher was in elementary school, President Kennedy had posted his father to El Salvador—a respected career diplomat sent to what had been considered a backwater posting, one strategy to show that the president was serious about his Alliance for Progress—and Ascher had been packed off to a boarding school in Connecticut.

"Being Wallace Ascher's son is a plus," Christopher went on.

"People on the Hill still remember your father. And you were posted in Costa Rica yourself during the years before the Nicaraguan revolution. You speak Spanish, you know Latin issues. But you've been out of the arena the last few years."

Before taking his Caribbean post, Ascher had served four years as political officer at the embassy in La Paz, Bolivia.

"That's good," Christopher said. "In the contra world, you're an unknown. Maybe best of all, in my view, as I understand it, you are a contra supporter, but you aren't rabid. You're a pragmatist."

That must have come from Kutler.

"Am I right about that?"

"Well, I guess so, more or less."

"You're just the kind of guy Congress will love," Christopher said, leaning back with a smile. Almost as an afterthought he added, "And I think you'd do a hell of a job."

"But what is this job exactly?" Ascher asked.

"Come on, let's have some lunch, and I'll tell you about it." Christopher pushed a button on the phone console next to his chair as they both got up and moved to the dining table.

Before they had spread linen napkins over their laps, there were two soft knocks on the door and in walked a black man wearing a starched white steward's coat. He stood beside the table and offered a slight bow of the head to each of them as he said, "Good afternoon, Mr. Christopher. Good afternoon, Mr. Ascher."

"Clifton," Christopher said, nodding back.

The steward handed each of them a single-page menu on stiff paper. *The White House*, it said at the top, just above an embossed gold presidential seal. Typed below in the shiny, precise lettering of a laser-jet printer was *Luncheon, August 8*, then the day's offerings.

"Gentlemen," Clifton said with the gentle, pleasing cadence of a black Washingtonian, "today we have as our appetizer course our baby lettuce salad with garden tomatoes, fresh basil, and a vinaigrette dressing, or we have our cream of avocado soup with a touch of brandy.

"For our main course we have fresh Chesapeake soft-shell crabs with a sliced-almond-butter sauce. We also have rack of lamb *aux flageolets.*" His accent wasn't bad. "Or we have a fresh Dover sole with lemon, butter, and tarragon, just picked."

Ascher saw the desserts on the menu—raspberries with *crème fraîche*, peach pie, cheeses with fresh fruit—but Clifton did not discuss them. Christopher waved his hand at Ascher, and he ordered the crabs.

"Good choice," Christopher said. "The same for me."

Clifton opened a bottle of Northern California chardonnay, wrapped it in a towel, poured, and left with a slight bow. Watching all this pomp for a work lunch, Ascher clenched his teeth, trying hard not to smile. To hide his mouth he reached for the wine.

"*Salut,*" Christopher said, quickly picking up his own glass. They both took a sip, and Christopher said, "Okay, let me tell you the situation. As you know, the president has grown quite committed to the contra cause. The Sandinistas left him no choice. Senator Van Nostrand and I are going to do everything in our power to help him succeed with the program, and now as we approach a reelection year it's even more important that we make progress—without getting into trouble." He stopped for a moment to butter a hard roll and take a sip of wine. Ascher drank his water. Alcohol amplified the Valium's effect, and he wanted to be alert.

"I think it's fair to say that all of us here in the White House understand the necessity of the contra program, even though not every one of us might be quite as passionate about it as the president has become. Speaking for myself, even if I didn't like the contra program"—and the way he was saying this, Ascher suspected he didn't—"I signed on to serve and support the president in *all* his causes. And I intend to do that.

"Besides," he said, worried, perhaps, about his previous phrasing, "I think the contra program makes sense.

"Anyway, as you know, to get funding last year, we agreed to divide management of the program among several agencies, to spread responsibility and reduce the chances for the kinds of excesses we've had in years past. That's been done; the new contra RIG's been meeting almost a year.

"We've got CIA, State, and Defense working together, in a manner of speaking," Christopher said. "But the problem, frankly, is that the interest level on the part of some of these career people isn't very high. These guys seem more interested in getting on and off the RIG without incident than in making the program work. That's the sort of person you get when appointments are subject to congressional approval.

"If we get new funding next month, it's possible that this could be the contras' final year, if the elections don't go our way. And if events continue as they've been going in Nicaragua, that will affect our chances next year. It's important; the president talks about this all the time. We have *got* to make the most out of the forces we've created before we lose Nicaragua altogether."

He stopped for a moment as Clifton came in with the salads. After Clifton left, Ascher asked, "Why couldn't the president just ask the agencies to order the people on the RIG to show more initiative?"

Christopher laid down his fork and leaned toward Ascher before answering in a low, confiding tone. "Well, the president has encouraged that. Still does. But to be perfectly honest, after all the problems with this program, most of the people in the agencies aren't real enthusiastic about it either. And with that old clause in the law saying we can't use the money to 'overthrow the Nicaraguan government,' we can't make a big fuss about it.

"This president," Christopher said, his voice emphatic, "is not going to get in trouble by ignoring the will of Congress on contra aid, in spirit or in fact."

He looked straight at Ascher, trying to gauge his reaction. Ascher showed none. He was looking down at his salad, trying to break up a large leaf of Boston lettuce without spewing oil on his necktie. Christopher plunged on.

"So we decided that the most effective thing we could do was to put our own man on the RIG. Terry, the president would like you to administer the RIG." Ascher looked up. "We want you to be the new White House representative, the president's own man. We'd hope you could apply the same sort of problem-solving initiative that you showed over there in the Caribbean. You'd move over here to the White House. I'll give you the outlines of the job, but the president wants to talk to you about this himself." Ascher jerked in his chair. Christopher didn't seem to notice.

"You'd be a deputy assistant to the president, but you would not lose your foreign service ranking. We'd pay you a salary of eighty thousand plus"—a large raise. "You'd be the RIG's secretary, the White House representative, a full member of equal standing with the three departmental members. A new position. You'd report directly to me. We'd ask you to promise to stay on the job through the elections. In exchange, in the next term the president will give you an ambassadorship or make you an assistant secretary. If somehow we lose reelection, well, if you comport yourself well in this difficult assignment, I can't see how any person who becomes president would not see you as a very valuable player."

"But what happens if Congress doesn't reapprove aid next month?" Ascher asked. The current appropriation for the contras ran out September 30.

Christopher shook his head. "I don't think there's much chance of that, particularly with the new information on the Soviets' accepting military landing rights. That intelligence has been shared privately with all the relevant congressional leaders, and it made quite an impact. And maybe you heard—the Sandinistas seem to do something stupid every day. This week they closed the Catholic radio station. Didn't like the archbishop's sermons. That made Congress even madder. But the other side of it is, we're being told that the House Democrats are not going to change their insistence on leaving the same spending limitations in place—including administration of the program by the same RIG.

"Still," Christopher said with a dismissive wave, "if for some reason we don't get the aid, then you'd stay where you are. Otherwise, we'd like you to straighten up affairs over there at State and be ready to start here in October."

Ascher showed no reaction. Christopher was silent, picking at his salad. Clifton came back in, cleared the plates, and served the crabs from under silver domes. They let off clouds of steam. He poured more wine and left. Still neither of them spoke. Ascher wondered if Christopher was having second thoughts. Should he have asked more questions? Should he be showing more enthusiasm?

Finally Christopher quietly asked, "Terry, will you at least think about it?" For a fleeting moment his manner made Ascher wonder if others had been here to lunch before him, only to turn the job down. But Ascher had no doubts. His life was looking up.

"Rich, I'll do it," he said.

Christopher flopped back in his chair with a thump and for a moment just stared at Ascher, his mouth open a quarter inch. His hand still gripped a forkful of crab; butter sauce dripped into his lap. Then slowly a smile spread across his face. "That's great, that's just great," he whispered. Then he stood all of a sudden, spilling his napkin onto his plate, and nearly bellowed, "This is great news, really great news!" He reached to shake hands, still smiling. "Wonderful, wonderful. Just wonderful.

"Terry, welcome aboard."

*   *   *

Ascher didn't get back to the office until almost two-thirty. He hurried through the work that had to be done this afternoon as fast as he could. Already it seemed irrelevant. Just after four he packed his briefcase, slipped on his jacket, and left. He had no special plans this evening but looked forward to pondering the new life ahead.

Pulling his BMW out of the State Department's underground lot he drove straight to his regular video store on Connecticut Avenue, looked around for a minute, and then bought a copy of the new Francis Ford Coppola Vietnam War movie, just in. He loved video war movies, collected them, and had been waiting for this one. Then he drove straight home.

He lived in a three-story Georgian-style townhouse on California Street in Kalorama, a block up from the Malaysian embassy. The five-bedroom home was not large for this neighborhood of million-dollar houses, but for a man living alone some parts seemed almost like wilderness territory. He'd bought it during his first tour in Washington, before going to Costa Rica. He was desk officer for Colombia then, an entry-level job, and the house had been far too expensive for a junior foreign service employee. But Ascher had a trust fund. His mother's family was wealthy, owners of the largest chain of auto dealerships in Cleveland. Ascher had been almost twenty when she died, and word of the grand inheritance did little to relieve his grief. But now the money made quite a difference.

He listened to a soft jazz station on the radio as he made dinner, washing each bowl and utensil immediately after use, cleaning splatters and spills from the countertops almost as they occurred. Ascher's whole house was immaculate, as if a white-gloved drill sergeant were due for an inspection in thirty minutes. His Guatemalan maid came three times a week and most days had a hard time finding anything useful to do. She washed towels that hadn't been touched since the last washing and vacuumed plush carpets that still showed wheel marks from the vacuuming a few days before. Throughout the house, down sofa cushions were fluffed, throw pillows stood on their points.

On the kitchen table Ascher set one place for himself. He had always been single but assumed the condition was temporary, though he hadn't gone out with anyone he considered a possible marriage partner in a while. Actually, every time he got involved with someone it seemed to end badly.

Ascher believed he'd been in love with his last girlfriend, Karen, a desk officer over in Western European Affairs. They'd been together almost three years, but toward the end she'd seemed to grow distant.

"It's just a phase," she'd explained. But then she was offered a post in West Germany and accepted it without even the tiniest hesitation. She wouldn't even listen to Ascher's attempts to talk her into staying, and she didn't call or even send a postcard after she left. A few weeks later, Ascher read a wedding announcement in the *Foreign Service Journal.* Karen had married Morris Burton, an officer who'd been working with her in Western European Affairs. He'd been transferred to West Germany at the very same time.

Ascher hadn't thought about all that in months. But he'd also stopped making much of an effort socially. He saw his longtime Washington friends now and then and accepted most of the dinner invitations he got—attractive single men were sought-after guests in Washington; they filled out the seating chart. But truth be told, most evenings he'd just as soon stay home. Sooner or later, he figured, the right woman would wander his way.

He ate slowly, listening to the jazz as he ran through a series of pleasing fantasies about what his life would be like at the White House. The scenarios grew more elaborate, more pointedly sexual, as he got halfway through a bottle of wine. He could see himself standing at one of those Washington cocktail receptions, sipping scotch as he was introduced to a tall blonde in a low-cut dress.

"And what do you do," she would ask, already looking over his shoulder to see who else was there.

"I work at the White House," he'd tell her.

"Ohhh," she'd say, tilting her head a bit as she looked back at him with a suddenly interested smile. When Ascher got up to clear the table he was smiling and erect.

He stumbled a bit as he put everything in the dishwasher. Downstairs in his "video room" he turned on all his electronics and pulled down the ten-foot theater screen for his projection television. With the Dolby Surround Sound system he'd bought a few months before, the room was ringed with speakers, like a movie theater. A special coded strip on tapes recorded with this format sent slightly different signals to each of the speakers, filling the room with sound.

Ascher poured himself a brandy in a fat snifter and punched the remote control. He liked the movie, more for the big-screen visual effects and the dramatic sound track—lots of shooting, explosions, and Huey helicopter rotor noises—than for the plot.

A couple of times he found himself imagining what it would have been like to work at the White House during the Vietnam era, trying to influence war policy. Would he have gone for a win or pulled out right away? He couldn't decide.

He poured more brandy, and by the time the movie ended just after ten he was sleepy and drunk. He staggered upstairs and, smiling, fell into bed.

THE WHITE HOUSE

Greta hadn't even escorted Ascher all the way back out to the lobby that afternoon before Christopher was on the phone to Kutler.

"It was amazing," Christopher said. "He bought it right away. You were so right about him. He could hardly keep his eyes in his head looking around my office. It was like a tourist from Kansas."

Kutler smiled. "Terry's a hell of a worker. But he's predictable. It's easy to push his button."

"One big problem solved at last," Christopher said with a sigh. "I never thought we'd find someone for that damned job. You remember that last guy, from Defense, he wouldn't even come over to talk about it. But, Art, let me ask you, are you sure about Ascher? I can't put my finger on it, but there's just something about him."

"He is a little odd. You know, sometimes I'll stick my head in his office, and he'll look up at me kind of startled, like I'd just caught him at something. It's unsettling. But he's a real worker, a role player. Not a great originator of ideas; I don't think we've got a natural-born leader here. But for what you want, an aggressive administrator who'll accomplish what he's asked to do, I think Terry's perfect. When you give him an assignment he works at it with this kind of frenzy, almost as if he's afraid you're going to take it away from him.

"You know, I'll be real sorry to lose him. His was one bureau I never had to worry about. I didn't always know how he did it, and sometimes I didn't want to ask. But he got some amazing things done for me over here."

"God knows, I'm thrilled to get that job filled. One less headache. Thanks, Art. Thanks a lot."

"Anytime. But listen, Rich, look out for Terry for me, will

you? His father was something of a mentor for me. For Wallace Ascher's sake, at least, I want Terry to do as well as he can. Watch out for him, will you, Art? Don't let him hurt himself."

"I will," Christopher said. "I promise."

CHAPTER FOUR

PHOENIX, ARIZONA, AUGUST 8

STANDING BEHIND THE DAIS, THE JUNIOR WHITE House press aide wore a Biltmore Hotel T-shirt and a gaudy pair of Jams swim trunks. But for the moment he was bathing only in the glare of television flood lights. "The briefing will begin in five minutes," he announced to the raucous crowd. "The briefer will be Fred Hillard." He started to step away from the microphone, anxious to get out of the spotlight, but a tech shoved a sheet of white paper at him.

"Hey, I don't want to do this," the aide protested.

But from the back someone shouted, "Whadya think, we wanna color balance on that abortion of a bathing suit you got on?" The aide took the sheet and rolled his eyes in disgusted surrender. Outside of the Federal Penitentiary at Leavenworth, there could hardly be a less appealing group of people than the traveling White House press corps.

He held the white sheet in front of his chest, and a dozen TV cameramen focused on him, adjusting their settings until the paper looked white, and as a result, all the other colors were in balance too. After a minute a cameraman bellowed like an Army noncom, "All right, you can go." As fast as he could, the aide left the room.

Fifty reporters, cameramen, soundmen, and still photographers milled about the pressroom drinking coffee, making wisecracks, complaining, and slowly taking their assigned seats behind six long tables facing the dais. Many were dressed in tennis clothes or swim trunks. The president was on vacation here in Arizona, and in a way, so were they. There was little news to report. Still, every morning they had to cover the White House press briefing.

Most mornings, the chief spokesman had little to say, and the journalists couldn't think of much to ask. Traditionally August was, by executive order, a no-news month. Still, the reporters couldn't wander far. As much as anything, White House reporters were on a deathwatch. If something happened to the president and one of them had taken the day to drive up to the Grand Canyon, more than likely he'd be out of a job when he got back. So most of the reporters spent the day at the pool or the tennis courts or out on a drive to look at the cactuses, within easy reach of a phone.

"Tough duty, but somebody's got to do it" was the common quip.

Just before noon the three chief TV network White House correspondents, familiar faces to most Americans, arrived, wearing dark suits and red silk neckties. Ignoring their assigned seats, they walked to three chairs lined up just to the left of the dais. Chris Eaton, a reporter sitting a few rows from the front, watched, shaking his head. He got perverse pleasure from watching the broadcast journalists display their petty vanities. Larry, Moe, and Curly, he liked to call them. Belittling these guys, whose salaries were ten times his own, helped Eaton feel better about the major drawbacks of his own job.

Setting up the press center here in the Arizona Biltmore's ballroom—a high-ceilinged convention room with sliding-door walls, probably used most often for Kiwanis luncheons and H&R Block training seminars—the White House had put the three network correspondents in their usual place, in the first row next to the wire-service writers. Other reporters were arranged in five rows behind them, ranked roughly by the number of people they reached.

But the CBS correspondent hadn't liked that arrangement. When his cameraman shot cutaway footage, showing him listening to the briefing with suddenly rapt attention, the tape couldn't help but show some of the other reporters in the frame as well. So the viewers saw their half-million-dollar-a-year correspondent as just one more reporter in the common, roiling mass.

Well, that wouldn't do. After a couple of days, the CBS man

had pulled his chair in front of all the others, just to the left of the podium. It made a nice cutaway, out there at the briefer's elbow, and all during that day's briefing the ABC and NBC men had glared at him with undisguised bitterness. In the night, apparently, each of the other two had crept in and moved their own chairs up front too.

Now, as most mornings, the three of them sat there, adjusting their ties, arranging their hair, looking bored and irritable as they waited. When Fred Hillard, the chief White House spokesman, took his place behind the dais, he looked down at them, sneering as he shook his head.

"You boys a little cranky this morning? Whatsa matter, didn't get your naps?" Everyone laughed while the TV boys glowered. And so the men who gave the world its news started their day.

"All right, the presidential report this morning," Hillard went on, and then read a statement that had been almost word-for-word the same the last two weeks.

"The president and first lady ate breakfast together this morning at eight A.M. The president signed some papers and read some of Richard Nathan's new novel. The president and first lady then took a horseback ride, and the president intends to spend the rest of the day swimming and catching up on his paperwork."

From the back someone shouted, "That's yesterday's report. Come on, give us today's." That brought a few small giggles, but Chris Eaton fidgeted, brushing at the forelock that barely hid his receding hairline, a nervous habit. His Tandy portable computer was on, screen flipped up, and he was rereading a story he had written yesterday, published in today's New World newspapers. First thing this morning he had checked the Associated Press and United Press International printers in the back of the pressroom, only to find that no one else had picked up his story.

These were the depths of August, the slowest news days of the year. The only item on this morning's UPI daybook, the list of today's scheduled news events in Washington, read: "District of Columbia Fire Chief Robinson to hold briefing on fireboat issue. Dockside, 10 A.M." Even on a day like this with nothing going on anywhere, Eaton's story fell into a void. Nobody noticed, nobody cared, even though, Eaton believed, he covered one important issue, the contras, more thoroughly than anyone else in the world. A run through his office clippings file would suggest he might be right.

His company, New World News Service, owned a chain of

small and medium-sized newspapers in the Southeast, including the number two paper in Miami. The Cubans in Miami and Latin American immigrants in several of the other Southern cities bought New World's papers looking for just the kind of news Eaton liked to cover. So Eaton's editors in Washington encouraged him. But, boy, it was frustrating sometimes. His stories didn't make it into the mainstream. They never got picked up in *The New York Times* or *The Washington Post* or on the TV news. So they never became a part of the national debate. His editor promoted him, gave him merit raises, and even pretended not to care when the White House attacked or denied Eaton's stories, as inevitably happened on occasion. But Eaton felt he was filing his stories into a deep, dark hole. He hungered for recognition, dreamed of being interviewed on National Public Radio or appearing on *Meet the Press.*

Hillard was muttering on about the president's signing a proclamation declaring National Asthma and Allergy week as several reporters simulated loud, tortured breathing. Eaton raised his hand.

"Chris," Hillard said, pointing at him.

"Fred, does the White House have any comment on the contra action a couple of days ago knocking out power to half of Managua?"

Up front somebody shouted, "Get off it, Eaton. Where'd you get that? Can't you write about anything else?" But behind the dais Hillard was shuffling through his papers looking for something. Watching, Eaton's mouth dropped open. They've given Hillard guidance on my story, he thought. Hillard began reading from a sheet:

"The United Nicaraguan Resistance announced this morning that they carried out their first major commando raid inside Managua on Wednesday, blowing up the main electrical substation and cutting off electricity to most of Managua, including virtually all of the Sandinista government's offices. The Resistance Directorate declared the operation a complete success."

The room erupted in a storm of shouted questions.

"Fred, Fred, you mean to tell me the contras cut off electricity to half the people they want to win over to their side?"

"What kind of policy is that?"

"Who paid for this?"

"Who authorized this?"

"Was this a CIA plan?"

"Was the U.S. embassy blacked out too?"

"What good's this kind of thing do?"

"Where'd they get the bomb . . ."

Eaton smiled. This was his story. Apparently the contras had put out an announcement this morning, and the CIA had prepared press guidance telling Hillard what he could say.

Hillard read from his sheet again. "Standard guerrilla warfare doctrine calls for acts of sabotage that show the people that the ruling junta is not all-powerful and cannot maintain control over even their own territory. Inevitably civilians will be inconvenienced, but it is hoped that they will also come to respect the resistance fighters for the boldness of their acts while the popular position of the government is weakened. That, as I understand it, is the general doctrinal theory behind actions like this.

"This was not a CIA action. This was an action planned and carried out by the United Nicaraguan Resistance."

"Aw, come on, give me a break," someone moaned. "The contras couldn't do something like this alone."

"By the way," Hillard added, "the United States embassy has its own on-site power generator."

Eaton raised his hand again. Hillard pointed at him. "Chris, did you have this story already?" Eaton broke into an involuntary grin but asked, "Fred, is it true that the electrical substation was built by the Agency for International Development while Somoza was still in power, and the CIA gave the contras plans and diagrams that they'd gotten from the Army Corps of Engineers in Washington?"

"You're kidding," a radio reporter said.

"Son-of-a-bitch," said the reporter from *Time*.

Hillard looked at Eaton, a bare smile on his lips as he told the group, "I'm sorry, as a matter of policy we don't comment on intelligence matters, as all of you know."

As the other reporters started on their stories, most of them working quickly to meet deadlines on East Coast time, Eaton quietly zipped his computer into its case and walked to the door. Most everyone noticed him leaving. He'd beaten the nation's press on an important story, and although hardly any readers or viewers would ever know that, the other reporters did. It was a rare moment. Even the resentful grimace he got from a *Los Angeles Times* reporter brought a warm glow.

He walked back to his large room with its Art Deco motif. Frank Lloyd Wright was said to have designed the hotel. The

White House made hotel reservations for the traveling press corps at the Sheraton but stayed at the $200-a-night Biltmore themselves. The big-time reporters stayed at the Biltmore anyway, convincing their editors that they needed to be nearer the White House staff. This year Eaton had persuaded his editor to let him stay there too. If he couldn't work for the national press, at least he could live as they did on the road.

In his room he called Tegucigalpa, Honduras. Contra headquarters.

"Jorge, they picked up my story!" he blurted out to the man who came on the line. "It'll be all over the papers tomorrow. And look at the TV news tonight." Honduras pirated network broadcasts from U.S. satellites.

"Did they get the part about the CIA giving out the Corps of Engineers blueprints?" the man on the other end asked.

"Yeah, I'm pretty sure. I had it in my story, and I asked about it at the briefing. The White House had no comment, but it was kind of a confirmation no comment."

"Good story, Chris. Our Miami office read it to us."

"Jorge, thanks for helping me—hell, for giving me the story."

"It is my pleasure again."

Jorge Paladino was a member of the eight-man United Nicaraguan Resistance Directorate. He spoke perfect English and was also the senior spokesman for the contras, based half-time in Washington. As he often complained, being the spokesman usually meant reading statements the CIA handed him, many of them untrue. On the few occasions he had volunteered information without checking with his American handlers first, he'd been dressed down with veiled threats of cuts in American aid. Paladino was not a great admirer of the CIA.

He was an educated man. Like many upper-class Nicaraguans he'd been sent to college in the States—Cornell, in his case—and he still dressed like an Ivy League preppie: button-down shirts, cotton chinos, and the ever-present tasseled loafers.

Before the revolution Paladino was a high school principal in Managua. He was one of the civic leaders who helped mobilize public opinion against General Somoza. But soon after the revolution, when Paladino saw the direction the Sandinistas were taking his country, he left for Miami. For a couple of years he'd been a contra dilettante, volunteering for odd jobs here and there. But two years ago, when the CIA had gone through its annual repackaging of the contra leadership, trying in vain for a combination that would finally satisfy Congress, they'd found

Paladino. With flawless English and a perfect appearance, Paladino was just the sort of man midwestern congressmen might like to see running Nicaragua one day.

But the CIA misjudged his politics.

Unlike Paladino, most Nicaraguans were philosophical about the North American manipulation they were forced to endure. It had always been so. Most of the contra leaders genuflected to Rafael Mendoza and the other CIA handlers because they knew the agency was the only game in town. But ever since the movement's beginning, there'd always been a director or two who'd bristled and complained. Years ago it had been Edgar Chamorro. Eventually he quit in disgust, complaining about incompetent and venal CIA management. Today it was Paladino. His constant complaints put him at odds not just with the agency. He'd argued so long and loud against Mendoza's choice of Major Paz for high-profile operations that he made the others on the Directorate uncomfortable too, though they knew he was right. That's why Chairman Alfonso Coronel had assigned Paladino to spend so much time up in Washington. Coronel simply didn't want to listen to him anymore.

"Jorge, why can't you go along with the game," he had shouted at Paladino when he ordered his transfer earlier in the year. "You're messing it up for all of us."

Coronel was a little man with oily slicked-back hair; he'd been a men's clothier in Managua before the war. But now he lived in a big house in Tegucigalpa the CIA had bought for him. They'd given him a condominium in Miami, too, and from there he gave interviews and took calls from State Department officers and *Meet the Press*. Coronel had no trouble accepting all manner of direction and "advice" from the CIA, and it infuriated him that Paladino wouldn't go along.

So Paladino had been sent to Washington, where he'd met Eaton. They became friends. After all, they had complementary needs. Paladino could get back at his CIA handlers by leaking some of their outrages to Eaton, whose stories got noticed in the Nicaraguan exile community but weren't generally picked up nationwide. Eaton could get back at the national press by beating them repeatedly on coverage of the contras. But even then they had an understanding. Eaton knew that although Paladino was always happy to embarrass the CIA, he wasn't about to give away anything that would harm the contras. Behind all the bluster, he was a true believer.

"Chris, you ought to come down here and go out on a mission

with one of our squads again," he said. Eaton had traveled with a contra unit inside Nicaragua a few years earlier. They'd seemed badly equipped and poorly trained then, and his story had made that clear.

"We've got some real professionals now. Not all of our people are out there running stupid CIA ops. I'd like to send you out with Comandante Venganza."

"Venganza, wasn't he that Sandinista lieutenant who defected a year or so ago?"

"Yeah. He's our best."

"Well, sure," Eaton said. "Just say when."

"We'll figure it out when I get back to Washington in a couple of weeks. I'm also hearing some interesting things down here we can talk about."

"Oh?"

"Yeah, I think the White House is getting back in the game. I hear they got permission to put their own person on the RIG, a new position. Somebody from your State Department."

"Oh, yeah?"

"Don't know yet. I need to find out more. But you know what everybody says about the RIG as it is now."

"Uh-huh. It's got the courage of a sparrow and the inventiveness of a slug. You think this means the White House wants to charge things up a bit?"

"Maybe," Paladino said. "Let me find out some more. We'll talk about it when we're both back in town."

"Okay. Let me know. And be careful, Jorge."

Most afternoons at the Biltmore, Eaton would hurry by the swimming pool—on his way to make a phone call, to do an interview, or to write a story—only to see that most of the other reporters were stretched out on lounge chairs, chattering as they got a tan.

But Eaton was always hungry, ever on edge, scrambling to uncover something and get ahead of the others. When he did get a good story, though, nobody seemed to notice. So he had to find another one. On and on it went.

Today he'd done as well as he could. Walking across the lawn back to his room, he had been content—an emotion he rarely felt. The day was warm, beautiful. The temperature was creeping up toward 100 degrees, but it was "dry heat, dry heat," as Arizonans never tired of saying with a smile. If someone had added the smell of cedar planking, Eaton would have sworn he was in a sauna. Now and then a slight breeze stirred. The sky was so clear he could see hot-air balloons floating what must have been fifteen miles away. Eaton had smiled to himself. By God, for the first time, today he was going to head for the pool.

It wasn't quite noon, but as usual nearly all the lounge chairs were taken. The Biltmore had two pools side by side; the larger one seemed to be the domain of the retirees, who held forth from beneath the striped awnings around its perimeter.

A fountain splashed in the center of the smaller, round pool, and chaise lounges were placed around the edge. This morning, bathers lay elbow to elbow.

As Eaton stepped inside the gate, the pool attendant, a pretty blond college girl, smiled at him from under her terry-cloth sun visor.

"Can I set you up in a seat? That one over there?" she asked, pointing to one on the end of a row, the only vacant lounge facing the sun.

Eaton looked around to see if any of his friends were here. No, everyone was still over at the pressroom, working.

"That'll be fine," he said and followed the girl, standing behind her as she spread two plush towels over the plastic-web chair. Lying on the next lounge was a woman in a two-piece suit not quite skimpy enough to qualify as a bikini. A small gold ring linked the two well-filled cups of her suit top, and Eaton could see a pearl-white circle of untanned skin just beneath it, set off against deep brown. She lay on her back, eyes closed, face up to the sun. God, what a wonderful body, Eaton was thinking.

Her face showed clear vertical creases on either side of her mouth. Her brown hair was cut in a flawless modern pageboy, and she had chosen not to pluck out four or five long silver strands. He looked at her hands, accurate barometers of age, he thought—she might be thirty-five, thirty-six, he guessed. Suddenly the woman opened her eyes to see who was standing over her. Eaton was smiling but quickly looked away. He was not the sort who liked to leer at women. Better to pay no attention than to hunger for something you can't have.

"Thanks," he said to the pool girl and gave her a dollar.

"If you want anything, drinks or lunch, we have full pool service. Just call me."

"I will."

As he sat down, he spotted a Motorola walkie-talkie with a stubby rubber-covered antenna on the lounge chair beside the woman. White House staff, Eaton thought, but he didn't recognize her. A secretary or executive assistant probably, but to be staying here at the Biltmore she must work for somebody pretty senior.

He stretched out and opened his book, the new Richard Nathan novel, the same one the president was reading. It was at the top of the hardcover bestseller list. Half a dozen people around the pool were reading it too.

Eaton didn't put on any suntan oil. He was moderately dark-skinned and didn't burn easily. Overall he was an ordinary-looking guy—light brown hair carefully arranged to hide the thin spot in front that seemed to have grown thinner every time he looked in the mirror. A pleasant but unremarkable face. Average height. Not the sort of man most people remembered on the basis of appearance alone. He was quiet, reserved, most of the time. But he tended to speak with a deep-voiced authority when he had something to say, belying a larger-than-average dose of self-doubt. He'd just turned thirty-two and believed he still had much to prove.

Most women didn't notice him. But every once in a while one found him extraordinarily appealing because under that veneer of quiet male authority she saw a certain neediness, a vulnerability. It showed through now and then in a momentarily pained expression in his eyes or a brief uncertain tone in his voice— quick-flash glimpses of an inner self crying out.

Eaton didn't know he sent out these almost subliminal signals, and the vast majority of people never noticed. But to some women his need was a powerful silent plea, and it instantly caught their attention. All his adult life he'd wondered why, every once in a while, one woman or another had quickly seemed to fall for him, though he'd made no special effort. He'd married one of them, right after college. But three years ago, when he was offered the job in New World's Washington bureau, Julie hadn't wanted to leave Miami. He had to choose, and he picked the new job. Married six years, they'd been growing apart anyway. The separation was painful but not as anguished as he'd feared. They had no children, and earlier this year they'd finally gotten a divorce. Eaton had begun dating again, but his social life in Washington was generally lackluster. He spent many a Saturday night at the office.

The pool girl with the visor stopped by, holding an order pad on a little round tray.

"Lunch?"

"Yeah, what do you have?"

"Whatever you want. Today we do have a really nice turkey-breast-and-avocado sandwich with sprouts and an all-natural mayonnaise on pita. It comes with a guava garnish." The girl grinned. "I reaaally like that one."

Eaton smiled the condescending smile of an East Coaster. "Yeah, that'll be fine. And a Diet Coke, please."

"Yes, sir."

Beside him the woman said, "Bring me one of those sandwiches too, if you would, please. And some iced tea. With Sweet 'n Low."

"Yes, ma'am." The girl wrote it down and moved to the next chair.

Eaton looked at the woman. She had turned over, lowering the back of the lounge chair, and was lying flat on her stomach with her head turned his way, eyes closed, her shiny brown hair tucked behind an ear. She had not unfastened her suit top, Eaton noted. Didn't mind tan lines across the back.

"Southwest fare if I ever heard it," he said to her.

She didn't move her head but strained her eyes up to his face, squinting, and gave a weak smile. "Yeah" was her only answer before she closed her eyes again. Eaton quickly turned back to his book. She thinks I'm coming on to her, he thought.

Twenty minutes later a young man wheeled in a cart carrying the lunch orders. The pool girl walked with him from chair to chair, handing out lunches and writing room numbers on the checks. Around the pool one by one people sat up, squinting and stretching as they leaned forward to pick pineapple spears and thick-cut potato chips off their plates. Eaton didn't look at the woman as they ate. But when her walkie-talkie screeched with a burst of static all of a sudden and she reached to lower the volume, he turned to her.

"You White House?"

She nodded, turning halfway to look at him only briefly.

"Where do you work?"

Still without looking directly at him, she asked, "Who're you?"

"Oh, I'm sorry. My name's Chris Eaton. I'm White House correspondent for The New World News Service. New World owns a chain of papers in Florida and—"

"Yeah, I know what New World is," she interrupted. Eaton looked away. Tough lady.

After a long silence she finally turned to him, saying, "My name's Leslie DeSalles."

"Hi, Leslie."

"Hi," she said, looking directly at him with a hard smile that seemed a challenge, almost a threat. She didn't look away, wide brown eyes staring right at him until finally Eaton found he had to jerk his own eyes away and turn back to his food. He picked up his sandwich and slowly took a bite, looking down at the plate.

A full minute passed before she said, "The NSC."

"Huh?"

"You asked where I work." She spit her words. "The NSC. I work for the NSC."

"Hey, I'm not trying to pry. I'm sorry I asked." It came out with a little more emotion than he had intended. He sounded almost anguished, and she looked at him, a puzzled expression on her face. He turned away; his right hand brushed at his thinning forelock. She stared at the side of his face.

"Look," she said in a softer voice. "I'm sorry. I don't mean to be so unfriendly. It's just that I'm new at this job. I haven't had a lot of direct experience with reporters before, and you hear so many things."

"I know," Eaton said. "Lots of those stories are true. I'm in a strange business, and it isn't always so honorable."

"I know you'll be shocked to hear this," she said, "but you could say the same thing about the government business too." They both laughed.

"So what do you do over there?" Eaton asked.

"I'm General Dayton's scheduler and aide."

"Oh!" Eaton sounded surprised, impressed. General Dayton was the president's national security advisor and head of the National Security Council. Being scheduler meant she was his note-taker and traveling aide de camp. She must sit in on even the most secret meetings. This was a woman to get to know.

"That's quite a job," he told her. But her response suggested she wasn't so impressed. She gave him an exaggerated burlesque smile, lots of teeth, clearly a reflexive artifice intended to hide some contrary view.

"So you took Carolyn's place," Eaton said, trying to ignore it.

"Yeah, she went back to the Pentagon last month."

"Where were you before?"

"I was over at politico-military affairs at State, executive assistant to the director for security assistance and sales."

"Oh, foreign aid, military sales credits, and things like that."

"Yeah."

"Lots of cuts in your budget, huh."

"Gutted. Congress really wiped us out."

"I can hear it now: Why give money to South Yucatan when we've got hungry people on the streets of Columbus? And then, before you know it, you can't get these allied countries to cooperate with us on our foreign policy initiatives."

"Yeah," she said. "America the undependable ally and all that."

"Next thing you know they've decided to get their RPGs from the Soviets and East Germans instead of us, right?"

"We'd be lucky if it was just rocket-propelled grenades."

They went on like that awhile, making Washington shoptalk, laughing at shorthand inside jokes. Eaton looked her over as they spoke. She was a mature woman, though certainly not matronly. She took good care of herself; she was trim, appealing. Relaxed with herself. Yes, sexy. She wore no rings. If she was divorced, she must not have had many children because she had the slender waist of an eighteen-year-old. But her most extraordinary feature was those large brown eyes. When she turned them on him, opened wide, they seemed to irradiate him. He felt he might dissolve. He had to look away.

"How do you like the Biltmore?" he asked after a pause.

"Oh, it's a great place. A little boring after a while, though. The general spends most of his time out on the tennis court."

Then with a roll of her eyes, she said, "He doesn't require me to take notes on that."

So that's it, Eaton thought. She thinks she's underemployed.

Eaton was quiet for minute but then, his voice tight, he asked, "Hey, can I buy you dinner one night?"

She gave him a long look, studying, obviously trying to figure out what he was up to. Eaton worried for a moment: maybe she didn't know that in Phoenix it was common practice for the press corps to take White House staffers out to dinner. Few of them had anything else to do at night, and among the reporters, some officials were notorious for accepting invitation after invitation, insisting on going to the most expensive places and then saying not a single interesting thing.

The first summer here, the reporters found they were climbing all over each other to take the senior people out to dinner. The officials could accept only a few invitations, so the people they refused were angry and resentful. The next year the major-media reporters formed little dining societies and dubbed them "tongs" after the secret oriental criminal organizations. *The New York Times*, CBS, and *Newsweek* were one tong. *The Washington Post*, NBC, and *U.S. News & World Report* were another. One tong member was named secretary each year and arranged a month of Phoenix dinners in advance. The first of August, tong members arrived at the Biltmore to find a typed schedule of roughly twice-a-week tong dinners waiting for them at the hotel. The deputy chief of staff on the twelfth, national security advisor on the fifteenth, assistant to the president for domestic policy on the twenty-third . . .

Well, that was wonderful for the national media, but they made arrangements only among themselves. People like Chris Eaton were left out. With so many invitations from the big-time people, the ones whose stories really made a difference, how many White House officials were going to make time for dinners with reporters from Christian Broadcasting, McGraw-Hill, and The New World News Service?

The tong dinners were one more source of resentment for Eaton. He'd tried relentlessly to make dinner appointments of his own but usually wound up dining with deputy press spokesmen, people like that. Once, walking past the tennis courts, he'd run into Admiral Fowler, an influential assistant to the president. When Eaton introduced himself and offered to buy dinner, the admiral looked stricken, as if he'd just taken a bite from a bar of Dial soap.

"No, I don't think so" was all he'd said before turning away.

It was in this spirit that he asked Leslie out, though he had to admit she also seemed nice for an older lady.

Noting her puzzled look, he told her: "Leslie, out here journalists go out to dinner with White House staff all the time. You've probably scheduled some of those dinners for the general. I'm not expecting anything in return. You deal with a lot of sensitive classified materials, I know. It's illegal to discuss that stuff, and I respect that. Please don't worry."

At that she gave another smile, but this one was genuine. She seemed pleased, maybe even flattered.

"All right," she said. "Tonight?"

"Sure." He smiled. "How about Edward's?"

"Don't know it."

"It's nice, wonderful view. Casual. You'll like it. How about seven-thirty, in the lobby?"

"Okay."

"Great." And then, a little self-consciously, Eaton turned back to his book.

At seven-thirty he was waiting. She was right on time and looked stunning in tight white jeans, a mauve, low-neck cotton sweater and a single strand of pearls. He could see just the top of that little white circle the gold ring on her bathing suit had branded on her chest. A little mascara and a touch of dark lipstick—with the tan, that's all she needed. Not a pinup girl, she was a confident adult who exuded a mature sexuality with no effort at all. She smiled easily.

"Hi."

"Hi," he said, smiling too.

He drove, and they didn't say much on the way, though the atmosphere between them was not uncomfortable. At Edward's, Chris asked for a table on the porch, and they were seated right away. It was a classic West Coast–style nouvelle cuisine establishment: triangular tables, canvas Wassily chairs, salmon-colored walls, and the restaurant logo in neon over the bar. The menu was on blackboards, written in an affected feminine script. Lots of pasta and fresh mahimahi. The restaurant was on a bluff, and from their table they saw the city's lights below them in the distance. Desert evenings grew cool quickly, so Eaton was glad he'd worn a sport coat.

He ordered a beer, she a glass of chablis. She put her elbows on the table and joined her hands under her chin, gold bangles clanking, and when Eaton looked he was visibly startled. On her left hand was a bright gold ring with a diamond the size of a pistachio nut.

She saw him staring and smiled.

"I take off my jewelry before going to the pool," she said, leaving him totally flustered.

"I didn't ask you to dinner because I thought . . . I mean I wasn't . . . uh . . ." She reached over and touched his sleeve, smiling and gently shaking her head as if to say: Calm down, it doesn't matter. He took a sip of beer and glanced at her over his glass. She looked back with those eyes that could melt ice. Suddenly he was aroused.

"What's your husband do," he said, looking away.

"He's a pollster."

Eaton responded with a quick questioning frown. "Not

Wyche DeSalles?" She nodded. "God, I should have guessed. I'm sorry."

"Why should you have guessed?" she asked, a little irritated now. "You assume I couldn't work in the White House without—"

"No, no. That's not what I meant. I mean, DeSalles is not a common name in Washington. I didn't mean to imply anything."

"Oh, I'm sorry, Chris. You know it's tough. Sometimes I overreact." They both sipped their drinks.

Wyche DeSalles was the president's pollster. He sampled public opinion for the White House, helped the president know which proposals would fly and which would flounder.

"I talk to your husband now and then," Eaton said. "God, you must never see him. Every time he calls back he's on the road somewhere. And you probably travel a lot too." Elbows on the table, both hands holding her wine, she looked at him over the glass with an unsmiling affirmation that seemed to carry some message Eaton couldn't quite fathom. Curious woman.

"How long you been married?"

She hesitated before saying, "Fourteen years." She paused another beat and then asked, "How about you?" glancing down at Eaton's own hands. He wore his gold wedding band on his right hand, a curious affectation he had adopted when he moved to Washington, a reflection of the ambivalence behind his decision to leave his wife.

"Divorced, apart three years," he whispered, looking down. And then, suddenly breezy, he asked, "So, where'd you grow up?"

Louisville, Kentucky, she said, though she pronounced the city "Looo-vulle." Then came her life story in capsule form.

Her father was a Jefferson County School Board administrator nearing retirement. She'd gone to the University of Louisville, majored in political science, planning to get a master's and go into government herself. Then right after graduation she got a job as the mayor's executive assistant, to earn money for graduate school. She'd met Wyche there in city hall. He was the mayor's closest political aide, even though he was only a few years out of the University of Kentucky himself.

They got married almost right away. But then the mayor was elected to Congress, and Wyche moved with him to Washington. The new congressman got Leslie a job on Capitol Hill. She had to work; she needed more money to go back to school, especially in Washington, where it would be so much more expensive.

"I guess it's my fault," she said at last. "I wanted a career, but it just never happened. I kept going from job to job, and now here I am." Then came that burlesque smile again.

"But you're at the NSC," Eaton said. "Most people would kill for your job."

"Taking notes?" she asked, eyebrows raised. "Oh, I'm sorry. I guess in some ways I am lucky, but . . ." She shook her head.

They ordered their dinners, and Eaton started pressing—slowly.

"You know it must have been interesting for the general, who certainly has views of his own on things like Central America, as an example, to have watched the president go through such a dramatic change of opinion on the subject."

Chris knew it had probably been more than interesting; it was certainly gratifying. General Dayton was a firm contra supporter, preferring the rebels to the fearsome specter of sending U.S. troops into Nicaragua, into "another Vietnam" that would tarnish the Pentagon, hindering recruiting and budget appropriations for another decade.

But Leslie offered none of that. "I guess military men are accustomed to carrying out orders no matter what their personal opinions might be" was all she was willing to say.

They talked easily through dinner, Eaton gently probing, looking for openings. She didn't give away any government secrets. But she lit right up when Eaton asked for her own views.

"I'm not a policymaker," she would say as introduction, but then she'd tell him exactly what she would do if that weren't so, even phrasing her views with all the proper Washington jargon. About the Middle East, for example, she told Eaton: "It seems to me the United States has a lot of moral authority in the region that we could be exploiting more to convince the parties to talk. Nobody else is so respected by both parties to the conflict." Then came that toothy mock grin again. Here was a secretary with views she wasn't entirely sure she had the right to speak.

But Eaton encouraged her, treated her as if she *were* a senior policymaker, saying, "That's an interesting approach" or "I've never heard it framed quite that way." After a while she began to relax. Her smiles seemed genuine, and a streak of gentle warmth began to show through.

Over coffee he asked, "You have any children?"

"No." Her voice betrayed regret.

"Both of you too busy, I guess, huh." She didn't answer.

"You've been together fourteen years?" Eaton asked. "You must have been out of college only about thirty-six hours when you got married."

She smiled. "If you want to know, Chris, I'm thirty-seven." He grinned—you caught me—and they smiled at each other a long moment. An electricity was there, unspoken but obvious. Eaton felt it, and he sat up in his chair, tugging at his jacket sleeves as he said, "Better get the check."

Eaton compartmentalized women right away. They were available or they were not, and he allowed himself to feel nothing more than casual fondness for someone he knew he could not have. He'd always been rigid about that, so he was all business on the drive back to the Biltmore. Leslie seemed bemused. He pulled into the hotel's circular drive and stopped in front of the entrance. A hotel doorman opened her door and stood back waiting. Eaton laid his hand lightly on her shoulder and said, "Thank you, Leslie, I really enjoyed it."

"Yeah, I did too," she answered with an impertinent smile. She patted him twice on the knee and climbed out, saying, "See you around." He watched as she strode into the lobby without looking back.

Eaton didn't go back to the hotel pool the next day or the next, though on the second day he did contrive a reason to walk past, peering over the bushes on his way. She was there, stretched out on a lounge, wearing that same gold-ring two-piece suit. He had been thinking about her but couldn't quite figure out what he wanted.

The president's summer break was drawing to its end, and the White House staff was desperately trying to vacation. White House officials took off to visit desert sites, the Grand Canyon. A couple of them flew over to Santa Fe. The president, according to Fred Hillard's morning accounts, was still swimming and reading.

None of the reporters had written anything in a week, and they were complaining. After a month of tong dinners they'd wrung all they were going to get out of their guests, and they had used up the canned stories they'd brought from Washington. At the morning briefings, they'd whine to Hillard: Come on, give us something, anything.

On Friday, two days before they were scheduled to leave and three days after his dinner with Leslie, there was no briefing, and just after eleven Eaton went to the pool. Half the lounges were empty this early, and Leslie was not there. Eaton was disappointed, even though he had decided she was a futile distraction. Explaining to himself, he figured the only reason he was sorry he wouldn't see her was that she could have been an important news source. But half an hour later there she was at the gate, and from across the pool he peered at her from behind his book. The pool girl asked her something, picking up two towels, and Leslie looked around, then pointed at the lounge chair right next to Eaton's. He pulled the book up, pretending not to see.

"Hi there," she said with casual warmth but also a trace of indifference.

"Oh, hi, Leslie, how are you." Eaton immediately regretted his fake surprised tone.

Standing at the foot of the lounge, she turned her back to him and lifted her translucent white caftan over her head. Looking at her long brown body, even from behind, Eaton was aroused.

"So, what have you been up to?" she asked as she lay down. He looked, and once again she was not wearing her rings.

"Oh, not much. Things have been pretty quiet. No news. You know, it's awfully pleasant out here, but I'm ready to go home. Aren't you?"

She smiled. "It is pleasant out here. It's great to be away."

"Yeah, Washington's no treat in August."

"What do you like to do back in town?" she asked.

"Oh, I don't know. I work a lot." He regretted the paucity of his social life and sounded a little sheepish as he answered. She gazed at him a moment but then turned away. He wasn't looking at her and in a low voice, almost to himself, he went on: "You know, I've been alone a couple of years now. We were married a long time, and it's hard. A strange city, a job that's frustrating more than anything else. I don't know . . ." His voice trailed off. He brushed at his forelock.

They were silent a moment, and when Eaton looked up Leslie was staring at him, her brown-eyed gaze so intense he could feel it weakening him. But then she jerked her head away and took a deep breath.

"Chris," she said, almost whispering, "you're a bright, appealing young man. You're going to do just fine." They were silent a moment.

When they started talking again, they chattered about all sorts of things. By the time they sat side by side eating lunch more than an hour later they were engaged in easy unaffected banter, smiling at each other often, gazes lingering a bit longer than necessary. Sometimes she reached over and touched him on the arm to accent a point. He grew less shy about looking at her lovely body, and if she noticed—all women must notice those things—she didn't seem to mind at all.

Nothing explicit was said. But after a while Eaton began to realize it was inevitable. It wasn't that she was coming on to him. No, it was beyond that. She had accepted him, and though they hadn't spoken of it, he knew the decision had been made, ratified, and sealed. All that remained was the act. He figured he ought to make some move, but he couldn't, wasn't even sure he really wanted to. He did, but he didn't. He was frozen, afraid. He didn't know what to do.

When the boy with the cart cleared away the lunch dishes, they both still sat up, leaning forward in their lounges, looking down as if the plates were still there. Awkward silence was beginning to settle over them, electricity sparking between them, when Leslie suddenly smiled to herself and made a move that stunned him. He would remember it forever. Without a word she got up and slowly pulled on her caftan, then slipped on her sandals. She stood over his lounge, looking at him for a moment, hands on hips, and then reached down between their chairs to Eaton's book. His room key stuck out of it, a bookmark. She plucked it away and then closed her hand around the key in a tight upside-down fist that she held under his eyes for the barest moment, looking him directly in the eye, smiling her wide Cheshire grin.

He was riveted. Then she straightened up and walked to the gate, shoulders erect, not looking back as Eaton sat there, unable to move.

The door to his room was slightly ajar, and he paused before pushing it open, wondering if he'd end up telling her he didn't want to go through with this. He took a deep breath and slipped inside, closing the door behind him. When he spotted her he stopped. Wearing only her bathing suit, she lay back in the armchair, her bare legs propped up on a chair she'd pulled over from the desk. Her head was thrown back in a lazy repose. The caftan was draped over the end of the bed.

Only the outer lace curtains were closed, so the room was

moderately bright. She'd lit the gas fire in the stone fireplace. Steady blue flames hissed over fake metal logs.

He didn't move, and she just smiled up at him. His head spun. He supposed this was the sexual fantasy of a lifetime, and he couldn't say he hadn't helped propel it along. But at the same time he sniffed trouble. Why was this happening?

Then she stood up and walked over to him, stopping a foot away. Barefoot, they were almost the same height and looked eye to eye. Gently smiling, she reached over and ran fingers through his scant forelock. Her hands settled on his shoulders and didn't move at first. His arms still hung lifeless at his sides; he was in a daze. Then she carefully slid off his pool shirt. It was unbuttoned down the front and fell easily to the floor. As he watched, his ears hummed. Softly she stroked the backs of her hands up and down his chest, and he was caught, as aroused as he had ever been.

Eaton was not a sexual naïf. But this older woman had an appeal he had never known and even later could not explain. Almost automatically he reached to unfasten her suit top, and as it dropped to the floor his mouth fell open. She looked down, smiling, as he traced a finger around the little white circle in the valley between her breasts, then reached over and carefully held them. He felt like a thirteen-year-old boy at the bicycle store running his fingers slowly over the magnificent expensive Bianchi racer he knows he cannot have. Why me? Then she took his hands, lacing her fingers through his, and led him to the bed.

They made love through the afternoon, and Eaton was astounded by her uninhibited energy. There was nothing she didn't want to do. He'd never been with a woman who knew so well what would make him feel good, both physically and inside his swirling head. He worried that he wasn't giving enough in return, though, God knows, he was motivated. What he felt wasn't just passion. It was wonder. And behind all her energy there was tenderness that told Eaton she must care about him, too.

They kept going long after he was ready to lie back and take a nap. She gave up only when none of her varied and exotic entreaties could bring him back to life. It was dusk when she lay on her side, head propped up on an elbow. Outside, the desert night seemed to be falling like a heavy curtain.

"You're really something," Leslie told Eaton, leaning over to kiss him on the shoulder.

He'd been gazing at the ceiling feeling spent and warm, but

he turned to her in disbelief. "*I'm* really something. Jesus, Leslie. You're the most magnificent woman I've ever met." She tugged at his ear a couple of times.

After a pause he turned and asked simply, "Why?"

She didn't answer right away but then asked, "You mean, why you? Or why anyone at all?"

"You pick," he said, and she fell back on her pillow, her hand resting on his arm.

"There's an expression around town, a cocktail party maxim. Maybe you've heard it: 'Washington's full of powerful men and the women they married when they were young.' I think that's the way Wyche feels about me."

"I can't believe that," Eaton said.

She squeezed his arm and went on. "We were drifting apart before, but since his candidate became president he's been on another planet. I guess it can't help but affect you. I wanted to have a profession of my own, still do, but instead I got a bad marriage. Now, at least I want to have kids. For three years he's been saying he doesn't have time. Well, I'm almost out of time, and how much time does it take? We don't have much of a love life anymore, haven't since early in the term. And now he's getting ready for another campaign. He helped me get a job in the White House to see if he could bring me along with him, I think. But it's too late."

"So why don't you leave him?"

"I don't know. Inertia. Maybe I should. But he is a good man inside, and he does depend on me. Still, it's empty."

"So you fool around?"

She whipped her hand away from his arm, insulted. But then, realizing where she was, she must have seen it was ludicrous, so she put her hand back.

"I don't go cattin' all 'round town," she said, a little irritated. "And I've never had a real affair. But I'd be lying if I said I'd never had an encounter like this before."

With that remark Eaton grew quiet. But when he spoke at last, his voice was hoarse, tight.

"Leslie, I hope maybe this time it isn't just an 'encounter.' I think you're special. I'd like to see you again."

"Oh, Chris, you are dear. You're the one who's special, not me. You are a wonderful young man, and I'm flattered. Really. But this is impossible. You can see that. Just think about it for a minute, what you do for a living, what I do for a living, what my husband does. Hell, if they ever come around for a security-clearance lie detector test I'm already in trouble."

"They've stopped doing polygraphs in the executive offices."

"Chris, you know what I mean."

"Leslie, I'm not proposing marriage or a full raging affair. I'd just like to see you again."

She turned over and kissed him with what felt like genuine affection. Then she got out of bed and stood looking down at him, hands on her naked hips. He looked back, imploring. But after a moment she picked up her bathing suit and stepped into it, saying, "Maybe I'm a fool. No, I *am* a fool. But better to do this now, Chris. We'd only get ourselves in trouble, maybe even legal trouble, and I think you know that's true." She pulled on her caftan and bent down to kiss him once on the forehead, one hand on his hair. He didn't move. She stood and looked at him only briefly, then without a word turned and walked out, softly closing the door. Eaton lay still long into the darkness.

He didn't go to the pool the next day, their last day in Phoenix. But he did walk by a couple of times. She wasn't there. At lunchtime he drove over to the Biltmore shopping mall and found a florist who delivered. He asked for a deluxe custom arrangement, seventy-five dollars, and gave Leslie's room number at the Biltmore.

When the florist handed him the card, he didn't hesitate at all. He had thought it over and over and over, all night and all morning long.

"I love you," he wrote. "Chris."

As he sealed the card in the little envelope he nodded to himself, convinced this was not an impulsive act born of a fleeting infatuation. What he wrote was the truth. He didn't feel love easily, and he wasn't going to deny it to himself and spend the rest of his life with a dull regret because he hadn't even tried.

Eaton asked the florist for a confirmation, and at about three in the afternoon the store called to say the flowers had been delivered. He waited and waited, ordering room-service food he didn't eat, switching stations on the TV because none of them seemed able to hold his interest. The blue gas fire still flickered. He'd never turned it on before but now couldn't bring himself to turn it off. At eight o'clock, the deadline for Air Force One baggage call, he took his suitcases downstairs and loaded them onto the truck. At ten the phone still hadn't rung. Nothing had been slipped under his door. So he took a Dramamine pill and under the heavy chemical weight he finally fell asleep.

The press plane, a Pan American charter, always left at least an hour before Air Force One. That gave the network cameramen time to set up at the other end so they could film the president's arrival. Since the president always liked to be back in Washington early enough so that the arrival footage could make the evening news, Eaton and the others had to climb aboard buses for the National Guard air station at six in the morning.

Between the Dramamine and the early hour, Eaton's head was such a muddle that he could hardly recognize his distress. At the airport, the buses rolled right onto the tarmac, past some F-4 fighters and then some F-16s. Beyond them, four planes were lined up in a row. At the far end was a large four-engine jet, a C-141 Starlifter military transport painted in brown-and-green camouflage. It carried White House vehicles, including the president's bulletproof bubble-top Lincoln, from stop to stop. The plane's rear drive-up ramp was lowered, waiting. Behind it were two Boeing 707s painted in the distinctive blue-and-white motif of Air Force One. The planes were virtually identical so no one could tell which one carried the president. Set into the struts just above the engines were odd-looking cylinders about the size of a gallon paint can. They held electronic countermeasure devices intended to defeat the guidance systems of heat-seeking surface-to-air missiles.

One plane carried secondary staff members. The other was for the president, his immediate staff, and the press travel pool: six or seven reporters and technicians who represented the entire press corps and had to share anything they learned with everyone else. That job was rotated, and hardly anyone wanted it. Why work when someone else would do it for you? The rest of the press corps, along with a few White House staff members—overflow from the staff plane—flew in the fourth aircraft, the press charter, a conventional Pan Am 727. It had better food.

The press bus stopped at the foot of the steps, and about fifty reporters, photographers, and technicians clambered off. Seating on the plane was assigned, designated by little blue cards stuck atop the seats. Here too, assignments were according to caste. The White House staff members got the best seats, up front. The TV networks, news magazines, and major newspapers also sat in first class, if there was room. Grumbling, Eaton usually found himself over the wing.

Suitbag over his arm, he dragged himself up the steps, nodded at the flight attendant, and then began scanning the seat tops, looking for the blue card with his name, already resentful over the bad seat he was sure to get. But then, just a couple of feet down the aisle, he stopped so suddenly that the radio technician behind him piled into his back.

"Hey, come on. What are you doing?" the tech growled. But Eaton didn't hear him. Just ahead, poking above a window seat toward the back of first class, was a head of brown hair, a page-boy with just a few strands of silver. He stopped, mouth open, eyes fixed, hands sweating.

Leslie was staring out the window. But then the technician remonstrated again: "Come on, Eaton, move your ass. What do you think you're doing?" Eaton hardly heard him; he just stared. But with that, slowly and deliberately Leslie turned to look at him. Right away her wide brown eyes fastened on him, irradiated him, as if she'd known he was there all along. When he thought back on this moment later, as he did over and over again, Eaton figured he must have been projecting abject distress.

For a second or two Leslie just stared at him with no expression, none at all. But then slowly her lips pursed. Her teeth clenched, her eyes narrowed, and she was stabbing him with a look that was impossible to misinterpret. On her face was an expression of utter, unequivocal contempt.

Then, just as deliberately, she turned away.

CHAPTER FIVE

NORTHERN NICARAGUA, AUGUST 8

MAJOR PAZ, TIGRILLO, AND BALITA KNEW ALL THE safe roads and precautionary tactics for driving from Managua north to the Honduran border. The Sandinistas seldom varied the locations of their checkpoints, even when they were looking for someone, as they must be now that they'd discovered the wreckage of the electrical substation. So Tigrillo anticipated the roadblocks and pulled around them, bumping over rock-strewn fields or driving through alleys and cluttered yards in little villages along the way. By late afternoon the breeze pouring through the old Plymouth's open windows began to grow less steamy, and the three of them started to relax a bit.

They were in the Highlands now; the hills were turning into mountains. The only people they passed were campesinos pulling lazy donkeys and old women carrying plastic-net shopping bags that held a few potatoes and a couple of onions, if they were lucky. The border wasn't far. But then, just north of San Juan de Río Coco, they hit a problem.

"Convoy!" Tigrillo warned all of a sudden as they came around a turn in the road, and the other two jerked up in their seats, peering ahead through the windshield. Rolling slowly along around the bend just half a mile or so up the pocked asphalt road was a line of about twenty military vehicles: armored personnel carriers, troop trucks, tank transports, and a fuel tanker. It stretched almost five hundred yards.

"What do we do? What do we do?" Balita whined. It was at moments like this that the first part of his nickname "the child-fighter" seemed apt. When he could shoot and fight as he had been trained to do since before puberty, Balita could be ferocious. But here—trapped, scared, with no weapon—he whimpered like the naïve child he really was. The others were used to it, and this time they were nervous too.

Tigrillo looked left and right for a place to turn off. There was none, just coffee bushes on both sides of the road. Because they'd come upon the convoy around a bend, they were already so close, Tigrillo knew, that it would look suspicious if they suddenly slowed down or turned off—especially this far north, in contra country. So the next thing the three of them knew, they were driving along thirty yards behind the Soviet-made armored personnel carrier that took up the convoy's rear, staring up the barrel of a 50-caliber rear-mounted machine gun. The gun's cartridge belt flapped in the breeze, and the soldier standing with his hand on the palm grip looked down at them with an expression both threatening and bored. The weapon was certainly cocked and ready to fire, the three of them knew. And unquestionably the fifteen or so other troops sitting forward in the APC's bed had loaded weapons at hand. Up here in the Highlands, Sandinista forces were ever alert for ambushes and probably wondered if this car appearing out of nowhere might be the rear watch for an attacking contra force.

As they drew close, Paz scrunched down onto the floor below the back seat. His orange hair, he knew, was a beacon.

"What do we do, what do we do?" Balita whimpered again, his voice faltering as they pulled along at about thirty miles an hour. Nobody said a word; none of them had an idea. They could tail along behind this slow-moving convoy for hours; passing all the vehicles on these hilly, winding roads was virtually impossible.

But then Tigrillo saw the soldier standing above them abruptly turn to his right and lift his Cuban-style steel helmet. An officer was shouting something into his ear. The young Sandinista turned back and looked straight down at them with an evil sneer, and just then the convoy slowed almost to a halt.

"Oh shit, shit, shit," Tigrillo muttered. On the floor in the back, Paz reached into the kit bag that lay at his feet and pulled out his Beretta. Sneering still, the soldier waved them forward, motioned them to pass.

"They've got us," Tigrillo said, his voice grim, as he pulled the Plymouth around to the left. Paz dragged himself onto the back seat and stretched out, pretending to be asleep and using his arm to cover as much of his hair as he could. Tigrillo drove as fast as he was able on the rutted road, maybe forty-five miles an hour. There was seldom much traffic up here; too many ambushes. But oncoming cars weren't a real problem anyway. Oddly enough, the entire convoy had pulled onto whatever shoulder there was beside the road to let them pass.

That must have taken quite a bit of radio coordination, Tigrillo thought. They must really want us.

He looked up front to see who or what awaited them. But the road was clear. Then Tigrillo looked up at the faces of drivers in the vehicles they were passing, and that's when he began to realize what was really going on. All of the soldiers were smiling—grinning, really. Some were actually laughing as they pointed at the car.

"Major," Tigrillo said over his shoulder as the car drew near the convoy's head. "I think we're just bait." And sure enough, as they pulled around the lead vehicle, another APC, everyone aboard was smiling down at them.

The convoy now had a point car. That's all this was. If contras had planted any antivehicle mines up ahead, the Sandinistas figured, it would be these farmers in the Plymouth who got blown up first.

Half a mile up the road, Tigrillo broke into nervous laughter, and Balita began to imitate him with nervous laughter of his own. Paz pulled himself up in the back seat and put his Beretta back in the bag. He too was relieved. But at the same time, as they drew nearer the border, he began to feel dread. When they got back to Camp Cascabeles, the major knew, he would have to pay for his mission's failure, for the death of Alvarado, the electrical engineer.

They left the Plymouth at a prearranged spot in Jalapa and followed a well-known foot trail to the Honduran frontier. All along the way they passed contra forces heading south. The other fighters smiled and nodded at them. Hardly anyone had been told of their mission, so none of these fighters knew of their failure. After a couple of hours, they were back in Honduras, their home these last years.

The Hondurans didn't much like the Sandinistas but weren't terribly fond of the contras either. The presence of a large well-armed foreign army on their soil made them more than a little uneasy. Still, Honduras was the hemisphere's second-poorest nation, and over time, massive American aid had forced Honduran government officials to begrudgingly accept their guests.

Back at Camp Cascabeles, Paz radioed the comm center at El Cuartelón, the main base, a few miles down the road. No messages. Not a word. Clearly Mendoza had cut them off cold.

For two days Paz ran the Pena de Muertes through endless firing-range exercises and assault drills, waiting for the CIA man to come to Cascabeles with his new commando squad. The Pena de Muertes would have to pack up and move back to the main camp. Then early Thursday morning a courier from El Cuartelón pulled up in a jeep while the men were running through tree-stump bayonet drills.

"Major, Rafael Mendoza would like to see you at base camp right away," he said. "You can come with me."

Stoic as always, Paz climbed into the back seat and told Balita to carry on.

Paz stepped up to the screen door of Mendoza's "command hut," off by itself in an open meadow a short walk from base camp. On the top step he stood at attention, waiting to be noticed. The inside door was open, and Mendoza was talking to a large blond gringo lounging in an armchair next to the little Cuban's desk.

Unlike all the other huts, this one had interior walls, not just frames. Must be for soundproofing, the major had figured the first time he'd been here. Maps of Honduras and Nicaragua were stapled to bulletin boards. Insulation was tacked to the plywood ceiling above the exposed rafters. Heavy padded shutters, open now, hung beside the windows. A secure telephone sat on the maple desk. But Mendoza hardly ever used any of these precautions. He must know he's among friends, the major assumed. In fact as Paz stood at the door waiting to be recognized, Mendoza glanced at him but finished what he was saying to the gringo before greeting him.

"And so I'm told he got congressional confirmation, and he's going to take the RIG job," Mendoza was saying. "He'll be leaving State and going over to Pennsylvania Avenue in September or October. In the meantime I've got a special asset who does some work for us over at State, and I'm going to send her over to see what we can learn about our new man. We'll see what she comes up with." Then he swiveled in his desk chair and turned toward the door.

"Paz, Paz, please come in, my friend," Mendoza said, gesturing with his arm. Paz stepped just inside and stood at rigid attention, Ray Bans pointed at the far ceiling rafters.

"Paz, I'd like you to meet Colonel Eric Gustafson, United States Marines," Mendoza said, pointing to the big man in the armchair. With that introduction—United States Marines—Paz's back stiffened even more.

"This is the man who's been giving us all that good intel from Managua," Mendoza said.

Gustafson got up, walked over to Paz, and almost stepping on his feet, looked down at the little major.

"How ya doing," he said with a grin, reaching down to slap Paz on the back before sitting down again.

"So, Paz, please tell us how it went."

"Sir, the target died. A heart attack," Paz said. "We tried to save him, but he died. We failed."

"What do you mean you failed?" Mendoza asked with his warm grin. "You destroyed the station. You got our target away from town. All of you came back alive. This was a success. We didn't accomplish everything we hoped for, but few operations are perfect. We learned a lot. Even Chairman Coronel sends you his congratulations." Coronel was Mendoza's toady.

"Come on, sit down, Paz," he said, motioning to a chair. The major didn't move.

"Well, Paz, you've got to tell us how it went," Mendoza went on. "We want to know everything. How the overnight housing worked. What security forces, what deployments you encountered. Problems, lessons. We want a full debrief."

Paz lowered his gaze from the rafters. Through the Ray Bans, Mendoza couldn't see that Paz was puzzled.

"Come on, my friend, tell us," Mendoza said, a bit impatient now. "We need everything. We've got very big plans for you and your men."

CHAPTER SIX

STATE DEPARTMENT, WASHINGTON, SEPTEMBER 22

FOR ASCHER THE LAST MONTH HAD BEEN HECTIC. HE'D been doing all his regular State Department work while also reading for his new job—intelligence reports that detailed the true state of the contra forces while also recounting the increasingly desperate living conditions for the poor people of Nicaragua. The Defense Intelligence Agency was reporting that some Nicaraguans actually wanted the United States to invade. The reporting seemed eloquent and convincing, but Ascher didn't quite know what to make of it.

By secure diplomatic pouch, Rafael Mendoza, the CIA station chief down in Honduras, had been sending him friendly notes and small packets of materials: monographs on Latin guerrilla strategy that Ascher found particularly interesting. They showed that Latin revolutionaries often succeeded through daring acts of bravado, not shrewd politicking. And out of it all, Ascher had grown convinced that the contra program was mismanaged. He couldn't figure out what the contras' American handlers were trying to accomplish. All they'd done so far was keep the rebels in the field shooting at nothing in particular with no master plan or identifiable goal. In more than a dozen years they'd shot up some coffee plantations, blown up a few dams, killed some Sandinista soldiers and probably as many women and children.

More recently they'd taken to blowing up infrastructure built years ago by the United States. Clever CIA. In a rusty file cabinet somewhere in the government's archival bowels, the agency had found some old Army Corps of Engineers plans. And so the contras had carried out their most daring act to date: They'd cut off electricity to thousands of their countrymen, the very people they were trying to recruit. What stupidity, Ascher had thought when he'd read about that in the newspapers. The intelligence reports explaining it in guerrilla-warfare doctrine did little to change his mind.

The program's stagnant, he thought. The United States is squandering the contras. Why can't we go in there and really accomplish something with this army we've created, the largest guerrilla force in Latin American history? Ascher believed he was being given a unique opportunity to turn things around, make a difference.

Just last week, the leaders of the key congressional committees had approved his appointment to the RIG and sent him a letter wishing him the best. This new job could make his career. And, at last, he would prove himself to his father.

Almost as soon as he'd accepted the White House job he had decided to tell his father. Talking to him was never easy, but he had to let Wallace Ascher know that finally he'd made it to the top. So one Sunday Ascher called him first thing, as soon as he'd finished his morning session under the sunlamp.

Wallace Ascher was seventy-two and still lived in the big family house across the river in Virginia. A year earlier he'd had a stroke. He had recovered, except that now he walked bent over and leaning heavily on a cane. But Wallace was more than six feet tall and still an imposing figure. He had been at least fifty pounds overweight ever since he was thirty years old, but because of his height, the effect was not of a fat person but of a big powerful man. He had a large patrician nose, ruddy cheeks, and a full head of hair that had turned silver-white more than thirty years ago. All his life he had been the man who stood out in a crowd.

Terry was never sure if he should ring the doorbell and wait in front of what had been his own home. But he always did. Wallace opened the door and said, "Hi, son," with a small benevolent smile. He patted Terry on the back and laboriously made his way back to the sun porch, where he sat on a cushioned wrought-iron sofa in the shade. On the coffee table were a tray holding a coffee carafe and the Sunday newspapers.

Without asking, Wallace poured Terry a cup. "Cream and sugar, right?"

"Yeah, thanks, Father," he said and watched as Wallace pursed his lips ever so slightly, pulling his mouth into the barest of grimaces as he picked up the sugar spoon. The casual observer probably would not have noticed the expression. If he had, he could have read it in a hundred different innocuous ways: as a tiny grimace of concentration, a reflection of a fleeting, irrelevant thought, or an old man's reflexive habit that held no meaning at all. But Terry didn't miss it; he never did. To him it was his father's grimace of disapproval, and a wounded expression sprang to his own face every time he saw it.

Wallace Ascher had always been an arrogantly confident man. So rigid was he, so certain that his was the only way on all matters big and small, that he couldn't even accept Terry's way of drinking his coffee. Wallace drank his black, and once, a year or so ago, he'd snapped at Terry, "If you're going to put all that sugar in there, you might as well just have a Coca-Cola."

That was consistent with his general view of others. Opinions that conflicted with his own were without foundation, the work of feeble minds. But only those who knew him well could read his disapproval. Wallace was the consummate professional diplomat, and even when he was away from work, the range of emotions he displayed had long ago been compressed within a very narrow band.

Growing up, Terry had developed a refined ability to read and react to his father's emotional twitches, like a deer that bolts at a sound other animals can't even hear. And how better to win his father's approval than to imitate him?

In Wallace Ascher's time, the postwar era, the countries of Western Europe were the prestige postings, the places all ambitious foreign service officers hoped to go. By the 1960s, demographers, economists, and others were suggesting that Asia and Latin America would gain importance in the decades ahead, for better or for worse. But the foreign service was not eager to change and didn't—the lesson of Cuba notwithstanding.

Wallace hadn't much liked his posting to Madrid in 1958, but he had considered it an acceptable way station. Spain was, after all, an important NATO ally. But when President Kennedy sent him to Venezuela, and then to El Salvador, Wallace knew he was ruined, his career irretrievably stunted by one president's irrational whim. Hell, until the 1940s the State Department hadn't even sent full ambassadors to Central America.

Wallace never talked about this at home; that was not his style. His wife could tell, of course, but as far as Terry knew, his father had accepted his Latin America assignments with equanimity, just as he'd accepted all the others. And so it was only natural, given Terry's own emotional makeup, that at Harvard he would learn Spanish and take courses under the history department's Latinists.

Thinking back on that later, Terry was sure he had discussed it with his father, though in the years after his mother's death he hadn't visited often. That's why he'd been not only crushed but completely baffled by his father's reaction when he told him he had selected the Latin America track for his foreign service career.

Eyebrows arched, Wallace Ascher had stared back at Terry, saying, "Son, I just can't believe you took this on by your own choice. Whatever got into you? I wish you'd talked to me first." But by then it was too late to change, and Terry plunged ahead, disconsolate and confused.

In the last dozen or so years, of course, Latin America had in fact grown to be an area of major diplomatic importance. There had been the Latin oil boom and then the debt crisis. The Grenada invasion and the Falklands War. Democracy had come to what seemed like scores of countries that had formerly been ruled by heavy-handed military tyrants. And then there was Nicaragua. The contras.

Terry had never discussed the issue with his father but supposed he was a contra opponent. Not his style. But at the same time, Wallace was fiercely anti-Communist, so Terry really didn't know where he stood on the Nicaragua issue. He'd thought a lot about what he would say. He was nervous.

"Father, I've got something to tell you," he blurted out with no warning, leaning forward as he spoke. "I've been given a new appointment. I'm going over to the White House. I'm going to be a deputy assistant to the president for the rest of this term."

That certainly got Wallace's attention. He put down his coffee cup and looked at Terry with a smile not so much of pleasure as of amazement, his head cocked a bit.

"Terry, that's some news. Tell me about it. What happened? What are you going to be doing?"

"Well, Father, the president is unhappy with the new RIG that's directing the contra effort. It's lacking in ideas and initiative. I'm going to be the fourth member, the president's own representative and the full-time administrator. In effect, I'm going to be the chief of staff for that program."

Wallace's smile disappeared. He wasn't disdainful, Terry thought, he simply hadn't yet figured out what to make of this. Still, the dread began to seep in.

"I know the contras are controversial, maybe even risky from a career standpoint. But I don't lose my foreign service ranking. No matter what, I can go back. And the president has promised me an ambassadorial posting or maybe even an assistant secretaryship when I come out of this."

Wallace breathed a heavy sigh. "You really think the president, if he's reelected, could keep that promise if the contras fuck up while you're in charge? And given their performance to date, they will most certainly fuck up before the next eighteen months have expired."

Terry began sinking. His father almost never cursed, and as Terry tried to respond, the pitch of his own voice rose. "But Father, maybe I can help straighten them out, make some good of this." His father just looked at him—didn't smile, didn't frown, didn't say a word. Terry knew this technique: Answer with a solemn stare, say nothing, wait, and the other side will blather on, trying ever harder to evoke some kind of reaction. Terry knew the tactic and blathered on anyway.

"Father, you know in our work that it's the officer's job to represent U.S. interests as best he can, even if he disagrees with the policy. And, agree with it or not, this is a very important policy."

"Come on, Terry, don't quote credos to me. And that one doesn't apply here anyway. Your duty to represent your country as best you can does not require you to accept suicide postings. The contras are greedy Latin mercenary killers. They've never amounted to anything and they never will." At least Terry now knew where his father stood on the contra issue.

"The program was stillborn; any Latinist will tell you that. And if you take this new job, you're unlikely to survive. If you can get out of this, then do it, because it's a dreadful mistake."

There was no recovery from that. Terry's shoulders slumped; he was bent over looking at the floor, rocking slightly up and down, arms wrapped around his stomach as though he'd taken a beating. He could hardly speak and only whispered, "Father, please, you're being too harsh. It's a risk, I know. But it's a White House appointment."

His father didn't even answer this time, just stared back again, his face now locked in that brutal pursed-lip grimace. Terry was defeated, too weak to say more. As he usually did at times like this, Wallace changed the subject and made small talk, as if nothing had occurred. Vacations, Washington weather, what he was growing in the vegetable garden out back.

Slumped over and monosyllabic, Ascher waited a decent interval, then got up and slunk out of the house. As soon as he'd closed the car door he reached for the little envelope in his glove compartment and took five milligrams of Valium.

Ascher never recovered easily from one of those sessions with his father. But one day out of the blue appeared what, for him, was the most effective antidote.

The State Department INR offices, intelligence and research, were just down the hall, and every once in a while he'd glimpsed an exquisite strawberry blonde going in or out of INR's cipher-lock door. He'd asked about her and been told she was an intelligence analyst, probably on loan from the CIA. The couple of times they'd passed in the hall Ascher had given his come-on smile, but she'd ignored him. In two years he had seen her only three or four times; those spooks didn't seem to come out into the sunlight very often.

But then, a few days after the episode with his father, he began seeing the woman almost every day, and every time they crossed paths she gave him a warm smile. She wore tight skirts and blouses that showed off her figure. Despite the blond hair, something about her coloration and features suggested she might have some Latin blood. She was gorgeous. Every time he saw her, he couldn't stop thinking about her. Then one day he was eating lunch alone in the cafeteria when all of a sudden there she was, standing over him, smiling.

"May I join you?"

"Well, of course. Please." Ascher stood up, almost knocking over his chair.

"I'm Laura Perez. You're Terry Ascher, aren't you?"

"Yes, I am. I'm glad to meet you."

"No, no. I'm glad to meet you," she said with a more-than-engaging smile. "I've seen you around."

"I've seen you, too," Ascher stammered, his own smile maybe a little too broad. He straightened his tie and felt grateful that he'd taken the time to sit under the sunlamp this morning.

"I hear you're going over to the White House."

"Yeah."

"That must really be exciting," she said with an expression of wonder.

"Well, I hope so."

"Going on the contra RIG?"

"Yeah. How'd you know?"

"I'm in INR. We know everything." Her smile was almost salacious.

They talked for a while, State Department banter, but she was all smiles and long-lashed alluring gazes. This woman was fascinated by him, Ascher could see. It would be great if the White House affected every woman this way. He felt like a school kid on his first date. She'd bat her eyes or flip her hair; he'd drop some cole slaw in his lap. Once he even knocked the pepper shaker onto the floor, but she didn't seem to notice.

As they were finishing their desserts, casually she asked about his views on the contra program, and he told her, "In a general sense I think we could be doing more with the contras than we are. But I'm new at this, so I want to see the lay of the land first."

With that she took a final bite of chocolate cake and then, looking directly at him, she began to lick her fork ever so slowly. Astonished, Ascher stared back. Finally she set the fork down and her wide brown eyes sparkled as she told him, "Well, Terry, if ever I can help you figure out 'the lay of the land,' you just call me."

Ascher's breath caught in his throat. His hand drawing a coffee cup up to his mouth seemed paralyzed. But then her expression seemed to change. The smile faded as her eyes flicked up and down, studying, calculating, appraising. And a moment later she sprang from her chair with a dramatic whirl and strode from the room.

Ascher didn't move for a couple of minutes, until he realized he'd been sitting there a long while with a silly grin on his face. Back in the office he looked her up in the State Department directory, jotted down the number, but decided he'd wait until tomorrow to call.

First thing in the morning he dialed her extension.

"INR," the secretary said.

"Laura Perez, please."

"May I ask who's calling?"

"Terrence Ascher.

"Just a minute, please." She put him on hold, then came back and said, "She's in conference right now. May I take a message?"

"Yes. Please ask her to call me. Extension 8692."

She didn't call back right away, so he tried again after lunch. The secretary took another message. And another one the next morning. And another that afternoon. Ascher wondered what was going on. Wandering the halls hoping to see her again, he was in and out of the office so much that Linda, his secretary, gave him funny looks. Before, he'd been seeing Laura two or three times a day. Now she wasn't anywhere around.

When a week had passed and she hadn't returned any of his phone calls, Ascher stopped trying. He had all kinds of theories. Maybe she was married and had had second thoughts. More likely, he figured, a man from the White House intimidated her. Still, it certainly seemed like an encouraging sign for his social life.

A week later, Congress finally got around to voting on the president's new package of aid for the contras: $240 million to be spent over the next eighteen months, enough to carry the program into the next presidential term. For the two weeks before the vote, strident supporters and opponents had been shouting the decades-old arguments for and against renewed aid. But, as always, in most congressmen's minds the question came down to this: No one wanted to invade, but no one wanted to give up either. Most of all, no one wanted to run for reelection against an opponent who could tell constituents that their congressman had "lost Nicaragua to the Communists."

"We don't want another Vietnam, but we don't want another Cuba either" was the tired old refrain. Still, it worked, and as always the contras were the compromise answer.

Terry stood in his State Department office watching the vote on C-Span, the cable TV station that covered Congress. For a moment the numbers were frozen on the TV screen, 182–182, and then there was a burst of last-minute voting from congressmen who'd hung back to see how the count was going before deciding how to cast their own vote. The fifteen-minute voting period was drawing to an end, and the digital vote clock on the screen was ticking past the thirty-second mark. Both the yeas and the nays flipped past 200, then froze. In red letters the message flashed on the screen: "Vote on final passage of amendment to Defense Authorization Act, 222 Yea, 208 Nay. Amendment approved."

Ascher slapped the side of the TV and opened his mouth in a smiling silent scream. He threw open the door and stood behind Linda, hands gripping her shoulders.

"We're going to the White House," he said. She was leaning her head backward to smile up at him when the phone buzzed. She picked it up.

"Mr. Ascher's office. Okay. I'll tell him." She hung up and said, "Art wants to see you."

"Be right back," he said, and hurried down the hall.

Kutler was waiting for him, his own TV still turned on to C-Span. "Hi, Terry. Congratulations," he said, standing up and smiling as they shook hands.

"Thanks, Art." Kutler sat behind his desk, Ascher on the other side, looking at his boss over the clutter.

"You've got quite an adventure ahead of you," Kutler told him.

"I know. It's exciting."

"Listen, Terry, I just wanted to tell you what a privilege it's been having you working for me. You've done some great things over here. You're one officer I always knew I could rely on, and I told Rich Christopher just that. I want to wish you the best of luck over there. I know you're going to do well."

"Thanks, Art. I've learned a lot over here."

"I know. I'll bet you come back and climb right over me on the ladder."

"No chance," Ascher said. Both of them were grinning.

"Listen, Terry, you know you've got to be careful over there. You can't step over the line working with the contras. It's too visible. You'll get in career-ending trouble."

"I know, Art. The contra program, it's cut short some fine careers."

"Be careful. Take it slow," Kutler went on. He paused, frowning, then said, "Running the contras, you can't pull things like that stunt with the Bahamas and the drug-trafficking list."

Ascher didn't say anything, tried to show no reaction.

"I don't know why he waited so long," Kutler said, "but your friend the attorney general was talking to Abramson at an embassy reception in Nassau and asked him sort of casually about the drug list, how countries get on it. After Abramson told him, the attorney general told Abramson what happened."

The deputy chief of mission in Nassau, Andy Abramson, was no friend of Ascher's and probably passed the information to Kutler with glee.

"The Right Honourable Mr. Wilcox was right angry. But I think he agreed it was in all our interests at this point to keep it quiet."

"Oh" was all Ascher could say.

"There's no way I'd have approved that little trick if you'd asked me. It was a stupid, dangerous thing to do." But then he paused, scribbling absently on his blotter, and without looking up said, "Just between you and me, though, I'm kinda glad you did it." He looked up, grinning. Ascher grinned back tentatively. "I don't think we'd ever have gotten the treaty without that game you played, and now that the first one's signed I think we may be able to get Panama too."

But Kutler's smile was gone in an instant, and his manner was dead serious when he said, "My point in going into this is that I want you to remember: The press is all over the contra program. Tricks you got away with in the Caribbean aren't going to fly in that arena. Working with the contras, you've got to be an absolute straight arrow. No stepping over the line. No second chances. My office is in this too, and I don't want anybody to get hurt. Understand me?"

"Yes, Art." Ascher felt like a schoolboy.

"Good enough." They stood and shook hands.

Ascher walked slowly back to his office, looking at the floor, preoccupied, trying to decide what other transgressions Kutler might have discovered. It was terrible to consider, but as it turned out, he didn't have much time to ponder the question. His secretary was trotting down the hall toward him, clearly agitated.

"Terry, Terry, the White House is holding on the phone for you. They say it's urgent."

He hurried back and took the call.

It was Rich Christopher, ebullient as he said, "Terry, ol' boy. How you doing?"

"Hi, Rich. How are you. Congratulations on that vote."

"Yeah, thanks. It was sweet, wasn't it?"

"Sure was."

"So what do you think, Terry? Any second thoughts?"

"Nope. I'm all set."

"Good. In that case, the president wants to see you."

"He does?" Ascher had wanted to sound nonchalant when this moment came but he failed. "When?"

"Right now."

This time Christopher met him in the West Lobby. The pretty receptionist knew he was coming and buzzed the deputy chief of staff right away.

"Hi there, come on with me" was all he said as they shook hands and then rushed out the door. Ascher tried to look around but found Christopher's pace so fast he hardly had time to focus on anything. Other people they passed seemed to be rushing too, as if everyone in the West Wing was in a speed-walk competition, or caught in some sudden emergency. From what he'd heard, that was always the pace here when the president was in town.

They walked swiftly through a handsome meeting room with salmon-colored walls and a fireplace, the Roosevelt Room, and then, before Ascher could catch his breath, they were at the open door to the Oval Office. Secret Service agents standing on either side stiffened for a moment and gave Ascher a malign look. A bored-looking military aide sat beside the door, next to the defense-alert phone.

"Listen, Terry," Christopher whispered, "I'm going to leave you with him, and you've got about ten minutes. Okay?"

"Sure."

A young man in a dark suit, the president's personal aide, stepped out of the Oval Office and said, "You may go in now," then set off down the hall. They went in. To their right the president was sitting behind his massive carved-oak desk—Queen Victoria had given it to President Rutherford B. Hayes—looking into a thick file folder. This president, everyone knew by now, was a voracious reader. Ascher and Christopher stood silently for a moment, and then the president rose and walked over to them, a smile on his face.

"Hello, Rich," he said in that warm, deep, and familiar voice.

"Good afternoon, Mr. President. I'd like you to meet Terrence Ascher."

The president shook Ascher's hand. "It's Terry, isn't it?"

"Yes, sir, Mr. President. I'm honored to meet you."

"Well, Terry, I'm delighted to meet you. I've heard great things about you, and we're all happy to know you're going to be joining us, working on a very important program."

"I'm going to leave you two alone," Christopher said and quickly left, closing the door behind him. The president put his arm around Ascher's shoulder and led him slowly over to the sofas in front of the fireplace, looking down as he said in a soft, almost conspiratorial tone: "I want to be frank with you, Terry. As you probably know, I wasn't one of the contras' greatest supporters when I came into office. So many things had gone wrong."

They were standing by the sofas now; the president's arm was still around him.

"But what I learned once I got here is that the blunders and scandals and overpromises weren't so much the contras' doing. They were ours. We can't blame them. And with the way the Sandinistas have been behaving these last months, I came around to seeing that we just can't sit back and let this go on.

"Just look at what they've been doing," he said, shaking his head. "This month that fellow Zelaya put some more of their political opponents in his torture prison. And now he has nationalized nearly all of the remaining private business—just took them away from good business people. They're harassing the Catholic Church. And now this business of giving the Soviets military landing rights at their airports. The Lord only knows where they'll go from here. We can't let this continue."

"Yes, sir, Mr. President. I think you're right." Ascher sat on a sofa, the president beside him in a Martha Washington chair.

Through another door set almost invisibly into the back wall, a White House staff photographer walked in and began taking flash pictures, with the small ornamental fire flickering in the background. Like all White House appointees, Ascher knew, he'd soon be given one of these photos, signed with a personal greeting from the president. He'd hang it over his desk.

The camera motor-drive was whirring in the background as the president said, "I met your father once. He was a fine officer."

"Yes, sir."

"How is he?"

"He's retired, lives here in town. He had a stroke, but he's mostly recovered. He's doing well."

"Good. I'm glad to hear it. He's a fine man. You do credit to your father and his proud professional accomplishments."

Ascher smiled. As the photographer left, a steward came in with a silver tray, quickly poured two cups of coffee, and left.

The president dove right in. "Terry, I asked to see you alone like this because, well, I want you to know how important this is to me. Congress saddled us with that Restricted Interagency Group."

Ascher started to open his mouth, but the president held up his hand. "I know, I know. I agreed to it, and I signed the bill without complaint. Given the history, I wanted some checks and balances this time, too. But I never realized how cautious, maybe even cowardly, the bureaucracy could really be, and from here I'm finding it almost impossible to do anything about it—especially since, the way the law is structured, those guys are essentially congressional appointees."

Sweeping his hand toward his desk, he said, "The recalcitrant bureaucracy has been the bane of everyone who's sat in that chair."

He sat forward and looked right at Ascher, eyes narrowed.

"Terry, I hope you can straighten out that RIG for me, get some enthusiasm back into the program. We're going to stay well within the law; I don't want to see any stories in the press that the president or his new appointee is violating congressional intent, trying to push the contras to overthrow the Sandinistas.

"But you're a doer, I know. That's why we're so glad to have you over here. They told me about that treaty you got with the Cayman Islands. First one, wasn't it? And I want you to do great things here, too."

"Thank you, sir. I will do my best." Ascher jerked in his seat. But if the president had known so little about the Bahamas treaty that he'd gotten the islands confused, he certainly couldn't have been told about the drug-list trick.

"Mr. President, I think we have a great opportunity with this new aid package and with the contras already up to speed. Maybe we can make more out of our assets than we have before."

"Terry, I couldn't agree more. I realize now that the Sandinistas are true Communists. Now that I sit here and see the actual reporting from our boys over at the agency, I am convinced. The resistance really is the only thing that keeps Nicaragua from becoming another Cuba on the American mainland, a Soviet base in our own backyard."

"Yes, sir," Ascher said. "And now I think we can have the contras do more than they have so far. With better-defined tactics and a real strategy, I think the contras don't have to be just a harassment force. I think they can make a real difference."

"You're right. The resistance can make a real difference. That's my strategy, and I'm glad to know you share it. I've met a lot of them now. These are people who care about their country. I'm not going to allow the United States to let them down. I'm not going to let the people of Nicaragua down either. If it wasn't for the resistance, we could end up fighting a war. Nobody wants that. Terry, I want you to get the program moving. Help me keep us out of a war. Will you do that? Will you?"

"I will, Mr. President. I certainly will," Ascher answered, his voice exuberant.

They stood, and the president put his arm around Ascher's shoulder again as he led him to the door. They stopped for a moment, side by side, and the president's hand gripped Ascher's shoulder.

"Terry, I'm glad we feel the same way about this. I really mean it when I tell you that this is very important to me. Some people think I should be worried about how it will look if the contras make a mistake and we get blamed just before the reelection. They say we shouldn't take any risks right now, just go along. But I'm not going to let politics interfere. It's too important. You're in charge. Don't allow anyone to let the contras down. You have my full support. If anyone tries to make you back away from doing the best you can to bring democracy to Nicaragua, you tell them that."

"Yes, sir, I will," Ascher said. He felt charged, as if he'd spent the last ten minutes plugged into a wall socket. The president was asking him to carry out his most important job, and Ascher assured him, "We will make a difference."

"I know you will, Terry. I know you will."

When he got back Linda was aglow, eager to know what had happened. She followed him into his office—for her a rash act. Normally she was all shy reserve. But today she was all smiles, and her words came in a rush "So tell me what happened!"

Linda was in her early thirties, divorced. She was conservative in appearance and manner—usually she looked at the floor when she smiled. Her figure was trim and her face warm and pretty, her eyes a pale blue. But her cheeks were pitted, not disastrously, though enough so that people often remembered that as her pre-eminent characteristic. In Terry's mind, that alone disqualified Linda from consideration for any sort of social relationship. Besides, he thought, you don't get involved with your secretary. It just isn't done.

But every once in a while she smiled directly at him, eyes shining, and Ascher would wonder if Linda had somehow developed feelings for him. When he worked late, without being asked she stayed as long as he did, sometimes past midnight, even if she had nothing to do herself. "You might need me," she'd say, looking at the floor. But no, Terry would always think, surely she knows that a relationship isn't possible.

Today Ascher was excited and said, "Why don't you close the door."

She was startled but did as she was told. He didn't even wait until she'd sat back down.

"Linda, he was wonderful. He seemed to know all about me. He confided in me, told me what he really thought and put me in charge of doing what he said he can't get anybody else to do—make the contra program work. Shake up the RIG. And I'm going to do it!"

"I know you are, Terry," she said, her voice warmer than it had ever been. "I know you will. You can do it. You always do."

OLD EXECUTIVE OFFICE BUILDING, WASHINGTON

Ascher loved his big new office. He had his things moved from the State Department over the weekend, a couple of days after he saw the president, and first thing Monday morning he went to an office-supplies and furniture store to buy all the new appointments he wanted. Walnut bookshelves. A chrome "executive water pitcher" with glasses that he would put in the middle of the big conference table, where RIG meetings were to be held. An oriental throw rug. A high-back leather desk chair, and a folding screen to hide the combination-lock file cabinets, ugly but essential, since he would be dealing with classified materials.

The White House, he figured, would give him battered hand-me-downs. He paid extra for immediate delivery.

Ascher had hoped to get an office in the West Wing, but after studying the staff list he realized that was impossible. The building wasn't that large, and only the most senior people had offices over there.

Instead he was given a suite in the Old Executive Office Building, the grand Victorian–Second Empire edifice just across Jackson Place from the White House. Once it had housed the War, Navy, and State departments in their entirety. Nineteenth-century cannons and ships' anchors still sat out front; crossed swords and Civil War battle flags were molded into the brass door knobs.

Today the EOB held the National Security Council and a variety of other White House offices. Inside it was Victorian-grand: well-worn black-and-white marble parquet floors, polished brass banisters that wound up circular stairways, ornate plaster friezes, and extraordinary fifteen-foot ceilings.

Monday night after all of his new furniture and accessories

had been placed and everyone else had gone home, Ascher sat behind his big desk, leaning back in his fat chair, smiling to himself. He leapt up every few minutes to adjust a chair, rotate the new ficus tree's pot half a turn, untangle the cord of the telephone over by the sofa. He took the burn-bag stand holding a small paper sack with the word BURN, appropriately enough, printed on it in bold black and moved it out beside his desk. It was ugly, but Ascher liked the effect.

It was almost ten o'clock when he locked the suite's front door, pausing for a moment to look at the new sign on the wall: TERRENCE W. ASCHER, DIRECTOR OF ASSISTANCE TO THE NICARAGUAN RESISTANCE.

Ascher called the other RIG members before he left State, trying to make appointments to see them. But they had already decided that the most practical idea was to hold a RIG meeting right away. It was scheduled for ten-thirty Tuesday morning.

They arrived together, causing Ascher to wonder if they'd met among themselves first. But as they sat around Ascher's table everyone was all smiles—wonderful to meet you, great to have you aboard. Legal pads and a couple of sharpened White House pencils were set at each place, and at Ascher's request, Linda had arranged to have a steward deliver coffee and some croissants. He sat at the head of the table, Linda behind him to the right. She was the recording secretary. A topographical map of Central America sat on an easel over in front of the fireplace.

They chitchatted for a couple of minutes. "Hey, great office," Scott Ames said in that sarcastic tone of his. "Really like those screens over there in front of the files. Nice touch. You pick out that paisley fabric yourself?" Ascher just smiled. Ames was the State Department representative, the only RIG member Ascher had known before. He was deputy assistant secretary for Central American Affairs, a position theoretically equivalent to Ascher's former Caribbean post, though several notches higher on the political scale. They were rivals, about the same age, and didn't much like each other. Ascher thought Ames was cocky and sneering. He liked to call people "old boy," as in "Well, Terry old boy, I like your tan, but I hope you don't get sun poisoning over there in the Caribbean while we're over here fighting a war."

"Good layout here, Terry," offered Winthrop "Win" Cater, a cool Army colonel who was the Defense Department representative. He didn't wear his uniform because his office was political, not military. Cater was the military analyst in DoD's Office of Inter-American Affairs. Ascher figured that was not a posting the Army would give an officer on the fast track. Still, Cater tried to exude the firm, confident air of a military officer on the rise. Maybe he could command troops, but it was clear he couldn't control a razor. His chin was a welter of shaving scars.

"An officer who knows how to go along with the program" was how Christopher had described him.

George Basham, the CIA representative, didn't say much. He just watched, eyes darting, and gave quick strained smiles when necessary. A career intelligence officer nearing retirement, he was chairman of the agency's Central America Task Force. As Ascher understood it, Basham had been station chief in several Latin countries years ago but had been out of the field more than a decade. Long ago he had molted into just another survival-minded bureaucrat. He was a balding, sour-looking man. Heavy bags sagged under his eyes, and his chin was a broad flesh parachute that hung down to his necktie before swooping back up to his throat. It jiggled when he coughed.

"The only thing Basham wants is not to make a mistake and jeopardize his pension," Christopher had warned.

They'd been sipping coffee, talking relatively amiably about troubles in the Persian Gulf—none of them wanted to seem one-issue men—when General Dayton, the NSC advisor, arrived with his own personal aide, a striking brown-eyed woman who held a steno pad.

"I'm dreadfully sorry to be late," he said, sweeping into the chair facing Ascher at the table's other end. He offered a brief businesslike smile. His short military crewcut—his head looked almost shaved—suggested that in his heart General Dayton was still a soldier.

"We're happy you could come, General," Ascher said. "We haven't really started yet."

The general's aide sat behind him to the left, facing Linda. Ascher gave his broadest come-on smile before he noticed her oversized diamond ring. She ignored him anyway, and he could feel Linda glaring.

No one had really expected Dayton to show up. The way Congress had set things up under the funding law, the NSC advisor was an ex officio member of the RIG. He had no vote except in the event of a deadlock, when he could cast the tiebreaker, as the vice president did in the Senate. As it turned out, the general didn't attend many RIG meetings. Everyone figured he didn't much like being a passive player, especially given his enthusiastic public support for the contra cause.

"General, sir, we're glad you're here," Colonel Cater told him. "Maybe we'd better get into it.

"Terry," Cater said turning to him, "usually we start with the military situation report. That okay with you?"

"Good idea."

A folder lay on the table in front of him, SECRET stamped across it in red, but the colonel didn't open it and looked one by one at the RIG members as he gave his report from memory.

"The northern resistance forces number about 12,560 men today, down, we estimate, about 200 from last month. Fighting has been heavy, casualties running at about 100 to 150 a week.

"As all of you know, resistance forces have managed to exfiltrate their bases in Honduras and are generalized throughout the north and north-central provinces. Thanks to your people, George"—he nodded at Basham—"supply lines have been steady.

"The resistance reports for the last month indicate that they carried out 468 actions in Jinotega, Zelaya, Matagalpa, Boaco, Chontales, and Río San Juan provinces. These, as you know, were mostly small-scale raids and ambushes. But we have had two important developments."

He got up and moved over to the map, taking a pencil with him. Standing there, he had to keep pushing a twig of Terry's new ficus tree out of his ear.

"Early this year, as you know, the resistance managed to seize some territory inside Nicaragua for the first time, on the Bocay River in Jinotega." He pointed to the spot on Nicaragua's border with Honduras, about halfway between the Caribbean and Pacific coasts.

"For the first time they've been able to hold some Sandinista territory." One reason, Ascher had read, was that the place was so mountainous and remote that for a long while the Sandinistas hadn't even known the contras were there. "And as a result, last summer they decided to move their main base to just north of there, in Honduras, since they had that nice buffer on the other side. The whole area is known as El Cuartelón, the Fortress.

"Well, early in September the Sandis managed to drive our people from the Nicaraguan side of El Cuartelón, back over the border. But not without a price. One of our commandos shot down a Soviet Hind helicopter gunship. He used one of the shoulder-fired Redeye SAMs we've been sending them. The resistance loves them, and the Sandis have made noticeably less use of their gunships now that they know we have finally trained the resistance to make effective use of the surface-to-airs.

"The Sandinistas did occupy our new territory for a while, even took press tours up. That worried us because it made the main base especially vulnerable. But last week, I'm delighted to say, we drove them back out.

"So now, gentlemen," he said with special emphasis as he stood up straight, shoulders back, hands clasped behind him, "the resistance has retaken control of El Cuartelón." Slowly he moved his gaze from face to face, giving each man a thin, deliberate smile.

"Now, in the interior, our U.S. Army–trained commandos followed up their successful attack on the Los Mártires electrical substation in Managua with a wholly successful attack on the main telephone switching station and microwave relay station in Estelí last month. The city of Estelí was without telephone service for eight days, and the Sandinistas were forced to bring in Cuban engineers to repair the exchange."

He returned to his seat and leaned back in his chair, saying, "Imagine, those people had come to know and rely on the fine Bell system we gave them way back in 1973. And now they'll have to learn to live with Cuban phones. Think of that. *Cuban* phones." He smiled at each of them again.

"In sum, we are satisfied with our progress this month, and we expect to be able to maintain current operational status with the new aid we have." With that he folded his arms and sat back in his chair.

"Well, thank you," Ascher said.

"Usually, Terry, the agency report is next," Cater said. Basham frowned and glared down at the table as he spoke. He had brought no notes or files.

"We have nothing unusual to report this month." Basham's voice was low, bored. "Our air drops are running according to plan. As you know, Terry, we have shifted most of our drop flights out of Ilopango in Salvador. That's the main military and commercial airport in San Salvador," he said as a weary, condescending aside to Ascher, who nodded as if he already knew.

"We've shifted most of them to El Aguacate in southern Honduras. That, Terry, is an 8,000-foot strip about 45 klicks from the Sandinista border." Army combat engineers built it behind the shield of Big Pine II, large-scale U.S. military maneuvers in Honduras in the early 1980s. They pretended the airfield construction was just a field exercise.

"Anyway, we're flying out to the Caribbean and then into the interior over the Caribbean coast, since that's where their radar is weak." He was talking directly to Ascher now, lecturing. "We're also starting to use Swan Island, off Honduras in the Caribbean. We use C-47s and DC-6s mostly, and we've had no casualties this year. We know where all the AA emplacements are. The only danger is if we happen to fly right over a Sandi holding a SAM.

"Our lines from U.S. warehouses are steady, all according to established ops plans. We anticipate continued smooth ops on current schedules through the new funding cycle. As far as we are concerned, we can keep this up at current levels as long as it's authorized. Questions?"

No one said anything, so Basham then turned to Ames, who sat up straight, looking briefly at General Dayton, who was taking a bite from a croissant.

"Conditions for useful negotiation improve," he intoned, slipping into confident State Department–speak. "The Sandinista economy continues to weaken. Oil shortages grow more severe. Food supplies dwindle, popular discontent with the GON continues to escalate."

Ames ticked off a number of new GON—Government of Nicaragua—austerity measures and cited a few isolated acts of protest, all of them small stuff, then ended by saying: "Our embassy continues to maintain useful back-channel contacts with important members of the Sandinista Directorate. And Ambassador Weinberg, our regional envoy, visited the region last month and had meaningful discussions with Costa Rican, Honduran, and Salvadoran government officers. We feel the conditions are continuing to mature toward the point where the GON will find itself in an environment where it has little choice but to carry on *serious* peace negotiations of the sort that they've managed to evade or torpedo until now. Minister Zelaya's unyielding positions cannot hold sway much longer if current trends continue."

Finished, he sat back, and glanced quickly at Dayton.

"General, do you want to say anything?" Ascher asked.

"No, Terry, it's your show."

Ascher leaned back and asked, "Well, where do we go from here?"

Ames looked startled at that, as if the answer were perfectly obvious. He glanced at the colonel, who showed no intention of responding, and then started in himself: "Well, of course, Terry, we keep the contras fighting as they are, keep the pressure on the Sandinistas so that popular discontent continues to mount and the GON has no choice but to negotiate into democracy."

"Yes, I know, but what kind of strategy can we use to step this up?"

Deep-voiced and confident, maybe a bit condescending, Colonel Cater said: "Ascher, the resistance is motivated but limited, both in prospects and abilities. These are peasant fighters, far outmanned and outgunned by the Sandinista army with all their Soviet equipment. Tactics like we've been using are about all we can expect of them."

Ames was tapping one of Ascher's carefully sharpened White House pencils as he added: "Terry, old boy, as my report made perfectly clear, the time will come soon when the GON has to give in and talk."

"Look, we all know the Sandinistas are committed Marxists," Ascher said. "And there is reliable intelligence indicating that they are willing to let their country fall into ruins before caving in to the Yanqui imperialists and their mercenary fighters. I think we need to do more."

General Dayton had started doodling but laid down his pencil and looked up at Ascher, who plunged on, falling into his own diplomatic voice-of-reason. He'd rehearsed this, whispering to himself in the shower this morning as he waved his arms through practiced mannerisms. One knocked the Wet Tunes shower radio off the soap shelf.

"Let's take a lesson from the last successful Nicaraguan revolutionaries. The Sandinistas. As all of you know, for fifteen years they tried strategies similar in some ways to our own. In the *foco* phase, they accepted the Che Guevara–Régis Debray revolutionary doctrine. Then, in the *tercerista* phase, they tried to build support among all the disaffected business and social elements in both urban and rural areas. Those and other strategies were failures when carried out by themselves."

Around the table, Colonel Cater listened attentively with no discernible reaction. Basham grimaced, arms folded across his chest, parachute chin flattened against his green-striped necktie. And Ames sat forward in his chair, palms flat on the padded arms as if he were about to leap up in protest. Only General Dayton continued to listen with clear interest.

"As with many other Latin revolutionaries, notably Castro,"

Ascher went on, "the Sandinistas succeeded only after several dramatic and celebrated acts galvanized support behind them."

Ascher was trying not to quote from them directly, but those monographs Rafael Mendoza had sent him from Honduras had been a big help.

"There were other big events, but as you know it was Edén Pastora's, Commander Zero's, grandstanding guerrilla raid on the National Palace in 1978 that had the largest effect. That action, more than anything, showed the dictator's weakness and brought the Somoza government down. Perhaps we should be looking for dramatic acts for our own revolutionaries?"

"Terry, that's the reasoning behind our raids on electrical and telephone stations," Colonel Cater explained, still calm. "They let the people know in a dramatic way the Sandinista Front's weakness."

"But there's a difference," Ascher said, "between our raids and having a personable and immensely popular guerrilla commander taking the Nicaraguan Congress hostage for three days and riding off into the sunset, to the cheers of thousands. There's a difference between that kind of dramatic act and our own fighters skulking into Managua, blowing up an electrical station that services the very people they want to recruit, and then sneaking away into the night." Ascher had loved the sound of that in the shower this morning. But before he could give his practiced closer, Basham broke in.

"Son," he said with an undisguised air of weary wisdom, bovine eyes peering out from under fleshy hoods. "We just don't have a Comandante Zero anywhere in this group of barefoot boys. You're new at this, and I suppose we ought to admire your youthful *zeal.*" He stretched out that last word with a heavy derisive tone. "But if there's one thing my years of experience with this little war have taught me, it is this: Never underestimate the contras' ability to fuck things up."

He paused for effect, then said, "If you want to take this fight into a new arena of dramatic, theatrical acts, you'd better find yourself another army to carry them out because this one can't do it. And you'd better not count on help from the CIA, because I'm not laying my career on the line for this tag-along troupe of tacos."

Colonel Cater coughed, and even Ames looked stunned by Basham's blunt bigotry. Ascher pulled out his ace.

"Gentlemen, I didn't have a specific idea to lay on the table for you right this minute. I just wanted to give everybody something to think about. And I also want to let you know that the president has specifically charged me with trying to move this program forward." Nobody seemed to like that at all, except General Dayton, who smiled.

The discussion deteriorated after that. Ames asked Ascher to be patient, give the program a chance to work. Ascher nodded. And soon after, the meeting adjourned until next month.

When everyone had left, Ascher waited only as long as he figured it would take Dayton to get back to his office, then he called to ask for an appointment. The secretary turned his call over to the aide who'd been with the general at the meeting.

"Leslie DeSalles."

"Hi, Leslie, it's Terry Ascher."

"Yes, the general suggested you and he might want to talk."

"Well, that's why I called, as a matter of fact."

"How about four-thirty this afternoon?"

"I'll be there."

"Terry, I admire your approach," Dayton said as soon as Ascher had settled back into a sofa in the general's large, bright corner West Wing office, down the hall from the president's. The carpet was clean white, the furniture genuine Queen Anne. A late snack from the commissary, tuna salad and potato chips, sat waiting on a tray over on the conference table. A glass of crushed ice for an unopened can of Diet Coke was carefully covered with Saran Wrap.

"I just wish I could be more help to you," he was saying. "But as you know, in this one area of foreign policy I am virtually impotent. Congress has hamstrung us, due, I guess you could say, to the misdeeds of my forebears." He smiled, resigned.

"General, you've watched that RIG. Any advice?"

"I haven't watched them that much. It seems like such a cover-your-ass group that I couldn't stomach sitting through those meetings. I've tried taking it up with their bosses, the two secretaries and the DCI"—the director of Central Intelligence—"but frankly, between you and me, those fellows on the RIG work for people who are just as spineless, now that we are getting near reelection season. More than anything else they are worried about screwing up and losing the election, so they'd have to go back to their old jobs at Merrill Lynch or someplace." He shook his head.

"I can tell you, I have spent many a morning listening to the president talking about this. He's right, in my view, and I know you're on the right track."

"Thank you, sir."

"If you can get those guys off their tails, the president will give you a medal. And if ever there's a tie vote, you can count on me to break it in your favor. The problem is, the way things looked this morning, I don't think you're even going to get a tie."

Ascher knew the general was right. He had to find a way around the problem. He'd done it before. If he could do it again, he'd make his career.

CHAPTER SEVEN

JINOTEGA PROVINCE, NORTHERN NICARAGUA, SEPTEMBER 25

COMANDANTE VENGANZA WAS THE FIRST TO HEAR THE low hum of the approaching airplane. At first it had been masked by the steady drone of jungle mosquitos. He ducked under some foliage, brushing wet plantain leaves aside as he ran to the middle of the open field, M-16 ready, ammunition clip locked into place. A second clip was taped upside down to the first, ready to be flipped over and shoved into position when the original was expended.

In the middle of the field, Venganza detonated a smoke bomb and dashed back to cover as plumes of purple smoke hissed skyward.

In a minute Eaton saw the C-47 lumbering over a line of palm trees. Really it was just an old DC-3 flying so slowly it seemed a miracle that it was able to stay in the air. The plane was unmarked, not even an N-number, and circled the clearing a couple of times just two hundred or three hundred feet up. Then it gained some altitude, up to maybe five hundred feet, and two white parachutes popped open under it. As soon as they were away, the plane banked left and turned east. A moment later two pallets slammed to the ground, parachutes settling beside them at the far edge of the clearing.

"Shit," Venganza muttered. He stood and waved his men to

their feet. Quietly, about twenty contras started to make their way around the clearing's perimeter, still under the cover of brush. If there are any Sandinistas here, Eaton thought, certainly they already know where we are.

Before Eaton left Washington, Jorge Paladino, his friend the contra spokesman, had promised he'd be sent on an easy, safe patrol, and Eaton thought he knew the politics behind this trip. Comandante Venganza was the highest-level defector ever from the Sandinista Popular Army, and by all accounts the contra Directorate considered him their best commander. Certainly he was the most valuable in a political sense. But, from what Eaton had been able to piece together, the CIA favored some other comandante for the high-profile raids. So Eaton figured he was being sent out with Comandante Venganza for promotional purposes. If the patrol went well, maybe his newspaper story would change the agency's mind.

Under these circumstances, Eaton had figured Paladino would not send him out with a squad that was likely to run into heavy fighting. But as they had waited for the supply drop he'd heard Sandinista rockets slamming into a hill that couldn't have been more than a mile or two away. The dark smoke pouring into the sky looked as if it was coming from behind just the next line of trees.

"It always looks closer than it really is," Venganza had reassured him.

"Oh" was all Eaton said. That had been their longest exchange in three hours here.

Venganza's nom de guerre meant Revenge, and it seemed as if that was all he had on his mind. When the guide had dropped Eaton off early this morning, Venganza had not seemed displeased to have a reporter there, but the contras weren't coddling him. Now they were marching through the brush double-time, ignoring the vines that caught at their feet and the wet banana-tree leaves that slapped them in the face. Eaton was winded after only a couple of minutes. He wondered if they were trying to impress him or displaying Latin machismo. Probably both.

Actually, Eaton thought, these coffee-colored guerrillas looked pretty impressive. Most of them had scraggly black hair and the broad, smooth features of northern Nicaraguan Indians, few of whose ancestors had intermarried with white-skinned people. They appeared disciplined, but you'd expect that with a squad good enough to be sent out with a *Norte Americano periodista,* a reporter.

All of these men wore fitted "tiger suit" camouflage fatigues with matching brown-and-green-mottled floppy hats. Flashlights, knives, and hand grenades hung from their shirts. Canteens flopped against web belts; cigarettes and squirt bottles of insect repellent were strapped into their hatbands.

They carried M-16 assault rifles with attached 40-millimeter grenade launchers—really just tubes bolted under the rifle barrels—and M-60 heavy machine guns with collapsible legs. Ammunition bandoleers were strapped across their chests. Three men carried new-looking computerized field radios that transmitted in code. Two others held army-green canisters about the size of trumpet cases, innocuous-looking except for the white stenciled lettering: ROCKET AMMUNITION WITH EXPLOSIVE PROJECTILE. Redeye infrared heat-seeking antiaircraft missiles, Eaton knew. Redeyes were largely out of use in the United States, replaced by the Stinger. But they were still quite effective against helicopters and other low-flying craft, and they were the contras' favorite weapons, America's gift. These men babied the cases as if they contained fine crystal. They cradled them under their arms, shifting them back and forth to be sure the cases didn't bump into anything. If one of those Soviet-made Hind attack helicopters came swooping down, they had a defense.

At the clearing's opposite edge, six of the guerrillas darted out and quickly dragged the two plywood boxes into the brush, white parachutes with them. The cartons had cracked open with the impact, and one of them left a trail of white powder. Eaton saw the corner of a torn packet of Carnation powdered milk sticking out of a shattered corner, dribbling its contents into the dirt.

The guerrillas stacked the supplies in piles. Beans here. Flour, rice, field-ration packs, and medical supplies there. Ammunition over there. Then without a word the guerrillas divided it up, each of them stuffing his share into a backpack.

"Break," Venganza said, and the men plopped to the ground, packs still strapped to their backs. They leaned against trees, and almost all of them lit up cigarettes. Eaton sidled over to Venganza and pulled out his reporter's pad. Exhaling smoke, the comandante gave the notebook a sidelong glance and said only, "Wait. After the operation." Eaton put it away and tried to relax but couldn't stop his nervous fidgeting.

At the base camp no one had told him exactly what he was in for. Operational security, they'd told him. And since he'd joined the squad this morning Venganza hadn't uttered even a dozen words to him. Still, Eaton couldn't complain. He'd asked for this, and it was unusual for the contra Directorate to permit one of these trips. Normally the contra leadership allowed American reporters out with their men in the field only once a year, before Congress was to vote on new funding. Then they needed the press. Afterward, typically, field trips were not permitted for another year, until the issue was before Congress again.

Venganza glanced at his U.S.–issue field watch on a green canvas strap and then barked, "Let's move." Quickly the men field-stripped their cigarettes, peeling back the paper and scattering the remaining tobacco and paper bits into the breeze. War must raise the incidence of lung cancer, Eaton figured. It was hell to field-strip a filter cigarette, so these men didn't smoke them.

They set off south through the brush toward the Nicaraguan interior, still at double-time. The line of men stretched a considerable distance because the guerrillas walked with enough separation to keep the man ahead just in sight. That reduced exposure in case of an ambush. Without slowing a bit they climbed hill after hill, some of them probably high enough to qualify as mountains, and after half an hour Eaton was panting, sweating through his shirt, struggling to keep up with these men who seemed to move effortlessly, even though they were loaded down with weapons and gear while Eaton carried only a couple of pens and a notepad. The base-camp comandantes had made him leave his camera bag in the car. Probably afraid the men might screw up somehow, and then the resistance would be haunted by the photos. They'd never forgotten the one that appeared in *Newsweek* years earlier purporting to show a contra fighter disemboweling a screaming Sandinista prisoner lying in a wet, shallow grave he'd been forced to dig for himself somewhere here in the jungle.

Once, the column halted in place when the lead man spotted a piece of paper stuck to the branch of a bush beside the trail. One word was written on it: *Emboscada.* Ambush. The guerrilla trotted back and showed it to Venganza. Eaton looked over his shoulder. The note had been written with a fountain pen, presumably by a local contra sympathizer who wanted to warn them about a Sandinista trap up ahead. But the ink had run in the rain. The paper looked old. Venganza balled it up and tossed it away, muttering, *"Piricuacos"*—beggar dogs, the favored epithet for the Sandinistas.

"Let's move," he shouted. Eaton wished he were as confident that there was not an ambush ahead.

But Venganza was right. They marched for another hour without incident until they came to a ridge and looked down at a village. Just some huts along dirt streets where the chickens and black pigs outnumbered the cars. Gray smoke drifted lazily from mud-and-brick chimneys. The only structure higher than one story was the church steeple.

"Wiwilí," Venganza whispered. A Miskito Indian village. That meant they were about fifteen miles south of the Honduran border.

Venganza looked at his watch and then waved them forward, saying, "More speed. Keep proper intervals." They marched on through thick forest-jungle for another thirty minutes until they got to a narrow dirt road. There they stopped. It was just after four in the afternoon.

Venganza pulled a plastic pouch from inside his shirt and unfolded a large multicolored contour map of Nicaragua, also showing southern Honduras and northern Costa Rica, the Pacific Ocean to the west, the Caribbean to the east. To the right of the large map were some smaller maps and charts. One superimposed Nicaragua over the state of Georgia, showing that they were about the same size. Another pinpointed the country's relative position in the hemisphere: roughly 1,000 nautical miles from either Orlando or Bogotá, 2,000 miles from New York City or La Paz. Colored charts showed population density: 80 percent of the people were in the east, in Managua and nearby towns; ethnic composition: 69 percent mestizo, 17 percent white, 9 percent Negro, 5 percent Indian; economic activity: mostly farming—coffee, cotton, and sugarcane; and land utilization—that was easy: Most of the land was unused "dense broadleaf woodland," like the jungle they were crouching in right now. At the bottom right was the legend "Central Intelligence Agency."

Venganza pointed to a spot and in Spanish told Eaton, "We are here," just south of Wiwilí, which, according to the map, was a town of fewer than 5,000 people. Considerably fewer, from what Eaton had seen.

"We've come a long way, haven't we," Eaton replied. Growing up and working in Florida, he'd had little choice but to learn Spanish and spoke it with ease. Venganza nodded.

Venganza shouted to his men, "*X* formation—now!" He ticked off names of lieutenants, "Pedro, you and your men in that brush. Mike, all of you there . . ." Then he turned to Eaton and pointed to a low mound overlooking the road. "You, reporter, up there with the radioman." Eaton immediately did as he was told. He crawled into the brush and introduced himself to the little radio operator, who called himself Mono, or Monkey. Strange choice.

Eaton asked what they were waiting for.

"Ambush," Mono whispered.

"I know, but an ambush of what?"

Mono suggested it would be best if they kept quiet. So Eaton looked down toward the other men. They had finished their preparations and melted into the foliage, silent, invisible. Remembering where the men had stationed themselves, Eaton could see that the four fire squads did form an X, and whoever or whatever got caught at the center would be wrecked by four lethal interlocking fields of fire. On his side of the road, he knew, two fire squads looked down from other spots on this low ridge, while across from them the others were stationed in a shallow depression. Eaton didn't know much about small-unit military engagements, but common sense suggested that the contras had a good tactical position.

Now the place was quiet, save for the rustling of trees, the low whistling drone of a million insects at work, and the occasional squawk of an angry tropical bird. If the radio was saying anything, Eaton couldn't hear it because Mono wore plastic-tube earphones. Eaton scooted back into the brush a couple of feet and leaned against a jacaranda tree. He felt suddenly alone.

He'd arranged this trip mostly because he figured it would be distracting. Of course time spent with the contras in the field always added perspective and authority to the reporting he did in Washington, and he hadn't been here for several years. But a larger reason this time was that a month after Phoenix he still hadn't been able to shake Leslie from his head. With this trip he'd hoped to immerse himself in his work again.

Just before he left Washington, Eaton was no longer finding himself lying in bed wrapped in anguish, as he had for the first week or so after that awful moment on the press plane. The torment had moderated, but he was left with a low pain that rose to consciousness anytime his mind settled into neutral. It was showing no signs of fading away, and in some ways he welcomed it. Though he was miserable, he also felt alive in a way he had not since his divorce. Strangely, the pain reassured him, made him feel as if he were still in touch with Leslie somehow. Sometimes he felt absolutely certain she was feeling it too, though he'd had no communication with her at all, hadn't even caught sight of her walking in or out of the West Wing.

He did try to arrange an appointment with General Dayton, to discuss the contras and other matters. As his scheduler, the request would fall to Leslie, and if things went as usual she'd have to call him to confirm a time. He put the request through the NSC spokesman, as per the routine, but two weeks later he'd heard nothing back. He figured Leslie had killed the request. But then in late September, right after the contra-aid vote and before he was to leave for Honduras, the general's secretary, not Leslie, had called to say Dayton would see him. They picked a time the week after he got back from Honduras, and Eaton had been looking forward to this with the fervor of a high school student counting the days to his first prom, even though he knew he would probably just get a glance of Leslie as he walked quickly past her desk. Long ago he'd decided what he was going to wear that day, though he was anything but a sartorial sort.

Eaton jerked to attention as he picked up the low rumble of a vehicle approaching from the west. Mono didn't move. Through the brush Eaton saw a motorcycle pulling into sight, heading toward town. As it got close, he saw two soldiers, rifles slung over their shoulders. Involuntarily Eaton dug his hands into the dirt as the targets heedlessly neared the center of the *X*, the death spot, wind whipping back their shiny black hair and contorting their faces into sneers.

But in barely a moment the motorcycle was gone, roaring past toward Wiwilí, and nobody in the bushes on either side of the road had seemed to move a hair. Eaton looked at Mono, who shook his head. But in less than a minute Mono hunched forward and put his hands to his earphones for a moment, listening, then whispered "Understood" into the microphone tube that hung below his mouth. The other radioman must have been sent up the road to warn when the real target, whatever it might be, approached.

Mono leaned out of the brush and whistled three low, sharp tones left and right down to the road. For a second Eaton heard rustling in the bushes, and then the tips of rifles and grenade launchers poked into view.

Eaton heard the rumble of heavy vehicles approaching. He tensed, eyes big, adrenaline rushing, as he thought: This can't be real. Only a couple of evenings earlier he'd been sitting in bentwood chairs eating shrimp and pasta salad with a couple of friends at a glitzy Italian café in downtown Washington. That was his life, and the greatest danger was boredom. Now he was deep in the rain forest, about to become part of a deadly Latin guerrilla battle. For a moment it felt as if he must be watching TV.

But then he saw the target approaching, a convoy of some sort with a heavy armored personnel carrier in the lead. Even from a hundred yards away Eaton could see two mounted machine guns pointing his way, soldiers standing behind them, steel-pot helmets on their heads. He crawled back behind the jacaranda tree for cover. Mono flattened himself on the ground, rifle pointed straight ahead.

The vehicles were moving slowly, maybe twenty-five miles per hour. The dirt road was so rough that they didn't have much choice. Behind the armored personnel carrier was a covered troop transport truck and behind that a jeep loaded with soldiers and another mounted machine gun, gunner standing behind it, ready.

Slowly the vehicles pulled into the death-X, Sandinista gunners relaxed as they looked straight ahead. They weren't expecting trouble. Eaton's position was near the center of the X, and the APC in the lead rolled right by him. Really, it was just a heavy six-wheeled truck. The bed was open, and maybe a dozen helmeted soldiers in olive-green uniforms sat at ease on benches inside, several of them smoking as they bounced around. The sides of the truck bed were heavy reinforced steel, like the sides of a tank, so the soldiers could duck behind them for cover. Up front, hinged steel plates hung under the cab's windows, ready to be pulled up to seal the driver and passenger inside. Eaton could see that the windshield was heavy glass, certainly bullet-proof. This was an East German BTR-152. Eaton recognized it from the periodic State Department/Defense Department picture booklets on the Sandinista military.

The troop transport, another East German import called an IFA, lumbered past, and Eaton could see two soldiers, rifles in their laps, sitting at ease on either side of the canvas opening at the rear. Jesus, Eaton thought, if this truck is loaded with troops we're vastly outnumbered. Still coming was a jeep carrying four or five soldiers. But then, without warning, up ahead the road exploded, and the APC skidded left, its front left tire shredded by a remote detonation antivehicle mine. The soldiers threw themselves behind the reinforced sides of the bed, but it did no good. The jungle ridge on the left immediately exploded in fire; rocket-propelled grenades tore out of the brush and detonated inside the bed, throwing the machine gunners to the ground before they could get off a shot. Two or three soldiers remained alive inside. They crawled over to the left and began firing into the jungle from which the rocket-propelled grenades had come. Eaton could see the APC driver's arm reach out the window, hand desperately scrabbling to grab the steel window shield. He had it halfway up when his arm jerked and then fell limp before snaking back inside the cab, dragged down as the driver's body slumped to the floor. Apparently the fire team on the other side had gotten off a burst before the passenger could raise the steel plate on his own side.

Eaton watched fascinated, as if this were a play. Behind the physical protection of this tree and the psychological shield of being a reporter who never did more than observe, he felt as if he were looking through a window. But suddenly behind him there was a burst of machine gun fire and a couple of rounds spit through the brush in front of his nose. The gunner back there in the jeep was laying down a wide pattern in the jungle, and a couple of rounds slammed into the jacaranda tree just above Eaton's head. He slid around the side for cover, realizing he was exposed to fire from the soldiers in the APC now. He pressed himself into the dirt.

But then the jeep exploded, bodies flying, as it was struck by two rocket-propelled grenades from the left rear fire team. One of the soldiers thrown to the road managed to crawl into the jungle—right into the lap of the other rear fire team. Beside Eaton, Mono was whispering urgent directions into the radio: "Team B, all clear your side. Now!" Eaton saw two contra fighters up front on the right drag themselves out of the brush and crawl the few yards back down the road to the side of the APC. The surviving soldiers all were huddled behind the opposite sidewall, occasionally daring to poke their rifles up to get off a purposeless shot into the jungle on the other side. Apparently they hadn't realized the right side of the road held a fire team too. Quietly the two contras pulled themselves up to the APC, backs against the big rear tires. Each peeled a grenade off Velcro fasteners on his fatigues, pulled the pin, and stood up, waiting five or six seconds before lobbing it over his shoulder up into the truck bed. The soldiers heard the little bombs rattling around on the floor, and one screamed "Grenade!" as they stood up to leap out of the truck. But it was too late. Both grenades went off, spewing shrapnel at close range. Spotted with blood, the soldiers slumped to the floor.

Just in front of Eaton the troop transport truck sat motionless and quiet. It had taken no fire, and Eaton had seen two soldiers leap out the back, wide-eyed as they pulled themselves behind the rear tires. What the hell's going on? Eaton thought. Here's a whole truck full of soldiers right in front of me, and the contras aren't even firing at it. He nudged Mono, pointing at the truck and frowning a question. But Mono shook his head and said nothing, concentration fixed on the road.

Eaton pulled farther behind the tree, cowering. Still no one else jumped out of the truck. But one of the two soldiers hiding behind the tires did spot the two contras up ahead, pressed tight against the APC as their grenades exploded inside it. Unaware that the Sandinista soldier down the road was watching, one of the contras jumped to his feet and yanked open the APC passenger door, rifle ready, but apparently the driver and passenger were already dead. He relaxed. Suddenly there was a rattling burst of fire from behind him. He threw up his arms as he fell to the dirt.

The Sandinista soldier in front of Eaton had sprung to his feet and started firing. But then there was a deafening burst of noise in Eaton's right ear. Mono was firing his M-16, and the Sandinista standing there in front of them dropped, loosing a couple of rounds into the air as he went down.

Then as quickly as it had begun, all was silent. No more soldiers piled out of the troop truck. No one moved, no one made a sound for fifteen or twenty seconds, until from inside the cab of the troop transport truck someone shouted, "Don't shoot, don't shoot!" Slowly the driver's door opened, and a mustached fat man wearing a white *guayabera* and a heavy gold watch stepped to the road, hands on his head, clearly terrified. Mono covered the radio microphone with his hand and shouted down: "You, behind the tire, weapon away and come out!" Immediately an AK-47 slid out, and the young soldier crept out, bent over, hands on his head.

"Lie on the ground, face down," Mono shouted, and that's just what the soldier did, right away.

Down the road behind them four contras—one of the rear fire squads—had climbed out of the brush and were walking cautiously up the road toward the troop truck, rifles raised, aimed inside the truck's canvas opening. Hard-faced, surely ready to kill without thought, the lead man screamed, "Out!" and within a moment men began scrambling over the tailgate. They were civilians, campesinos.

Of course, Eaton thought. It was Friday. These were farm workers being escorted back to town for the weekend after a week on a Sandinista coffee cooperative. Ten or twelve of them stood there, smiling with clear relief.

"Bueno, bueno," one of them yelled to the approaching contras.

"Sit!" the lead contra shouted back, and the men instantly plopped to the ground.

Up front the other two teams were crawling through the APC, making sure everyone was dead. A couple of rifle reports indicated that a contra had found someone still alive.

Venganza appeared among the group of contras gathering behind the troop truck. The last fire team was walking up from the jeep, escorting a Sandinista prisoner.

"Count off," Venganza shouted, and in sequence the men shouted their numbers, up to twenty. Only number twelve had failed to speak up.

"You two," Venganza ordered, pointing to a couple of guerrillas. "Take our brother Rayo up the trail. The rest of you, we have little time. The garrison from Wiwilí will be out here soon. Check the vehicles and then deal with them."

Contras searched the truck and the APC—the jeep was still burning—looking for documents or other useful matériel. One came back with a Soviet RPG-7 shoulder-fired grenade launcher, but that was all.

"All right," Venganza said to the campesinos. "Who wants to come with us? One dollar a day. Uniforms. Your own weapons." He held up his automatic rifle. "And you can help us take out the Sandinista Communists and make our country free again." Tentatively a couple of men stood up. "Come over here," Venganza commanded, pointing to a spot at his feet, and as the two men stepped forward a third one rose quickly, pulling something out of his boot.

"You killed my sister," he screamed at Venganza. "You Yanqui mercenaries raped my little sister and slit her throat!" He was waving an old revolver he'd pulled from his boot and began firing at the cluster of contras without taking careful aim. He caught one guerrilla in the shoulder before half a dozen others opened fire, spraying the man with bullets until his body fell over the back of another campesino and slumped into the dirt. The two campesinos who'd volunteered crouched down and were duck-walking backward toward their terrified fellows.

"You two, come with me," Venganza ordered, pointing to

them again, and they froze in place, still crouching, looking up, their faces full of fear. "Tomás, take care of Manuel's wound." The paramedic pulled a pretreated iodine bandage from his pack and peeled off the sticky paper facing while Manuel opened his shirt. He didn't appear to be badly hurt. Just a glancing wound.

"Guillermo, lead the others away," Venganza barked. "Team B, blow the vehicles and let's move out of here."

A contra led the other campesinos down the road toward Wiwilí. They were skittish, clustered together whispering nervously, obviously unsure what this guerrilla intended to do with them. But fifty yards away he sent them off with a wave of his rifle and turned back. The campesinos scrambled off toward town, some of them darting instantly into the jungle, others looking backward, stumbling as they ran down the road.

The guerrillas assembled at the head of the trail and briefly looked back over the carnage, bodies spread all over the road. Venganza nodded, and Team B threw grenades under the gas tanks of the APC and the troop truck. The group was hurrying into the jungle when both vehicles exploded.

A short distance ahead, Rayo's body waited for them beside the trail, where it had been dragged. It was carefully laid out, arms crossed, eyes closed. The contras gathered around and stood in silence. Several crossed themselves. As homage, one tossed a pack of Camels on top of Rayo's body. Venganza said simply, "Our brother, a freedom fighter." Eaton choked. That phrase had been President Reagan's invention; he hadn't heard it in years. By now almost everyone had accepted the term "contra," short for counterrevolutionary, though the phrase "democratic resistance" still popped up now and then. Eaton shook his head and jotted the anecdote in his notebook as three guerrillas buried Rayo under just a few inches of dirt.

Minutes later, they set off at double speed without another word, the two now-reluctant recruits up front, ahead of Eaton and Venganza. The prisoners were near the rear.

Eaton didn't know what he thought about the engagement just ended. It was exactly the sort of operation he knew the contras favored, killing Sandinistas, saving some campesinos from their clutches, picking up a couple of recruits, and demonstrating to all who saw or heard that the Sandinistas could not really protect them. And one dead contra to nearly a dozen Sandinistas—they could hardly have done better. No matter, what were they really accomplishing? More than a decade of this, and where were they?

Behind them Eaton heard a short burst of automatic weapon fire. Neither Venganza nor the other contras slowed or even flinched. Only Eaton and the two recruits turned, tripping on vines as they tried to march while looking backward. But they couldn't see anything that far back through the jungle.

"What was that?" Eaton asked Venganza.

"Probably trouble with one of the *piris,*" he said.

So that's it, Eaton figured. They'd actually executed a Sandinista prisoner, a *piricuaco,* as they were marching along the trail. The contras had been doing that for years. Eaton had written an outraged story about the practice a couple of years earlier, after a former contra told him about it. But Paladino had explained it to him, and though Eaton still found the practice repugnant, at least he understood. Some of these patrols stayed in the jungle for weeks at a time and couldn't escort prisoners around with them in battle. Even if they got the captives back to base, the contras had no prisoner camps; they hardly had permanent camps of their own. If they let the prisoners go, surely the soldiers would come back and kill them or some of their fellows. So, most often they asked their captives one at a time if they wanted to join up. Each one who said no was shot dead on the spot. After the first one, they usually found the others to be eager recruits.

They stopped only when the last light of day was almost gone and made camp in a small clearing.

"No fires," Venganza warned. Sighing, the men took off their packs, leaned back on them, and lit up cigarettes. One of them handed around a flask-sized bottle of Early Times bourbon.

"Where'd you get that?" Eaton asked with wonder.

"*Americanos,*" one of them bragged with a broad grin.

It was almost dark now, and the talk quickly broke into animated chatter about the day's operation after someone said, "We really kicked those Communists, didn't we."

"They didn't even know what hit them."

"I killed four of 'em myself, sent 'em sailing downstairs to see their true maker."

"You see those Commies in the truck jump when they saw those grenades bouncing around? They'd have died of fear if the grenades hadn't gone off."

"Jumped even more after the grenades did go off." Hilarious laughter.

"What's that coffee-picker talking about, we raped his sister?

Hell, his sister looked anything like him, I wouldn't do her the favor of sticking it in." They laughed some more.

"Rayo fought hard," one said. "His family can be proud."

"Yes, yes," the others echoed, serious for a moment.

"We really blew them away," someone said. "Splattered 'em all over the road."

"That's some Communists we won't have to worry about anymore."

"Didn't even know what hit 'em, did they."

Venganza sat beside Eaton and handed him an army rations packet, a fat foil pouch.

"They call it ham steak," Venganza said.

"Thanks." He'd eaten from army rations packs before. Feeling in the dark, he found the notch in a corner of the packet and tore off the top strip. Then he squeezed the semisolid lump up to the opening and bit off a chunk. Ham steak it was, bland, but right now it tasted pretty good. He hadn't eaten since morning.

Eaton finished it quickly and was still hungry. He'd brought some cinnamon-raisin granola bars and pulled a couple out of his pocket. Venganza sat beside him, smoking, so Eaton handed him a granola bar.

"What is it?" Venganza asked.

"Granola bar," Eaton said in English. He didn't know the Spanish and doubted there was an equivalent.

"Don't know granola bar." Venganza repeated the English words with a thick accent.

"Try it."

He tore open the packet and downed the bar in three bites. "Good. You have more?"

Eaton smiled and handed over his last one. Venganza reached in his pack and gave Eaton a small bag of fried banana chips.

"Where you from?" Eaton asked.

"Nueva Segovia. But the Communists moved my family to one of their cooperatives in Jinotega three years ago, after I was in the army. I was transferred to Managua then, and later I left and joined the FDN." The Nicaraguan Democratic Force had for a long time been the largest contra army; finally all the disparate groups were consolidated under the FDN name. "Now I guess I'm from Las Trojes, Honduras."

"What did you think of your operation today?"

Venganza didn't answer at first. But then with more than a trace of bitterness he asked, "What did you think? You are a

North American. You paid for it. Our brother Rayo died for you, too."

"Venganza, I'm a reporter. I just try to tell the people of my country the truth about what your fight is all about."

"Do you tell the people of your Congress who fight against us what it's about? Do you tell them we are fighting Communists?"

Eaton had been through debates like this before and knew where it would lead. Frustration ending in anger and no useful information.

"Venganza, let me tell people what you are accomplishing, and maybe it will help."

"We are showing the Communists that they cannot have our country without a fight. We are killing as many of them as we can."

"You killed a great many Communists today. But where does it take you? There are lots more of them, you know."

"We cannot fight the Sandinista Communist army directly. They have artillery and helicopters and many more men." That was certainly true. The Sandinista Popular Army had sixty thousand men, active and reserve troops—four or five times more than all the contra forces.

"We would like to do more. Maybe carry out special operations in the cities. Killing Communists up here is fine; all of us like it. But the only way to really catch the Sandinista comandantes' attention is to be in the capital. I know. I was there."

"Well, you did take out the electrical station in Managua," Eaton said.

"Stupid," he spat. "CIA stupid."

"Why stupid?" Eaton asked, but Venganza didn't answer.

"We have good rifles now and computers and maps and radios," he said after a long moment. "But still the North Americans won't let us win."

"But I thought you said you can't win."

"I don't know. I like killing the Communists, but I think we could have better operations. We need to be in the cities. It's the Americans that don't want us to win. They say they just want us to 'keep pressure on.' "

"Why do you think?"

"They're scared men, they're not fighters."

Eaton nodded. As several American officials had told him time and time again, Washington worked under one abiding maxim: Keep the contras in the field, but don't let them screw up. One State Department official who, Eaton suspected, really worked for the CIA, liked to say, "Those boys down there need twenty-four-hour adult supervision."

That's one reason Eaton had been fascinated when Paladino told him that the president had appointed his own man to the contra RIG, suggesting he was impatient with the ever-cautious strategy in place now.

"Venganza, have you noticed any change in the kind of advice or direction you've been getting from the North Americans recently?"

He shook his head but then said, "The CIA does its own operations with other comandantes, but I don't know about them."

"Other comandantes?"

"The Americans have their own people they like to use for special operations, that's all." He was trying to sound nonchalant, but his voice was laced with resentment.

Eaton slept on a blanket one of the fighters gave him. Two rolled-up plantain leaves made a pillow of sorts. The next morning the two volunteer-recruits were gone, escaped in the night. The Sandinista soldier was still there, under guard. He'd stripped off his green Sandinista uniform shirt and wore a U.S. Army Special Forces T-shirt one of the contras had just given him—loaned him, more likely. The Sandinista gazed down at the ratty shirt, smiling as if it were an extraordinary prize. Eaton shook his head at the paradox.

They marched back to the road near the clearing where Eaton's base-camp escort had first passed him over to Venganza's squad. Just after noon a jeep pulled up to take Eaton and the prisoner-recruit back to El Cuartelón. Venganza briefed the driver on the operation; then it was time to leave. Eaton thanked Venganza and shook hands all around.

"Make us famous," one of the fighters shouted after him as they pulled away. "Tell the Americans we killed many Communists."

EL CUARTELÓN, HONDURAN-NICARAGUAN BORDER

Eaton was dropped off at one of the command huts, and a friendly-looking little man in civilian clothes greeted him.

"Mr. Eaton, I'm Augustín Salazar," he said in near-perfect English.

"Señor Salazar, I'm happy to meet you. We can speak in Spanish if you like, though your English is excellent."

"No, I like your language. Please come in."

They sat at a rough wood table. A couple of other men in civilian clothes sat at desks; neither of them looked up. An old black metal-blade fan turned in slow motion, clacking against its cage. The hut's wall studs were exposed; the only ornament was a Honduran calendar from a Tegucigalpa machine-tools store, tacked to a stud. Though it was late September, the calendar was still opened to July. That month's model wore a jumpsuit with no shirt, the suspenders just covering her nipples. She cradled a phallic-looking submersible water pump on her knee.

"I don't think we've met before," Eaton said to Salazar.

"No, I've been in Tegucigalpa most of the time. I'm communications officer. So tell me about your trip. How did you find Venganza's squad?"

"Very impressive," Eaton said. He'd been expecting a debriefing. He wasn't going to give anything away.

"Tell me about the operation," Salazar asked. Eaton explained what had happened, using nonjudgmental, almost clinical language.

"Yes, very good," Salazar said. "And what did you think of that?"

"Señor Salazar, I am a journalist. My personal opinion doesn't matter."

"Yes, of course. You are right."

"But the men do wonder why they are limited to this sort of operation, why they can't expand and carry out ops in the cities."

"Oh, of course there are many reasons," Salazar said. "But you know we have had operations in the city very recently."

"Who carried those out?"

"One of our best commando squads."

"Which one?"

"Oh, we cannot say who. If the Sandinista Communists knew, there could be reprisals."

"But isn't it the CIA's special squad?"

Salazar smiled. "Mr. Eaton, of course I cannot comment on that. The North Americans are our very good friends."

They chatted for a few minutes, Eaton wondering who this fellow would report to after he left. From the sound of it, Salazar was tight with the CIA, but he was trying hard to be friendly.

"Would you like to see our camp?" he asked. Eaton was about

ready to start the five-hour drive back to Tegucigalpa, but he did want to see the contras' facilities.

"I've got to go soon, but sure, show me around a little bit."

They got up and walked out into the dirt yard. Fighters milled back and forth, many of them shirtless in the heat, some with lazy, braless women by their sides. Off toward the mess tent, several contras wearing braces, bandages, and casts sat sleepily in the shade on upturned beer crates and soft-drink containers. Every once in a while one of them would swat slow-motion at a fly. Half a dozen giggling little boys played in the shade of an unmarked hut, tossing spent bullet-casings into a circle drawn in the dirt.

The discards of war lay all around the yard's edge: worn-out boots and other bits of military clothing, ammunition crates bearing the markings of half a dozen countries of the East and West: France, Czechoslovakia, America, Israel, the Soviet Union. The contras' CIA arms buyers clearly showed no ideological preferences.

Salazar walked him through the field-hospital tent, where doctors and nurses in camouflage fatigues ministered to several dozen men in bloody bandages, body casts, and wheelchairs. The place was quiet, save for the whir of fans and an occasional low moan. This was a side of the war Eaton had rarely considered.

Eaton could tell that Salazar was keeping him away from sensitive areas. But he did show him the firing range, the mess, the family living quarters—a field of plywood huts. And then they walked over to the weapons depot, maybe three hundred yards from camp. This was a low building, half underground and covered with dirt to help absorb any possible accidental explosions. In addition to that precaution, military doctrine dictated that ammunition and fuel storage areas should be separate from living and working areas, in case the depots blew up.

"We keep our sophisticated weapons here," Salazar explained. "Mortars, grenades, and of course our Redeyes." The contras' spokesman spoke of the antiaircraft missiles almost with reverence, and Eaton remembered how the contras on patrol had babied those Redeye cases. The security out here reflected that attitude. Half a dozen heavily armed men surrounded the building. "Some of our best men," Salazar explained. "Being away from the camp, we have to keep a close eye."

Eaton nodded. To his right, three men were leading a train of mules carrying ammunition crates off to fighters at the border.

As they walked back toward Eaton's rental car, Salazar said,

"Mr. Eaton, we have read many of your stories. Many of our compatriots live in Florida." Eaton smiled. At least somebody was reading his work.

"In Washington," Salazar went on, "I guess you talk often to Jorge Paladino?"

So that was the game. Trying to figure who his source was. Contra intrigue.

"Well, sure I know Mr. Paladino. He's your spokesman and a member of the Directorate. Whenever I need a statement from the contra leadership, Mr. Paladino's the one I'm supposed to call."

"Yes, of course," Salazar said. "That is so."

They walked on, and just ahead Eaton spotted a long-legged woman with a mass of shiny black hair that swept down her shoulders in exotic tangles. She wore paramilitary fatigues custom-fitted to her extraordinary body.

Eaton smiled. It was Francesca, widely known among reporters as "the contra vixen." She was a Nicaraguan beauty, the perfect central casting "Latin revolutionary woman." She was trotted out as tour guide and translator for influential "codels"—congressional delegations—and for carefully selected American officials who came down on "fact-finding" trips. He couldn't see from here, but Eaton knew her shirt would be unbuttoned far enough so that anyone who cared to look could see a tiny gold cross bouncing about deep in her cavernous cleavage. She was famous for coming on to her charges, but Eaton had never figured out whether she actually slept with them. He'd never been lucky enough to be given one of the golden tours, as reporters called them. None of them had ever written a story about her, probably hoping they might get a "tour" themselves one day. He and Paladino always joked about that, although Jorge didn't seem to think it was all that funny.

"She belongs to the CIA," he'd said once. "Francesca's the agency's secret weapon; they decide who she sees. She won't even associate with Nicaraguans." Eaton couldn't tell if he was kidding, though his tone of voice suggested he was not.

Francesca was walking with a tallish American, her arm tucked solicitously under his. This guy wore a safari suit with a many-pocketed khaki shirt, starched and pressed—straight out of a Banana Republic box.

Because of his tan, he looked at first glance as if he had been down here a long time. But though his face was a golden brown, his arms below his rolled-up shirt sleeves were stark white. A sunlamp? In any case, Eaton could see that the man was enjoying Francesca's attentions as they turned into the communications hut.

"So who's that with Francesca?" he asked Salazar.

"Somebody from Washington."

"Must be a pretty important man for the CIA to give him Francesca," Eaton said with a leering smile.

Salazar smiled back. "So you know of our Francesca?"

"It's hard to miss her."

"Don't believe everything you hear," Salazar said. "She's really a very nice girl." But he gave a smile that said the opposite.

"So who is this man from Washington?"

"I haven't met him. His name's Ascher. Supposed to be from the White House, but then lots of North Americans who come down here say that."

"Ascher, huh?" Maybe this was the new guy on the RIG. "Which Ascher is it? You know his first name?"

"Terry, I think."

Eaton wrote it down in his reporter's pad.

CHAPTER EIGHT

TEGUCIGALPA, HONDURAS, SEPTEMBER 26

BEFORE ASCHER LEFT WASHINGTON, GEORGE BASHAM had made it clear that Rafael Mendoza, the Honduran station chief, wasn't one of his favorites. So Ascher had figured he would like Mendoza. He'd called Basham over at the agency on his new secure telephone to ask whom he should see on his orientation trip. Basham had given him a few names and then almost as an afterthought said, "When you're in Teguc, I guess you better go see Mendoza. He's the senior control officer. But he's not my kind of man."

Basham had dismissed Mendoza with a phrase: "Bay of Pigs syndrome." But Ascher figured people like Basham sometimes mistook the patriotic anti-Communism of many Cuban émigrés for thoughtless zealotry. Still, Ascher had looked up Mendoza's file. He was a Bay of Pigs veteran of sorts.

The file showed that the agency had recruited him as an "asset" in 1960, when he was only twenty-one and still living in Cuba, working for Castro. Mendoza's father had been a comandante in Fidel Castro's guerrilla army, but he was killed in the famous Moncado army barracks attack of July 26, 1953. The revolt failed to topple the Batista government, but in a larger sense it was a success. It made Fidel Castro famous, even though he was caught and imprisoned. When Castro got out of prison a couple of years later he named his guerrilla organization the

July 26 Movement—and the incident was still another argument for the thesis forming in Ascher's head that Latin revolutions galvanized around bold guerrilla stunts.

After Castro took power he gave young Mendoza a job in the new government. Meanwhile Mendoza had made friends with a case officer at the U.S. embassy, and while working for Castro, he began reporting little inconsequential things to this American. The reporting got better as Mendoza's disenchantment with the new government increased, until finally he defected. The CIA, suddenly aware that its Latin America division was wholly inadequate for the times, hired Mendoza and some other Cuban emigrés right away. But few of them had stayed in the service as long as Mendoza.

He hadn't been part of the actual Bay of Pigs attack force. He helped coordinate the operation from its launching point: Puerto Cabezas in Nicaragua. (General Somoza's eagerness to let the Americans launch the invasion from his country helped explain why Castro was just as eager years later to help the Sandinista guerrillas as they were throwing Somoza out of office. At least one thousand Cuban "advisors" remained in Nicaragua.)

Like most Cubans, Mendoza was crushed by the Americans' desertion of his country's fighters. But Mendoza decided to stay in the agency and try to make a difference the next time. He'd never married and had served in several Latin American posts over almost two decades. He was on the Latin American desk at CIA headquarters in Langley for four years before he was named Tegucigalpa station chief a year ago.

Now Mendoza was in his fifties, but to Ascher he seemed possessed by the smiling energetic enthusiasm of a man twenty years younger. In fact, when they first met, Mendoza scared him.

They had arranged to meet in the lobby of Tegucigalpa's Maya Hotel at 8:30 A.M., but Ascher got up a little early and after breakfast walked out into the cool morning, down the city's hilly, winding—and noisy—streets. By the sound of things, car buyers here must as a matter of routine crawl under their new cars and remove their mufflers before driving off the lot.

Every few yards Ascher crossed cobblestone side streets or alleys that were so steep that it seemed as if cars driving down them would topple over and roll front over tail to the bottom. He tried to get the street names so he wouldn't get lost, but there were no street signs.

Terry was looking for a *farmacia*. It was time to replenish his

Valium supply. He'd never had a prescription; he'd always managed to pick some up here or there, on trips like this one. Here, he knew, it was sold over the counter. He walked only a couple of blocks before finding a pharmacy, a large green cross over the door. The little woman behind the glass counter happily sold him all she had, four 25-tablet bottles of five-milligram pills. She charged an inflated price, he was sure, but Ascher didn't care. It was illegal to smuggle the pills into the United States, but he wasn't terribly concerned about that either. With his black diplomatic passport, Ascher knew Customs wouldn't check him. Still, he was a little nervous carrying these clinking bottles of contraband in his pockets. So when he walked back into the Maya lobby and a little man came through the door behind him, then slapped an arm around his shoulder, Ascher almost jumped out of his safari suit. Had someone been following him?

"What's a matter, my man? Think it's Minister Zelaya come to take you away?" Mendoza quickly introduced himself, and they both laughed, Ascher nervously at first. He was sure Mendoza must have felt the bottles bulging in his pockets. If so, Mendoza didn't say anything.

Mendoza was a little man, maybe five feet four, with skin the color of coffee with lots of cream. He spoke with the barest of Spanish accents and gave Ascher a smile of childish innocence.

They sat and chatted for a moment in the dark-paneled lobby bar, Tegucigalpa's best-known meeting place for spies and others involved in all manner of intrigue. Around them many seats were full—particularly those with backs to the wall. Hondurans spoke accented English in low tones to crew-cut gringos who peered with interest at anyone who came through the lobby door. Even at this early hour, high-priced prostitutes in long shimmering dresses were leading men up from the Monte Carlo Casino to the elevators.

"Let's go," Mendoza said after a few moments. It was clear he didn't like spending much time here, and given his position, Ascher could understand why. The hotel security officer standing just outside the front door carried an automatic rifle, as if to underline the point.

Mendoza's car sitting in the driveway seemed to belie his non-threatening appearance. It was a Dodge with heavy bulletproof Plexiglas plates bolted to all the windows. They couldn't be rolled down. And Mendoza's driver, a Honduran national, had a bulge under his zip-up jacket that suggested he was carrying a shotgun in his shoulder holster. Pretty impressive security for a junior political officer.

CIA officers in embassies around the world all had cover jobs. Usually it was something like first secretary in the political office, a post that didn't carry many responsibilities because they had to do that work, to maintain the cover, and handle their CIA jobs as well. The embassy in Honduras actually had two political offices, Pol 1 and Pol 2. Pol 1, downstairs, carried out all the important diplomatic work. Pol 2, across the hall from the ambassador's office upstairs, was actually the CIA station. Innocent visitors passing down the hall must have wondered why "political officers" needed padded metal doors with heavy cipher locks.

Ascher and Mendoza drove the short distance along Avenida La Paz to the embassy, Mendoza pointing out the sights along the way, both of them aware the driver was listening.

The embassy sat on a bluff overlooking the street, and like all other embassies it had been protected against truck bombs. The antivehicle barriers were raised.

Inside the front door, Mendoza smiled and waved at the Marine guard standing behind a green-tinted bulletproof window, and without hesitation the sergeant buzzed them through the electric door. They walked directly to Mendoza's little office upstairs. Here there was no overt indication that Mendoza was anything but a political officer, except for the secure telephone.

As soon as they sat down Mendoza asked, "So, tell me what the White House wants to do with our little war?"

Ascher took a deep breath. He had expected to be the one asking questions and hadn't really prepared a pitch.

"Well, I wish I could give a simple answer. I was put on the RIG partly because the president thinks it's too passive. With the funding-law restrictions in place now, he can't make a stink and shake things up without getting into trouble himself, especially with the election coming up. I didn't get the impression that he has a sophisticated view of what the contras should be doing exactly, just something more. So he's putting me on the RIG to see if I can change its view."

"What's that view?" Mendoza asked.

"Keep the contras in the field as they are now, carrying out low-level ambush-type stuff and occasionally something grander, like sabotaging utilities. Make a show of action without actually accomplishing anything."

"Uh-huh" was all Mendoza said.

"I'm kind of new at this, but there doesn't seem to be a lot of confidence in the contras' ability to do anything more. That's one thing I was hoping you could help me with."

"When you say 'a lot of confidence in their ability to do more,' what do you mean by 'more'?"

"Well, I think we could be more ambitious, move this war forward now that they're fully funded, equipped, and trained. Quite frankly, I talked to the president about this, and he agreed."

His expression serious, Mendoza stared at Ascher for several seconds. Then he stood up.

"Terry, come with me" was all he said as he walked out the door. Ascher followed to the basement and down a hall past a Marine security officer. Mendoza unlocked a heavy steel door and locked it behind them again. They were in another short hall, maybe two or three yards long. Ahead up a short ramp was a second door with acoustic padding. Mendoza opened that door and then another just behind it. Inside he locked both doors behind them. They were in a small low-ceilinged chamber, bare except for a simple conference table and half a dozen hard wooden chairs.

"A bubble room?" Ascher asked. Mendoza nodded. Ascher had never been in one before but knew what they were. It was really a room built inside a room, surrounded on all sides by several inches of acoustic damping materials to assure that nothing said inside could be monitored or overheard. The walls were clear Plexiglas, insulation pressed right up against it; no bugs could be planted without being seen.

They sat across from each other, and Mendoza said, "So, Terry, tell me what you mean when you say you want to be more ambitious with the contras."

"Rafael, I—"

"No, no, my friend. Please call me Raf."

"Okay, Raf. Now this is just my view, and I can't pretend to be an expert yet." He paused and gave an embarrassed smile. Mendoza nodded that he understood. "But I can tell you the general idea I have without knowing for sure whether it's possible."

Ascher then went through the full spiel he'd given during that first RIG meeting, complete with the hand gestures he'd practiced in the shower. He talked about the failure of the *foco* and *tercerista* strategies during the Sandinista insurgency, and he opined that successful Latin revolutions seemed to be built around bold guerrilla actions, like Pastora's seizure of the National Palace and Castro's raid on the Moncado army barracks.

Mendoza listened quietly at first. But as Ascher got further into his pitch, Mendoza began nodding his head slowly, rhythmically, sometimes closing his eyes in concentration. When Ascher got to the part about Pastora and Castro, Mendoza sat up at full attention, smiled, and cut him off.

"Terry, my man," he said, beaming, arms outstretched. "You don't have to say any more. You're just the guy from Washington I've been waiting to meet."

Ascher gave a questioning smile.

"We have a major guerrilla force, the best-equipped in Latin American history and ten times as large as either Castro's or the Sandinistas' ever was." Mendoza was still standing, waving his arms. "They are armed, trained, ready and eager to do something worthwhile. It's time the resistance moved forward, and it sounds to me like you know just the way these things are supposed to work.

"Let me ask you," Mendoza asked, "have you met my boss, George Basham?"

"Yes, I know George." Ascher was smiling. "Somebody should go ahead and give the guy his pension so he could stop devoting every bit of his energy to protecting it."

They both burst into warm empathetic laughter, and then Mendoza said, "Terry, my friend, I think maybe you and I can do some good for the world."

"But, Raf, I need some help from you. You've got to tell me how good the contras really are. And I've also got to know how you think the ordinary Nicaraguan people would react if we did suddenly change the tactics. Is it conceivable the contras could ever attract a large popular following? You know the RIG wants to leave things just the way they are, and if anything is to change, I'm going to have to make a pretty strong case."

Mendoza stood up, walked around the table, and laid a hand on Ascher's shoulder. "I've got somebody you've got to meet," he said and then started to unlock the bubble-room doors.

On the way out, Mendoza called the embassy in Managua on the secure phone and sent a cable to El Cuartelón while Ascher waited in another room. Ascher asked what he was planning, but Raf offered an enigmatic smile and said only, "You'll see." Ascher dismissed the hint of intrigue as the ingrained manner of a spook.

He'd asked to visit El Cuartelón, and now they were driving out of the mountains downhill to Palmerola, the "temporary"

United States military base. From there they'd fly down to the contra base.

Palmerola, just outside the little town of Comayagua, had most features of a major foreign military base, including a fifty-thousand-barrel fuel depot, munitions storage areas, a sixty-bed military hospital, and a thirteen-thousand-foot asphalt runway, big enough to accommodate any military plane the United States owned. About fifteen hundred combat troops were stationed there, more or less permanently. The only incongruity was that all the structures were tents and huts. That was the thin thread from which the Pentagon hung its contention that Palmerola was just a camp, not a permanent base and possible launching spot for aggression against Nicaragua.

Most of Palmerola's troops didn't have much to do (which is why Comayagua had nearly as many prostitutes as ordinary residents), but the aircraft maintenance techs were busy. Several SR-71 Blackbird spy planes were based here, used for high-altitude surveillance-photo flights over Nicaragua. These planes were supersonic, and once, many years ago, the president had used them for another purpose. When the Sandinistas had seemed about to acquire some Soviet MIG fighters, a development the United States had said it would not accept, the Blackbirds were sent up to accelerate through the sound barrier over Managua, setting off volleys of sonic booms. That sent the Sandinistas into a frenzy. They put their military on full alert, and as it turned out, the Soviet Union never delivered the fighters.

These days the work at Palmerola was routine, and as they drove up Ascher saw dozens of shirtless men playing volleyball amid choking clouds of dust in a field of volleyball courts. When they got out of the air-conditioned car, the heat struck with a stiff punch. They were in the dry lowlands now.

To keep the troops busy, Ascher guessed, gravel walks flanked by shade palm trees had been laid between the tents and other important spots. They followed one to the helicopter pad. Palm fronds rustled in a slight breeze.

A CIA pilot was waiting for them beside a small Hughes-500 helicopter, and they took off right away, heading south. Soon they were over rugged wooded mountains. Ascher was reminded of the Honduran official who'd balled up a piece of writing paper and dropped the crumpled sheet on his desk, saying, "This is a topographic map of my country."

Shouting over the rotor noise, Ascher and Mendoza continued

amiable chatter about Latin revolutions, what made them work, what failed, the likelihood that an entrenched Marxist regime could ever be removed from power through political means. They'd obviously read many of the same books, and they exchanged relevant quotations from obscure Latin scholars.

By the time El Cuartelón came into view, Ascher was thinking he should have met Mendoza years earlier.

An hour later, Ascher stood before a long table lined with more than a dozen Tandy personal computers, green screens blinking in the darkened room as their contra operators tapped at the keyboards. Fifteen cooling fans hummed.

"With your government's help, we are able to intercept almost a thousand Sandinista military messages a day," the contra intelligence officer was saying, "and with these new computers we can decode them and pass enemy troop positions to our men. Come, let me show you."

Ascher followed the officer. But he wasn't really paying attention. He was in love. Francesca, the "contra vixen," was leaning against him, her arm in his, her hand caressing his in the dark. He could smell her fragrant hair on his shoulder and the earthy scent of woman rising from her clothes. Outside he hadn't been able to keep from looking down her shirt at the moist spot where her breasts pressed together just below a tiny gold cross. God, she seemed to have fallen for him in a big way. What a woman. Now he was having trouble walking.

Thirty minutes earlier, Mendoza had turned him over to Francesca for the tour.

"Enjoy yourself, my man," he'd said with a grin. "I'll wait here."

"Oh, uh, thanks, Raf," Ascher had stammered, staring at Francesca as she took his arm and led him from the S-2 tent.

Now, as they stood just outside the pool of light falling on the communications message board, Francesca dropped his hand so she could reach behind and squeeze his cheeks. Ascher closed his eyes and gave a solemn, silent thanks to his new friend Rafael.

Before coming to the communications hut, Francesca had taken him to see the intelligence hut, command HQ, comandantes' barracks, firing ranges, and training fields. They'd stopped in to meet Chairman Coronel, who happened to be in camp, and Ascher had reached down to shake the little man's hand.

"Anything we can do for you—anything—just let me know anytime," Coronel had said with a sickly-sweet smile, nodding his head. The overhead light shone on his oily hair.

The computer building had been the last stop. And now as they stepped outside, squinting in the bright sun, Ascher could think of nothing but getting her into bed.

Francesca put her mouth to his ear and whispered, "Now I think it is time I showed you where I stay."

Ascher could hardly breathe. As she took his hand, he felt a flush all over his body. They were surrounded by dozens of people, but none of them looked twice as she led him to the family barracks area. Women sat in dirt-colored hammocks bouncing babies in their laps.

Francesca had a new-looking plywood hut, larger than the others and nicely maintained, given the limitations here. Still holding his hand, she led him up three wooden steps. Inside she closed the door and twisted the lock, then fell back against the door with a thump and looked up at Ascher, on her face a smoldering expression that seemed to pull him to her. He crushed her against the door, prying open her mouth with a hard kiss, grinding his body against hers. Ascher was burning. As he reached behind Francesca and squeezed her warm round cheeks through her thin fatigues, she moaned into his mouth and thrust her hips at him. Ascher lifted her clear off the floor. She wrapped her legs tight around him, and he hugged her with a strength he didn't know he had.

They couldn't have been locked in this embrace for even a minute before someone knocked softly on the door just behind them. Francesca's eyes popped open, and Ascher froze in place for a moment. But then he squeezed her again; he intended to accept no interruptions. Whoever it was knocked again, this time harder, and they could feel the rapping through the door.

"Terry, Terry. It's Raf. We've got to go now, my friend."

"Oh, shit," Ascher muttered as he set Francesca down. He sat on the edge of her cot to collect himself, head in his hands.

"Just a minute," he moaned after a moment. He was wondering how Mendoza had known where they were and why he had picked this very moment to come get him. But then Francesca sat down beside him, on her face an expression of clear regret as she stroked his upper thigh.

"My beautiful man, I too am sorry," she breathed in that sultry voice of hers. "This time it was not to be. But there will be other times if all goes well."

"I certainly hope so, Francesca. I've never met anyone like you." Her smile was curious. It seemed to say, yes, I understand. She gave him a deep goodbye kiss.

Outside Mendoza patted Ascher on the back. "So you liked our Francesca, huh? I think she liked you too."

"Raf, you're a good man, but your timing's terrible."

"Oh, Terry, we have an important appointment back at Palmerola. It's getting late, and nobody wants to fly over country like this in the dark."

"Yeah, but . . ."

"Terry, I promise you, if things go well, you'll see Francesca again. Maybe she can come for a visit in Washington." That remark sent a dozen wondrous fantasies spinning through Ascher's head.

They didn't talk much on the flight back to Palmerola. Ascher gazed absently out the window, and Mendoza didn't interrupt his reverie. When Palmerola came back into view, Ascher roused himself and shook Mendoza's knee.

"So what have you got on the agenda now?"

"The man I said you needed to meet is joining us here for dinner," Raf said. "Colonel Eric Gustafson's the name. He's our senior military attaché in Managua, and I think he can answer some of your questions better than anybody. He's been doing some interesting analyses of how the populace in Nicaragua feels about the regime and possible alternatives."

"Military attaché, huh. Is he the one putting out those DIA analyses saying the Nicaraguans want the United States to invade?"

Mendoza looked startled. "Well, some of them have come out in final form with that kind of spin on them," he answered a little defensively. "But his work's more sophisticated than that. You'll see."

From the helicopter, they walked over to the CO's hut, a not-quite-so-temporary wooden building on cinderblock stilts. The secretary, a Honduran, greeted Mendoza warmly.

"Hi there, Raf. The CO's expecting you. Go right in."

In the office a bird-colonel was relaxing with a big blond man in civilian clothes.

"Colonel Bob Teeley, I'd like you to meet Terry Ascher, from Washington," Mendoza said quickly to the CO. The colonel nodded. "And this here, Terry, is our man from Managua, Colonel Eric Gustafson. Eric, say hi to Terry Ascher."

Gustafson stood up and walked over. God, he's tall, Ascher thought. He had that unmistakable bearing of a determined, overconfident military officer, and he came so close that the tips of their shoes almost touched as they shook hands. His grip was more than firm.

"Terry, good to meet you," he said looking down. Ascher smiled back. Then Gustafson slapped Mendoza hard on the back a couple of times. "Good to see you too, ya little spook," he said through a smile. "How ya doin'?"

"Better and better my friend," Mendoza answered, smiling back. "Bob, we've got to move on," he told the CO.

"Nice to meet you, Colonel," Ascher said to Teeley as all three of them left and headed for the mess, a large open-sided tent on poles with enough tables and benches to seat a hundred or more. A few dozen men were eating off to one side.

Ascher, Mendoza, and the colonel went through the chow line: Salisbury steak with gravy, mashed potatoes, green beans, and apple cobbler. They set off for the far end of the tent, where they'd be alone. Halfway there Gustafson and Mendoza stopped, conferring. Ascher turned to them, questioning, but Mendoza waved him on.

"Be right there, Terry. Excuse us for a second. A personal matter." Ascher sat down. When he looked back at them, Gustafson was nodding agreement to something as they started over. Both of them sat across the table facing him.

"So, Terry," Gustafson said. "I hear you're on the contra RIG now. White House representative, huh?"

"Yeah."

"Gonna shake 'em up, are you? They sure need it." Ascher smiled.

"Eric," Mendoza said, "we asked you up here because Terry and I were discussing some of the things you and I have been talking about off and on. A new strategy. Terry, why don't you tell him."

"Well, it seems to me that we're wasting our resources down here," Ascher said, figuring he didn't have to beat around the bush with this guy. He took a couple of bites of the chopped beef, then gave a much abbreviated version of his by now familiar soliloquy, trying to vary it some so it would sound spontaneous to Mendoza, who'd heard it just that morning. He added some detail from his conversation with the president, saying at the end, "The bureaucracy is sitting on its hands, but the president wants to move forward, and he's asked me to try to do it." Gustafson nodding approvingly.

"If I'm to make a pitch in Washington that has any chance of success, I've got to have some idea how a change in strategy would be received by the Nicaraguans. That's what I was hoping you could help me with. I've read some of your stuff, the invasion scenarios, in the DIA intelligence summaries."

"Well, Washington puts a spin on some of those things that makes it sound like we're talking just about invasion, but that's not really what my work's about—though I have to say, my reading is that the ordinary Nicaraguan would not stand in the way of Americans coming in to take out the Sandinistas." He glanced quickly at Mendoza, who was frowning.

"Anyway," Gustafson went on, "from what you've been saying, your question is whether the ordinary Nicaraguan people might rise up in support of the resistance if they were to carry out some bold guerrilla acts in the city, right?"

"I guess that's right," Ascher said.

"Okay, we'll get to that in a minute. First, Terry, let me tell you what I do. Nobody else from any of the other intelligence agencies does this." He grinned at Mendoza, who rolled his eyes.

"I travel around Managua and Estelí and Chinandega, talking to people about what their problems are, what they think of the Sandis. Been doing it for two years, and the answer is always the same. They're plain fed up. They can't even get flour and beans. They complain and they lose their ration cards. They run out of toilet paper and they gotta pay some kid to stand in line for a couple days to get half a roll. Their cordobas don't buy anything anymore, and they can't get dollars. Their standard of living is dropping so fast, soon they're gonna have to reach up to touch bottom.

"I've been talking to these people, lots of them, for two years now. I am utterly convinced that if an attractive alternative presented itself, they would flood forward in support."

Looking over Ascher's head as he talked, he drifted into recalling an interview with the owner of a Managua print shop who complained that severe cuts in government paper allotments had destroyed his life, leaving his formerly middle-class family virtually penniless and hungry.

He told about forced recruitment for the army—kids kidnapped at the bus stop and then, a few months later, sent back home to their mommas in pine boxes. "That army's not going to fight long for those Sandi bastards," he spat.

He told about the man in the vendor's stand who'd sold him the orange drink. "This old man told me, and I quote, 'If the contras came in here tomorrow, I wouldn't stand in their way.' " He looked over at Mendoza, who was smiling.

"Now I would not be totally honest," Gustafson said, looking directly at Ascher, "if I didn't say that part of my analysis is that many of these people see dollars. They think Nicaragua would get lots of American aid if the contras brought in a new democratic government."

"Well, I'm sure they would," Ascher offered without pause.

"Then, Terry, I don't think there's any question that the answer to what you are asking is yes. If we adopted a new strategy that thrust the contras into the public eye, I think they would have widespread popular support."

Ascher leaned back and smiled. "So what are you guys suggesting?"

"Well," Mendoza said, "I guess what all of us have decided here is that to be effective, the resistance ought to carry out a highly visible urban raid along the Castro-Pastora model. Right?"

The three of them smiled.

"So who do we get to do it?" Ascher asked.

"My pick is the unit that carried out the Managua utility raid," Mendoza said. "Major Paz and his Pena de Muerte commandos." Ascher smiled at the incongruous name. Major Peace and his Death Penalty commandos.

"That's peace in the eternal sense," Mendoza said, noticing Ascher's smile. "Paz is the best. He and his men got Special Forces training up in Florida not long ago."

"Who is this guy Paz?" Ascher asked.

"Paz is amazing. He's from the Caribbean coast, black family, but Paz is a mulatto. He likes to brag that his grandfather was a United States Marine. Paz was in the Guardia. He was one of the first contras. Lived in a motel in Miami for a while after the revolution. He was one of the Guardia that our old Bay of Pigs Brigade 2506 took care of for a while. Moved down to Guatemala, and I think he might have done some death-squad work for La Mano Blanca back in nineteen-eighty." La Mano Blanca, the White Hand, was the right-wing Guatemalan death squads that murdered thousands of suspected Communist sympathizers.

Ascher's eyes popped open at that, but Mendoza shook his head, saying, "Be forgiving. Those Guardia boys had a hell of a time making a living. The only thing they'd been trained to do was kill. Anyway, Paz was fighting the Sandis back when the contras just had twenty-twos and peashooters. But the one thing I like best about him is he follows every order, exactly to the letter, every time, no questions asked, no matter what the orders are. He's a machine."

Mendoza gave a dramatic pause and leaned over the table to whisper, "Paz can be a stone-cold killer. No questions, no regrets."

Ascher shuddered. "I guess I should have met him when I was down there this morning," he said, maybe a little tentatively.

Mendoza sat back and said, "Terry, you get this idea approved in Washington and you'll just have to come back down here to meet Paz." Then with a smile he added, "And you could get to know Francesca a little better, too."

Ascher grinned. Rafael sure knew how to motivate a guy.

CHAPTER NINE

NATIONAL PRESS BUILDING, WASHINGTON, OCTOBER 3

BY THE TIME EATON GOT BACK FROM CENTRAL AMERica, Washington had slipped into its brief but glorious fall. His plane arrived late, and he didn't make it home until almost midnight. When he got up around seven-thirty the next morning, he stepped out onto his porch to pick up the newspaper and just stood there for a moment, smiling.

The sun was low, and the oak tree out by the sidewalk threw a long shadow into the street. Most of the leaves were still green and rustled in a slight breeze. At last the city's temperature and humidity were just right, so the breeze felt like a warm caress. Eaton knew it wouldn't last long.

Since moving to D.C., he'd rented a small two-story, one-bedroom apartment off DuPont Circle, not far from downtown. Back inside, he sat in the living room reading the paper for a few minutes but grew impatient and finally just tossed it on the floor, dressed, and went in to work.

Almost as soon as he got to his desk, he looked up Terry Ascher's name in the federal staff directory. It listed Terrence Whitfield Ascher as Deputy Assistant Secretary of State for the Caribbean. Curious.

The capsule biography in the back said he was a relatively young career diplomat, a Harvard graduate who'd served in several Latin American posts, including Costa Rica. Eaton ran Ascher's name through Nexis, the computerized library of news stories, and picked up only three references, one on page A-16 of *The Washington Post* early this year and then two short wire-service pieces on the same subject. Obviously Terrence Ascher hadn't turned the world on its end.

STATE DEPT. WINS BAHAMAS TREATY, the *Post* headline said.

Eaton vaguely remembered this. Stories about the Bahamas got good play in Florida papers, and there'd been questions about why the Bahamas had signed all of a sudden. He called Ascher's State Department number, listed in the directory.

"Mr. Houghton's office," the secretary said.

"Oh, I guess I've got the wrong number. I'm looking for Mr. Ascher."

"Mr. Ascher's moved. Would you like that new number?"

"Yes, please."

The secretary gave him a number with a 456 exchange. The White House. So Ascher really was the new guy on the contra RIG. Eaton was intrigued. He was having lunch with Jorge Paladino today, and, depending on what Paladino told him, this was also something he could ask General Dayton when he finally went in for his appointment with the national security advisor on Wednesday.

Paladino met him at a seafood restaurant on the C&O Canal in Georgetown, a couple of blocks from the contras' Washington office on Thomas Jefferson Place. He was waiting at a table on the terrace overlooking the towpath. Water cascaded through a canal lock just behind him. Tourists milled along the brick paths on both sides of the canal, built in the last century so barges could navigate past the falls of the Potomac River.

Eaton and Paladino embraced, a Latin custom that Eaton didn't much like. But with Paladino it was different. Eaton was friendly with many of his news sources, but Jorge was a true friend. Often they got together for a drink or dinner, with little if any thought of work in mind.

Friend or not, Eaton smiled to himself at Paladino's clothes. Today he wore a paisley silk ascot, a blue double-breasted blazer with gold buttons, and pleated cotton chinos. When he crossed his legs, yes, he had those tasseled loafers on his feet. You'd think he'd grown up in New England.

"So how are you?" Paladino said.

"Oh, I've been worse."

"Still can't get that married lady out of your mind?" Eaton just smiled. Paladino was a moralist. "It will do you no good," he warned. "Back away while you still can."

"I wish I could."

"You will find a way. You have to."

His appointment with General Dayton was only two days away, so Eaton wasn't even trying to stop thinking about Leslie. He brushed at his thinning forelock a couple of times as he changed the subject.

"Listen, Jorge, who's this guy Terrence Ascher? I saw him down at El Cuartelón."

"Terry Ascher. Yes, he's the one I mentioned to you last month. He's the new White House man on the RIG. The way I have it, the president put him on to get things charged up. He told our people that the president ordered him to get the program moving. We don't know what that means exactly, but it sounds good."

"Could mean a lot of things. So what do you know about this guy?"

"Not much to tell, far as I know. He was in Costa Rica during the revolution, so he probably got to know some of the Sandis. But he doesn't have much of a background in our issue that we can find."

"Who's he getting to know?" If Ascher was on the RIG he would become an important player, so it would be interesting to see who was shaping his views.

"Well, he was brought through the camp by somebody from the agency. That's all I know."

"You mean that's all you can say," Eaton complained with a sour smile. Paladino smiled back. Eaton had pushed on this front before but given up. Of course Paladino knew that Rafael Mendoza had taken Terry through the camp. Paladino was a member of the Directorate. He knew everything. But the real identities of CIA officers were sacrosanct secrets. Not even to a friend like Eaton would Paladino give that away—even when the agent was Mendoza, an officer he disliked.

"Well, I do know that Francesca sunk her teeth into Ascher pretty deep," Paladino said.

"So that means the CIA is trying to cultivate him, am I right?"

Paladino smiled. "Sometimes you're too clever." But then he was serious as he said, "I can't speak for Francesca. She doesn't associate with us."

"Oh, I see." Eaton grinned. "Jealous, huh?"

Paladino did not respond.

On Wednesday, Eaton was out of bed at five in the morning. He gave up trying to sleep. All night he'd rolled around in the sheets, as charged as if he'd drunk three cups of coffee before bed. He hadn't taken a Dramamine to help him sleep because he didn't want to feel muddled in the morning. His twenty-minute appointment with General Dayton was at eleven.

He'd had his hair cut last week. He wanted it neat but not still showing the precise lines left by the barber. And now he was shaving with extraordinary care, pulling the razor slowly over those well-known nick-spots.

He put on his "power suit," a dark blue pinstriped number—the style that seemed to be favored by the men he interviewed here in Washington. Back in Florida he'd have worn a suit like this only if somebody had died. With a light blue shirt and a red silk necktie, he looked every bit the serious Washington man. So far, he realized, Leslie had seen him only in sport clothes, a bathing suit—or nothing at all.

THE WHITE HOUSE, WASHINGTON

Sitting in the West Lobby, waiting for the NSC press assistant to escort him, Eaton began to think he didn't really want to be here. When he walked past Leslie's desk into General Dayton's office, she might stab him with another of those contemptuous stares. But at the same time the idea of never seeing her again was even worse.

In the end, the whole long-awaited enterprise was over before he knew it. Or so it seemed. Kent Borstein, deputy press secretary for the National Security Council, sat down only long enough to say, "You know you've got fifteen minutes, and when that's up I'm going to have to cut you off cold, okay?" Eaton nodded. "All right, let's go."

They walked swiftly out the door, swept down the hall in a rush, and were moving into the general's reception area before Eaton could catch his breath. The general was standing in his office doorway waiting to greet them, and Eaton had only about half a second to look around before reaching up to shake hands. An older lady sat at the desk on the left. FLORENCE MUELLER, the nameplaque on her desk said. She was the general's personal secretary. The desk on the right was empty, though a cup of coffee, still steaming, sat on the blotter. LESLIE DESALLES, that plaque said.

Just as it dawned on Eaton that Leslie had left the office to avoid seeing him and would probably be gone again when his interview ended, the general was reaching to shake his hand. In another instant Borstein had shuttled him into the office and closed the door.

"General, I'm delighted to see you," Eaton said, trying hard to paint an interested expression on his face as the disappointment sank in. He'd set up this interview only so he could see Leslie; he didn't expect to get much news.

Eaton always programmed these short White House interviews by writing down key-word summaries of the most important questions on the edge of a sheet of paper. He would slide his little sheet into his legal pad and pull the edge of it out now and then. At a moment like this when his mind was far away, his little sheet was a godsend. He proceeded through the interview by rote.

They had established the ground rules: background. That meant anything the general said would be attributed only to a "senior administration official." In Florida anyone who insisted on that would have been greeted with a stare of disbelief. But in Washington, Eaton had learned, that's the way the game was played. If an official said something but then regretted it after seeing his words in print, he could always deny he ever said it, confident the reporter wouldn't give him away because he was sworn to protect his "confidential sources." Reporters who wouldn't accept the ground rules didn't get interviews.

Given the relative safety of speaking to a reporter behind this shield of near-anonymity, General Dayton was attentive, even frank. But to Eaton it seemed a hollow exercise. Still he read his script. He asked about the chances for a summit conference with the Soviet Union in light of the Nicaragua-landing-rights issue, and Dayton said they'd received an informal message from the Soviets saying the general secretary would be willing to meet and discuss the matter in Geneva. That was certainly a front-page story, but Eaton noted it with barely academic interest.

Eaton asked about the Middle East, but then the general's phone buzzed. Eaton looked, and the green button was lit.

"Excuse me a minute," Dayton said. "Yes, George," he said into the phone. The green button must be the chief of staff, George Van Nostrand. Borstein reached over and turned off the tape recorder, signaling that anything said during the phone call was completely off-the-record. He needn't have bothered.

"Uh-huh, uh-huh. I'll do it" was all Dayton said before hanging up. "Sorry. Now where were we?" Terry got through his Middle East questions, then turned to the one thing he really wanted to know.

"General, I understand a new man has been added to the contra RIG, Terrence Ascher. Why is that?"

"Well, the president decided he needed a full-time White House representative. As you know, with the way the Congress set up the RIG, the only White House representative is me. And I am only an ex officio member, plus my schedule is such that I can't always attend. The president wanted his own man, and after some talks with congressional leaders he was given permission to appoint his own representative."

"What's this I hear that the president has ordered Ascher to get things 'charged up,' as one person put it. To get the program moving again." The general thought for a moment and started to answer, saying, "I guess that's true, though not exactly in the way you are implying." But then the phone buzzed again. This time when Eaton looked over, the red button was lit. He already knew whose line that was. Dayton gave Borstein a sharp look as he reached to push the button, and Borstein immediately stood up.

"Chris, we have to wait outside while the general takes this call." Without fully realizing what was happening, Eaton followed Borstein to the door. As they opened it Eaton heard the general behind him saying, "Yes, sir, Mr. President . . ." And then he was in the reception area and Borstein was motioning him into a seat as the door closed shut behind him.

He took a deep breath and after a flustered couple of seconds, slowly he looked up. Leslie wasn't looking at him. She seemed startled, disconcerted. She was yanking blue Kleenexes out of a box, trying to wipe coffee off her blotter. Apparently she'd spilled it this instant.

As he looked at her there, upset and disconcerted by his unexpected presence, shiny brown hair falling into her face as she looked down, everything flooded back, all the feelings that had since been replaced by the dull pain. He had been losing the clear memory of her face. She was beautiful. Involuntarily he relaxed, leaning back in his chair, and his face melted into a smile. As he gazed at her she continued dabbing at the blotter, agitated, distracted. But then gradually her jerky motions slowed, until finally her hand plopped on the desk, still holding a ball of wet Kleenex. Her head was bent down, her eyes lowered, but then she turned to look at him, mouth open half an inch, brow furrowed.

This time Eaton was the one in control and wanted only to reassure her with his warm and devoted gaze. She looked at him for several seconds, anxious eyes open wide, before her own face began to relax. A moment later, the door burst open behind him and General Dayton said, "Mr. Eaton, I'm terribly sorry." But Eaton didn't even hear him. Gathering on Leslie's face was the beginning of a soft smile.

CHAPTER
TEN

OLD EXECUTIVE OFFICE BUILDING, WASHINGTON, OCTOBER 10

ASCHER BELIEVED HE MIGHT ACTUALLY BE ABLE TO convince the RIG to approve the raid. It was such a wonderful plan. But if he failed, he was ready to go directly to the president.

He'd worked out the idea with Mendoza and Gustafson before they left Palmerola. Actually, he admitted to himself, he hadn't done much more than nod at the right places as the two of them created the plan there in front of him, settling on details so quickly that it almost sounded as if they'd drawn it up long before and were re-creating it there for his benefit. But, no, he'd described his ideas for the contras only a few hours earlier. Mendoza and Gustafson couldn't possibly have devised all this in the meantime.

In the weeks since his trip, waiting for the next RIG meeting, he'd sat on his patio at home, yellow and brown maple leaves falling from the trees around him, and made notes on a yellow legal pad, working on his pitch.

The plan was almost poetic. Roughly once a month the Sandinista Directorate, all nine comandantes, went to see a show. Surrounded by several hundred loyalists and their families, they'd spend an evening at the Rubén Darío Theater watching a Managua theater company's Spanish-language performance of some Soviet or East German play. They'd all laugh at jokes they didn't completely understand and sigh at the exposition of European or Asian dilemmas that had no real pertinence here. All this was to show that Nicaragua didn't have to rely on the Yanqui art that had made up so much of the country's cultural heritage before the revolution. And it was also intended to taunt Somoza, who, the Directorate hoped, was looking up at them from hell.

Somoza had built the theater to be a scaled-down version of the Kennedy Center in Washington. It was a sweeping modernist structure intended to impress visitors from the States.

Well, the theater was the target. The entire Sandinista Directorate would be together in a public place at a known date and time, surrounded by several hundred people, including women and a few children. A day or two before the performance, Major Paz and his Pena de Muerte troopers would filter into Managua and stay with friends or family in the lakefront barrio down Calle el Triunfo from the theater, just as they had before the electrical substation raid.

Show night, five separate six-man teams would assemble at designated locations. That way the whole thirty-man squad wouldn't be seen together until the raid was under way. If one of the squads got caught, the plan could still be carried out by the other four.

They'd have good intelligence on the security details. On show night last month, Gustafson had wandered by the theater and noted the arrangements.

Major Paz and his men would take out the guards. Then they'd burst into the theater, firing at the ceiling, and take the group hostage. Major Paz would demand the release of certain political prisoners and order them brought to the theater. There might be other demands, too, not yet formulated.

Ideally they would hold everyone for at least twenty-four hours, giving the contra commandos a full cycle of worldwide attention in the news media. They'd have food delivered, maybe give some interviews, too, talking about freedom and democracy. By the end, thousands of Nicaraguans would surely have crowded into the streets outside, waiting to see what would happen. Then the guerrillas would order buses brought to the theater and a plane readied for them at Sandino International Airport. Taking with them one or two Directorate members as hostages, they'd drive away to the cheers of thousands—just as Pastora did in 1978. Landing in Costa Rica, they'd release the hostages there on the tarmac, and the world would see film footage of Minister Zelaya, beady eyes glaring, widow's peak reaching for his nose, as he walked alone and angry to the terminal building.

Powerful stuff. It was beautiful. How could it fail? After they'd laid it out for themselves, Ascher, Mendoza, and Gustafson hadn't been able to stop grinning at each other.

And now the climate seemed just right. Last week had come word that Minister Zelaya had decided to expel the Sandinistas' longtime antagonist the archbishop. The Vatican was furious, and so was the president.

"What arrogance," he'd said to a television interviewer, throwing up his hands. "I just don't know how much more heedless and belligerent they can get. How much longer can the free world put up with this?"

Ascher had smiled to himself when he saw that tape. How could the RIG resist taking action after that?

But in fact, the second RIG meeting was going just like the first, same cast, same location. As last time, General Dayton had arrived a little late, his attractive aide in tow. Everyone had taken off his suit coat, to demonstrate that they were now a relaxed working group. First Cater, then Basham, then Ames had given his status report, and to Ascher they already seemed redundant. All three of them spoke in a monotone. Any animation he might have seen in their reports last month had been affected to impress the new man. Or so Ascher guessed.

As before, General Dayton listened, and when his turn came to talk he deferred to Ascher, who was ready to give his pitch. This one he had practiced and practiced. He knew Mendoza was standing by in Tegucigalpa, waiting to hear what happened. And he also figured that if the RIG bought the idea, he'd have to head right back down to Honduras to get the plan moving. He'd meet Major Paz. And he'd get to see Francesca again. For Ascher, a lot seemed to ride on this moment.

"Gentlemen," he said, "I spent a few days in the region last month, visiting El Cuartelón, getting oriented. It was impressive. All of you ought to go down. George, you been down there recently?"

Basham looked particularly sour at the question. "We have a rather large contingent in Honduras" was his only answer.

"Got a pretty good tan for just a couple of days, didn't you?" Ames sneered. His white broadcloth button-down shirt was so heavily starched that Ascher figured it could probably stand up on its own.

"It's my opinion," Ascher went on, ignoring Ames's crack, "that we fail to appreciate what kind of assets we've built down there. We have by far the largest, best-trained, best-equipped guerrilla force in Latin American history. It's true that they couldn't win a frontal war against the Sandinistas. And obviously not every one of our twelve thousand men would make it through the U.S. Army's officer candidate school. But we've got some good men, like Major Paz and his commandos. And as previous Latin revolutions have taught us, all that's really needed is a small highly trained unit that can carry out a spectacular action or two, backed up by the image of a large force behind it. Castro, you remember, took power firing hardly a shot toward the end. Well, we have a highly trained commando unit and far more than the image of a large force behind it."

They were listening, expressionless. Well, not completely expressionless. Ames sneered and Basham scowled, but those were the faces they wore at rest. Ascher moved to stage two.

"Now, as I mentioned last month, the president wants to get things moving, be more aggressive. I know you all have mixed feelings about that." Basham nodded with a grunt.

"But I have a proposal that I've formulated along with several of our field officers in the region. I think it is workable, carries a minimum of risk, and is potentially quite effective. Let me describe it." With that, Ascher laid out the proposal step by step.

Colonel Cater looked down at the table, concentrating on Ascher's words, eyes fixed on a spot on the table—the military professional evaluating the plan.

Basham, not surprisingly, began shaking his head the minute the general idea became clear. His parachute chin jiggled. Ames looked at Ascher with bemused astonishment. And Dayton listened with clear interest.

Ascher was interrupted only once, when he got to the actual assault on the theater, taking out the guards.

"Wet or dry?" Colonel Cater asked, looking up for the first time.

"Our intent would be to take no lives unless we had no choice. We'd prefer to knock the guards over the head and tie them up. From a propaganda point of view, we think the whole exercise would be much more effective if there was no shooting."

Ascher continued without further interruption and finished, saying, "The end result, we believe, would be to make the contra fighters major figures in the popular imagination of Nicaraguans while also radically lowering the standing of the Sandinistas." With that Ascher stopped and leaned back in his chair, looking around the table.

"Ludicrous," Basham belched right away. "You been talking with Mendoza?"

"Why ludicrous, George?"

"Those bumbling coffeepickers would fuck it up before they ever set foot in the city. Then Zelaya would have a propaganda bonanza—Yanqui-mercenary terrorists arrested. He could make up any kind of story he wanted about what your boys had been intending to do. Poison the water supply, murder the cardinal. Whatever he wanted."

Ascher had vowed not to overreact to Basham's polemics. Going in, he knew he'd never get Basham's vote. "George," he said, "members of the unit will filter into Managua alone or in pairs. If a pair of Nicaraguans gets picked up carrying a disassembled rifle, what can the Sandinistas do with that? The unit will not be together until the assault is under way. Even if somehow the assault on the theater fails, I think we still gain. Castro's Moncado army barracks attack failed, after all. But he got credit for the boldness of his plan."

Basham started to respond, but Ames burst in first.

"Terry, this is precisely the wrong time for this kind of stunt. We're too close to forcing the Sandis to the table again and working out a new treaty. The internal situation is getting desperate." Ascher knew the State Department too well to fight that line. Foreign service officers were promoted if they won diplomatic agreements, just as military officers rose through the ranks by winning battles.

"Scott, what better way to force the GON to the table for serious talks than to raise the popular esteem of the opposition?" He hadn't much hope of turning Ames around, so he turned to Cater, the only one who had not been utterly dismissive. Gustafson, a Marine colonel, had thought the plan was workable from a military point of view, so he figured Colonel Cater might, too. If he could win the colonel's vote he'd have a tie, and Ascher was confident General Dayton would break it in his favor.

"What do you think, Win?"

His answer was precise and wholly lacking in emotion. Cater was not an officer with strong politics. As he spoke, Ascher couldn't keep his eyes off the collection of shaving scabs on his neck.

"Terry, I think the idea has military promise," he said. "There are some possible downside problems, but I think they could be addressed. My problem is, I don't have authorization to approve an operation of this sort. My shop specifically ordered me to support the operational direction we have right now, not to reduce it, not to enhance it. Those are my orders, and they couldn't be clearer. I can't sign on."

"Do you think you could go back to them with this and see if you can get it approved?"

"Well, I can try. But knowing the interests of my superiors, I can't hold out much hope."

Ascher was stymied. He looked to General Dayton for support, a desperate question on his face. The general was leaning back in his chair, running his hand over the stubble that served as hair, but then quickly pulled himself up, saying, "Terry, I am here mostly as an observer, as you know, and I can't honestly evaluate the quality of your plan at this time. But I like your initiative, and if it were a tie vote I might be inclined to proceed with study of the proposal."

Hardly an unqualified endorsement, and Ames seized the moment. "I suggest we have our vote and then move on to the next matter. All those in favor, say aye." Ascher muttered the word.

"Opposed, no," and the other three spoke up, Basham and Ames almost bellowing their disapproval.

Dayton called an hour after the meeting broke up.

"I meant what I said. I do admire your initiative. I wish to hell I could be more help. But you know I have to go up to the Hill and appear before the intelligence committees every few weeks. Unlike some of my predecessors, I absolutely will not lie to them. And if they find out that the NSC is in any way taking an active role in directing the program, breaking the funding agreement we made with Congress, all of us will regret it. Not to mention what would happen if the press ever found out. It would undermine everything everybody's trying to do—and with an election year coming up, too."

"I understand, General."

"Sometimes I think I shouldn't even come to the meetings. I hate sitting there like a bump. But I'm in your corner if you can get a tie. That much at least the president and Congress specifically authorized me to do."

"Well, General, I appreciate the support you are able to give," Ascher said before he hung up. He had no choice now. He would take this directly to the president. He called Christopher for an appointment.

The next morning, Ascher got a kick out of walking across Jackson Place and into the West Wing, directly to the deputy chief of staff's office, without an escort, no questions asked. Greta waved him right in.

"Terry, how are you?" Christopher said, pixieish, ebullient as always. "How are you settling into the job?"

"Fine, Rich. Just fine." They chattered for a few minutes about the Redskins and Christopher's recent weekend on Skyline Drive in the Shenandoah Mountains, looking at the fall foliage. Finally Christopher asked, "So, tell me what's on your mind, Terry."

"Rich, I need to see the president."

Christopher didn't say anything, waiting for Ascher to explain.

"As you probably know, the president charged me with getting the program moving, making the contras more aggressive." He studied Christopher, trying to see if the president had repeated their conversation. No reaction.

"Well, I was down in the region talking to our people, and we came up with a plan for an operation that would significantly raise the popular standing of the resistance. I think it's just the thing."

"You mean the Rubén Darío raid," Christopher said, with no judgment in his voice. Ascher smiled, not really surprised that Christopher knew.

"Yeah. Now you know as well as I do that the departments— State, DoD, and the agency—just want to keep the program going without causing any unpleasant incidents. Well, I think the only way to jolt the bureaucracies is if they got a call from the president. I'd just like to explain it to him, see if he buys the idea. If he does, great. If he doesn't, well that ends it once and for all. I could run through it for him in ten minutes, max."

Christopher answered without pause: "Terry, you're enthusiastic as can be, and that's why we brought you over. But we don't work that way over here. The president can't listen to operational proposals from individual staffers like that. That's how some people who sat here before us got in trouble, running their own cowboy ops. Everything has to be vetted. I know it's bureaucratic, but it's the best way.

"What you need to do is prepare a written report on your proposal, and we'll send it through the system just as fast as we can. We've got to give the relevant parties the opportunity to comment. That's the only way we can make an informed decision. Then we here in this office will make a recommendation and forward it to the president. Okay?"

Ascher took a deep breath and murmured, "Okay." He knew what Christopher was really saying. Sending a report to the "relevant parties" meant giving it to the naysayers at CIA, DoD, and State. It would come back covered with red. There was no reason even to try.

Suddenly Terry remembered how ambivalent Christopher had seemed about the contra program when they'd first talked in August. Christopher was one of them. The plan had been scuttled. Hardly anyone around the president gave a damn.

Ascher was stymied. Back in his office he called Mendoza on the secure phone.

"I'm not surprised," Mendoza said after hearing the story. "Basham wouldn't be sitting on the RIG if that wasn't the majority view in town."

"But, Raf, this is what the president wants. I know it. He's not being well served by these people, and I can't get to him to explain."

"That's Washington, my friend. Welcome to the world of power games."

"Raf, I've run out of options. What do I do?"

"Terry, we really shouldn't be having this kind of conversation even on this kind of line. Secure phone or not, somebody's always listening."

"Understood." The National Security Agency, Ascher knew, monitored conversations on the government's secure phones, ostensibly to make sure they were working properly. But that meant someone out at Fort Meade might be listening even now.

"Terry, I'm going to be up in Miami or D.C. for meetings soon."

"Yeah?"

"Don't lose hope, my friend. Trust me. We'll do some good for the world yet. I have an idea."

CHAPTER ELEVEN

WASHINGTON, OCTOBER 20

IT WAS SUNDAY AFTERNOON, AND EATON WAS HOME alone, lying on his living-room sofa, staring at the ceiling as he castigated himself over and over again. Never had he been through such an emotional wringer. One day he was happier than he could ever recall. Now, less than a month later, he was flat on his back again. This time he'd really screwed up.

He'd tried so hard to be honorable, but he should have known Leslie would think the worst. How could he have been so stupid? Leslie was the best thing that had ever happened to him. But once again he'd let his professional ambition take control and run roughshod over his own good sense. Now it looked as if he'd lost her—again. They hadn't spoken in almost a week. Finally she'd called this morning, her voice frosty, and in an hour or so she was coming over for a talk. The way she sounded, this was almost certainly the end. After what he'd done, who could blame her? And it had been going so well.

Leaving General Dayton's office two weeks ago, Eaton had no doubt what Leslie's budding smile had meant. She was not at her desk when he left, but she'd already sent her message. So as soon as he started back to his office a couple of blocks away, he began trying to figure out how he'd reach her. It wasn't such a simple matter. He couldn't call her at work. The secretary would certainly ask who was calling, and Eaton didn't want to leave a trail that might cause them problems later. Sending her a note at work carried the same risk. Their home phone was certainly unlisted, and Eaton didn't even know where they lived.

At the office he had to write a story, so he didn't have time to give the matter much thought during the day. But he was back at it as he left about seven-thirty. Then, as he walked through the lobby, the guard at the reception desk called to him.

"Delivery for you, Mr. Eaton." The guard handed him a plain white business envelope with his name typed neatly on the front. Eaton was walking down F Street toward the Metro station as he tore it open. He took one look and stopped dead. It was a sheet of White House stationery with one hand-written line.

"Call me on Sunday at 4 o'clock. Leslie." Then a phone number.

A couple of passing pedestrians smiled at Eaton, standing there staring at a sheet of paper; the grin on his face was so broad he looked as if he'd just won the daily lotto.

He figured she'd sent him the note right away to keep him from calling her at the office or making some other incautious move that might haunt them later.

At home, he looked up her telephone exchange, 654, in the front of the phone book. Chevy Chase, over the District of Columbia line in Maryland. A wealthy and exclusive suburban neighborhood. Suddenly he found himself looking around his modest one-bedroom townhouse wondering what she'd think. Shag rugs, a mottled brown Herculon sofa, cinderblock-and-board bookshelves. If he wasn't impressed by it, she certainly wouldn't be. After all, her husband must be wealthy.

Decorating had always been his wife's job, and now that he was living alone, he hadn't bothered. But he had three days, so he decided he'd buy a few pieces of furniture and make some other home improvements. He had no idea what would happen after the phone call, but if he could convince Leslie to come over, he wanted the place to be ready.

By Sunday he had a new armchair, throw pillows for the fold-out sofa in the living room, matching brass lamps, a compact-disk player with a small selection of jazz and classical CDs, a digital microwave oven, some other new kitchen appliances, and—a hopeful purchase—bright new queen-size sheets with a handsome down-filled quilt. The place was vacuumed, scrubbed, and dusted. The only problem was he thought he could still smell the disinfectant he'd used to soak down the bathroom.

By three o'clock he was pacing, pulse racing. By three-thirty he was searching for excuses to call early, sometimes laying his hand on the kitchen phone for a moment before shaking his head and pacing some more.

As the second hand ticked up toward four, he held his hand on the receiver, waiting to lift it. But when four o'clock struck he decided it would be imprudent, overanxious, to call on the dot of the hour. Beginning to sweat a little now (he had showered at two-thirty) he managed to wait until four minutes past four.

"Hello," she said in a neutral, anybody-could-be-calling tone.

"Hi, Leslie. It's Chris." His voice sounded almost mournful. Would this somehow turn into a rebuke?

"Hi, Chris. It's good to talk to you." She was warm but certainly not gushing.

"Leslie, I can't tell you how good it is to talk to you."

The line was silent for a moment.

"Chris, I'm sorry for what happened on the press plane. Your flowers were lovely, and your note, well, I was really touched. I reacted badly. I saw a major complication rising in my life, and I resented you for it. That was wrong. I'm sorry."

"I understand. I have to admit, it shook me up. But I guess I can see what you're saying."

There was an awkward pause, then Leslie asked, "Would you like to get together for a drink later? Someplace neutral? I'm alone this weekend."

"Sure."

"Any ideas?"

"Yeah, how about Afterwords." He felt a little devious. Afterwords, a café at the back of a bookstore, was only two blocks from his house. But she agreed right away.

Afterwords was crowded and noisy, as always on Sunday evenings. All sorts of people from the upwardly mobile urban neighborhood sat around drinking coffee and reading the Sunday papers.

He'd been there fifteen minutes, had already drunk a beer, when Leslie walked in. Seeing him, she smiled awkwardly; he was swiping at his thinning hair as she walked up. She looked great in snug jeans and an open-collar white silk blouse, a slender gold chain around her neck. They said hello, and she gave him a benign kiss on the cheek. They sat smiling, darting nervous glances at each other for a few seconds. Then she leaned toward him over the small round table, melting him again with her direct brown-eyed gaze. She spoke softly so as not to be overheard. The next table was only a couple of feet away.

"Chris, I wish I knew exactly what I wanted to say to you."

"You don't have to say anything. I'm just very happy to see you."

She went on as if he hadn't said anything. It was clear she had something she wanted to tell him, despite her opening remark. Leaning closer to him, she looked alternately at his face and at her own hands in front of her on the table.

"You know, I'm a lucky woman to have met someone like you. But after we got back from Arizona, I was still trying to keep myself angry at you, even though inside I knew I was tricking myself. After a couple of weeks I managed to force myself to stop thinking about it. About you. Well, not completely. But you know what really got me going again?"

"No. What?"

"This'll probably sound funny, but it's that story you wrote from inside Nicaragua. I saw it in *News Summary*."

Eaton couldn't help smiling at that. *News Summary* was a daily White House publication reprinting important stories of the day from the nation's newspapers. Copies were put on every desk. Some White House officials were so busy that *News Summary* was the only "newspaper" they had time to read. The *Times*, the *Post*, and the *Wall Street Journal* got into *News Summary* every day, but the White House reader-editors looked through an array of other papers too. Eaton hadn't known of a New World story's being chosen before, but then he seldom saw it.

"Chris, that was a really moving piece. Dramatic and touching. That's your main area, the contras, isn't it?" He nodded.

"You know, what really got me was all of a sudden I was worried about you, down there in all that shooting. Obviously you were okay, because you'd come back to write your story. But that kind of woke me up." She squeezed his arm.

"I know it sounds funny, maybe even condescending," she said, looking at him now, "but that story in News Summary made me see you all of a sudden as a serious young man. You're very accomplished at what you do, you know."

Eaton just smiled. He figured Leslie didn't know she had pushed his own special button.

"Anyway, I don't know what happens now. Probably nothing. But I wanted to apologize for the way I treated you last month."

She glared at the couple at the next table, who looked as if they were trying to overhear. Eaton put his hand on her arm.

"Thank you, Leslie. What I said in my note to you in Phoenix I still mean."

"What I'm trying to say is, yes, my marriage is unhappy, but I'm not the kind of woman to have an affair. I'm going to leave Wyche sometime, I know it, but I can't say when. And it would be unfair of me to ask anything of you." She turned to the other table again.

Eaton hadn't planned this exactly, but now it seemed to make sense on several levels.

"It's hard to talk here," he said. "I live a couple of blocks away. You want to come over and have a cup of coffee?"

She looked startled and stared at him a second. Finally, sounding almost resigned she sighed, "Okay."

Eaton hadn't thought it was possible, but this time was even better than before. They embraced inside the door and moved easily, gracefully, upstairs and into the bedroom without even stopping in the living room. The lovemaking was every bit as varied and energetic as the last time. As before, she gave up only after nothing she tried would work. But now they held each other with clear affection that had not been there the last time. And as they lay in each other's arms, Eaton closed his eyes and smiled in the dark. They didn't say much. They didn't have to.

After a while Leslie sat up to look over at the blue numbers on his clock-radio. It was almost ten P.M. She got out of bed. All of a sudden Eaton remembered a scene like this one not long ago. But then she told him, "If I'm going to spend any time over here, we're going to have to put in another phone."

"Huh?"

"Well," she said, as if all this were perfectly obvious, "if I'm going to be away from the house, I don't want to have to come up with excuses every time Wyche calls and I'm not there. If we put another phone in here somewhere," she explained, sweeping her hand around the darkened bedroom, "then I can put my phone on call forwarding before I come over, and we won't have to worry. It won't interfere with your using your own line either."

"Well, sure. Okay," Eaton said, taken by her matter-of-fact presentation of something that would never have occurred to him. But as soon as he grasped all the wonderful implications, he said, "Of course. I'll order one first thing in the morning."

*   *   *

When the phone man came the following Friday, Eaton had him put the line behind his dresser. As the man went to work Eaton stood behind him, smiling to himself at the incongruity of getting so much pleasure from watching a telephone being installed.

Leslie called later. He told her the phone was in.

"Great," she said. "You know I guess the best thing would be if you just ignored it. If it rings when I'm not there, don't answer it. That way we can't get in trouble if I forget to turn the forwarding off when I get home."

"Sure, of course." He was getting into the swing of this.

When Eaton chose to think about it, really this was not an ideal situation. She was married and had only vague plans of leaving her husband someday. She was six years older; she'd be forty before long. If Leslie ever did get divorced, she might be too old to have children safely by the time they could get married. All of that skittered through his mind a couple of times. But he was so happy to be with her, even under these circumstances, that it didn't seem to matter much. And at the same time, he imagined that going out with a younger man might be a fantasy come true for a woman Leslie's age.

They never talked about it. The closest they'd come to discussing the future was their decision to put in the second telephone.

The next weekend she came over on Saturday night. Wyche was away, and Eaton made her dinner. At the table, Eaton gave a shorthand life story. Born in Miami, father a tax lawyer. Emory University. Married young. Divorced. Worked his way up the newspaper ladder. Been in Washington two years. Frustrated with his position in Washington and the White House journalists' hierarchy.

Watched Miami become an ever more Latin community as he grew up. Fascinated with Latin America issues. Drawn into the contra story.

"And soon," he went on, "I think it's going to be time I started looking for a better job. Maybe the *Post* or the *Times*." She smiled; that would be fine with her. Leslie would never say this to him, but she'd feel a lot better about Eaton if he had a major job.

"It's tough," he was saying. "I've got expertise and good clippings. But so do a lot of other people. You know, around here you need to have a good job to get a good job. Nobody notices my work, and the people who get hired by the big papers are names the editors have already heard of when the applications land. I guess I've just got to try harder.

"The contras are still a big, big story, and I've got to work real hard," he murmured, looking down at his plate. Deep inside he believed that getting a better job was the key to winning her.

"You will," Leslie said. "You're good. If that's what you want, you'll get it."

Eaton cleared the plates and served coffee brewed in his brand new Toshiba automatic coffee grinder and brewer. He'd had a hell of a time figuring out how to program the computerized device and felt some relief to see that it had actually worked.

"You know, I never paid much attention to the contras before I started this new job," Leslie said after taking a sip. "But going to these RIG meetings with the general is pretty interesting."

Eaton was so startled he slopped some coffee in his lap. She didn't notice.

"Oh yeah?" was his only response, trying to sound as neutral as he could. God, was Leslie really going to start talking about classified contra-RIG meetings? She was new at the White House; was it possible she didn't know any better?

"You know they really have some bozos on that thing," she was saying. "It's perfectly obvious they don't care anything about it, just want to get in and out without screwing up."

"Yeah, that's what everybody says."

"So the president puts this new guy on from State, and he's all charged up, trying to get these other guys off their tails, but they aren't buying it. Not one bit."

"Terrence Ascher, you mean?" he asked, trying to seem casual, looking over at her as he took a sip of coffee.

"Yeah, how'd you know?"

"I'm working on a story about him." There. He'd said it. So if she went on, she'd know this was not just idle banter.

"Well, he's really something. Came in with this plan earlier this month for a big raid in Managua. I didn't understand all of it, but it sounded like he was trying to imitate something this guy—Pastor, is that it?—something he did during the revolution."

"Edén Pastora? Commander Zero? The raid on the National Palace?"

"Yeah. That's it, that's it. Well, he'd just come back from a trip down there."

"I saw him when I was down there."

"Did you really? Well he wanted to send some contras, the same guys who bombed the electric station, into Managua to seize the theater they have in town . . ."

"Rubén Darío?"

"Yeah, take that over while all the commanders are in there watching a play."

"You mean the comandantes, the Sandinista Directorate?"

"Yup. He was going to have them take all of the comandantes hostage and demand freedom for some political prisoners, then ride out of town. Cause a big splash in the press. Sounded kind of exciting to me, but I don't know enough about it to know if it makes any sense. The DoD guy on the RIG, a colonel, sounded as if he thought it could work, but he didn't have authority to vote for it. The other two guys laughed him out of the room."

"Really," Eaton said, trying not to sound too interested even as he took notes in his head. "So what happened?"

"I don't know. I think the general liked the idea, but he couldn't get involved. He's real religious about not doing anything more with the contras than he's allowed to, and that's almost nothing. Everybody else is scared to death about doing anything unauthorized, except this guy Ascher. There's something about him, I don't know."

"What do you mean?"

"Well, it seems like he's trying too hard. I can't figure it out, but I don't think I trust him."

"Humm."

Monday morning Eaton thought it over long and hard. Certainly he couldn't write a story based on their dinner conversation, though he didn't know how he'd ever get anything better than that firsthand source. But this was important. Surely it would be okay if he got the same information elsewhere.

He called Terrence Ascher. He'd been planning to try to go in for an interview anyway.

"Mr. Ascher's office," his soft-spoken secretary said.

"Hello. My name is Christopher Eaton. I'm White House correspondent for the New World News Service. Is Mr. Ascher in?"

"Mr. Ascher's in conference. May I ask what this is in reference to?"

"I'm writing a story I was hoping he could help me with."

She was quiet a moment, then said, "Mr. Eaton, I'll have to call you back. Can I have your full name and number?"

He gave it, and she called back half an hour later.

"Mr. Ascher does not give interviews to the press," she said. "May I suggest you talk to Kent Borstein in our public affairs office?"

"Well, yes, I'll talk to Mr. Borstein. But would you tell Mr. Ascher that the story involves him directly, and I was hoping I could talk to him, even if it's off-the-record, to make sure I don't get anything wrong."

Not surprisingly, Ascher never called. And after Eaton laid out his story for Borstein, he got the accustomed response.

"Chris, you know we can't discuss operational matters like that, even to confirm or deny that any such plans exist."

So Eaton turned to the source of all "secret" information in Washington: Congress. After all the contra scandals of the last dozen years, the congressional oversight committees—intelligence, armed services—watched every footstep the contras and their government handlers made, waiting to catch the administration "violating congressional intent," the one unpardonable sin on Capitol Hill.

Some of the tenured staff members on the oversight committees had been following the contra program from its inception. They'd been talking with the same staff people over at Defense, State, CIA, for years. After RIG meetings, people involved with the program gossiped, and by now the congressional staffers had been in this gossip loop for years.

He waited until after six P.M. to call his favorite source, Eric Drury, a balding, sour young man on the staff of the Senate Select Committee for Intelligence. He dialed Drury's home number. All calls to his office were entered on a log; if ever there was a leak, the first thing the staff director did was look at the call log. So Eaton and Drury had an understanding. They never got together in public and talked on the phone only when Drury was at home. Drury had worked through the Iran-contra scandal years earlier. He was a wizened cynic and didn't believe *any* administration could be honest and straightforward about the contras.

"Can you believe it?" he asked Eaton. "Sending them into Managua to take the Directorate hostage during a play? Does that sound to you like they aren't trying to use Congress's money to overthrow the government of Nicaragua? Does it?"

"But the RIG didn't buy it, did they?"

"No, not this time," Drury said. "But with a White House rep on the RIG now, it's only a matter of time before they step over the line. Trust me. I've been through this before. It's only a matter of time."

"Who else can I talk to about this?" Eaton asked.

"Try Snell over at State. He works for Ames, and word has it that Ames hates this guy Terry Ascher."

Eaton called Snell—at home—and since he already knew the details of the story, Snell agreed with only a little reluctance to fill in the few remaining holes. After all, it was a dead plan; he wasn't giving away any operational details.

So Eaton had the story. And he didn't have to rely on anything Leslie had told him; he'd gotten all the same information, and even a bit more, from other sources.

It was late, and he went home. But the next morning, right away, he described the story to his editor, Walter Abel, Washington bureau chief for New World. Abel seemed enthusiastic too.

"Great story," he said. "You say you got it from several sources who heard from people actually in the room?"

"Yeah, but I can't be real specific in the story."

"Okay, but are you really sure about this one?" Abel asked.

Eaton sighed. He didn't like Abel's tone. With his long experience on this beat and special sources such as Paladino and now, in her own way, Leslie, Eaton often got information no one else had. Sometimes the White House denied his stories, even though Eaton knew full well they were true. That was to be expected on occasion. It came with the job, and for a long time Abel had taken the knockdowns, as they were called, in stride. But of late it seemed as if Abel's confidence was not so firm.

"Walt, this story is good," Eaton assured him. "Believe me."

Abel thought for a moment, then said, "Okay. Let's go with it."

Wednesday morning Eaton stopped off at the office to check the wires before heading over for the daily White House briefing. Look at that. The AP had picked up his story.

The daily schedule of Associated Press stories that would be put out for today's afternoon papers listed this one:

WASHINGTON—Administration considered raid on Managua theater, taking Sandinista Directorate hostage, according to story by New World News Service. Plan rejected, indicating fundamental disagreements in Administration over direction of contra policy. 600 words.

Not a big story on AP, but it was bound to come up at the briefing. Walking over to the White House, Eaton worried about what might happen. Maybe Fred Hillard would confirm his story. Just as likely, the whole press corps would fall on him in a pack, trying to tear the story apart so they wouldn't feel bad about missing it. If that happened, he wouldn't look forward to telling Abel that another one of his stories had been knocked down.

The White House briefing room, sandwiched between the West Wing and the residence building, was crowded as always. Correspondents sat in eight rows of assigned theater seats, which had brass plaques showing the names of their news organizations. Eaton's seat was in the second-to-last row.

From a platform in the back a dozen Sony and Ikegami TV cameras recorded the proceedings. The White House allowed them to shoot video but not audio footage of Fred Hillard giving the daily briefing. The reasoning was that the president's voice, not Hillard's, should be the one speaking for the White House. Newspaper photographers stood on ladders in the aisles so they could shoot over all the other heads.

After Fred Hillard recited the president's schedule for the day, reporters asked a few predictable questions about the stories of the moment. Would a new Labor secretary be named today? Any progress on Middle East peace talks? What about the trade rift with Japan?

Then the AP correspondent asked: "So, Fred, what about this story on a proposed raid on the dinner-theater in Managua?" Several people laughed.

"You mean he Rubén Darío Theater?" Hillard asked.

"Yeah, I hear they serve a great Sunday buffet," someone quipped, to more giggles. Eaton squirmed. Fred was smiling as he shuffled through his papers looking for the guidance.

"We have no active plans to carry out any such raid, and there have never been any active plans," he said at last.

"Well, are there any passive plans?" the AP writer asked.

"I don't know where that story came from exactly," Hillard said, looking back at Eaton for a second, "but I can tell you the United States has no intention and never had any intention of carrying out a plan like this. Whether somebody, somewhere, discussed this at some point, I can't say. Lots of people discuss all kinds of things. But I can't give this story any credence at all. Next topic?"

Around the room reporters uttered dismissive grunts. A complete knockdown. Eaton slumped in his chair.

The mail boy dropped a copy of today's *News Summary* on Leslie's desk about nine A.M. It lay there awhile; Leslie was transcribing some meeting notes into the White House computer.

At noon she was supposed to go to lunch in the White House mess, but Sheila, her lunch partner from down the hall, was running a little behind. Waiting, Leslie flipped casually through the *News Summary*. The first page had this morning's White House story from *The Washington Post*, a report on the president's speech yesterday extolling the wondrous state of the nation's economy after almost three years of careful ministration under his leadership. Flipping through the pages she glanced casually at various versions of the same story in other papers.

But then she got to page eight. Leslie froze. Quickly she looked around to see if anyone was watching. No, she was alone.

"White House Discussed Plan to Seize Nicaraguan Comandantes," it said. "By Christopher Eaton." She read to the bottom, clenching her teeth. This was their dinner-table conversation with a few elaborative details, though most of it was attributed to "administration officials and other knowledgeable government officers."

That son of a bitch, she thought. How could he do this?

First Leslie called Sheila. "I'm sorry," she said, struggling to keep her voice calm. "Something's come up. Can we do this later in the week?" Then she dialed Eaton's number, stabbing the buttons on her phone.

"Chris Eaton," he answered.

"How could you do this?" Leslie hissed.

Eaton sounded scared and defensive at the same time. "Leslie, what's wrong? What do you mean?"

"You know exactly what I mean, you son of a bitch. How could you do that to me? Were you sitting there taking notes under the dinner table? Is that what this is about to you? How could you?"

"You mean the story?"

"Do I mean the story," she repeated slowly, in a derisive tone. "Of course I mean the story. Don't play stupid with me."

"Leslie, I told you I was working on a story about Terrence Ascher." His pitch was rising. "I didn't use anything you told me, per se. I called and got all of it from other people. All of it. Honest."

"You never told me you were going to write a story about things we talked about over the dinner table. I never would have talked about any of it if I thought it was going to get into the newspaper. There's no excuse. None. A source—is that what I am to you?" Her voice dripped contempt. "And did you even stop to think about what this might do to my job? Did you? Did you?"

"Leslie, I'm sorry. I just assumed—"

"You assume too goddamned much!" And she hung up.

Leslie snapped at so many people through the rest of the day that they started giving her funny looks. She was still angry the next morning when a messenger dropped Eaton's note on her desk. Risky, she thought, but no one noticed.

Dear Leslie:

I'm sorry. Very sorry. You are right. I was wrong.

I meant it when I said I didn't use anything you told me; I got all of it from other people. But I should have just ignored the whole damned thing. I had no right to take our private conversation and use it even passively. No right at all. It will never happen again. You have my word. If you don't believe me, we can promise each other right here that we will never, never discuss things like that again. Never.

I love you. Please forgive me.

Chris.

Not bad, Leslie thought. And over the following couple of days her thinking about the whole episode underwent an interesting transformation.

Eaton's story caused a small stir. The vast majority of people in the White House had never heard of Terrence Ascher's scheme. Several people asked if it was true. Some were impressed by the plan, some were appalled.

More interesting to Leslie was the reaction of the people who had known, like the general. They started trying to guess who had leaked the story. And the consensus, as General Dayton put it, was that "the agency put it out. Trying to double-kill a plan they thought was stillborn to begin with." Leslie smiled at that. In the beginning she'd been terrified they'd figure out she was the leak. There were only seven people at the meeting, and she was the only one who knew Christopher Eaton. She'd lose her job.

But of course nobody knew she was seeing Eaton. And as for the small number of people at the meeting, every one of them talked to other people. That story could just as easily have come from any number of people at State, CIA, or Defense. After years of futile effort the government had long ago stopped trying to track down the source of routine leaks. Ninety-nine times out of a hundred, it just wasn't possible—the field of potential leakers was far too large. Besides, when the president came in he had abandoned the widespread use of polygraph exams, started in a previous administration. Every time the lie detectors had been put to use it had caused such a stink in the press that it just didn't seem worth the trouble.

At the same time, as everyone knew, the monitoring of people who had a security clearance was a joke. There was a recheck once every seven years or so; for years, the reinvestigation backlog for Top Secret clearances like hers had been more than 250,000 people. When the FBI finally got around to it, a rookie agent interviewed her and asked some predictable questions: Have you visited any East bloc countries lately? Do you take drugs? Do you gamble or have large debts? Then he talked with some of her friends and gave the records a cursory review. That was that. Really there wasn't much to worry about.

Then toward the end of the week she heard that the president had noticed the story in *News Summary* and asked about it. Was it true? Why hadn't he been told about it? Sounded like a good idea to him. But the deputy chief of staff assured him it was a bad story, not true. Nobody'd ever proposed any such thing, and a plan like that couldn't work for any number of reasons.

For Leslie, all this was quite an education. By unintentionally leaking to Eaton, she'd had an impact on the White House for a few days. Last month the gossip had been that Ascher wanted to take his plan directly to the president but couldn't get an appointment. Well, without intending to, she'd done it for him, and now everybody was talking about the plan—including the president.

Leslie didn't know if she liked Ascher's plan. But it was exciting to have shaken things up—in her own way she was having a direct effect on administration decisions. She was a policymaker of sorts. And at the same time she was helping Eaton.

No, she did not intend to find herself in a position like this again. She'd never dealt with reporters before, and now she knew she had to be more careful. It was just too dangerous, on several levels. But this one time . . . maybe the episode wasn't such a terrible thing after all.

She let Eaton stew through the week. But finally on Sunday morning she called and told him she wanted to come by for a little talk.

Eaton had the shades down so the living room was dark, matching his mournful expression. A fire was burning, the room was warm. Leslie had taken off her shoes and tucked her feet under her on the sofa. She asked for a glass of wine, and Eaton almost bowed as he rushed to get it for her. He didn't know what was coming, but she didn't seem as angry as he had feared.

"First," she said. "You had no right whatsoever to take advantage of me that way. Don't ever make assumptions about me."

"You are right," Eaton whispered, his head lowered as he brushed at his bangs. He couldn't look her in the eye. "It was stupid." Leslie frowned. Maybe she didn't like him as a penitent supplicant, but he couldn't help it.

"Second," she said, and her voice softened. "It's not the end of the world." Eaton looked up, startled.

"In fact"—she was smiling now—"it was kind of a kick watching those guys scrambling around because of your story."

"Huh?" Eaton cocked his head.

"Yeah. We really had 'em running."

She grinned. Eaton stared.

"But listen. These are the ground rules from now on. I'm never going to talk about these things again. It's too dangerous. If I slip sometime, you've got to stop me. Is that clear?"

"Well, uh, sure."

"Now, why don't we order some Chinese takeout."

CHAPTER TWELVE

BAL HARBOUR, FLORIDA, JANUARY 3

THE SLIDING GLASS DOORS TO THE BALCONY WERE open, and a soft ocean breeze fluttered the lacy curtains, taking the edge off a hot Florida afternoon. Outside, the sky was bright and clear; the blue-green surf glistened in the sun.

Ascher was calmed by the clean salt smell and the sound of the rising tide tumbling up the sand five stories below and just about one hundred yards away. The living room was light and cheery, decorated with bright posters and pastel fabrics. It was not what Ascher had imagined when he thought of a CIA safehouse.

For weeks, ever since the turmoil over that newspaper story about the Rubén Darío plan, Mendoza had been inviting Ascher down here for a strategy meeting. But he'd had a hell of a time getting away. After only three months, Ascher was already smothered by his new job. His life was an unending string of meetings and other commitments. Even though the contra program seemed to be going nowhere, his assignment carried a numbing array of administrative tasks. So like most everyone in the White House, he worked ten or eleven hours a day, six and sometimes seven days a week.

Finally, early in January, Ascher found a free Sunday. The president was on vacation in Arizona again, and Congress was in recess. So he told Linda to call the White House travel office.

Ten minutes later he was booked in a first-class seat on a flight leaving National Airport at 7:30 A.M., with a return flight at 4:45 the same afternoon.

Ascher had looked forward to the trip. Mendoza had promised there'd be other "special guests" waiting for him. And now that he'd finally managed to get here, sure enough, Francesca sat in a dining-room chair over by the doors to the balcony. Sunlight filtered through her crown of curly black hair, and leaning back, wrapped in skintight Calvin Klein jeans, she had one long leg stretched out in front of her, the other draped casually over the chair's lower arm. Her foot wagged a sandal. With her right hand she toyed with the gold chain around her neck, absently pulling the little cross up into view and then dropping it back down her open shirt to the seraphic spot below. Her eyes were fixed on Ascher while he tried without complete success to concentrate on what Mendoza was saying. Colonel Gustafson sat on the couch beside Mendoza, nodding.

"We've got to figure Basham did it," Mendoza was saying. "He's counting the days till he leaves the RIG, and anything threatening to disrupt the status quo he's going to fight. What better way than to leak a story to the press?"

"It may have been Ames," Ascher suggested. "We never got along very well."

"Possible," Gustafson said. "But I know those State Department types too well. You want my view, they're too gutless to try anything like that."

"Okay, okay," Mendoza interrupted. "Let's move on. We've got to work out some strategies among ourselves to do what needs to be done."

"What do you mean?" Ascher asked.

"Well," Mendoza told him with a conspiratorial grin, "the best thing we can do for our cause right now is to give ourselves a little independence."

Ascher looked a bit confused, but Gustafson sounded as if he were stating the obvious when he said, "The president wants action. He's been subverted by these gutless wonders who work for him. We've got to see that the commander in chief's orders get carried out."

With that, Mendoza glanced briefly over at Francesca. And when Ascher looked back a moment later she was still staring at him, eyes unblinking, moist red lips barely parted, one hand still at her throat. But now she was tracing a long-nailed forefinger from her throat slowly down into the beginnings of the dark valley inside her shirt. Ascher swallowed hard.

"We'll have a plan," Mendoza was saying, "a new one, a better one. Because of that newspaper story we're going to have to wait a little while until the dust settles. But that gives us time to get ready." Ascher wasn't listening. His mind was filled with Francesca as he watched her hypnotic finger. After a moment he had to uncross his legs.

"Terry, I want you to open an offshore bank account."

"Huh?" Ascher said, looking up.

"Where do you think is best?"

"Best for what, Raf?"

"Best for a confidential bank account."

"Well, right now I'd say the Caymans."

"Good, good. Why don't you open one there."

"I must have missed something. What are we doing?"

"Terry, we're going to set up some minimal independent capabilities of our own. It's what's required now. We need a bank account we can get into and out of without notice. A contingency fund. It's SOP. I can't do it because the agency monitors field officers too closely."

"But what are we going to put in this account? What am I going to open it with?"

"It doesn't matter for now," Mendoza answered with a wave of the hand. "A little of your office contingency funds, a little of your own money. Anything at all. The point is just to get it open so we have it in case we need it later."

Ascher didn't say anything, not sure where this was leading.

"Next thing we're going to do," Mendoza went on, "is change the staffing in the resistance's Washington office."

"What's that do?" Terry asked.

"Jorge Paladino talks to the press. That's his job, but he's not a friend. Let's bring up a spokesman we know we can trust and who can let us know what's going on. That protects you, Terry."

Ascher looked back at Francesca. She was nodding.

"I'm going to send up Augustín Salazar as the full-time spokesman," Mendoza said. "He's ours. Totally trustworthy. He met this Eaton reporter character down at El Cuartelón, and he'll report to us on what's going on."

"Okay," Ascher said.

Then Mendoza nodded to Francesca. "You want to get the equipment?" She got up and walked into the bedroom, and

Terry's eyes were fixed on her rear as she passed through the door. He sighed. Mendoza smiled.

"Don't worry about her, Terry," he said. "Francesca's totally trustworthy. She's with us. She's ours—yours. We can talk about anything in front of her. So can you."

"No, that wasn't what I was thinking about. I mean, I wasn't worried about that...." He was stammering, but then Francesca came back into the room carrying what looked like a portable typewriter case. She sat next to Ascher on the sofa. Her leg rubbed against his as she laid the case on the coffee table.

"Open it," Mendoza told Ascher. Inside he found a portable computer. It had a small screen just above the keyboard. Ascher looked up, puzzled.

"It's a KL-43 secure phone transmitter," Mendoza told him. "They're very good. Completely secure. Both Eric and I have one. To protect ourselves, prevent leaks, we've got to communicate with these from now on."

He told Ascher how it was used. The phone cable is unhooked from the back of the telephone and plugged into one cable of a Y-cord that plugs into the computer and also back into the phone. A little tape cassette holding the transmission code is plugged into a slot on the side. Conversations are typed instead of spoken, transmitted in code over the phone, decoded on the other end, and then displayed on the liquid-crystal diode screen.

"Take it with you wherever you can, in case it's needed. But be discreet. These are highly classified devices. They belong to the National Security Agency, and we only have them on loan. Be careful, or the NSA will come take them back." Ascher nodded, distracted. Out of view, Francesca was squeezing his leg.

"I've got a couple of other things for you here," Mendoza said. "Just precautions." From a drawer in the end table Mendoza gave Gustafson and Ascher each a miniature tape recorder and an ordinary-looking Parker ballpoint pen that, Mendoza explained, was actually a high-power remote microphone for the tape recorder.

"Just keep them in case you need them," he said. Gustafson took his without remark. Ascher frowned a moment but then shrugged and laid the stuff beside the KL-43 computer.

"And these." Mendoza held out two small beige capsules. "Just slip them back in your wallets."

"What's this?" Ascher asked, turning the little pill over in his fingers.

"Cyanide," Mendoza said. Ascher looked up, startled. Gustafson smiled, shaking his head.

"It's in a hard plastic jacket." Mendoza's tone was matter of fact. "It's shaped so it can be held behind the gums without notice. If it's swallowed by mistake, it goes all the way through without opening up or doing any harm. To activate, bite down on it hard."

But Ascher laid his down on the table and shook his head. "This is crazy," he insisted. "What the hell do I need a poison pill for? And all this other stuff?"

Mendoza started to answer. But Gustafson stopped him, holding up his hand as he said, "Terry, we gotta humor the little spook. This is the world they live in. Just take all this junk." He gave a dismissive wave. "Stick the pill back in your wallet somewhere and forget about it. Believe me, it's easier than listening to him try and explain what we would ever need all this crap for."

With a sigh, Ascher pulled out his wallet and stuck the pill back behind his credit cards.

"I know all this seems kind of silly," Mendoza said. "But I've been at this a long time, and sometimes things develop you never expected."

"Rafael, nothing's ever going to develop that I'm going to need a suicide pill for."

"I'm sure you're right," Mendoza said. "I just want all of us to be ready for whatever happens. If everything goes as it's supposed to, what harm's a little pill going to do back there in your wallet?"

"Look, all this is great, but what is it you've got in mind that we're going to do with all this stuff? What's really behind all this?"

There was a note of irritation in Ascher's voice, and Mendoza stood up and said, "I've got one more surprise for you, but not for another twenty minutes or so."

Ascher frowned, tired of Mendoza's infuriating need for secrets and intrigue. Why couldn't he ever answer a simple question? But then Mendoza said, "Terry, it's one o'clock. Why don't you and Francesca go take a little walk on the beach and be back here by one-thirty."

Ascher looked at Francesca with a startled smile. Immediately she took his hand and led him out the door.

*   *   *

The CIA safehouse was really a beach-front condominium, part of an apartment-hotel in Bal Harbour, a wealthy little town just up Collins Avenue from Miami Beach. A high-price shopping mall with a Saks Fifth Avenue was across the street. The beach was groomed and cultivated: palm-tree groves were planted at regular intervals above the high-tide line and watered automatically each night by an underground sprinkler system. But hotel rooms and apartments here were so expensive that the beach was almost deserted. The denizens of Bal Harbour were retirees, more often than not, who spent afternoons under their cabana awnings up by the pool. Most would spend weeks here without ever touching sand.

Ascher and Francesca left their shoes and sandals in the CIA's own swimming pool cabana (the name tag over the door said Arturo Ambrose), rolled up their pants legs, and walked down to the beach hand in hand. The temperature was in the mid-eighties, a normal, pleasantly warm January day here. The way the breeze rustled Francesca's exotic sweep of hair reminded Ascher of film scenes he'd seen showing fashion photographers stationing fans in front of their models to flutter their hair just so.

Ascher himself was an odd sight. His face had a deep brown sunlamp-tan. But his legs, exposed now up to the knees, were chalk white.

As soon as they got to the surf line Francesca dropped Ascher's hand for a moment and started to unbutton her shirt. Ascher didn't say anything, just stood there gawking as she took it off and tied it around her waist.

She was wearing a tight yellow tube-top underneath, and her nipples were straining to press through. Ascher sucked in his breath. Standing ankle-deep in the surf, Francesca turned, pressing herself hard against him as they embraced in a long, heated kiss. As their lips parted, Ascher stood numb for a moment; then she took his hand and started walking down the beach again.

"Francesca, isn't there someplace we could go?" he asked, his voice tight.

"But where?"

"The cabana. Anywhere."

"Terry, my love, we have only a few minutes. I look forward to spending a long night with you in my arms, not a hasty moment on the floor."

"But when?"

"Soon. I know it. Very soon. Trust me."

"But . . ." She put a finger to her lips, shushing him, then reached down to the surf with both hands and splashed him, laughing as she ran away down the beach. Ascher chased, tackling her, and they rolled around in the warm water, kissing and laughing. Ascher barely noticed that he was getting his clothes all wet.

When Ascher's waterproof wristwatch said it was almost one-thirty, they walked back to the hotel in silence, hand in hand. At the last palm grove, she stopped and pressed him against a tree in one final, fervent embrace, her hands up and down his body.

"God," Ascher gasped when they pulled apart. She backed a few inches away and looked at him with a curious smile, close to triumphant. Then she turned and swaggered back to the hotel, her head high. Ascher stood for a long minute, leaning against the tree and watching until she was out of view. Finally, with a ponderous sigh, he pulled himself together and followed.

"Terry, I'd like you to meet Major Paz," Mendoza said as soon as he walked in the door. Mendoza's hand rested on the shoulder of an unsmiling man no taller than he was. "Paz, this is the very important man I told you about from the White House, the personal representative of the president of the United States of America."

Ascher didn't feel very important. He was still soaking wet, and sand stuck all over his clothes and in his hair. He reached to shake the major's hand, but instead of taking it, the little man snapped to attention as if Ascher were a comandante. Ascher gave him a crisp nod. So this was Paz, the ruthless Guardia major who carried out any order without question. He didn't look the part. Actually he didn't seem to fit any particular part. Major Paz just looked odd—brown-splotched skin, orange hair, and Ray Ban sunglasses, even indoors.

Paz's jaw was set hard, as if he was clenching his teeth. His chin was high, shoulders stiff. He wore a zip-up jacket over a striped sport shirt, and Ascher could see the holster bulge under his arm.

"Paz, why don't you wait here a minute while Mr. Ascher dries off," Mendoza said, and then gestured Ascher into the bedroom, following and closing the door behind them. Francesca sat on the couch filing her nails but looked up smiling when they came in. She threw Ascher a damp towel that lay at her feet.

"Terry, I think it would help if you gave Paz a pep talk," Mendoza whispered. "We ask a lot of him, and we are going to be asking even more still. It would be good for him to know it's not just me talking but the United States government. Tell him how important he is, how he's doing the president's work and so forth. Lay it on thick about the president. You know what I mean?"

"Yeah, sure, okay," Ascher said as he rubbed the towel through his hair. "But a pep talk for what?"

"For whatever operation we decide to carry out."

Ascher shook his head at the non-answer. Back in the living room, he sat on the sofa and gestured Paz to a chair. But Paz still stood at attention, his Ray Bans pointed at a spot on the wall just over Ascher's head.

"Why don't you sit down," Ascher said finally.

"Yes, sir," Paz barked, giving a hint of the Caribbean accent in his English, and sat on the edge of a chair, his posture still suggesting he had a two-by-four stuck in his shirt.

"Major Paz, my good friend Mr. Mendoza tells me wonderful things about you, how valuable you are to our effort. You and your Pena de Muerte commandos have done some great things." He waited for Paz to respond, but the major looked straight ahead.

"Well, I want you to know that the president appreciates everything you are doing. I am going to tell him all about you." Paz seemed to sit up even straighter, if that was possible, but still didn't say anything or look directly at Ascher.

"When you do work for Mr. Mendoza, you are working for me and you are working for the president of the United States," Ascher said.

"Yes, sir," Major Paz answered. Ascher had never played a role like this. He was winging it, but it seemed to be working.

"Major, we don't know what's ahead, but there may be some difficult assignments. I want you to know how important you are to the cause. When you carry out an assignment you are helping not only the resistance movement but all of your countrymen, my countrymen, the president of the United States, and the cause of freedom everywhere."

Ascher looked to Mendoza over at the dining table behind Paz to see how he was doing. Mendoza and Gustafson were smiling and nodding at each other, their grins inexplicably broad.

A short time later Ascher had to head back for the airport. Carrying the KL-43 with the other craftware tucked inside the case, Mendoza followed him to the lobby and outside to the windy parking lot.

Standing beside Ascher's rental car, Mendoza said, "You did our cause a great deal of good with your little talk to Paz. I know him; he's ready to fight. You'd make a great general."

"Yeah, sure," Ascher said with a frown.

"We're going to do some good. Just wait."

"But Raf," Ascher said, unable to hide the exasperation any longer. "You told me you had an idea. What is it? Come on, tell me, what is it you want to do?"

"We're carrying out my idea just by meeting here and getting ready. We have to wait a little while longer. Trust us and be patient. Soon we will come up to visit you when it is time to move. Or maybe you can come down and spend a weekend in Tegucigalpa with us." He grinned. But Ascher's smile was strained. He was growing weary of all the mystery, the frustration, the waiting for who-knows-what. Shaking his head he took the KL-43 and turned to the car, wondering if in the end all of this wasn't just a waste of time.

But then Mendoza said, "Oh, I almost forgot a little something I brought for you." When Ascher turned back, Mendoza was reaching into his pocket. Smiling he pressed two little brown bottles into Ascher's hand, then immediately turned and started up the driveway without looking back.

Ascher glanced at what Mendoza had given him and, startled, stared after him. In his hand were two 25-tablet bottles of Honduran Valium.

CHAPTER THIRTEEN

FOR EVEN A MODERATELY POPULAR INCUMBENT PRESI-
dent, the conventional wisdom goes, reelection is a lead-
pipe cinch. And for this one, the nomination was assured.
No one had dared oppose him. Still, the stunted presidencies of
Gerald Ford and Jimmy Carter remained fresh in the minds of
everyone in the White House, even all these years later. So as
the gray of winter settled over the capital, and West Wing strate-
gists looked out their steamed-up office windows to watch the
grounds-keeping staff carefully brush mounds of snow off the
South Lawn boxwoods, warnings against reelection overconfi-
dence grew to be ritualistic chants. This, after all, was primary
season.

True, the opposing party hadn't fielded a candidate so daz-
zling that it hurt their eyes to watch him. In fact hardly anyone
had guessed that Senator Robert Kelly of Ohio would be the one
who rose out of the pack.

He'd been like all the others, talking about new ideas without
ever explaining what they were, promising to erase the lingering
budget deficit without quite saying he'd have to raise taxes again,
suggesting it was time to begin making new peaceful overtures
to the Soviet Union while also pledging to maintain a strong defense.

But on one issue Senator Kelly was unambiguous, and that

was the contras. He had no use for them, never had. He'd voted against the program from the beginning. In his view, the United States had no business meddling in Nicaragua's internal affairs. As long as the Sandinistas didn't bother their neighbors, he liked to say, the United States shouldn't bother them. And when he was elected president, he promised without equivocation, the contras wouldn't get another dime.

Well now it looked as if Senator Kelly would be the nominee. No one had been sure who would win the caucuses in Iowa, the primary season's first test, but it had turned out to be him. With that boost, Kelly won the New Hampshire primary too. And now the polls said he was leading in the South as Super Tuesday loomed.

Campaigning, Kelly sometimes talked about the contras. "All these years later, and what have they done?" he liked to ask. "They've driven the Nicaraguan people deeper and deeper into the arms of the Soviets, and that's about all."

The line didn't usually draw much reaction or applause, so his speech writers advised him to drop it. But on this issue, the senator was a true believer. The president and his men took the Sandinistas' angry march toward totalitarianism to be the most convincing argument for the contras. But Senator Kelly contended that if it weren't for the contras, Managua would have no need to act this way. The line stayed in his speeches—even as the Sandinistas seemed to grow more threatening by the day.

More than a dozen years of war had so drained Nicaragua that the government could no longer provide for even the most basic needs of the people. United States intelligence was picking up reports of severe malnutrition among campesinos in some remote areas. The Sandinistas couldn't do much about that, so they tried to turn the anger of their hungry people toward the north. From Managua Minister Zelaya and the comandantes were speaking out against the United States with ever greater bombast. In Washington the president was growing angry, largely because there really wasn't much he could do.

Though no one in the bureaucracy really thought Senator Kelly stood much chance of winning, even the slim possibility that he would come to office and simply sweep the contra-aid program away exacerbated the limp-wristed timidity that had already plagued the program's management. And when interested foreign governments—particularly the Hondurans—heard the Sandinista bombast in one ear and Senator Kelly's anti-contra rhetoric in the other, they started growing restive, and worse.

To those who paid attention, there was a palpable sense that the situation was deteriorating. But no one could conceivably have anticipated the chain of events all this would set off.

Leslie had been telling Chris how frustrated General Dayton and some others in the White House were growing about Nicaragua. Now that the campaign was the central preoccupation in the West Wing, her husband, the pollster, was working at a frantic pace, trying to measure the effect state by state of each new speech, every stratagem. With all the work and travel, Wyche was never home these days, and so neither was Leslie.

She and Eaton had begun daring to go out for dinner now and then, as long as they chose restaurants their friends were unlikely to visit. Tonight it was La Plaza, a Mexican restaurant in the Adams Morgan neighborhood, home to many Latin American emigrés.

"People coming out of the Oval Office say he's asking about the contras almost every day," Leslie was saying as they drank their after-dinner decaf. "He wants to do something, but he doesn't know what. When the general goes in to give his national security briefing at nine-thirty, the president keeps telling him, 'Think of something we can do, think of something we can do.' "

"You think they'll actually do anything?"

"Naw, absolutely not. Nobody's proposing anything. Most people just roll their eyes and humor him."

"Leslie, this is kind of interesting. You mind if I use a little of this sometime?"

"No, go ahead."

That's how it had worked since the blowup back in November. Now and then she'd make conversation about goings-on at the White House—mood, atmosphere, the gossip of the moment. Nothing more than that, never anything that was classified or even terribly exclusive. It was the sort of information other reporters got from their own White House sources with little difficulty. Still, Eaton would listen and if he found any of it interesting he would make sure to ask before using it. So far she'd always said yes, and there'd been no problems. She even seemed to get a kick out of helping him. In fact, as far as Eaton was concerned, their relationship was wonderful—no, even better than that. Apparently Leslie thought so too.

Back in December they'd had their own Christmas dinner, on

December 23 while her husband was out of town. He roasted a goose, and they exchanged gifts in front of the fire. He bought her a gold necklace with a small diamond, suggesting she tell her husband she'd bought it for herself. She was flushed with delight as she put it on.

Before Chris could open his gift, Leslie's phone rang up in his bedroom, the call forwarded from her own home. Eaton felt sour when she ran up to chat with her husband for a minute, but after she came back down, Leslie looked at him with her searing brown eyes as he read her gift card out loud, choking over the emotion-laden greeting. Inside the box was a beautiful wafer-thin Piaget wristwatch. He hugged her, and afterward they made love. As they lay together, moist and warm in each other's arms, Leslie had whispered in Chris's ear, "I love you."

Now, almost three months later, they were coasting along, still delighted with every minute they spent together. And as they grew more comfortable with each other, Eaton began daring to think about the future. He still believed that if he wanted to win Leslie, he had to make a name for himself and get a better job. And the only way to do that was to follow the Nicaragua story as aggressively as he could. Something was about to happen. He just knew it.

One clear indicator had been the sudden and inexplicable reassignment of his good friend Jorge Paladino. He'd been sent back down to Honduras all of a sudden, replaced by Augustín Salazar, the slick spokesman he'd met at the end of his last visit to El Cuartelón. "He's the CIA's man," Paladino had explained bitterly.

Eaton was almost as upset about the change as Paladino; he threw a little goodbye party for his friend at a local restaurant and missed him now, though they still spoke on the phone a couple of times a week. At the same time, though, Salazar had proved to be surprisingly helpful, even solicitous. Still, the sudden changeover seemed odd, to both Eaton and Paladino. Chairman Coronel had sent Paladino to Washington to get him out of the way. Coronel certainly didn't want him back. It had to be the CIA, burying the man who had been something less than an agency cheerleader here in the United States.

Or, Eaton wondered, was Terrence Ascher, angry about the Rubén Darío story, showing off his newfound power?

Late in the month the contra RIG held its regular monthly meeting, but the group was not its normal desultory self. A lot was happening, and the RIG was right in the middle. There was an air of excitement as the members sat around Ascher's conference table and gave their reports. Leslie sat beside General Dayton taking notes, and his manner made her think he was going to be a force here as he had not been before. Even Basham's voice betrayed a note of interest, although he certainly wasn't allowing himself to get carried away with enthusiasm. Gravely, he explained that the new bellicosity coming from Managua was scaring the Hondurans. They wanted to expel the contras and close down their bases on Honduran territory. "They don't really know how to read the political situation up here," he said, "and with Senator Kelly clearly opposed to the program, they are afraid he might win. Then the ride would come to an end; aid would be cut off again, and this time they think the contras would just give up.

"General Ramirez, the army chief of staff, told us they don't think the United States could keep the Sandis from retaliating against them for supporting the contras all these years. They want the contras out now, and it's hard to fault them. If I were the general I sure wouldn't want twelve thousand well-armed guerrillas roaming around my country all of a sudden, looking for something to do."

"Recommendation?" Terry Ascher asked. To Leslie he seemed as assertive as ever. They hadn't clipped his wings, and he was behaving as if he had something up his sleeve.

"Well," Ames said, "this afternoon our people are going over to the Presidential Palace to tell President Suarez he's got to put in an immediate request for forty million dollars in emergency military aid. It's already been approved at this end. We're hoping word of that will get back to Managua and maybe knock some sense into the Sandis, show them we're standing strong behind our Honduran allies.

"I suspect it will also lubricate some palms in Tegucigalpa and maybe make them a little more tolerant," he added with a grin. As Leslie jotted that down, she wished she could pass this on to Eaton. She knew she couldn't.

"But let's not give up on diplomacy here," Ames was saying. "We don't want to ratchet this up so far that we can't pull back. I think when push comes to shove the Sandis will settle."

To that Ascher gave a theatric roll of the eyes. It was now his turn. Leslie watched him, and he seemed absolutely delighted with himself. His secretary, the woman with the pitted checks, placed a small cassette tape recorder in front of him on the table and looked up at her boss with an expression that, to Leslie, made it perfectly obvious she was or wanted to be his lover. But Ascher barely seemed to notice she was there. He was too eager to get on with whatever show he had planned.

"I can't tell you exactly how this recording was made—sources and methods," he said with a quick, nervous grin as he took the tape Gustafson had sent him out of his shirt pocket and slipped it into the player. "But the two voices you hear are Miguel Zelaya, whom you all know, and Mrs. Carrión, editor of *La Prensa*. They're speaking in her kitchen. It's just after seven A.M. the day before yesterday."

Then he played the tape. It was scratchy but clear enough. They could hear Zelaya limping across the kitchen floor, and the mockery in his voice was recognizable even to those who didn't speak Spanish. Ascher translated simultaneously as the tape played.

> MINISTER ZELAYA: "Good morning, Señora Carrión. I hope I am not disturbing you."
> MRS. CARRIÓN: "Minister, no, come in. Please sit down."

Chairs scraped; apparently they sat around the kitchen table. She offered coffee, and they could hear it being poured. The microphone must have been on or under the table.

> MINISTER ZELAYA: "Señora, I come with necessary information. We have been generous to you, allowing you to publish your newspaper without interference, even with the war, and we have made sure you were supplied with newsprint despite the shortages. But you have not returned our kindness. You have published much misinformation. You have been a tool of the North Americans, a friend to the counter-revolutionaries. With the international situation as it is today, we cannot allow that to continue."

Mrs. Carrión's voice quavered slightly, betraying the edge of panic.

> MRS. CARRIÓN: "No, Minister Zelaya, you cannot censor us again. We could not stand it. The international community would not tolerate it. You cannot. No!"
> MINISTER ZELAYA: "Señora, you do not understand. We are not going to resume censorship."

There was a silent moment. Leslie pictured Mrs. Carrión giving him a questioning look; his beady eyes probably bore down on her.

MINISTER ZELAYA: "We are closing *La Prensa.* Today's issue is the last."

Mrs. Carrión gasped.

MRS. CARRIÓN: "No, no, you can't do this. You can't! How can you get away with this again? You just can't do it!"

Zelaya's voice was matter-of-fact.

MINISTER ZELAYA: "But señora, we are at war."

Leslie watched Ascher turn off the tape recorder and look around the table, smiling. His gaze lingered on Ames, who looked despondent. For a moment there was silence, but then General Dayton held out his hand, saying, "Terry, I'd like to borrow that tape, if I may, and play it for the president."

"Certainly," Ascher chirped and immediately handed Dayton the cassette before giving Ames a triumphant look. Oh, the games, Leslie thought.

"Things may start moving fast," Dayton said. "I suggest we reconvene here again same time the day after tomorrow."

Eaton was the first to report that the United States had ordered the Honduran government to put in an emergency request for $40 million in military aid. He'd been chatting with a friend in a hallway of the Rayburn House Office Building when he saw Thomas Driscoll bustling in to see the chairman of the House Foreign Affairs Committee. Driscoll was the State Department Latin America division officer who most often made the required notifications to Congress of foreign aid disbursements that were outside the regular sums set in the budget.

Chris asked around and quickly found out what was up. It was no secret. Without being explicit, his story made it clear that the offer was a bribe. But Eaton beat the pack by only a day. Within twenty-four hours it was all over the hemisphere's press. Honduras was certainly happy about the unexpected largesse, but all the attention embarrassed President Suarez and may in fact have hardened the Hondurans' resolve to evict the contras—especially after they saw how the Sandinistas reacted.

The Nicaraguan government was anything but chastened. Immediately the Sandinista Directorate stepped up the draft; reports from Managua said Interior Ministry enforcers had begun carrying out wholesale kidnappings of young Nicaraguan men, who were being carted off to boot camp by the truckload.

In the next morning's *Barricada*, the Sandinista party newspaper, Minister Zelaya announced that opposition political parties—they were no more than stunted symbols anyway—were now illegal.

At the RIG meeting two days later, General Dayton reported what everyone at the table already knew. The president was enraged.

"Gentlemen," he said, "we have decided on a number of actions. We have watched this steady march toward complete totalitarianism long enough. The president is afraid that if the United States does not show firm resolve now, before the Sandinistas continue much farther along this path, it will be too late. This country will be left with no reasonable recourse. So here is what we are going to do.

"First of all, the president has asked me to direct you to step up the resistance's offensive actions. Wherever possible, we want them in the field fighting as hard as they can, making as much trouble as possible. And we want their operations coordinated with the other action I am about to describe."

"What kind of fighting do you mean?" Ascher asked.

"Ambushes, sabotage, all the things they've been trained to do." Ascher took some notes.

"Now collateral to that," the general was saying, "we are reviving elements of our 'perception management' program from several years ago. We're sending up the Blackbirds for sonic effects, as we did back a few years ago."

Colonel Cater nodded at that. "Sure scared the hell out of them last time."

"I hope it scares them this time, too," Dayton interrupted, cutting Cater off. "Because if it doesn't and the Sandinistas continue on their present course, the president has ordered us to be ready for a second action. An Operation Bright Lights, just over the border in Honduras. We've already notified the Hondurans."

"Bright Lights?" Ascher asked.

"I know that name," Cater said, shaking his head, trying to remember. "I know it. . . ."

"Bright Lights," Dayton explained. "Like we did over the border from Libya back a few years ago when we wanted to put a little scare into them. I hope we don't have to do it here."

Cater looked up, eyes wide. "You mean . . ." He paused, mouth open, then whispered, "Holy shit."

That night, the president requested network airtime for a speech. NBC, CBS, ABC, and CNN all gave it to him, even though there was predictable grumbling that he was using his office to get free campaign-season airtime. Chris and Leslie watched in Eaton's living room. The president spoke from the Oval Office, with silver-framed photos of his family on the table behind him. He looked directly at the camera, and his manner was grim.

"My friends, what we have all feared is happening. The Sandinistas in Nicaragua are hardening their regime, removing the last shred of doubt about their true intentions, and victimizing the freedom-loving people of their country."

The president recounted the recent events in Nicaragua and quoted from the tape recording of Minister Zelaya's conversation in Mrs. Carrión's kitchen, repeating Zelaya's last line with melodramatic emphasis:

"But señora, we are at war."

Then the president held up *La Prensa*'s last issue. Its large black headline said simply: IT IS ALL OVER.

"We will not allow this to happen," the president said. "We will not allow a Communist base, a feeding ground for instability and insurgency, to take root in our own backyard. The democratic resistance must continue to be supported despite the misguided policies of some would-be leaders"—a barely veiled reference to Senator Kelly.

"We will stand by them. And if the Sandinistas continue their headlong march to darkness, if necessary we will act ourselves."

Excited, Chris turned to Leslie. "He's going to attack them, isn't he? Isn't he?"

Leslie shook her head. "No" was all she said, her voice controlled. Eaton knew this tone. She knew a lot, he guessed, and probably wished she could tell him. But he couldn't press, though he did stare at her for a moment, until finally she whispered, "He's just going to scare 'em."

PALMEROLA AIR BASE, CENTRAL HONDURAS

Even as the president spoke, flight crews were readying four SR-71 Blackbird spy planes, the fastest, highest-flying airplanes in the world. So unusual were they that it took twenty-four hours to prepare them for a mission. There were no real hangars at Palmerola. After all, the base was just "temporary." So the Blackbirds, each more than one hundred feet long, were housed in concrete revetments covered with translucent camouflage nets to hide them from Soviet reconnaissance satellites that made passes over Honduras twice a day. Takeoffs and landings were timed to avoid the satellite overflights—one spycraft sneaking into the air out of sight of another. But for the Blackbirds today, surveillance was only the secondary mission.

Working under the long black titanium hulls, the crews stepped through puddles of JP-7 jet fuel. Blackbirds flew so fast—up to 2,189 miles per hour, or almost Mach 3—that their fuel tanks were built with loose seams so they could expand without buckling when friction from the air pushed the fuselage temperature above 800 degrees Fahrenheit, as it usually did, even in the rarefied atmosphere at the Blackbirds' top altitude: 86,000 feet—more than sixteen miles up. The fuel puddles weren't dangerous; JP-7 had such a high flashpoint that it would drown a lit match. It had to be that way. Otherwise at the extraordinarily high operating temperatures the planes would explode in flight.

The next morning the two-man crews ate high-protein, low-residue preflight meals: steak and eggs. Once locked in their pressure suits they couldn't eat or go to the bathroom. An hour or so before takeoff they zipped into their bubble-helmet pressure suits and began the change to breathing oxygen. Before eleven A.M. the first of them climbed into their planes. The lead plane was to be high over Managua near noontime. While the pilot taxied to the end of the runway, the RSO—reconnaissance systems officer—checked surveillance and astro-inertial navigation systems.

From above, the plane looked like a flatworm with wings. A wide ledge, a continuous horizontal fin, wrapped around the fuselage and tapered as it moved back toward the short, triangular wings. The planes used ram-jet engines—virtually perpetual-motion machines, since they used the force of the air pouring into the engines' front, augmented by the jet's power, to create thrust out the back—and they were as big around as the fuselage. Ram-jets aren't as efficient at low altitudes, so they screamed as the first Blackbird lifted off and headed east toward the Caribbean. Another plane took off almost immediately after, and the other two would follow in a few hours. At about the same moment, several other SR-71s were lining up for takeoff from Patrick Air Force Base, just south of Miami.

UNITED STATES EMBASSY, MANAGUA, NICARAGUA

Gustafson had seen the coded cable traffic. He knew what was coming and when. So at lunchtime he got a ham sandwich and a Coke from the Oasis, the commissary behind the embassy, and took them around front. He leaned against the hood of his car, watching the Mothers of Heroes and Martyrs marching up and down in orderly lines just outside the fence. He lifted his red Coca-Cola can as ostentatiously as he could, hoping the little women would see it. A couple of them did, although they pretended not to.

It was just after noon when Managua shook under a thunderous boom that seemed to roll over the city like a slow wave, from the mountains to the lake and then back. Nearby, Gustafson heard glass shattering, and through the fence he saw the little women suddenly breaking ranks and looking all around—up, down, back, forth—panicky as they bumped into each other, some of them dropping their placards. The rumble had barely rolled away when down came a second, this one even stronger. A women screamed, but the shriek was almost drowned by what sounded like a huge plate-glass window crashing to the sidewalk not far away.

Almost as a group, several of the women turned to look at Gustafson. He was still leaning against the car occasionally sipping from his Coke. But as they stared at him, eyes full of fear, the colonel looked back with what he liked to call his shit-eating grin. He lifted his Coke can as if he were toasting them. Ah, he was thinking, who'd ever have guessed you could do so much good with a little ol' sonic boom.

In shifts all through the afternoon, a dozen Blackbirds tore through the skies over Managua, timing their accelerations so they crashed through the sound barrier just above the city. Then they would decelerate over the Pacific, loop back east, and shoot photos of assigned intelligence targets before turning back to Managua, where they would rip easily through the sound barrier again. The booms struck the city at the rate of two or three an hour, and after a while people were running through the streets in panic. Most had no idea what was happening. They could feel the air shake, hear the glass shattering. But the planes were eighty thousand feet up in the air, just speeding specks in the sky. They didn't leave white contrails, and hardly anybody knew they were there. So to many Managuans, the rolling booms and shattering glass truly seemed to be the crashing wrath of God.

The United States had pulled this once before, though only for an hour or two. That first time, even the comandantes had panicked. They'd put the armed forces on full alert and readied themselves for an invasion. But a short time later they read in *The New York Times* that it had only been deliberate sonic booms, so this time they grimaced and looked up. They'd have loved to shoot the planes down but had no surface-to-air missiles effective at anything close to that altitude. In the minute or so it would take a SAM to lock on to its target, launch, and climb up sixteen miles to where the SR-71 had been, at full speed the plane would already have flown more than thirty-five miles away. As the comandantes knew full well, over the years the Soviet Union had fired more than a thousand SAMs at Blackbirds sent over their borders on radar-triggering penetration sorties. Not one had ever hit its target.

So the only thing the comandantes could do was blame the Americans, put the military on alert, and warn everyone that an invasion was imminent. The generals knew this wasn't true, but invasion scares were always a good way to keep the people's minds off their empty bellies. In late afternoon, orders went out for the city's antiaircraft gunners to man their weapons. Citizens were told to go home. That was no problem; after several hours of sonic booms, most people were already in their houses, cowering in closets or basements, clasping babies to their chests. The comandantes assembled down in El Chipote, the Sandinistas' below-ground command bunker next to the police prison, named after General Sandino's guerrilla headquarters up in the hills fifty years earlier.

But then at exactly five P.M. another boom echoed across the city, this one closer, more focused than the Blackbird noises. Down by Lake Managua, a large electrical pylon teetered on its legs and crashed to the ground, power cables arcing and crackling as the tower fell through a row of barrio shacks. At almost the same moment two other explosions echoed down from Las

Colinas, the wealthy suburb in the hills southeast of town. Two small bridges collapsed into streams.

At the sound of the explosions, AA gunners wheeled around in their seats looking through their sights for targets, and some of them shot at phantoms. Down by Lake Managua, one ZSU-2 AA gunner fired a short burst of 57-millimeter rounds at a target but then immediately released the trigger, leaning back embarrassed when he realized he'd shot down a crow. Down in El Chipote, the comandantes looked back and forth at each other in stunned silence. Had they been wrong? Was this really the invasion, at last?

But after a few minutes they realized the skies were clear. What the hell's going on? they asked each other. The answer came a moment later when their radios began crackling with reports of ambushes, explosions, and guerrilla attacks all across the country.

It was just the contras, the mercenary clowns, launching an offensive, doing the North American circus master's dirty business.

Deep in their hearts, Gustafson believed, the hard-core comandantes really wanted the United States to invade. When the events of the day had ended and it was clear all of it had been a ruse—"perception management," followed by a coordinated contra offensive—the colonel was convinced that some of the comandantes must have been disappointed.

"They know it's inevitable; we're coming in sooner or later," he was telling his aide, Major Rosen, over lunch in the Oasis commissary the next afternoon. "They thought this was it, and they'd finally get to shoot some real live gringos and then go back up into the hills like Sandino did, picking off our Marines one by one and getting pictures of our boys in body bags broadcast on the TV news every night. Don't you think?"

"Oh, I don't know," the major said. "Maybe that's the way they thought at first. But they seem pretty much at home in those Mercedes they drive around town now. I bet they'd rather be lying around in the swimming pools behind those embassy houses they've been confiscating from us than digging for roots up there in Jinotega."

"You mean you think the glory of the revolution isn't first on their minds now?" the colonel asked with a sarcastic grin. "The way things are, I'm not sure it's so much fun running this country anymore."

Just then a secretary poked her head in the door and called to Ned Frederick, who was sitting alone at an adjacent table.

"Traffic coming in, Ned," she said, and without a word Frederick stood up, grabbing the other half of his turkey sandwich to take with him.

"What's going on, Ned?" Gustafson asked.

"Don't know. Gotta go see."

"Can I come?" Gustafson asked as he got up. Frederick frowned, but Gustafson was already in step behind him.

Frederick worked for the National Security Agency, the nation's largest intelligence agency and one of the most secretive, in charge of electronic and photographic spying worldwide. Theoretically Gustafson wasn't even supposed to know who Frederick was, though in a post this small it was ludicrous to think it could remain secret, especially considering the abnormally large office the NSA kept here. One good reason the United States had not cut off diplomatic relations with Nicaragua, even though the two countries had been virtually at war for more than a dozen years, was that the embassy had become an important "intelligence platform," in the jargon of the trade.

Satellite reception equipment, so advanced, so secret, that not even Gustafson knew how most of it worked, scooped up the Sandinistas' most sensitive military message traffic and channeled it into the NSA's Cray supercomputers at headquarters just outside Washington. The Crays were the fastest computers on earth; they had to be. Their job was to take coded information and run it through every conceivable decoding permutation until finally they found one that worked. Each Cray operated at such an incredible speed and created so much heat that if its freon cooling system ever failed, even for a moment, the several-ton mass would melt into a puddle on the floor. These computers decoded the messages and then spit them out in plain English on printers in Washington, and here.

Gustafson followed Frederick across the courtyard and into the main chancellery building's back door. Frederick was a pale, stoop-shouldered figure who wore sleeveless undershirts even beneath his short-sleeved sportswear. He didn't look back at Gustafson. Down a hall, Frederick stopped at a door and punched a code into the cipher lock. Gustafson grabbed the door before it slammed shut and followed Frederick into the CIA-NSA wing, built on the back of the embassy in 1986. The intelligence wing was not cardboard; special bug-free building materials had been smuggled in among the monthly commissary food shipments flown up from Panama.

Frederick turned into a windowless office crammed with electronic consoles. The secretary handed him a message printed on white form-feed computer paper, and Gustafson read it over Frederick's shoulder.

"Great!" the colonel yelped, smacking a fist into his palm as he wheeled around to leave.

"Hey," Frederick called after him. "That's a code-word classified message, and you're not even cleared. Keep it to yourself."

"Yeah, yeah," Gustafson said over his shoulder.

Back in his office with the door closed, Gustafson pulled his KL-43 computer out of a locked file drawer and plugged its Y-cable into the back of the telephone. Then he called Mendoza in Tegucigalpa. Mendoza wasn't in his office, but Gustafson told his secretary it was important, so she said she'd go get him. A minute later Mendoza was on the line.

"Hey, Raf, got some news down here," Gustafson said. "Let's go on KL-43s."

"Okay, my friend," Mendoza said, and plugged his own computer into the phone, then hung up the receiver.

"On line," he typed, and the words were coded using the formula on the little microcassette code tape, transmitted to Managua at a speed of twelve hundred baud, then decoded by the mirror-image code tape in Gustafson's machine.

"On line," appeared on Gustafson's screen, and he hung up his own receiver, turning the conversation over to the computers.

"You hear what is happening from your people up there?" Gustafson typed.

"I heard that the Blackbirds were successful, and up here we got our troops out for a pretty good series of coordinated operations. Is there more?"

"Sure is, pal. The Sandis are going north again."

"Oh?"

"That is right. The NSA boys just got a military command message going to the BLIs up in the Highlands." BLIs were light infantry battalions, the Sandinista's eight-hundred-man irregular warfare units. They were the Sandinistas' toughest, most seasoned troops, charged with fighting the contras on their own ground.

"Three of them are ordered up to the border."

"Really? What else?"

"They're moving artillery up there too."

"Another firing-range exercise, you think?"

"Sounds like it."

El Cuartelón was so close to the border, only about seven miles north, that the Sandinistas could line up their Soviet artillery and lob shells at the camp without ever stepping a toe over the line.

The comandantes had ordered these artillery assaults before, every time they needed to show the Nicaraguan people that they could get tough with the contras. As part of the exercise, the BLIs were supposed to seal the border area, keeping any rebel troops inside Nicaragua from returning to help out at base camp.

"Another chastening exercise, huh?" Mendoza said.

"Yup."

"When is all of this supposed to begin?"

"Ten days," Gustafson said. "You know the Sandis. They're not what you might call a rapid-response army."

"Eric, are you thinking what I am thinking?"

"Sure am, pal."

"We can use this," Mendoza typed. "Finally it is time to cash in our assets. I will call Ascher right now."

CHAPTER
FOURTEEN

MAYA HOTEL, TEGUCIGALPA, HONDURAS,
MARCH 20

HERE THEY WERE IN ANOTHER HOTEL SUITE, THIS TIME a dark-paneled sitting room in the Honduran capital, getting ready to plan another operation. Mendoza hadn't told Ascher why he was needed for a full weekend, or even what exactly they were to discuss, except to say it was another urban guerrilla raid. But this time, Mendoza had said in a KL-43 computer call, events were speeding forward so rapidly that "we are going to have to go black."

In normal government parlance, "going black" usually meant turning the program over to the Central Intelligence Agency. But if a CIA officer used that phrase, Ascher guessed, it could only mean that the operation would be completely off-the-books. Ascher, Mendoza, and Gustafson would be out on their own; not even the RIG would know what was going on. Ascher was prepared for that. As the situation continued to deteriorate, he was convinced that the president must be as frustrated as he was. And he still hadn't forgotten that the president had directed him to get the job done.

Here at the Maya, Gustafson had a room across the hall. Ascher's bedroom was off the sitting room. And just after he arrived, as he'd set his suitcase next to his bed, through a half-open door to the adjoining room Ascher saw Francesca smiling at him, lounging on her own bed, the sheets turned down. He stepped to her doorway and said hello, lingering there until Mendoza gently patted him on the shoulder saying, "Later, my friend. We have important work to do."

Ascher agreed. With all the recent action, he was feeling an electric sense of urgency. But at the same time, the race of events gave Ascher the nagging worry that maybe even this "black" operation, whatever it was, would be too little, too late.

Reconnaissance photos taken in the last couple of days clearly showed the Sandinistas beginning to mobilize their heavy artillery for the move up to the border. The Sandinistas had lined up their guns and fired them across the border into Honduras several times previously, but to no good effect. Without a radio-equipped spotter looking down on the target, there had been no way to adjust the aim, so the shells had fallen randomly in the area around whatever they were trying to hit.

"This time, as you've seen from the intelligence, they've got precise coordinates," Mendoza was saying. "And with those, it's now no problem hiding a spotter up in the hills." Ascher and Gustafson were leaning forward on sofas in the sitting room. Francesca was still in her own bedroom—waiting, Ascher figured. Mendoza was spreading a map of Central America, a Defense Mapping Agency tactical pilotage chart, over the coffee table.

"They're really going to wreck the camp this time," Mendoza said, pointing to the spot in the Río Coco valley. "They're also bringing up their Hinds."

To protect the ground forces, the army's Soviet-made Hind attack helicopters—the world's most heavily armored helicopters; flying tanks, everybody called them—were being moved up to the region. If contra forces tried to attack the fixed-position artillery emplacements, the Hinds could wreck them.

"We had to tell the Hondurans what was coming," Mendoza was saying. "And now they really want us out, forty million dollars or no. We've got to move fast. We've got a plan."

Gustafson nodded.

"First thing when you get back, there are two big things you need to do for us," Mendoza said.

"Sure," Ascher told them. "Just tell me."

"The RIG meets the day after tomorrow, right?" Ascher nodded. "And you guys are supposed to formulate your strategy for dealing with this." Ascher wondered how Mendoza knew that but figured it was an obvious conclusion to draw.

"What you need to do is get the RIG to agree to move the resistance base back into Honduras, right away." He pointed to a spot in the Río Guayape valley, about thirty miles directly north of the border town of Las Trojes. The secret CIA airfield, El Aguacate, was just a few miles north of that.

"How the hell are they going to fight from all the way up there?" Ascher asked.

"We want them fighting in Nicaragua, not sitting in camp in Honduras." Mendoza explained. "This move has two purposes. First, it means our fighters can't easily duck back over the border when they're tired of fighting. It'll be a major effort to get back to camp, so they'll be more likely to stay in the field, which is where we want them.

"Second, if we move them way up here, the Sandinistas can't go in and take the camp out without a full-scale invasion. And we know they're not about to do that. Lining up artillery along the border isn't going to do them a bit of good. This will destroy their operational plan right now and put an end to the border incursions altogether. It'll also keep the Hondurans quiet for a while. This is very important for the cause. Can you sell it to the RIG?"

"I'll do my best," Ascher said, though he didn't quite understand this. Why didn't Mendoza just send the proposal up through channels if it was so important? But Ascher didn't say anything; he wanted to be a team player.

"Now another thing," Mendoza said. "Eric, you want to tell him about the Redeyes?"

Gustafson leaned forward and grinned at Ascher.

"First, congratulations, buddy."

"What do you mean?"

"You really did some good with that tape of Mrs. Carrión and that goon Zelaya."

Smiling, embarrassed, Ascher replied, "Well, when you send good material like that, how can it fail? How'd you get that tape anyway?"

"Just used some of that stuff this little ol' spook gave us," Gustafson said, gesturing to Mendoza. "I guess Zelaya didn't think it too odd to see a Parker ballpoint pen sitting on the kitchen table." Gustafson shook his head and added, "You even got the president to use the tape on TV. Boy, you got some pull up there, don't you." Ascher was blushing.

"Well, listen," Gustafson went on. "See if you can use a little of it for the cause. The Sandis pulled a hell of a stunt. You know they've got their Hind choppers up there at the border. Well, those Hinds are the best pieces of equipment they've got, and our Redeye AAs have already knocked a couple of them down. They don't want to lose any more of them. So you know what they did?"

"What?" Ascher asked.

"Sent some people up and stole our Redeyes."

"Huh?"

"Yeah," Gustafson said, shaking his head. "You've been to the base. You know where the ordnance bunker is, off away from the camp, up the hill. Well, some of our boys must have been asleep at the switch, because the other night the Sandis sent a squad up there that broke in and took all our Redeyes."

"How many?" Ascher asked.

"Two dozen."

"Jesus," Ascher exclaimed. "How the hell did they do that? What would the Sandinistas want with our Redeyes? And why didn't they just blow the place up?"

"Well, we figure they probably didn't have any remote detonation explosives. Besides, if they made all that noise they might not have been able to sneak back home. The Redeyes have been doing the Sandis a lot of harm. They probably wanted them for themselves, took 'em back to Managua as a prize."

"Pretty odd, a squad sneaking up seven miles and hauling away two dozen AA missiles," Ascher said.

"We didn't have the bunker guarded adequately," Mendoza said apologetically. "Late at night, just one man. They just smacked him over the head."

Ascher was frowning.

"Strange things happen in war," Mendoza assured him with a bare smile.

"Anyway," Gustafson continued, "Redeyes can't just be dialed up like M-16 rounds. Our boys need replacements, and fast. We'd appreciate it if you could call DoD and get that taken care of for us. Okay?"

"Sure, okay," Ascher said, hoping they'd get to the more substantive problems soon. He'd never intended to be a high-placed fixer for these guys. He wanted to hear the new plan.

They paused after that and ordered room-service lunch. Francesca joined them and sat next to Ascher, rubbing his knee and then his upper thigh under the little table. Ascher nearly swallowed the toothpick in his unusual Honduran club sandwich.

A bellhop cleared away the plates and left them a pot of coffee.

Francesca went back to her room, and Mendoza plunged right into their plan. This was to be a guerrilla raid quite similar in concept to the Rubén Darío plan last fall, complete with important hostages and lots of media attention. As Mendoza and Gustafson described the proposal in elaborate detail, Ascher was impressed with the planning and the intelligence Gustafson had gathered to make it work. If all went well, nobody would be harmed. Ascher liked that. It would be quite a show.

Certainly all of it was well thought out, but when Mendoza finished, Ascher said, "Raf, I think this is a brilliant plan. But what I really wonder is, with everything that has happened now, isn't this maybe too little, too late?"

Ascher caught the sudden startled look that flashed between Mendoza and Gustafson. But it was gone as quickly as it appeared, and right away Mendoza said, "Even with everything that has happened, I think the long-standing principles of urban guerrilla operations still hold true. And for us it is one of the few things we can do with plausible deniability. The resistance is perfectly capable of coming up with a plan like this themselves. After all, there's a long history of operations of this kind. So the beauty of this plan is that when it's over, we can say it was a surprise to us, too."

Ascher thought about that for a minute, took a sip of coffee, then said, "Okay. I'm in."

"Great," Mendoza said, clapping his hands once. "Now tomorrow you'll tell Paz."

"Huh?"

"First thing tomorrow the three of us are going down to Cascabeles, Paz's special camp, and we want you to give him another pep talk like you did up in Miami."

"Rafael, we can't have any White House fingerprints on this."

"Don't worry, my friend. There is no man in the world more tight-lipped than our Major Paz. You saw that for yourself. And for an important operation like this, it would really help if all of Paz's men got a word of encouragement from you."

Actually Ascher liked playing military commander. It might be fun reviewing the troops.

"Okay," he told them.

"Good," Mendoza said, grinning as he and Gustafson got up to leave. But Ascher stopped him.

"One thing, Raf." Ascher motioned Mendoza back to his chair. "Paz is a Somocista, and if we pull this off, the Sandinistas are going to label this a Guardia, a Somocista, operation. That will ruin the whole effect."

"Terry," Mendoza said in a low, dead-serious tone as he sat back down, "Paz is the only man we have who is trained and trustworthy enough to carry off an operation like this."

"Fine," Ascher said. "Send Paz. He can even be the commander. But send someone else too, somebody clean, who can take the heat, who can give the interviews and everything else, even if he's really only second-in-command to Paz. I feel strongly about this."

Mendoza and Gustafson were looking at each other, expressions grim. But Ascher wondered how in the hell they could not have foreseen this problem. If this operation got the press attention they hoped for and all of it centered on Paz—a notorious former Guardia officer under Somoza who'd even done odd jobs for La Mano Blanca death squads in Guatemala—their grand plan would turn into a major embarrassment.

Somber, Mendoza asked, "What do you have in mind, Terry?"

"Well, let's graft somebody saleable onto this operation. How about that former Sandinista, Venganza, the one who got all the good press when he took that Eaton reporter out on a raid a few months ago? He'd look good."

Mendoza and Gustafson were looking at each other again. Clearly they were not happy.

"Terry," Mendoza said softly, "Venganza's men have never been trained for this kind of operation."

"Then don't use his men. Just send him along as co-commander with Paz."

"I don't know how Paz will feel about that."

Ascher shook his head. He was growing exasperated. "Paz takes orders, doesn't he? Just tell him."

Mendoza and Gustafson glanced at each other again, but then Mendoza slapped his knees and rose from his seat again, saying, "Okay, Terry, you're right. Consider it done." Then he and Gustafson headed for the door.

"So Venganza will be at Cascabeles tomorrow?"

Mendoza and Gustafson stopped. Ever so softly Mendoza shook his head. But then he turned to Ascher and, sounding resigned, said, "Yes, Terry, we'll get Venganza over to Cascabeles tomorrow."

Strange men, Ascher thought as they headed toward the door. But then Mendoza stopped again.

"Oh, by the way. One more thing."

Ascher looked up.

"We're going to need some special equipment for this. Can you put a little bit of cash through your Caymans account that we could use?"

"What money?"

"Well, we were hoping you could lend the 'enterprise' a little money. We're going to be getting all kinds of donors coming to us when it's over, lots of them, and we'll pay you back in full."

"How much are you talking about?"

"I think fifty thousand dollars should do it," Mendoza said matter-of-factly.

"You want fifty thousand dollars?" Ascher asked, eyebrows raised.

"Come on, Terry. It's just a loan. It's for the cause."

"I could pitch in some money from my pension fund," Gustafson said.

Ascher sighed. "No, Eric. I'll do it."

"Great!" Mendoza said.

It was just after two in the afternoon, and they agreed to meet at seven in the hotel steak house, next door to the Monte Carlo Casino. On the way out, Mendoza waved through the doorway to Francesca in the far room. She must have given him some questioning gesture because Mendoza stopped just long enough to give her a brief nod back.

As the door closed behind them, Ascher leaned back and sighed to himself. The work was over. Now he was wondering how to proceed. Should he just jump into bed with Francesca or take her to the bar for a drink first? But in a moment she answered the question. She was leaning in the doorway, smiling at him. She wore a long pink silk robe open halfway down to the belt tied loosely at her tiny waist. It was quite obvious she wore nothing at all underneath, because as she walked over, her grand breasts swayed. Hands on her hips, she stood over him, right between his outstretched legs, and looked down with her electric smile, tangles of shiny hair cascading over her shoulders. Ascher stared back.

Slowly she kneeled between his legs and unzipped his pants. Then she leaned forward, her breasts spilling out of her robe, and looked directly into his eyes as she took him in her mouth with such soft skill that Ascher moaned out loud, thinking: *God, she's a pro.*

For two hours Francesca led Ascher through every facet of

his febrile fantasy, first there on the sofa, then on the floor, then in the bathtub, and finally in her warm bed. They didn't talk much when they finished. Ascher was exhausted. He lay back, fantasizing about bringing Francesca to Washington for a long visit. He imagined showing her his big house, introducing her to envious friends, taking her to glitzy stores, buying her whatever she wanted.

As they lay there, Francesca seemed distracted. She picked at her cuticles or stared up at the ceiling, eyes open wide. As Ascher began to drift off to sleep, he pulled her to him, and for a moment she did lie in his arms, head on his shoulder. But as soon as he was asleep she rolled away.

When Asher woke an hour or so later she was sitting on the stool over by the dresser, pulling on her shoes. She'd already showered and dressed. It was a little before six, and without looking at him she started toward the door.

"Hi," he said softly.

"Oh, hi," she answered, startled as she looked back at him. "Did you sleep well?"

"Yes, very well. Why don't you come back to bed."

She shook her head. "Oh, no, it's late and I want to go down to the casino before dinner. Why don't you come? Maybe we can both become rich." She smiled, barely.

"Okay, wait a minute," he said, climbing naked out of bed. "Let me take a quick shower." But she was already heading for the door.

"See you down there," she shouted over her shoulder as the door closed behind her. Boy, she must really like to gamble.

OLD EXECUTIVE OFFICE BUILDING, WASHINGTON

The RIG agreed right away to move the contra camp up to the El Aguacate river valley.

"Makes sense," General Dayton told Terry. "Good thinking, Terry. This'll leave the Sandis sitting up there with nothing to shoot at. I like it."

Even Ames conceded that "it solves a lot of problems. I think the Hondurans will buy it." But while Ascher was quietly grateful to have accomplished this, he still wondered why Mendoza hadn't sent the suggestion himself.

The next request didn't go down quite so easily. As Ascher explained the problem with the Redeye missiles, Colonel Cater started shaking his head.

"The inspector general's going to have fits over this," he said. "The Sandis walking off with two dozen SAMs? There's going to be an investigation of this for sure."

"I'll take responsibility," General Dayton told him with a wave. "If the inspector general wants to investigate, tell him to come see me. My office will handle it. And in the meantime, get some more Redeyes down to the resistance right away."

"Yes, sir," Cater said.

Right after the meeting, Ascher called Mendoza in Tegucigalpa using the KL-43 computer phone.

"The RIG bought the new camp location," he wrote, "and I have also transferred the $50,000 into the Caymans account. It should be available to you now."

"Wonderful," Mendoza wrote.

"And you will also be getting the new Redeyes shortly," Ascher said.

"Great," Mendoza responded. "Good work, my friend. You really get things done."

"But the DoD inspector general might be sending someone down to ask some questions about the missing Redeyes," Ascher wrote.

"What do you mean?"

"Colonel Cater said this might trigger an investigation. Just be aware."

"We will handle it," Mendoza said.

"Everything else on schedule?" Ascher asked.

"Yes, my friend. According to plan. Your talk with the troops was perfect. They are charged and ready to go, General."

Ascher smiled. He had felt like a commanding general when their helicopter landed at Cascabeles. As he'd stepped to the ground, two dozen Pena de Muerte commandos snapped to attention, lined up in rigid formation. Tropical birds squawked in the trees, and Ascher thought he could hear steam rising from the dark, fragrant earth in the early morning heat.

Paz and Venganza both stepped forward to salute. Nobody else was around, and Ascher had stood in front of them giving the little speech he, Mendoza, and Gustafson had rehearsed on the flight down.

"Men," he had said, "you are being given a very challenging, important, and unusual assignment, the first of its kind in our effort against the Sandinista Communists. Mr. Mendoza and Colonel Gustafson will be telling you about it." He gestured to the two of them, standing off to the side, smiling at each other. Mendoza had told him that senior commanders weren't supposed to get into discussions of precise operational details. "Leave that to us," he'd said.

"We are giving this assignment to you because of your outstanding record and because of the great confidence the president of the United States has in all of you. I am behind you. The president is behind you."

Paz jerked to even stiffer attention with that, Ray Bans pointed at the sky. Venganza stood rigid.

"Listen well to your commanders. We know you will carry out your assignment with great skill and courage. Good luck, and take care."

Mendoza had patted him on the back as they'd walked away. And now, over the KL-43, he wrote: "You were right. Venganza is an important addition to the unit. Preparations are going well. They will exfiltrate right on schedule."

"Good," Ascher wrote. "And how is Francesca?"

"She is well. She thinks of you. She said to tell you she is sorry she did not get to say goodbye properly."

Ascher had been frustrated with their parting. He didn't get a chance to invite her to Washington. After dinner at the Maya steak house, she'd left, saying she had to see some important friends of the movement. She didn't come back that night, and they'd taken off for Cascabeles very early the next morning.

"When this operation is completed, we will celebrate again," Mendoza wrote. "Francesca looks forward to that."

"Me too." And with that they signed off.

In his embassy office, Mendoza didn't even unhook the KL-43. He simply went through the sign-off procedure, then signed on again and dialed Gustafson, who was waiting in his office in Managua.

"Ascher reports that the RIG gave us everything we wanted," he typed.

"Great going. We're rolling!" Gustafson typed back. But Mendoza paused almost a full minute before typing what he next wanted to say.

"You still there?" flashed onto his screen.

"Yes, Eric, I am here. Just thinking for a moment. Listen, everything is going along just as we planned. If all goes well, we will fulfill an important goal for our country, even for the world. It's what we have been talking about for a long time. But, my friend, you know it may turn out that we accomplish our goal at a cost—some personal sacrifice for you and me. With Ascher, we are insulating ourselves as best we can. But with something this big there's bound to be fallout.

"You and I haven't talked about the personal downside risks for both of us, and I want to make sure you have thought about it. It's not too late to turn back."

Gustafson's response came without pause.

"Old buddy, I'm a Marine. I swore to die for my country. Hell, this is nothing. Anyway, when the history of this is written, they are going to give us medals."

"Okay, my friend. I'm with you," Mendoza wrote back. "For me, more than 30 long years in the agency—this is what will make it all worthwhile."

In Washington, Ascher felt pretty good, too. Excited. Then on Friday Art Kutler came by his office for a little visit. He hadn't been here before, and Ascher liked the role reversal, leaning back in his own executive chair, talking to Kutler, his boss at the State Department for several years, from behind his own big desk.

"Quite a nice office, Terry."

"Thanks Art."

"You're doing a good job over here. We're all impressed."

"That's nice of you to say."

Kutler paused, looked away for a second—a signal, Ascher knew, that something was troubling him.

"Terry, what's really behind this business of moving the HQ camp up near to Aguacate?"

"Well, just what we're saying. Gets them out of harm's way, defangs the current Sandinista offensive, and ends those cross-border incursions once and for all so the Hondurans will calm down."

"But did anybody give any thought to the safety-valve effect of having the camp on the border? When the Sandis get upset, they can go up there and knock the contras around a little bit to deal with their own internal political problems instead of really going crazy and doing something stupid they can't pull back from. You move the contras all the way up to the Río Guayape valley, and that safety valve is gone. Who knows what they'll do next time."

"Art, the resistance isn't supposed to be punching bags for the Sandis' political problems. Maybe if they don't have the contras around for that, things will get worse for them at home and they'll be forced into making bargaining concessions sooner."

Kutler looked at Ascher for a moment, head cocked, eyebrows raised. Then he pursed his lips. "Terry, you're not starting to take all this stuff seriously, are you? Force them to the bargaining table and all that?"

"What do you mean, Art?"

"Come on. Be realistic. Don't be one of those people who starts falling for your own rhetoric."

"I don't know what you're talking about."

Ascher really hadn't known what Kutler was talking about. But it worried him. Kutler had caught him once before. The Bahamas treaty. Before coming to the White House, he vividly remembered, Kutler had said to him: "You can't step over the line working with the contras." And he sure as hell didn't want Kutler taking an interest in his work, especially now with this "black" Paz-Venganza raid coming up. If the raid went as planned, he'd be proud to take credit. But if something went wrong . . .

Then in his office the next day he got an unexpected visit. Linda called Ascher over the intercom to tell him: "There's a man here who says he's from the community and needs to see you. He says he's got ID, but he wants to show it to you."

"The community" meant the intelligence agencies, but probably not the CIA. They usually said they were from "the agency."

In a moment the man stood over Ascher's desk and showed him a National Security Agency ID card. Stephen Jasper from the technical services branch.

"I'm here for the KL-43," he said.

"What do you mean?"

"We're supposed to reinventory it. Got the orders right here." He showed Ascher an NSA memorandum calling for "reinventorying" of KL-43 number BR-4297-33. Ascher unzipped his KL-43 case and looked at the government property tag. The number was the same.

"Just a minute." Ascher sent Jasper back out to the lobby while he called Mendoza, using the machine. Mendoza came to the phone right away and hooked up his own computer.

"They want to take this computer back," Ascher typed. "What is going on?"

"SOP, Terry. Deniability. It is better if you are not on any unusual lists, like the KL-43 distribution list, once this op goes down."

"But how will we communicate?"

"We will make other arrangements. It is for the best. Do not worry."

But over the next few days Ascher did worry. Without his KL-43 there was no safe way to call Mendoza. He felt cut off, alone. At the same time he imagined Kutler sitting at his desk over there at State trying to put the pieces together, guessing what he was up to. Ascher was already taking a little more Valium than usual when another blow came.

On Thursday, George Washington University Hospital called after lunch. His father was in intensive care. He'd had another stroke.

Ascher rushed over; it was only a few blocks from the office. The doctor was reassuring. Mr. Ascher could have died, but he was lucky. The blockage had passed through quickly. He was incapacitated for the moment. But the paralysis was from trauma largely, and most of it would pass, maybe in a few days. He might recover fully.

For now though, with tubes running out of his nose, a heart monitor purring beside the bed, and smooth silver-white hair spread out on the pillow above him, Wallace Ascher would have been an unhappy sight to even a stranger. But Ascher took one look and sucked in his breath.

His father was awake and apparently alert. His eyes followed Ascher as he moved around the room. But he was paralyzed, his face frozen in a grimace, a sneer that seemed to communicate utter contemptuous disapproval. Ascher choked, squeezed his father's arm, rushed from the room, and went straight for the water fountain, uncapping his Valium on the way.

Ascher drifted through the two days before the raid only half awake. Saturday night, as the operation was supposed to be getting under way in Managua, he lay alone in his basement video room, gulping brandy, slipping deep into a drugged torpor, unable to focus his eyes as *Apocalypse Now*, his favorite superhi-fi video movie, flashed blaring across the big-screen TV.

CHAPTER
FIFTEEN

NORTHERN NICARAGUA, MARCH 22

SANDINISTA ARTILLERY UNITS WERE ON THE MOVE. Soviet-made KRAZ-255 troop transport trucks were bumping along the shell-pocked roads of the Highlands toward Jalapa, sending campesinos and their donkeys scurrying into ditches. Behind them the trucks pulled D-20 152-millimeter howitzers—five-yard-long guns on wheels. These were the most powerful cannons in Central America. Two dozen of them were being drawn from positions all over the country, along with another dozen D-30s, slightly smaller versions of the same Soviet weapon. All of them were on their way to stations along the Honduran frontier.

When the guns were in place, the Sandinistas planned to point them across the border at the contras' main HQ camp. El Cuartelón was seven miles north, but not far enough. A D-20 could hurl its ninety-six pound shell eleven miles or more. A D-30's range was just a mile less.

For the Sandinista Popular Army, this exercise had grown to be almost routine. When they got up to the Río Coco valley, they knew, they would have to dig new positions for the guns. After each previous "firing range" exercise, contra forces had destroyed the trenches and sandbag revetments just as soon as the Sandinistas withdrew. This time, positioning the weaponry would take longer; in none of the previous exercises had they used so many guns. That's one reason the army needed ten days or more to get ready. But when everything was set, the comandantes knew, they would be able to plaster the contra camp with a withering area-bombardment barrage.

Most of the comandantes were still in Managua, at the Defense Ministry or down in El Chipote, coordinating the complex repositioning of equipment and men. They were still angry about the Blackbird exercise a few days earlier.

The day after, they'd put Minister Zelaya on TV, where with his characteristic curled-lip sneer he'd told an interviewer from an American network, "You imperialist fools make a mistake if you think we are barefoot Indians who are going to crawl into a hole because of a few spy-plane noises. Just watch—it's your mercenary contra clowns who are going to pay for your ignorant misjudgment."

And now, as the comandantes radioed orders to move this howitzer or that Hind helicopter from here to there, some of them flexed their muscles, clenched their teeth, and puffed up their chests under their ribbon-bedecked uniform tunics. Like stock-car drivers gunning their engines before the race, the comandantes were savoring the power they were about to unleash.

But later in the evening, when they started getting the hysterical reports from the northeastern border, their macho bubbles burst. Hurriedly they issued orders in high-pitched voices that betrayed the edge of panic. They told defense positions throughout the country to go on immediate true-invasion alert. And they ordered all the artillery units to turn around and hurry back to protect Managua—to save them.

Earlier that day, four squadrons of B-52 Stratofortress bombers lifted off from a base in Nebraska and climbed to fifty thousand feet. They turned south just off the Pacific Coast and sortied two hundred miles off the coast of El Salvador for fifteen minutes or so. They didn't want to launch too late and arrive over Nicaragua after the Nicaraguans had turned off their radars for the evening. The Sandinistas manned most of their radar installations only about eight hours a day.

Normally, B-52s would be preceded by fighters equipped with radar-jammers and other electronic countermeasures. But for today's mission, Operation Bright Lights, jamming the radars would defeat the purpose.

At eight-thirty in the morning the heavy bombers formed up and headed east, dropping quickly so they were less than five hundred feet up as they roared across the Gulf of Fonseca and then over the marsh just south of the Honduran town of El Triunfo. When they were only a mile or so north of the Nicaraguan border, Sandinista radarscopes suddenly lit up—hence the name Bright Lights—showing multiple targets approaching from the west. Air defense captains up and down the border set off alert horns. Something big was approaching, filling their scopes, though from the radar signature they were not yet sure what it was. It didn't take long to find out.

A B-52 fully loaded with bombs, as these were, weighs almost half a million pounds; four pairs of large Pratt & Whitney jet engines are needed to pull it through the air. The noise is deafening, and the plane itself, 160 feet long with a 185-foot wingspan, is hardly inconspicuous, either on radar screens or thundering overhead. The newer B1-B bombers, in the rare moments when they worked properly, were faster, quieter, and less conspicuous on radar. That's why they weren't used for exercises like this one.

One by one, west to east, the Sandinista border defense stations watched, terrorized, hands over their ears, as more than a dozen B-52s roared past just across the border, trailing four fat black exhaust columns as they pulled up and down at low altitude over the hills, so close that United States Air Force insignia were clearly visible on the wings and fuselage. Cream-colored air-launched cruise missiles could be seen suspended under the wings. And so, one after another, defense station chiefs grabbed radios and sent screaming, hysterical bulletins back to Managua, warning that the vanguard of an awesome full-scale American invasion force was here.

But about sixty miles inland, just over the border from the Nicaraguan town of Santa María, the planes pulled up and loosed their loads of two-thousand-pound bombs on a deserted mountain the Hondurans had designated for target practice. The explosions could be heard for a hundred miles. When all the bombardiers had dropped their bombs the mountain was just a hill. The B-52s reversed course, and still at low altitude, they roared back along the border to the coast.

Managuans could hear the bombing off in the distance, until the heavy booms were drowned out by wailing alarm sirens all over the city. In the streets, soldiers ran from barracks to duty stations, pulling on uniform tunics as they went. Loaded troop trucks rushed back and forth, tires squealing. Tanks lumbered down narrow streets, flattening sidewalk trash piles and knocking over vendors' stands. As they had the day the Blackbirds flew, Managuans rushed into their homes.

In about thirty minutes the streets were deserted, the city quiet, save for the occasional growl of a military vehicle rolling past. Soldiers and AA gunners looked to the sky once again.

An hour passed and then another. Nothing. Again the skies were empty. Now the comandantes were really growing angry. When their intelligence officers told them what had happened—they'd been fooled once again—they cursed and pounded their fists.

If the president had intended to chasten the Sandinistas with the Blackbirds, instead he merely hardened the comandantes' resolve. And if Operation Bright Lights was supposed to scare the Nicaraguans, convince them to abandon their plans to shell El Cuartelón, this operation too had the opposite effect.

The United States had poked a stick into a hornet's nest. In angry, bitter voices, comandantes ordered their artillery units to turn around again and head right back to the border—double-time.

CHAPTER SIXTEEN

MANAGUA, NICARAGUA, MARCH 26

A COUPLE OF MILES FROM THE CENTER OF TOWN, IN A middle-class neighborhood just off Pista Benjamín Zeledon, Comandante Venganza stood in his former mistress's kitchen, giving her a long goodbye kiss as a van waited in the driveway, engine idling. The previous night Venganza had snuck into town in the back seat of a car. None of the soldiers at military checkpoints recognized him. The Americans had given him false papers, eyeglasses, and a fake mustache, and once in Managua, the twenty-four-hour wait had been bliss. He and Celia had spent most of the time in bed. But as much as he hated leaving, it was Venganza who broke the embrace first, eager to climb in the van and get the operation moving. At last, the counterrevolution was taking the initiative.

Venganza had known that the contra Directorate liked the newspaper story about his attack on the caravan down by Wiwilí. Everybody had joked and congratulated him, and even General Arcos, the contras' top military comandante, had patted him on the back. His standing had clearly risen, but even so, Venganza had never expected to be chosen for the role he was to play tonight.

When the CIA flew him over to Cascabeles for the meeting with the man from the White House, he'd been apprehensive at first. He'd had no idea what they would propose. Still, count on the Americans to come up with one more stupid idea. But when Rafael Mendoza and Colonel Gustafson began describing the plan, Venganza hadn't been able to resist breaking into a smile.

Apparently it was Gustafson's idea. Somewhere he had picked up intelligence that Colonel Huber Escalona was coming to Managua for a state visit. As head of the Cuban Foreign Ministry's Americas Bureau, Escalona was the Sandinistas' patron saint.

When Nicaragua ran low on oil, Colonel Escalona arranged a shipment. When the Kremlin grew irritated but refused to say why, Colonel Escalona would find out the reason and let the Directorate know. When new East bloc counterinsurgency weapons became available, Colonel Escalona shipped them to the port of Corinto or Cabezas right away. He'd been the one who arranged the first shipment of Hind attack helicopters. Even three years ago, when Venganza was still in the Sandinista army stationed in Managua, his comandantes had spoken of Escalona's ceaseless patronage in almost reverent tones.

Well, the dinner for Colonel Escalona and his wife was tonight. President Ortega and Minister Zelaya were in Mexico City for a couple of days, and most of the senior comandantes were up at the border, still assembling units and weaponry for their planned offensive against El Cuartelón later in the week. The Sandinistas apparently didn't know that the United States Army was assembling helicopters and troop transport trucks to move the contra camp to its new northern location starting tonight.

Even with the planned offensive only a few days away, Escalona was such an important guest that several senior comandantes had stayed behind to entertain him. They and their wives were hosting an evening at the Foreign Ministry.

"We want you to take all of them hostage," Rafael Mendoza had explained to Venganza, discussing the operation with him privately in the CIA command hut at El Cuartelón. To Venganza it was obvious that the little Cuban was in love with the idea of seizing a prominent Castro government official.

"Hold them for twenty-four hours, demand the release of all political prisoners, and then get the government to supply a plane out at Sandino Airport," Mendoza had told him. "When you fly away, take a couple of the prisoners with you and let them go only when you land in Panama."

It was perfect, Venganza had thought as they spoke—just like Edén Pastora's raid on the National Palace.

Toward the end of the briefing Mendoza had leaned over his desk and confided in him. "Let me be honest with you. Paz is a good man, and his unit is very professional. But he has an image problem, you know. He's a Somocista. It's his unit, so he's the one who is in command until you break into the dining chamber. But then you will become comandante and take over. Okay?"

That had been fine with Venganza. In fact it made this even sweeter, knowing he would take command away from his nemesis at just the moment of glory.

They'd explained it to Paz separately in what seemed like especially long private briefings. Venganza figured Mendoza and Gustafson had to do a lot of selling to convince Paz that it was okay to give up command. But when Venganza talked to Paz later, he had seemed to accept the plan, as best he could tell, given the major's less than voluble manner.

And now it was time. Celia held Venganza's hand even as the van door started to slide closed. Softly, he called to her as they pulled onto the street, but then Venganza leaned back and looked around at the five fighters in the van with him. These were Paz's men. He'd met them in Honduras, and they'd trained together for several days. But Paz's men had also insisted on training several hours a day without him, and he still didn't feel fully a part of the unit. Now, seeing them in these black Special Forces outfits with camouflage paint all over their faces, Venganza couldn't tell one from the other. All of them sat upright, gripping their weapons tightly, and when he nodded to them nobody nodded back, nobody smiled.

The Foreign Ministry was only a mile or so away. One of Managua's best restaurants, Los Ranchos, was around the corner, but the beef shortage was so acute that for the moment, at least, it was closed. Surrounding the ministry's other three sides were dark, empty earthquake fields. The van stopped once more on the way, to pick up another commando. With seven, this squad was only one man short. Then a couple of minutes later, lights out, the driver pulled slowly off the road and onto the far edge of an empty field. The ministry building, bathed in light, was about two hundred yards away.

Venganza stepped out and stood for a moment letting his eyes adjust to the dark. He had binoculars, and before looking at the bright building he turned left to the adjacent field, straining to see if the other vans were there. Sure enough, as he scanned he was able to make out both of them parked side by side, just where they were supposed to be. Then Venganza fixed the binoculars on one spot. Light was barely reflecting off Major Paz's own binoculars pointing back at him. From here the binoculars looked odd, oversized. But when Paz lowered them, Venganza smiled to himself. Even in the dark, Paz had not taken off his *Guardia* Ray Bans.

Then through his binoculars Venganza studied the single-story building. Most of the windows were dark. It was about seventy-five yards long and had an entrance at each end. He'd been in it many times.

Venganza counted four soldiers at this end. There were probably twice as many at the other end, the main entrance. But they were Paz's job. The major had two squads to Venganza's one. After Venganza's squad took out the soldiers here, they'd storm through the back door while Paz and his men poured in through the front.

The security was just as lackadaisical as Colonel Gustafson had suggested. Back here, the soldiers were lounging around, rifles over their shoulders or leaning against the side of the building. They weren't expecting any trouble. There'd never been a guerrilla raid like this in Managua, not since the Sandinistas' own, back before the revolution. Two soldiers were smoking cigarettes, feet propped up on the front bumper of a Mercedes limousine, one of several official vehicles lined up in two rows. Cuban and Nicaraguan flags hung from little poles stuck in holders on the fender. Over by the entrance the other two soldiers leaned against the wall.

Venganza looked at his watch, and as the second hand ticked up to 9:10 he gave whispered orders, sending two commandos straight ahead, toward the cars. Two more he sent off to the right, around the building's end. Across the way he could see Paz dispatching his advance teams, too.

The men heading for the cars ran halfway across the field and then dropped to all fours as they edged into the building's light. The other two skirted the building, staying in the dark.

Venganza whispered to the van driver, "Thank you. You can go now. Be careful." The man didn't answer. Then, waving his remaining two men along with him, Venganza ran toward the building. Ahead he could see that the first team had already made it undetected up to the first line of cars. Venganza and his little squad stopped and set up just outside the building's light. They lay prone and took aim.

The advance teams were supposed to knock the Sandinistas out and tie them up, all quietly. Venganza had managed to convince Mendoza that, for a propaganda raid, the fewer deaths the better. Once they got inside and took their hostages, the place would be surrounded by armed men anyway; leaving these men alive added no additional threat. Still, if his advance men got into trouble, the rest of the squad would open fire, and then they'd have to storm the building instead of sneaking in.

To his left, Venganza couldn't see Paz and his men anymore, which must mean they were in position too. It was all going so well. He checked his rear and saw nothing, except—the van was still back there. The driver hadn't moved. Strange. Why didn't he leave as he was supposed to? Well, that was the driver's problem.

Across the way, Paz crouched with several of his men in the dark. He could see his own five-man advance team under an empty bus parked maybe thirty yards from the main entrance. They too were prone, aim drawn, but unlike Venganza's squad, these men carried high-precision Remington Model 40 marksman's rifles equipped with silencers and twelve-power infrared scopes.

"The man from the White House bought them for you," Mendoza had told Paz with a grin as he handed the rifles over. Money from Ascher's secret Caymans bank account had also paid for the Startron infrared night-vision binoculars Paz was using.

Two Sandinista guards in pressed uniforms stood rigid and alert at the top of the steps on either side of the main entrance, next to a telephone. Four others in fatigues milled about at the foot of the steps and still another was walking a leisurely patrol, now headed toward the back of the building. Paz watched closely as the sentry turned the corner. This was the moment.

Back at Venganza's end, it was over in an instant. Two commandos slid along either side of the Mercedes limousine, giving each other hand signals under the car. Then at the same moment they leapt up with heavy grunts and grabbed the two soldiers, dragging them to the ground, hands over their mouths. Just as they'd been taught, each commando dug a knee hard into his captive's chest, one hand still covering the mouth while the other hand shook a long shiny knife directly over his prisoner's wide-open eyes.

The other two Sandinistas at the back entrance jumped up when they heard the scuffling and the rifles clattering to the ground. They grabbed their weapons but couldn't see their comrades prone in the dirt between the cars, and in that moment of confusion each of them suddenly felt a pistol hard against his own back, then a hand over his mouth. The other advance team quickly bent them face down into the dirt.

Venganza ran forward, beaming, almost effervescent as he whispered: "Outstanding work, men. No one hurt. Perfect. Fast—pull them aside. Tie them up. Outstanding."

Down at Paz's end, the action didn't take much longer. The desultory sentry had been gone around the building less than a minute when Paz saw little Balita, the child-fighter, stick his smiling head around the corner, looking through the dark in the general direction of the rest of the squad. He was waving a bloody knife high over his head, and with that as a signal, the five marksmen opened fire. Their silenced rifles made only slight spitting noises. First they took out the two sentries up beside the telephone, and the other four dropped almost right away. The Sandinistas couldn't really hear the rifles; none of them quite knew what was happening in the couple of seconds before each of them got hit himself. One of them shouted something. It sounded like a name, maybe the name of the soldier falling down beside him. But it wasn't very loud, and he was hit before he could open his mouth again.

As soon as all of them were down, Balita and his men ran around to the foot of the steps and fell on the soldiers. Some of them were still squirming in the dirt, but the fighters drove knives through their hearts with evident relish.

Paz and the rest of his men ran forward out of the dark. The major ducked around the side of the building for a moment and spotted Venganza down at the other end. Both men waved their rifles over their heads and ran to the doors.

A long center hall ran unobstructed from the front door all the way to the back. It wasn't well lit, but cooks, waiters, functionaries, and others would certainly be working and milling around up and down the distance. The attackers had figured there'd be armed guards outside the dining-room doors, exactly halfway down the hall. Inevitably they'd see the commandos coming at them, so the plan was to send two men from each squad rushing forward at full speed to neutralize the guards before they could open fire. For each of them the distance would be only about thirty or thirty-five yards, and the hope was that the attackers would be there before the guards could figure out what was happening. Meanwhile, the rest of the men would move quickly but methodically, dealing with others in the hall along the way.

At the last minute Venganza got an idea. He ordered his advance men to take the uniform tunics from two of their prisoners and put them on over their other clothes. They wouldn't be in full Sandinista uniforms, but Venganza figured the tunics would leave people confused for just long enough.

That done, with the advance men dashing ahead, Venganza and the rest of his men rushed down the hall, ignoring wide-mouthed waiters who got in the way. Anyone who seemed threatening got a sharp rap with a pistol butt in the back of the head, enough to knock him out.

As he ran, Venganza could hear Paz and his men charging in from the other end, but the hall was so dark he couldn't really see them.

Paz sent two attackers charging ahead as well, and with twice as many commandos, the major and his men had time to deal with all the people they passed in the hall. Every one of them got a smashing blow on the back of the head, and it seemed unlikely that some who crashed to the floor would ever get up. Ahead Paz saw one man in uniform and, lightning fast, the major grabbed him from behind. He had already slit the man's throat when he realized it was only a waiter.

Armed men running to the center from both doors, people falling to the floor along the way—all of this set off panic and a few screams. But the advance men got to the dining room entrance in a few seconds, and as it turned out there was only one guard seated outside the doors. When the full squads got there after less than a minute, one of Venganza's half-uniformed men had the guard disarmed, face down on the floor. He and the other advance-team commando were stripping off their Sandinista tunics as Venganza looked at Paz, his face aglow.

"Perfect! Perfect so far," he whispered. "I can't believe it." He slapped Paz on the back, but the major waved him off with a frown and shook his finger at the dining-room door. Venganza motioned to his squad and immediately burst into the room, his men right behind him. As soon as Venganza had turned his back, Paz reached down and grabbed the prostrate Sandinista guard by the hair. He jerked the man's head up and slit his throat with a single stroke.

When Venganza stormed into the room, most of the dinner guests were already standing, linen napkins in their hands. They'd heard the noise outside. Venganza raised his rifle and fired a burst at the ceiling. Plaster fell to the floor in heavy chunks. One of the women screamed.

"All of you, away from the table, hands on your heads," Venganza shouted as his men, weapons up, spread out around the table.

A moment later Paz and his men burst through the other door. Now nineteen commandos, dressed in black from head to toe, trained automatic rifles on about ten men and women. Most of the men wore white long-sleeved guayaberas and dark pants; the women were in simple gowns. The men looked grim and furious, lips pursed, eyes narrowed. A couple of the women clung to their husbands' arms. One was whimpering, two others stood quietly. For almost a minute all of them just glowered at each other.

Venganza lowered his rifle and climbed on a chair to look over his captives. Over here was the deputy foreign minister, there the vice president. And at the center place, Colonel Escalona stood in green military fatigues, medals hanging from red ribbons pinned over his chest. The Cuban's teeth were clenched, his eyes cold. But Venganza wasn't interested in Escalona. His eyes locked on the one man here he knew well: General Arcoza, hero of the revolution, member of the Sandinista Directorate, and Venganza's former comandante and mentor of years ago.

Arcoza spent most of the revolution in one of Somoza's prisons; he might even have been one of Major Paz's prisoners. But Somoza freed Arcoza along with the others when Edén Pastora seized the National Palace in 1978. Arcoza's fall into communism helped persuade Venganza to switch sides. So, all in all, Venganza found it fitting, even ironic, that the general was one of his captives tonight.

Arcoza looked back at Venganza quizzically, head tilted slightly. Venganza reached up and took off his stocking cap, using it to wipe some of the black and green camouflage paint off his face.

Suddenly Arcoza's eyes widened. "Lieutenant García," he murmured.

"No, I am Comandante Venganza now," he said with a cold smile, and then to the group at large Venganza shouted, "Ladies and gentlemen, you are now prisoners of the counterrevolution." Several of them gasped.

"We have certain demands. As long as you comply, none of you will be hurt. We have a list of prisoners, and you will . . ." But Venganza stopped in midsentence because suddenly at a hand signal from Paz all the commandos moved to the table and began grabbing the hostages by the arm, pulling and jerking them to the far wall.

"No, no!" one of the women screamed as all of them were lined up, faces against the plaster, hands on their heads. Commandos poked rifles in their backs.

"None of you will be hurt if you meet our demands," Venganza repeated, his manner less certain now. He jumped down from the chair.

Grabbing General Arcoza and his wife by their arms, Paz ordered, "Balita, take those two over to the side." Pointing at the general's wife, a large, quivering middle-aged woman, Paz said, "I hope this time, *this* one has a strong heart. Make sure not to hurt her." As Balita and another fighter pulled the two of them away, Venganza grabbed Paz's elbow.

"Major," he whispered, his voice hard, "just what the hell are you doing?"

Paz glared at Venganza, pulled his arm away, and then barked an order: "Now!"

Immediately the fighters backed fifteen feet from the wall and began spraying the hostages with automatic weapon fire, waving their rifles back and forth. Only a couple of people had time to scream before they slumped, groaning, into bloody pools. The white wall behind where they had stood them was pocked with more than one hundred bullet holes and streaked with sliding smears of blood.

The firing lasted fifteen or twenty seconds, and Venganza stood stunned. He didn't move as one fighter turned Escalona's corpse over with his toe. Clearly the Cuban was already dead, but the fighter pulled out his pistol and fired a single shot through Escalona's forehead. Off to the side, General Arcoza's wife broke into a high-pitched warbling scream.

Venganza grabbed Paz's right arm in a tight grip and shook it hard. With his chin thrust forward, slowly he hissed: "What the fuck have you done? You Guardia bastard, you are insane!"

Paz turned to Venganza and with his left hand pulled the Beretta pistol out of his belt. He raised it to Venganza's chest. Venganza looked down, eyes round.

For Paz, still this did not seem right. Killing all the Communists was one thing. That was what Mendoza had ordered, and he did it with pleasure. But when the CIA man told him he'd also have to shoot a fellow comandante—even if he was a former Sandinista Communist—well, that was different. His men didn't understand either. During the first pre-operation run-through, they'd asked him: "Why? Venganza is a hero. This must be a mistake. Why?"

His men were so disturbed that Paz had brought himself to ask Mendoza for an explanation—something he'd never done with a comandante before. All the Cuban would say was: "I know this is hard for your men. I can't tell you everything now. But you and the Pena de Muertes are setting off a course of events that will throw the Communists out of your country very soon. You can tell your men they will be heroes. But for now, you'll just have to trust me."

That hadn't eased many minds among his troops. But then that man from the White House had come to Cascabeles. He'd told them they were carrying out orders from the president—from the commander in chief of the U.S. Marines.

The Americans knew best. He'd never disobeyed an order before, not even one. And he wasn't going to start now.

Paz fired three quick rounds through Venganza's heart. His mouth still open, his hand still grasping the major's arm, Venganza crumpled to the floor. Even in death his eyes stared up at Paz in disbelief, but Paz gave the body a last vicious kick—for the president. And then on to the last of the plan.

"Everybody start back to the vans except Coyote and Tigrillo," he shouted. "You three"—pointing to a cluster of fighters—"take Comandante Vengan—no, Lieutenant García with you." The men lifted the comandante's body and joined the others trotting out the doors.

Paz walked over to Balita, who held General Arcoza and his screaming wife at gunpoint on the floor. Staring up at Paz's face, still covered with camouflage paint, Arcoza showed no recognition or fear, just clench-teethed contempt. Beside him his wife was sobbing. Her whole body jiggled. To Coyote and Tigrillo, Paz said, "Take hold of the woman," and each of them grabbed one of her arms from behind. She sucked in her breath. Her head flopped forward, chin on her chest, as she began to moan.

Balita crouched behind the general, grinning at Paz as he repeatedly jabbed Arcoza hard in the back with his pistol. Paz squatted two feet in front of him and looked directly in his face. Arcoza stared back, eyes narrow slits, breath hissing through his nostrils. His head trembled with rage.

Slowly Paz reached up and took off his stocking cap, and at the sight of his orange hair, Arcoza started. In almost a whisper he asked, "Major Paz?"

"That is right," Paz said, enunciating carefully in his leering Guardia voice. "I am Paz. Major of the Guardia."

And with that, Arcoza's wife watching, Paz pulled his knife from its leg sheath, grabbed the general by the hair, jerked back his head, and with little ceremony slit his throat.

The woman's moans had turned to wailing howls as Paz and his men walked swiftly to the door.

CHAPTER
SEVENTEEN

THE WHITE HOUSE, WASHINGTON, MARCH 28

THE UNITED STATES GOVERNMENT HAD NO CONNEC-
tion with the guerrilla action in Managua Saturday night.
All questions should be directed to the Nicaraguan resistance.

Normally the morning White House press briefing began with
a calm reading of the president's schedule for the day, followed
by announcements of trips or other special events. But this
morning, as Fred Hillard stepped into the briefing room he
cringed, wincing from the force of the shrill, hostile questions
hurled at him even before he'd reached the podium. Television
cameramen, far more of them than usual, moved in close and
stuck their lenses in his face. Some reporters stood in front of
their seats shouting and waving their hands as if they were
throwing tomatoes.

"Has the United States government apologized for slaughter-
ing all those people?"

"Who's responsible for this?"

"Who ordered this?"

The swarm of questions was so loud, so angry, that it was hard
to tell who was speaking—or shouting. Ignoring protocol, Hillard read the prepared statement right away, but the disclaimer
only seemed to make the hostile swarm angrier.

"Oh, come on!" a UPI reporter burst out. "The contras don't

do anything without checking with the United States first. Remember the mining of the harbors in Nicaragua? Remember the CIA assassination manual? Remember the arms sales to Iran? Remember all the lies since then? The White House lied and said the United States didn't have anything to do with any of those things either—"

"Don't tar us with the misdeeds of previous administrations," Hillard burst out. That always made him angry. But then he returned to his prepared statement.

"We have checked with all the relevant agencies and officials of the U.S. government," he shouted, holding up his hands to fend off the angry questions. "And to a man they are as surprised by this as you are. The resistance leadership is conducting an inquiry to find out what happened."

"You mean the contras didn't even know what their own men were doing?" asked the Associated Press correspondent.

"We don't know yet," Hillard said. "This very well could have been a renegade unit, but it's too early to know for sure."

Near the back, Eaton smiled to himself. He didn't have all the answers either, but he was certain no one here knew as much as he did.

The Sandinistas announced the massacre Sunday afternoon. President Ortega had been in Mexico but flew back right away and read a brief but dramatic statement on national television. With dark circles under his eyes, he looked as if he'd been up all night. His voice trembled and choked as he struggled to control his rage.

"Mercenary terrorists working for the president of the United States carried out an unprovoked massacre Saturday night, murdering our honored state visitor, Minister Escalona, Vice President Herrara, and General Arcoza, esteemed member of the Directorate and hero of the revolution. They were assassinated alongside other important and honored members of the Sandinista Front as they sat peacefully together at a state dinner. The only survivor, General Arcoza's widow, is hospitalized in shock. But she has managed to tell us of the terrorists, led by a notorious and murderous Somocista Guardia officer."

Here Ortega laid down his text and stared into the camera.

"The innocent victims of this senseless slaughter were unarmed. Among them were four heroic women gunned down in cold blood. All of them are revered martyrs of the revolution. The nation grieves with their families.

"The Nicaraguan people will not let this tragedy pass without acting. The people are now preparing to respond."

The camera lingered on his cold face for several seconds, and not even the overdubbed English translation diminished the dark drama. The footage had been aired on all three U.S. network news shows Sunday night.

As soon as Ortega finished, most of the news shows put on U.S. government officials, Cubans, Nicaraguans, and other experts who gave their views, explaining how deeply this attack would likely touch the sensibilities of the Nicaraguan people—especially if it had in fact been carried out by a former Guardia officer. No one in the United States, it seemed, could explain what happened. And clearly no one approved.

ABC caught Minister Zelaya getting off a plane at Sandino Airport. He set a black satchel down on the tarmac, and his little pellet eyes squinted as he looked straight into the lens, saying, "Last night's bloodbath reveals the venal snakelike character of your country. For America now, there can be no redemption. Even the fevered fires of hell are too good for you and your people."

Another network interviewed Directorate Chairman Alfonso Coronel on the balcony of the Miami condominium the CIA had bought him. He put his hand to his heart as he told of his shock and horror.

"Renegades," he insisted, shaking his oily little head. "Had to be renegades. My men would never do such a stupid thing."

Even the CIA put out an unusual public statement denying any knowledge or responsibility.

Whoever arranged this operation, all the commentators agreed, must have intended to enrage and provoke the Sandinistas. But to what end?

Sunday afternoon, Eaton's weekend editor had called from the office as soon as news of the attack came over the wire. He read Eaton a short, cryptic Reuters story. Right away Eaton called Paladino at home in Tegucigalpa. His wife said he was at camp. No wonder, Eaton thought. Actually Paladino was at the new Río Guayape valley HQ camp, helping get the place set up. But he called when he got home that night.

"Chris, we don't know how this happened. Our Directorate did not approve this. It is a terrible thing. The Sandinistas cannot let this pass. Whoever ordered this had to know that. I'll tell you, the CIA had to be behind this."

"Why?"

Two weeks ago, Paladino explained, his friend Venganza had suddenly been summoned over to Cascabeles for a meeting with the CIA.

"When he came back he was all excited. He said the CIA had given him a new assignment. He said something like 'At last we are going to take the initiative.' He was a little worried about the people he was going to be working with, but he said it could change the course of the war. I asked around, and no one on the Directorate was informed of it."

"Well, what's Venganza say now?"

"He hasn't come back."

"So you think this attack was what he was talking about?"

"I don't know, but I'm afraid it was. It must have gone bad."

Eaton knew the next question stepped beyond what he was supposed to ask; Paladino had always refused to give away the identity of the commando squad that worked for the CIA, saying it would set the fighters up for Sandinista retribution. But Eaton tried anyway. He and Paladino were friends. Jorge told him things he didn't give anyone else. Now was the time Eaton really needed him.

"Jorge, who's this notorious Guardia officer Ortega was talking about? Is that who Venganza was working with?"

On the other end, Paladino didn't answer right away. Finally he whispered, "Yes."

Eaton waited. After another pause, Paladino told him: "His name is Major Paz, and he's not back either. The Directorate's looking for all of them. Between you and me, I've been warning them about Paz for a long time. Paz has to be the one behind this. His unit reports directly to the CIA. We don't really control him."

"I got to know Venganza a little on that trip to Wiwilí last fall," Eaton said. "I don't think this is his work. Is this Paz character a renegade?"

"No, that's the funny thing. He's a tough dedicated killer, an assassin. But he's anything but a renegade. His reputation is that he follows orders, exactly, every time. We don't understand. Nobody could order so bloody and foolish a thing as this, unless he wanted to start a war or something. It must have gone bad."

Eaton's bureau chief, Walter Abel, had come into the office on Sunday, as soon as he heard word of the attack in Managua. He took his weekends seriously, so Eaton knew that Abel realized this was not just another small development in the long-running contra story. His manner drove the point home. The firm-set jaw and low, carefully modulated tone meant Abel believed he was making decisions of consequence.

"Because of you we've been out front on this story from the beginning," he said, standing over Eaton's desk, looking over Eaton's head toward the far wall. "We're at the edge of something here. I can feel it." He looked down now.

"I want us to stay out front. Push. Push hard. But be careful. It's a fragile moment, and I don't want us to precipitate something. Do you know what I mean?"

"Yes," Eaton said, though he didn't really.

"I don't want to go with anything that is not absolutely rock-solid. Some of your stories have gotten knockdowns recently. You've got to be careful."

Eaton sighed. Abel had been one of the few newspaper editors he'd met who thought beyond the headline of the moment and tried to anticipate social and political consequences. That was fine. But apparently it wasn't the only concern on his mind right now. He was still worrying about Eaton's reporting.

Yes, as most people in Washington knew, White House knockdowns often were carefully worded indirect denials intended to disguise the fact that the story was essentially true. Nonetheless, when the spokesman for the president of the United States stood up before national television cameras and declared that a story was wrong, it had an effect on even the most wizened and cynical editors. That was especially true since the rest of the White House press corps, the reporters who didn't have the story in question, usually gloried in reporting the knockdowns in their own follow-up pieces.

After several hard knockdowns, few editors could fail to worry—and doubt. And small newspapers were especially vulnerable. At *The New York Times* and *The Washington Post*, editors could lean back in their thick leather chairs, arms crossed, and shrug away the knockdowns, knowing that most readers believed that the big-time papers had unique access and special sources. What they printed must be true. But when little papers, like New World's, broke a big story, it was always a surprise. White House denials were easier to accept. So editors like Abel couldn't escape the questioning looks they got from their colleagues at the Press Club bar.

As Eaton sat at his computer Tuesday afternoon, Abel stopped by again and said, "This Nicaragua thing's spiraling down so fast I'm afraid of where it might end. Let's think carefully about what we write."

BY CHRISTOPHER EATON
NEW WORLD NEWS SERVICE

WASHINGTON—A special contra commando unit trained and directed by the Central Intelligence Agency carried out the bloody attack at a state dinner in Managua Saturday night that resulted in the deaths of four Nicaraguan government officers, their wives and a visiting Cuban official.

Although the United States government and the contra leadership today disclaimed any responsibility and suggested that the attack had been carried out by contra renegades, sources in the government and the contra movement said a special American-trained unit headed by "Major Paz," the nom de guerre of a former National Guard officer under President Somoza, carried out the attack.

An informed source said Major Paz and his Pena de Muerte (Death Penalty) commandos have been working under the immediate direction of CIA officers in the region, although it is not entirely clear what role, if any, the CIA had in this operation. In Washington, the CIA issued an unusual disclaimer denying any responsibility for the attack. Officials said the contra leadership cannot explain it either.

The contra Directorate "doesn't really control Paz," an informed source said. "His unit reports directly to the CIA." This source and others said that Major Paz is well known for following orders precisely, without elaboration.

For some time the contras have been trying to carry out urban guerrilla raids. Some previous plans, never carried out, have included schemes to take senior Nicaraguan government officers hostage, as the Sandinistas did during their own revolution in the late 1970s.

If that was the plan this time, a senior contra officer said, "it must have gone bad."

He and others said the contras and the American officials involved in the program were waiting anxiously to see how the Sandinistas would react.

"Having a former Guardia officer kill a visiting Cuban and a Sandinista war hero—in Nicaragua today that's just about the most inflammatory thing that could happen," a senior American official said. . . .

This time, the White House didn't comment on Eaton's story, either to confirm it or to knock it down. Eaton was relieved. He didn't want any more accusatory looks from Abel.

"Nobody here knows what happened yet," Leslie told Eaton over the phone from her office Tuesday morning. "I don't think they want to deny your story and then find out it was true."

"Are they giving Fred Hillard any press guidance to read?"

"Not from here at the NSC," she said. "We just don't know. Gotta go now. We're having a meeting."

A few feet away, General Dayton was ushering José Cristovar, the NSC specialist for Latin America, and Roger Strauss, the CIA's deputy director for operations, into his office. Leslie hurried in after them to take notes. The meeting was already beginning, and nobody took the time for pleasantries.

"General, this is very, very serious," Cristovar said. "No matter how this happened or who's really behind it, the Sandinistas blame it on us. Colonel Escalona was the Sandinista's greatest patron. And General Arcoza, well, he was a living symbol of the revolution. And slitting his throat with his wife watching, well . . ." He shook his head.

"The Sandis have to respond," Strauss insisted. "Yesterday afternoon there were large street demonstrations in Managua. They weren't Sandinista propaganda extravaganzas. We think they were truly spontaneous."

"They don't believe our denials?" Dayton asked, already knowing the answer. Both men shook their heads.

"So what are they going to do?"

"We don't know yet," Strauss said. "Their forces are still up at the border, and as you know they fired a few rounds at El Cuartelón Sunday afternoon, before they figured out that it had been evacuated. But they haven't sent out any new operational orders yet. For now they're just sitting there. But they are on full alert status, and they've called up reserves too. We just can't figure out who or what they're going to strike."

"Maybe now they really are going to march up to Austin," Cristovar joked, repeating the facetious wisecrack liberal congressmen sometimes used to rebut bloated arguments about the Sandinista military threat. Today nobody laughed.

"What do we do?" Dayton asked.

"My recommendation, sir, is sit tight for now, until we see what they've got in mind."

UNITED STATES EMBASSY, MANAGUA, NICARA-GUA

Later that day, in the embassy's intelligence wing, the NSA computer printer spit out a decoded message intercepted from the Sandinista military.

All the army's mechanized units—more than two hundred Soviet T-55 and PT-76 tanks, plus BM-21 multiple rocket launchers, fuel tankers, armored personnel carriers, and related full-scale assault armor—were being mobilized and ordered to join the forces at the Honduran border. Additional Hind helicopter gunships and Hip troop transport helicopters were already arriving at airfields up near Ocotal.

Their orders: "Locate counterrevolutionary forces. Do not take prisoners. Do not pull back until ordered from central command. Engage the enemy and fully destroy all installations, camps, and placements, wherever they are found."

Details followed. These orders, unlike those for previous strikes against contra camps, were sweeping, unequivocal directives for a full-scale, scorch-the-earth assault. But it wasn't just the aggressive tone that caused all the alarm and the pre-crisis emergency management meetings at the White House in Washington.

The problem was that, now, at Terry Ascher's suggestion, all the contra "installations, camps, and placements" had been moved thirty miles north of the border, deep inside Honduras.

CHAPTER EIGHTEEN

"'M SORRY, MR. ASCHER, BUT MR. MENDOZA STILL has not returned to the office."

"But hasn't he gotten my messages?" Ascher was shouting at the secretary. The line to Tegucigalpa was fading as they spoke.

"I'm sure Mr. Mendoza will call you back as soon as he returns."

"Where is he?"

"Mr. Ascher, this is an open line."

"But . . . " The connection went dead, as it often did. This time, though, Ascher wondered if the woman had hung up.

Shorn of his KL-43 computer-phone, Ascher had no secure way to talk with Mendoza, even if he did call back. Calling Gustafson in Managua was out of the question. They had no official relationship, and the call would leave a trail certain to catch up with them. Ascher didn't know what to do. He'd even tried sending a short, ambiguous State Department cable:

RAFAEL MENDOZA, FIRST SECRETARY,   MARCH 28
   POLITICAL OFFICE
UNITED STATES EMBASSY, TEGUCIGALPA, HONDURAS
   IMPORTANT YOU CONTACT T. ASCHER, EXECUTIVE OF-

FICES, EOB-346, WASHINGTON, AS SOON AS POSSI-
BLE.   WHITE HOUSE COMMUNICATIONS SECRETARIAT

But that had gone unanswered too. The emergency RIG meeting was less than an hour away, and Ascher was pacing the office, unable to concentrate on anything for more than a few
seconds at a time. Now not even the Valium was helping. Linda
had come in a couple of times, looking worried, asking if there
was anything she could do. He'd gestured her back out. God,
how could it have gone so wrong?

On Sunday morning Ascher had woken up with a bad hang-
over and a bleary-eyed sense of dread. He'd watched the morning
TV talk shows in his den, sitting forward in his lounge chair.
Nothing. Maybe the raid hadn't gone off after all. Instead of disappointment Ascher felt relief. But then about three in the afternoon Linda called. She was at the office, as usual, trying to catch
up.

"Something's happened down in Managua," she told him.

"What is it?"

"I don't know, but somebody from down the hall"—the National Security Council—"said there was some kind of big contra
incident, and President Ortega is supposed to go on TV to talk
about it in a little while."

Washington television stations played old movies on Sunday
afternoon, so he first heard about the massacre on all-news radio.

"Holy shit," he muttered to himself and right away headed
to the bathroom for another Valium. He turned off his answering
machine and didn't answer the telephone, though it started ringing at about four and didn't stop until late into the night. If he
hadn't had so many phone extensions all over the house, he
would have simply unplugged them.

Monday he got into the office a little early, before eight, and
already three message slips lay on his blotter, two from Richard
Christopher.

"Call right away," they said.

That scared him, but he let out a long sigh when he saw that
the third message was from his father. He was still in the hospital
but recovering rapidly. God, how was he going to explain himself
to Wallace Ascher? He decided not to think about that now and
called Christopher.

"You know anything about this?" Christopher asked as soon
as he came on the line. His tone was cold, accusatory.

"Not a thing, Rich. This is terrible. What do you hear?"

"Not a damn thing. We've got to get to the bottom of this and fast. I want to know who did this, whether any of our people were in on this. And I don't want to read about it in the papers first. You know our people down there, the agency people, right?"

"Yeah, somewhat."

"Well, I want you to get to the bottom of this, find out what happened, and report to me as soon as you know. Understood?"

"I'll try, Rich."

He needed to talk to Mendoza, and not just to find out what had gone wrong. He had to know the cover story so they didn't cross each other up. Finally, Monday afternoon, he'd called Basham over at the agency.

"So you wanted to send the barefoot boys into Managua for a guerrilla raid, huh?" Basham sneered. Ascher tried to ignore it.

"George, do you know what happened?"

"Yeah. Your boys fucked up, that's what."

"No, I mean how'd this happen. Have you been able to talk to Mendoza at the embassy?"

"We got a cable from him yesterday saying he was going down to Río Guayape to ask some questions. We haven't heard back."

"Well, what do you think?"

"I think your half-assed ideas about how to move this little war forward with an 'urban raid' got into the newspapers and gave those chili peppers some bright ideas. I think they sent some of their apes down there for a 'raid,' and the minute they ran into the tiniest bit of difficulty they did the only thing they know how to do—killed everybody in sight. That's what I think. And now we've got one hell of a mess on our hands, buddy boy."

If that was the story everyone settled on, Ascher would take only indirect blame. It could be worse. But surely with a crisis of these proportions the United States government would find out what really happened. He needed to know what Mendoza was going to say when he got back to Tegucigalpa. What if Ascher said the wrong thing?

The RIG meeting was postponed to the evening.

"Developments" was the only explanation from General Dayton's office. This time they met in the West Wing, the Roosevelt Room, across the hall from the Oval Office. Dayton presided, sitting at the end of the table. Teddy Roosevelt's Nobel Peace Prize sat on the marble mantel over his shoulder.

Christopher sat next to Dayton. Basham was there, but so was his supervisor, Strauss, the CIA's deputy director for operations.

"As all of you know," Strauss began, "the Sandinistas are massing two mechanized infantry divisions in Nueva Segovia alongside the forces they already have there, preparing for a thrust into Honduras to take out the resistance camp. And as you also know, the resistance HQ camp is now about thirty miles inland." He paused, and Ascher saw that Christopher was scowling at him.

"Well, here's the latest," Christopher said. "General Hodel over at NSA called the president this afternoon to read him a message just intercepted, sent from Managua to President Suarez in Honduras. I don't have the text with me, but in essence, President Ortega was notifying President Suarez that because of the massacre, the Nicaraguan military has no choice but to enter Honduran territory to retaliate. Ortega is asking Suarez not to take this as an act of aggression against Honduras."

"Rich," Ames said, "there are significant populated areas between the border and Río Guayape."

"I know." Christopher glowered at Ascher again. "Ortega is promising not to bother any Hondurans encountered on the way, but he's also saying this is the price Honduras has to pay for harboring the contras. So the real question now is how we are going to respond."

"The Nics are going to have a hell of a time," Colonel Cater said, shaking his head, looking down at the table. "There's only one road through all those mountain passes, and it doesn't even go all the way. They're going to have to send those old tanks up single file, lids open, drivers' heads sticking out, because T-55s aren't air-conditioned, and they've got to stop every couple of hours to refuel. Hell, we could take out that column of tanks in about twenty minutes without one single casualty. With the new F-5 fighters and TOW II missiles we gave them, even the Hondurans could—"

"Colonel," General Dayton interrupted, holding up a hand. Startled, Cater looked up, displaying his full array of shaving scars. Dayton told him, "Suarez called the president a few hours ago to say he does *not* want United States military involvement."

Then Christopher said, "The president met with the congressional leadership an hour ago. They were unanimous on both sides of the aisle. Congress would not support any direct use of

United States forces here unless specifically requested by the Honduran government. And none of this business of twisting their arm till they give us the request.

"The leadership from our side of the aisle was adamant," he went on, shaking a finger. "They think our party would get creamed in the next election if we attacked the Nicaraguans now. Remember—they're responding to a highly unpopular *massacre* by United States–supported forces, and as you may know, De-Salles's latest polling data show that the American people over-whelmingly disapprove of the 'raid.' " Christopher strung out that word as he gave Ascher a stare meant to shrivel.

"Terry," he said after a pause, "have you gotten anywhere fig-uring out how all of this happened?"

"Well, I don't have any firm answers." Ascher was straining to keep his voice even. "But I think it's likely that certain contra elements, frustrated by the progress they've been making, took up an idea that has floated around in public." At that Basham raised his face to the ceiling, opened his mouth, and rolled his eyes.

"I think they planned and carried out a raid that went bad, and somehow they wound up killing the people they were sup-posed to take hostage."

"Well, it doesn't matter for now," Christopher said waving his hand. "It's done, and now we have to deal with it. The presi-dent has made his decision. He met with the Cabinet and the National Security Council this afternoon and decided the United States will not become involved. We will help the Hondurans ferry troops to the area and provide whatever logistical assis-tance they may request. But that is all."

He stopped and looked at each man around the table.

"And now here's what we need you to do. George and Terry, when the Nicaraguans get up to Río Guayape, we want them to find empty camps. Get the resistance out of there. Let the Sandinistas blow up some empty buildings, then go home. We want the whole thing over with as fast as possible. Understood?"

Both men nodded.

"Win, how long do you project it will take the Sandis to get up to Río Guayape?"

"Two days, max," Colonel Cater said. "Maybe a day or two more once they get up there, if the camps are empty and they don't find any resistance, and then two more days, give or take, getting out."

"Okay, hold your breath, gentlemen," Christopher said.

"Let's see if we can pull through this next week without getting into a war."

SOUTHERN HONDURAS

The Honduran army kept an eight-hundred-man infantry battalion just outside Azacualpa, the little mud-street village at the end of the only hard-surface road leading up from the Nicaraguan frontier. If the Nicaraguan army hoped to attack the Río Guayape camp, they'd have to roll their tanks right past the little Honduran base. In that event, the battalion's orders were unambiguous: Stand clear.

To American intelligence, it seemed that President Suarez simply wanted to get the Nicaraguan "invasion" over with as quickly as possible. To do that, he was going to let a foreign army march deep into his country and out again, unmolested.

"Serves them right," Suarez spat at a Honduran reporter who asked the president how he felt about the Sandinistas' plan to destroy the contras. Nobody, not even the Sandinistas' enemies, liked the idea of American mercenaries shooting unarmed men and women sitting quietly together at dinner.

The main armored elements of the Nicaraguan army crossed the border Thursday, just five days after the massacre. They cranked up engines at dawn but didn't manage to get onto the Honduran highway six miles north until late afternoon. Bulldozers had to precede the tanks and trucks; there was no direct road link between the little Nicaraguan town of Teotecacinte south of the border and Cifuentes, Honduras, to the north. So the bulldozers cleared a wide path through the pine trees and brush.

Behind them rolled an assortment of troop transports and armored vehicles, including about almost two hundred vintage T-54 and T-55 main battle tanks. They were Soviet-made World War II–era diesels, similar to the Sherman tanks U.S. forces used to use, and several of them broke down on the way. But with a few fits and starts the rest made it noisily to the highway and turned right, leaving tread marks in the hot asphalt as they lumbered slowly north, belching clouds of exhaust.

The Sandinista soldiers ignored the few curious Hondurans who stood beside the road watching them pass. This part of the country was lightly populated—the last census showed only about thirty-five residents per square mile—and most of those people had been cleared out. The armored column had made it only about ten miles north of the border before it started growing dark. So they pulled off the road and made camp.

Up north just before dusk, three American government employees who wouldn't say what agency they worked for drove up to a field adjacent to the new contra camp in a large van that pulled a flatbed trailer. The van's roof bristled with antennas, and they parked it next to the helicopter landing zone.

"We're down from Aguacate" was all they would say to the contra comandante who walked up to inquire. "The Directorate knows." The comandante stood and watched as the three of them wheeled what looked like an oversized model airplane off the back of the flatbed. About six feet long with a twelve-foot wingspan, it was painted in brown-and-green camouflage on top, white underneath.

"An Aquila," the men explained to the contra, but it was clear the name meant nothing to him.

Aquilas were RPVs—remotely piloted vehicles. Drones. The men set this one on the ground, and one of them stayed outside to watch as the other two climbed in the back of the van and sat at a console. In a moment, the drone's rear propeller started up. The Aquila turned south, then started bumping along over the grass, lifting off after taxiing about fifty yards. It ascended quickly to an altitude of about three thousand feet and headed south toward the Sandinista camp.

The third American joined his fellows in the back of the van, and the comandante stuck his head in the door.

"Can I watch?" he asked. The men nodded. They were looking at a large black-and-white television monitor set into a console of buttons, dials, and little lights. The drone was broadcasting a wide-angle TV picture from its underbelly camera as it flew along, and to the left of the television monitor a videocassette recorder was taping the transmission.

In less than ten minutes the Aquila was right over the Sandinista camp. The Americans adjusted its course, and from the TV picture they could see the drone beginning to circle. It was almost dark now, but the monitor showed tents and even individual soldiers. One of the men at the console was taking notes.

"I see artillery, mobile D-20s, more than one hundred tanks," one of them noted. "Getting dark."

"Switching to IR," another of them said. He flipped a switch, and the infrared camera on board the drone took over. The picture on the monitor broke up for a second, then reappeared, only this time it showed dark patches and bright spots, heat sources. Most of the heat sources were men, hundreds and hundreds of them.

"I'd say five battalions, maybe six," one of the men said. But then suddenly a large bright spot appeared in the center of the screen.

"Uh-oh. A SAM," one of the men warned. "Say goodbye."

The Sandinistas had fired an SA-7 surface-to-air missile at the slow, defenseless drone, and as the four of them watched, the missile soared straight up at the camera, filling the screen until finally they saw the tip of the missile, and then the drone popped off the air.

The comandante looked shocked, but the Americans were nonchalant.

"Happens all the time," one man said as he turned off the VCR. "Anybody asks, we just say the equipment malfunctioned. We got what we came for, and RPVs are expendable. Better an RPV than a pilot."

"Gotta go now," another said, ushering the comandante out the back. "Need to get this information to your Directorate. You got a pretty formidable attack force coming up your way. You guys gotta get out of here."

The contras had already begun "dispersing," to use the word the Americans had suggested. They'd grabbed what they could and fled to no-one-knew-where. By morning all of them were supposed to be gone.

The Honduran base beside the road at Azacualpa had been emptied; the general staff officers in Tegucigalpa said they didn't want to offer "a provocation." With U.S. help, the Hondurans were setting up a special command HQ in a field a few miles west of Azacualpa, out of harm's way. The relocated Honduran battalion was charged with standing by to defend the little town in case of trouble. But they were to do nothing more.

All in all, as a military attaché at the U.S. embassy put it, the Hondurans were being "rather accommodating."

By evening the tents were up and communications lines were strung at the new Honduran command headquarters. Aides were unpacking the general's whiskey.

Just before five P.M., four twin-rotor Chinook troop transport helicopters brought down from Fort Bragg, N.C., lifted off from Toncontin Airport in Tegucigalpa. On board, in addition to the three-man U.S. Army crews, were about thirty-five Honduran communications specialists, technicians, and related support staff for the new Azacualpa headquarters. The ride to the camp, over rugged mountain terrain, took less than an hour. It was the second trip today, and the army pilots were taking it at low altitude, about six hundred feet. Even though the lead Sandinista units were camped more than forty miles south of their destination, the Americans wanted to keep below the horizon so they wouldn't present a visible target in case the Sandinistas had acquired long-range AA missiles the United States didn't know about.

Major Eddie Marker, a North Carolinian, was the electronic-countermeasures officer in the lead chopper and also senior communications officer for the squad. He was the one who communicated with the DoD air ops control center at Aguacate.

Major Marker spoke with the calm, even twang of the classic military aviator. His friends said he sounded kind of like Chuck Yeager, the test pilot from West Virginia who first broke the speed of sound. And when the recording of his distinctly proud American voice was played on U.S. radio and television for days, weeks afterward, it brought tears of pride and sorrow to millions of eyes. As they listened to the tape, repeated over and over again, Major Marker remained in firm, reassuring control—even as he tumbled to his death.

"Aguacate, this is Azu 1 over the Río Jalan valley," Major Marker radioed to the comm officer when the choppers were about twenty miles out. "We have incoming."

"Roger, Azu 1," the ground operator radioed back. "Please identify."

"Aguacate, could be SA-7s, but closer to Redeye signature," he said. "Flares away."

The radio operator from another chopper, his voice not quite so controlled, broke in then, saying, "What the hell are the Nics doing way up here?"

"Hold on, Azu 1," the Aguacate operator said. "We're notifying help."

"Too late," Marker radioed back in that unnerving monotone. "Must be a hundred of 'em down there. AA coming up like buckshot. . . . We're hit. Going down." In the background, behind Marker's composed narration, the Aguacate comm officer could hear panicked shouting, then the clipped first half of an explosion before the radio went dead.

"Azu 1, come in," the comm officer said. "Azu 1, Azu 2, Azu

3, Azu 4, come in. Please come in." Nothing came back but static.

A couple of the choppers managed to get flares away. And Sergeant B. J. Robertson, the gunner in Azu 4, did spot his attackers in time to get off a few 50-caliber rounds. But with not much more than one thousand feet to cover at near supersonic speed, the missiles tore up at the Chinooks so fast that none of the choppers had time to deploy effective countermeasures.

The flares and chaff and missile jammers probably wouldn't have made much difference anyway. The attackers fired such a concentrated volley of missiles—so many that in a couple of cases the missiles' on-board infrared guidance systems homed in on other missiles instead of on the target—that each copter took several hits.

One was more than enough, and all four choppers fell like bricks, crashing within a few hundred yards of each other, in a broad valley largely defoliated by decades of lumbering. A few people survived the crashes, but none without grave injuries.

In four squads, the attackers stacked their Redeye missile launchers in careful piles so they could be sure to pick them up again on the way out. They approached the burning wrecks cautiously, AK-47s at their shoulders. When a fuel tank on one of the Chinooks exploded, all of them fell to the ground. They were close enough now to hear the moans of survivors, and they made for them, rifle safeties off, fingers ready on the triggers.

"Tigrillo, take that one," Major Paz shouted, waving the squad toward the chopper straight ahead. "El Muerte, go up front. Balita, you and your men take the rear bird. Remember the orders: No survivors, and fire only your AKs, no other weapons. And don't forget: Shoot from a distance. To keep from getting into trouble, don't move close. Move fast. We have little time."

Balita's chopper was a couple of hundred yards back, and he started off at double time, his five men beside him. Behind, he heard scattered AK rifle fire.

Like all of them, Azu 4 was now a black twisted hulk, smoking and unrecognizable. Most of the passengers had died still strapped into their seats, but a few had been thrown out onto the ground.

"Pitufo, Tacho, check those Honduran fuckers over there," Balita ordered, pointing to two bodies lying in the scrub grass ahead. "I'll check around the other side." He trotted around the copter's tail, making a wide berth since it was still burning and might explode. He almost tripped over a body on the way, a Honduran lieutenant who was obviously already dead. Balita kicked the corpse and spit on the body. He had learned to have little respect for the Honduran army. Their generals were fat. But still Balita found it hard to believe that these men had taken money to help the Sandinista Communists.

"There will be bad men in these helicopters," the Americans, Mendoza and Gustafson, had told them. "These are Honduran traitors on their way to betray you and the cause of freedom. People who take money to help Communists are worse than the Communists themselves. You must bring them down, teach a lesson."

And so Balita had approached this special mission with relish. What better way, he figured, to show his loyalty to the Americans than to kill these Communist *judidos* (fuckers)? Before setting out this morning, Balita had fantasized, as he did before each of the special missions the Americans gave them. Once again he thought of his private pact with the major. Maybe if they carried out this mission well and impressed the Americans, at last he and Paz would get to go up to Camp Lejeune. They could be United States Marines, dress in American uniforms, and parachute out of airplanes. Still today, this was the child-fighter's comic-book dream.

Balita continued on and ahead, maybe thirty yards from what had been the Chinook's side door, he saw another man lying in the grass. He ran over but stopped several yards away and circled the body. Something was funny.

The man lay on his back. He was missing a leg; blood oozed from the stump at the knee. His face was black from smoke and drying blood. So was his uniform. Still, he looked up at Balita. His eyes followed as the little fighter walked around him fifteen feet away, keeping his distance as ordered. Odd, Balita thought. His eyes are blue. The man made no sound, and his expression betrayed no fear, no pain. Watching Balita he looked strangely at peace, maybe even reassured by Balita's presence.

But Balita had orders. These were traitors. Quickly he raised his rifle, took careful aim, and fired a round between the man's blue eyes. His body jerked just a moment. But in death the man still looked up at Balita with that expression of knowing calm.

Balita shuddered. He was supposed to keep his distance. But he just had to close the dead man's eyes.

He knelt over the body but stopped abruptly, his right hand stilled in midair. Then suddenly agitated, he brushed soot off the dead man's shoulder and stared for a moment, his mouth open. The flyer's shoulder patch had writing on it. Even though he had a difficult time reading Spanish, much less English, he knew what these words meant: United States Army, 82nd Airborne.

"Jesus, Mary, Holy Mother of God," Balita whimpered, "I have killed an American. An American! Why was he on this helicopter? The CIA man never said we would kill an American. Holy Mother, please forgive me."

Now Balita was gazing skyward, on the verge of tears. He crossed himself, then reached down and gently closed the dead man's eyes. He looked around quickly to see if anyone was watching him, then squeezed his eyes shut, trying hard to keep from crying. How could he and the major join the Marines now? They'd killed Americans. Americans! After a few moments he heard his men calling to him from the other side of the wrecked chopper.

"Coming, coming," he shouted. He crossed himself again as he stood and wiped his eyes with his sleeve, then started back toward his men. But after a few yards he paused briefly, then ran back to the dead American. With his foot he turned the body over. Carefully, using two fingers, he pulled the man's wallet out of his rear pants pocket and looked inside. The fat wad of twenty-dollar bills gave him a rush of excitement, but he didn't take the money. Instead he pulled the dead man's United States Army identification card from behind a little plastic window. The man in the ID photo stared back at him, an unselfconscious grin wide across his face. He looked as if he'd just told a dirty joke.

B. J. Robertson, the card read. *Sergeant, United States Army. Abilene, Texas.*

Balita didn't know for sure what he'd do with the card. But he'd killed an American soldier, a terrible thing. He would have to confess, tell the major what he had done. How would they ever join the Marines now?

Balita stuck the card in his kit pouch and then put the wallet back in the dead man's pocket, buttoning the flap again before rolling the body back over and running back to his men.

Minutes later, the commandos joined up at the edge of the field to pick up the spent Redeye rocket launchers. They'd kept the missiles hidden at Cascabeles these last weeks, since they'd snuck over to the El Cuartelón weapons bunker late one night, paid off the guards as arranged, and walked off with all the Redeyes.

When Mendoza had explained the plan privately to Paz, the major had wondered why they didn't use some Soviet SAM-7s—the CIA could get them easily enough—instead of Redeyes and save all the trouble of stealing them. That's what the Sandinista Communists normally used. Mendoza must have anticipated the question because, without being asked, he'd explained how difficult it was to procure two dozen of those Soviet weapons without being noticed by the CIA's regular foreign arms buyers. Besides, he'd said, "your men are trained on Redeyes. SAM-7s aren't the same. Training would take time."

Now, fulfilling the last part of the CIA man's instructions, they were supposed to dispose of the spent Redeye launchers so they wouldn't be found.

As everyone loaded up, Balita looked over at Paz. The major was staring back at him, and Balita could tell that Paz knew something was wrong.

Paz walked over. "What is it Balita?" he asked with that bare trace of warmth that crept into his voice on occasion.

"Major, Major, I . . . I . . ." he stammered. But Balita couldn't tell him. He looked down at his feet.

Paz whispered to him, "Balita, sometimes fighters have to do things that we never expected. It is war."

Startled, Balita looked back at Paz. Had the major already known there would be an American on the helicopter? No, no. That couldn't be. He just couldn't have known they were going to have to kill Americans and end their chances for going to America.

It just couldn't be true because if it was, then everything they'd talked about these last years, all their plans to be Marines, every bit of it would have to have been a lie.

For years, ever since the invasion of Grenada, the Defense Department press corps had bitterly complained that the military allowed no press coverage of foreign military operations. So, to shut them up, the Pentagon had begun permitting press-pool coverage of the frequent and usually benign military maneuvers in Honduras.

With that precedent established and the system already in place, the military could hardly refuse to allow pool coverage of real military actions in Honduras. That's how it happened that the first American forces to reach the crash site were accompanied by a dozen reporters, photographers, cameramen, and related technicians on their way back to Tegucigalpa from the press-pool station at Aguacate.

At first, the choppers circled the crash site, looking for the enemy. The wreckage still smoked; the crashes had occurred only about thirty minutes earlier. Gunners leaned out the doors, and the soldiers tried to keep the cameramen in their seats, but to no avail; photographers took shots hanging out the door. After the choppers touched down, the soldiers hopped out in full battle readiness as if this were a hot LZ. Noncoms ordered the newsmen to stay on board. But when it became clear that the attackers were gone, there was no holding back the press. Hell hath no fury like a TV cameraman denied good footage right in front of his nose. The NBC cameraman hopped off and started for the wreckage, tape running. He didn't even turn around when a sergeant barked, "Get back on board!" and raised his M-16. The cameraman kept walking and shouted back over his shoulder, "You're just going to have to shoot me." Shaking his head, the sergeant lowered his gun, and the other reporters followed immediately.

Back in Tegucigalpa, the army tried to impound the tape and film, but the press refused to cooperate. Later, orders came from Washington to back off.

By late evening, the pool writers had put together a sketchy news story, the photographers had printed and transmitted their pictures, all in time for first-edition morning newspapers. The TV footage made it on the morning news shows. And by the time the evening news shows came on, most everyone in the United States had heard something about the "Chinook massacre," as the incident came to be known. Tens of millions of Americans turned on their televisions.

"Good evening, this is the CBS Evening News. Sixteen American servicemen and thirty-five members of the Honduran military were killed last night when the Nicaraguan army shot down four United States Army helicopters in central Honduras in an unprovoked attack. The attackers used American-made Redeye antiaircraft missiles the Sandinistas had stolen from contra headquarters a few weeks earlier. The few Americans and Hondurans who survived the missile attack were murdered on the ground, executed, I should say, with bullets fired at close range as they lay wounded in the grass."

*   *   *

On all three networks the anchormen read the story in tones of grave import they hadn't used in years, not since the space shuttle *Challenger* exploded. Viewers were not spared vivid portrayals of the carnage, either. All three networks played the tape of Major Marker dying like an American hero.

"Aguacate, this is Azu 1. . . . We have incoming . . . could be SA-7s, but closer to Redeye signature . . . Must be a hundred of 'em down there. AA coming up like buckshot. . . . We're hit. Going down."

Then the clipped explosion and several seconds of static.

They also showed close-in shots of the twisted metal wreckage, and one network even offered a brief but close-up shot of Sergeant B. J. Robertson, his face peaceful, a small red hole between his eyes. Across the country Americans sat open-mouthed in front of their TVs. Some people wept.

The overnight *New York Times*/CBS News poll showed that 78 percent of the American people thought military retaliation against the Sandinistas was called for. Just over 40 percent said this was as bad as Pearl Harbor.

If the carnage at the Managua dinner party had inflamed Nicaraguans, the Chinook massacre united the American people in an angry cry for vengeance. The Defense secretary, the CIA director, and the joint chiefs of staff flew up to Camp David with the president for the weekend. By Sunday afternoon, National Guard and Reserve units were being called to duty.

The United States military was on full alert.

CHAPTER NINETEEN

MANAGUA, NICARAGUA, APRIL 5

SOME MANAGUANS MIGHT HAVE THOUGHT IT A LITTLE odd. But while people around the world waited to see whether the United States would attack Nicaragua, while Colonel Gustafson and other diplomats sent coded cables back to Washington detailing Sandinista preparations for war, the United States embassy was getting ready to throw a party.

It was tonight, just for the embassy staff and their dependents, about forty-five people in all. But ordering food, drink, and flowers for that many people, especially now, was enough to catch the Nicaraguan government's attention. Though it was widely reported that the United States military was mobilizing, as usual Washington was giving no hint of what if anything it intended to do. And Wednesday morning, when a *Barricada* reporter asked Ambassador Donald E. Blanchard why he was throwing one of his embassy parties just now of all times, he said, "Oh, you know, we have them from time to time. It's a troubled moment, and I think lots of people are worried. I just want to let my staff know that everything's okay."

Actually the leaders of the Sandinista government weren't paying close attention. They were preoccupied, rushing to get ready for . . . well, they weren't exactly sure what. Just a few days before, the great bulk of the armed forces had been up in Honduras, rolling north to strike the contras. But the operation was called off Friday morning, after Managua realized it was going to be blamed for the helicopter attack, their righteous cries of innocence notwithstanding. Once again, the troops and tanks were called back to defend Managua.

The comandantes didn't know who shot down the helicopters. Maybe it really had been some of their own men, renegades. But the generals also believed that the United States had been hungering to invade for so long—this Yanqui president, like the last ones, had probably been lying awake at night yearning for it—that the army might have ordered its own helicopters shot down just to make the excuse.

In any case, the troops in Honduras were recalled immediately. It was going to take several days of hectic preparation to get them back in place. So if the Americans were silly enough to throw one of their embassy parties at a time like this, well that was their business. It was probably just a bit of disinformation anyway, trickery meant to lull them into complacency.

The party was at Casa Grande, the imposing ambassador's residence that gleamed white on a hill over the city. The 1940 WPA building design had been repeated in several Latin American countries, including Panama. And in Managua, Casa Grande had come to symbolize the fat and wealthy American overseer looking down at Nicaragua from on high.

After the Sandinista revolution, the ambassador of the time moved to a less visible home, explaining that continued use of Casa Grande sent the wrong signal. Actually it had been to keep his wife happy. To make an artistic point that none of the residents ever quite understood, the WPA architect had built each room's Spanish-tile floor at a slightly different level, so walking about the house meant stepping up or down a few inches every time you went from one room to another. The first time the ambassador's wife tripped and broke her ankle she limped around and complained. The second time, they moved.

At that time—just after the Sandinista revolution, when the United States was still trying to be friendly—it seemed politically convenient anyway. Over several decades, Casa Grande had become a powerful symbol of American support for the rapacious Somoza regime.

Now Casa Grande was the embassy guest house and dining facility. If embassy officers didn't want to eat at the embassy commissary, they could drive five minutes up the hill. The Casa Grande kitchen staff served three meals every day. The old house, on a seventeen-acre estate, was also where the embassy held its parties, and Tuesday evening embassy operators made a "call-out," advising every American household of this party's particulars.

Early Wednesday morning, before the temperature had risen to the level of excruciating discomfort, everyone showed up at work carrying boxes and bags—party supplies, they explained to their gardeners, housekeepers, babysitters, and any other Nicaraguans who asked.

Outside the cardboard chancellery during the day, embassy staffers, Gustafson among them, helped people load their cars with other boxes from inside the building. Anyone watching Gustafson as he piled box after box into cars, positively effervescent with enthusiasm, would have figured the Americans were planning one hell of a party.

Up the hill, Sandinista sentries on desultory patrol outside Casa Grande's gate watched streams of embassy cars pass by all day long. Gringo drivers looked out, strained smiles on their faces. Late in the day a florist brought a vanload of fresh cut flowers, one of Nicaragua's few resources unaffected by the shriveled economy.

Although the Sandinista government didn't seem to have much interest in the party, officials were watching the Americans for other signs of unusual activity. It was almost certain that the United States would not attack Nicaragua without evacuating the embassy staff first, so Managua travel agents and airline ticketing offices were instructed to report immediately if significant numbers of embassy officers or their families booked flights out. So far they'd seen nothing unusual, just a couple of wives taking off for a few days of shopping in Miami: Marcia Kiernan, wife of the deputy chief of mission, and Jeannie Gustafson, married to that pushy colonel. Gustafson had driven his wife to the airport, and the Sandinista watchers saw her grow teary as they hugged at the gate. They wondered about that. Why such emotion for a shopping trip? But anybody married to that man, they figured, probably had emotional problems.

Sandinista security officers with binoculars also watched the embassy from atop a nearby building. One man was in charge of keeping his eye on the little chimney. The embassy had no fireplaces, and not one building in this tropical country had a heating furnace, so this chimney had only one purpose. It vented the burn vault, where sensitive papers were destroyed. The Sandinistas figured that if clouds of smoke, greater than normal, began billowing out all of a sudden, it would be a clear sign that evacuation was imminent. But what the Sandinistas didn't know was that the CIA had long ago installed a scrubber in the chimney that could eliminate all but the barest trace of smoke. It wasn't used for routine burn-bag destruction; the scrubber was to be turned on only for the final burn. Besides, the embassy's "burn-time"—the time needed to destroy all the sensitive documents—had been kept below an hour for several years, just in case.

Late in the day the Sandinista watchers did see a panel truck from the little British embassy up the street pull into the compound and around to the back door. The Nicaraguans hadn't made a major effort to identify all the British embassy officers, and the watchers did not recognize the driver and his assistant who went inside. But they did know the stoop-shouldered American who came back out with them carrying several large boxes that appeared to be quite heavy. After only two trips his sport shirt was soaked with sweat and showed the clear outline of a sleeveless T-shirt underneath. He was Ned Frederick, listed on the official American embassy roster as a junior political officer. But the Sandinistas knew that the Americans often liked to use "political officer" as the cover for intelligence agents. The watchers radioed this bit of information to their superiors, and immediately they put a man outside the British embassy—a small post, since the British didn't keep a full-time ambassador here. Soon enough Frederick and the two Brits arrived, unloaded the boxes, and carried them inside. Several hours later Frederick still had not come back out. The watchers weren't sure what if anything to make of this.

By dusk, when the Americans began leaving their homes for the party, the Sandinista military command had evaluated the Americans' activities during the day and decided that an invasion was not probable in the next twenty-four hours, unless the United States had decided to sacrifice its embassy staff. And that was not considered likely. Whatever was to come, the Sandinistas figured, they were probably safe for at least another day.

CASA GRANDE, MANAGUA, NICARAGUA

Reassured or not, the Sandinistas stationed trained state intelligence officers outside Casa Grande Wednesday night and ordered them to keep a close eye on the gringos' party. They peered through the fence with infrared binoculars.

Starting about seven-thirty, the Americans came, alone or

with their families, including infant children. As they parked
their cars and walked toward the big house the gringos didn't
look particularly festive. Tugging children, they seemed pur-
poseful at best. Some were clearly anxious. The ambassador had
his job cut out for him if he hoped this party would reassure his
staff. Everybody disappeared inside, and the sentries figured the
Americans were being served dinner.

Inside, the briefing was almost over, dinner was about to be
served and ambassador Blanchard, standing in his socks on a
silk-upholstered armchair, had a few last words for the entire
group assembled in the living room. The lights were low, the
windows closed, and the central air conditioning was blowing
to reduce the chance that anyone outside could point a long-
range microphone at the house and overhear what was being
said. The Americans didn't know for sure whether the Sandinistas had the Soviet Union's latest laser eavesdropping technol-
ogy.

In Washington, the KGB bounced laser beams off government
office-building windows, gauging the vibrations of the glass
caused by conversational sound waves bouncing around inside.
The laser beams carried images of the vibrations back to a computer that used them to reconstruct the speech. So in some offices, the FBI had built little speakers into the window frames
that played soft music all day long. Rather than picking up sensitive conversations, the Soviets might hear Mantovani instead.

Casa Grande didn't have those protections. So every curtain
and blind was drawn, and Ambassador Blanchard tried to keep
his voice low. A baby whimpered, but the others assembled there
were largely silent, expressions somber.

"As you know, we're being watched," Blanchard told everyone. "This is supposed to be a party. We've done everything we
could to make it look authentic." He swept his hand toward a
grand floral arrangement on a table. "But now we have our parts
to play, so let's make it convincing."

"I just got a report, acquired through our redeployed national
technical means, that the Sandinistas have sent out no communications evincing any awareness of what we are up to." "National
technical means" was the government euphemism for the National Security Agency's electronic surveillance equipment, in
this case Ned Frederick's operation, redeployed at the British
embassy.

"After dinner," Blanchard went on, "we've got to stand

around on the lawn where the people outside the fence can see us. Let's look like we're having a good time. I know this is difficult, but we're professionals and if we work together everything will be just fine. I'm proud of you all for your good work so far."

Gustafson was standing next to his deputy, Major Rosen, and his face was a picture of undisguised glee.

"Buddy, I almost wish I was going with you," the colonel said, slapping Rosen on the back a little too hard. "It ought to be quite a show."

"I wouldn't trade places with *you*," Rosen responded, and he wasn't smiling.

"Whadaya mean?" Gustafson asked, his face a mask of incredulous wonder as he turned to Rosen, almost stepping on his toes. "This is it. I wouldn't miss this in exchange for the rest of my life."

"That's just what it might cost you," Rosen said, backing up. Gustafson shook his head and walked away.

Dinner—a buffet of cold roast beef, boiled potatoes in butter, string beans, and a mixed green salad—was quiet, grim. The dining room couldn't seat everyone, so families sat together on the carpeted floors of the living room, the library, or the sun porch. No one talked; there was only the soft clinking of silver against china. Between bites some mothers reached over and stroked the hair of their children, who looked up perplexed, not sure why everyone was so serious.

After dinner, parents took infant children to the little nursery for a nap. Some mothers sat watching their babies sleep, softly caressing their cheeks and occasionally looking at each other with brave smiles.

With clear reluctance, most of the others left the cool cloistered security of the house and stepped out into the steamy Nicaraguan night, drinks in hand—club soda and Coca-Cola, nothing alcoholic. For the benefit of the Sandinista watchers, they stood around on the lawn and pantomimed jolly party behavior, forcing smiles and waving their arms theatrically as they made conversation. The only person who seemed to be having a good time was Gustafson, who strode around with a Stroh's beer in hand, smiling and joking with people, some of whom didn't seem to appreciate it.

"Jane, I'm gonna miss you," he told Mrs. Penders, a widowed middle-aged secretary who worked in an office down the hall from his. He used to flirt with her, tired jokes about what they could do together if he weren't married, and she always giggled appreciatively. As she looked back at him tonight her eyes grew wet, and her voice faltered.

"Eric, oh, Eric. Please be careful. Don't do anything foolish."

"Count on it, honey," Gustafson said, grinning. "When it's all done, I'm gonna come looking for you." He kissed her on the cheek and marched off.

The gathering had seemed so sedate, the partygoers so quiet, that the Sandinista sentries outside radioed in their midnight status report and then settled back against the fence to take a nap until the next report, when the people started leaving. Their reaction the instant they awoke, startled and scared with a blinding spotlight in their faces, was that their lieutenant must have arrived and caught them asleep on watch. But fear gave way to terror when, as their drowsy minds began drawing the world back into focus, they felt the fierce and steady blast of wind tearing at their clothes and hair, pressing them back against the fence, and they heard the deafening roar in their ears. Suddenly they realized a helicopter was hovering right in front of them, just a few feet over the road.

Before they could scramble to their feet, over the rotor noise an amplified voice bellowed in heavily accented gringo Spanish: "Do not reach for your weapons. Keep away from that radio. Lie face down in the dirt, *now*!" Looking up through the searing light they could see a machine gun, a 30-millimeter automatic cannon, pointed at them from an under-fuselage turret mount. The AH-64 Apache attack helicopter was gyrating in the air. But to compensate, the gun swiveled rhythmically in its mount, ever pointed at its target by the copilot-gunner, who aimed the cannon by looking through his target-acquisition/night-vision avionics helmet.

Multiple rocket launchers hung from stubby wings, and the spotlight in the chopper's nose had the sentries fixed in place. So both of them did just as they were told. As they lay with their faces in the dirt, the Apache copter gained a little altitude but kept its spotlight and machine gun on them. Almost right away the sentries heard several other choppers roar overhead, onto the Casa Grande grounds.

"Right on time," Ambassador Blanchard said when the two Apaches arrived, followed almost immediately by four Sikorksy HH-60 Night Hawks, which settled on large phosphorescent-cardboard *X*s that had been laid out on the lawn half an hour before. About fifty yards from each landing zone, the embassy staff and their dependents assembled in prearranged groups of eight or ten. Each person carried just one small suitcase—"carry-ons only that can fit under the seat in front of you or in the overhead compartment," the embassy's emergency evacuation coordinator had joked.

As soon as each chopper set down, rotors still turning for instantaneous lift-off, two combat-ready officers dressed in black from head to foot jumped out and ran to the group nearest them. Just outside each chopper door, a third officer stood in attack crouch looking left and right, M-16 ready. Gustafson, beer in hand, stood beside one jittery embassy group as the lead officer shouted over the rotor noise, "Ladies and gentlemen, good evening. I am Major Leonard, United States Army Delta Force. If you will fall in behind me in a line and follow quickly but calmly, please, we will get you out of here right away. Just follow me, and stay together."

Leonard turned and fast-walked back toward his chopper as the second officer fell in at the rear of the line. Sandwiched between the two of them, the embassy group picked up their bags and started moving. One older lady stumbled a bit but quickly regained her pace. A baby screaming in his mother's arms could hardly be heard over the rotor noise.

But just as all four groups started to move, everyone heard another noise coming up from the city, the shrill wail of military alert sirens. That meant Sandinista pilots were undoubtedly scrambling into their MI-24 Hind attack helicopters at the airport a few miles out of town, and if those choppers were prepped, they could be here in less than five minutes. At the city army barracks responsible for this area, soldiers and Zelaya's Interior Ministry security troops were certainly piling into trucks at this very moment as well. They, too, could be up here almost right away. At the siren's sound, several embassy staffers froze, causing others close behind to bump into them. A few people fell into the grass, and the Delta Force officers had to stop and try to get everyone up and moving again. All but one of the columns were stalled. People put down their bags to help the others back onto their feet; most of them were stumbling around in the dark.

Into a secure radio on one of the Night Hawk choppers, the communications officer said, "*Enterprise*, this is Ferret One, do you copy?"

"Roger, Ferret One."

"*Enterprise*, we have alert status here. No unfriendlies on scene. Cargo pickup ragged but under way now."

"Roger, Ferret One. We will move to Ready Two status. We show no bandits near your LZ. Will advise if conditions change."

"Roger, *Enterprise*, and out."

Forty miles off the Pacific Coast, two squadrons of fully armed FA-18 attack fighters circled three thousand feet up, and with word from their ship, the aircraft carrier *Enterprise*, they moved another ten miles closer to the coast—still outside Sandinista radar range but ready to tear full-throttle into Managua if needed. From that distance, just sixty miles from the city, the FA-18s could be over Casa Grande before the Sandinistas' Hinds got there from the airport five miles out of town.

About twenty-five thousand feet above the FA-18s, two Navy E-2C Hawkeye radar planes circled and sent back to the ship fully plotted positions for all aircraft flying within a three-hundred-mile radius. And another FA-18 fighter squadron sat charged on the carrier flight deck, pilots in ready rooms prepared to launch and replace those in the air if fuel levels grew critical.

Embassy evacuations of this sort had been planned and practiced for years and years, ever since Iranian students seized the American embassy in Teheran. But this was the first live test, and surprise was the key. As soon as Washington began to realize trouble was likely, the Delta Force extraction team was rushed from Fort Bragg in North Carolina out to San Diego. The *Enterprise*, which had been at dock in San Diego, had already left—it was just over a two-day steam south—when the Delta Force officers arrived. They had to be ferried out to the ship en route.

Eight specially equipped Night Hawk night rescue helicopters were also flown out from North Carolina aboard C-141 transport jets. Four were for the mission and four were spares; after the Desert One debacle in Iran, the army insisted on full replacement "redundancy" for all Delta Force missions.

The *Enterprise*, along with nearly a dozen support ships, had been sixty miles off the Nicaraguan coast, out of sight, for about twenty-four hours now. For the Delta Force, this operation had looked easy. The LZ was just a few miles inland, meaning no in-flight refueling was needed. The Sandinistas' Pacific Coast radar was patchy, and usually they turned it off at night. Although the U.S. forces couldn't count on inactive radar at a tense moment like this, they knew that Nicaraguans were unaccustomed to fighting at night. Neither side had ever done it, during this revolution or the last one. But the United States had been forced to learn night techniques in Vietnam, and U.S. Special Forces had long since accepted them as standard doctrine.

All six mission helicopters, the Apaches and the Night Hawks, were equipped with state-of-the-art night vision and radar guidance. Even in pitch dark, using Doppler radar autopilot systems, they flew into Managua at treetop level, darting up and down a few feet above buildings and hills—a nap-of-the-earth approach, as it was called, intended to evade detection. New pilots found the night nap-of-the-earth tests scary; the stick was controlled largely by computer as the copter bumped up and down just a few feet above trees and homes. But the radar autopilot had been in use for years now and was standard equipment on a broad array of helicopters, planes, and missiles. For this operation it had worked. The Sandinistas hadn't sent out the alert until the helicopters were already on the Casa Grande grounds.

Even with the spills in the grass, loading everyone took only about four minutes. The Delta Force officers hoisted older people on board, and copter crew members immediately strapped them into the choppers' web seats. Mothers hugged infant children almost suffocatingly close to their chests. Then, just under five minutes after they arrived—Gustafson timed them—the four Night Hawks lifted off. With an Apache in front and another taking the rear, all six choppers headed back at treetop level toward the Pacific at about 150 miles an hour.

As the rotor noise faded into the distance, Ambassador Blanchard walked across the lawn to Gustafson and stood quietly beside him for a moment. Before them, a Nicaraguan on the Casa Grande staff was running across the lawn retrieving the phosphorescent Xs and a small suitcase someone had dropped.

Moments later they heard troop trucks screeching to a halt at the end of the driveway. Sandinista officers barked angry orders that Blanchard and Gustafson couldn't quite make out. A Hind helicopter circled directly overhead for a minute but then turned around and headed back to the airport.

"Eric," the ambassador said, "the Lord only knows what we're in for now. A few of us had to stay, to demonstrate that we don't intend to start a war. But I'm a widower; I've got nobody to worry about me. You've got a wonderful wife in Jeannie. I'll never figure out why you volunteered."

"Don, I wouldn't miss it," Gustafson told him as if it were

the most obvious thing there could be. "Jeannie will be just fine, and I wouldn't miss this for anything in the whole wide world."

NATIONAL PRESS BUILDING, WASHINGTON, APRIL 5

The lull, the ominous quiet that had settled over Washington since the Chinooks were shot down screamed to Eaton that war, or something close to it, was on the way. But early in the morning, while the embassy employees in Managua were lying to their housekeepers as they hurriedly loaded boxes into their cars, everything in Washington seemed perfectly normal.

Eaton figured that maybe even the government was beginning to think, as he did, that there was something unusual about the whole Chinook episode. He could still picture in his mind how well the El Cuartelón weapons depot was guarded. And the contras, he remembered, babied their Redeyes as if the cases held their most precious possessions. How could the Sandinistas have simply marched up there and walked off with all those Redeyes, as the White House had explained yesterday? But if anyone else in Washington was suspicious, there was no sign.

Taking the subway to work—bracing against the raw early-morning chill that seemed almost pleasant because Eaton knew the first blooms of spring were only days away—he couldn't help but shake his head and smile at the clusters of midwestern tourists standing on the Metro platform, poring over their pictorial city maps. From the chatter, it appeared their only worry was whether they'd be able to get tickets for the film at the Air and Space Museum, even as their nation seemed about to go to war.

At the office, Eaton called everyone he knew at the Defense Department, on Capitol Hill, and in the other agencies, trying to get an idea what was coming. No one seemed to know.

If hostilities were imminent, the president would have to advise the Speaker of the House and the majority leader of the Senate, at the least. Some White House reporters and cameramen were staking out the West Wing's lobby entrance, just in case any of the congressional leaders came by. But they didn't. That meant nothing in particular. If the president wanted to ensure secrecy, he could handle the congressional notifications by telephone.

The White House press office had scheduled no photo opportunities for the president today, no moments when reporters or photographers could drop into the Oval Office for about thirty seconds to take pictures and ask two or three quick questions. The president's schedule for the day—reporters got it by calling a White House phone number and listening to a tape—showed he had the normal morning meetings with his staff and the ordinary ceremonial events that dot every president's daily schedule: posing for a picture with this year's Send a Kid to Camp poster child; reaching up to shake hands with new national college basketball champions from the University of North Carolina. If the White House was planning a war, the president might cancel those meetings. Or, Eaton knew, it was just as likely that the schedulers would keep them—they took only three or four minutes each—just to make everything appear normal. The president's schedule included several long, empty blocks of time, according to the tape, but that was true every day. So Eaton could draw no conclusions. There was nothing to do but wait. Still, there was something about this whole episode . . .

"I'm going up to the Hill and check on a few things," he told Abel, his boss, as he headed out the door for the Metro Center subway station. On Capitol Hill, he made directly for the Rayburn House Office Building, to the office of his friend Hunt Kinnard, the senior staff member of the House Appropriations Committee's Subcommittee on Military Construction. Kinnard was a freckle-faced southern boy with a subtle wit and warm drawl. His boss, the subcommittee chairman, was a moderate from Georgia, and the two of them had been tracking the contra program for a decade.

Of course, the Intelligence and Armed Services committees had the most direct oversight responsibilities for the contras, but half a dozen other subcommittees had a piece—Military Construction, for example, monitored Pentagon building projects in the United States and abroad. One of Kinnard's favorite pastimes these last years had been challenging the Defense Department's plans to pre-position equipment at Palmerola and other bases in Honduras, saying the tons of weaponry were there "just for field exercises." Since the department's Honduras projects also benefited the contras, directly or obliquely, the subcommittee had managed to grab a piece of that program too.

"Hey, Chris, how ya doing?" Kinnard said, standing up as Eaton poked his head into Kinnard's booth at the back of a windowless office in the basement, just down the hall from the public cafeteria.

"Okay, okay. How about yourself?"

"Busy, real busy," Kinnard said. "But sit down."

"I'll bet you're busy," Eaton said, plucking a pair of dirty running shoes out of the only other chair. "What do you hear?"

"Same as you. Nothing. But like you, I bet, that tells me we're in for something big."

"Listen, Hunt, I know you don't have much time. But let me just bounce something off you. You know the White House gave out this explanation yesterday of how the Sandis got those Redeye AA missiles. That's the first I'd heard they'd been taken. When'd you first hear the Sandis had walked up and stolen them?"

"Just after it happened last month. DoD put in an immediate emergency requisition for two dozen replacements. That's prepositioning of U.S. equipment. We get notification."

"What's the reason? Why'd they say the Sandis took them? It's weird."

"The contras had gotten pretty good using the Redeyes. Shot down two Hinds choppers, best we can determine. And the story goes that the Sandis didn't want the contras shooting down any more of them during the border firing exercise they were planning."

"Story goes, huh," Eaton said, grinning at him.

"Yeah, so the story goes." Kinnard smiled back. He had Top Secret clearance and didn't give classified information away easily. But long ago Eaton had learned his code phrases.

"So, how'd they get in and out of the depot without anyone seeing them? I've been down there. The contras baby those Redeye cases like they're the most important things on earth. It seems kind of funny that anyone could just walk in and make off with them."

As Eaton watched, a fleeting moment of concentration flashed across Kinnard's face, and in that millisecond Kinnard's eyes darted down to a stack of papers on his desk. But in just an instant he was smiling again.

"Story goes that there was only one guard at night, and they knocked him over the head," he said.

"Yeah, I see," Eaton said, stretching his arms and trying to look casual as he glanced down at the stack of papers. On top were galleys of a new subcommittee hearing report: "Prepositioning NATO Munitions and Spare Parts in Israel as Part of the U.S.–Israel Strategic Cooperation Agreement: What Will the Arab Neighbors Think?"

Sticking out from under that, Chris saw the corner of a government-brown envelope with a red-edged sheet paper-clipped to the top. The paper was the "limited distribution" list for classified documents. The date rubber-stamped at the top was March 25, just a few days before the Chinooks were shot down. The return address: Office of the Inspector General, Department of Defense.

"Anybody looking into the Redeye theft?" Eaton asked. "Seems like DoD might want to figure out how all those expensive missiles got away. Sounds like an inspector general's case to me."

Smiling, shaking his head, Kinnard reached over and straightened the pile of papers, burying the brown envelope under the others.

"You're good, Chris. Maybe too good. With things the way they are right now, I don't think the IG's going to push this investigation any farther."

"I guess you're right. But one last thing: Why'd the Sandis use the Redeyes on the Chinooks instead of their own SA-7 missiles? They're just as good, aren't they?"

"Soviet SAM-7s are comparable, I'd say. The story here is that the Sandis wanted to cover their tracks, use American equipment to make it seem like maybe the contras shot the helicopters by mistake."

"You believe that?"

Kinnard smiled a long moment, but then he just shook his head. "Can't do that, Chris, just can't get into this now. You know. But I can suggest one thing you might want to think about. It takes some practice to learn how to shoot a new AA missile accurately, doesn't it?"

"Huh?"

"You're a smart boy. Just think about that. You can't just walk off with sophisticated AA missiles you've never used before and then hand them over to green troops and expect them to use them with any precision without any practice first, any more than the contras could pick up Soviet SAM-7s and be expected to shoot them right away. All of these different shoulder-fired AA missiles have their own sophisticated and complex target-seeking and firing protocols. It takes practice, even for educated people. Just think about that."

Eaton looked back at him, thinking.

"Anyway, I wish you luck with this. You'll need it. If you're on to something, and maybe you are, you're not likely to get much help. With the mood of the country the way it is right now, it would be political suicide for any of us to get into this issue now."

Eaton nodded. "Thanks, Hunt. You helped a lot."

THE WHITE HOUSE, WASHINGTON

As Wednesday wore on, Leslie too knew something was up. General Dayton was in and out of the Oval Office and the Situation Room, and no one was brought along to take notes. They wanted no leaks. The Joint Chiefs were marching around in the West Wing with grave, determined expressions, but nobody was talking. Certainly the United States was about to do something down in Nicaragua. But no one outside the inner circle knew just what.

First thing Monday morning, the State Department had issued its highest-level travel advisory recommending that every American in Nicaragua leave right away.

"With the anarchic conditions that resulted in the downing of four American helicopters, and the senseless slaughter of all the Americans and Hondurans on board, the United States can no longer remain responsible for the safety of Americans in Nicaragua," the advisory said. "The situation is such that we recommend that all Americans leave Nicaragua immediately."

The Washington Post's lead story the next morning describing the advisory began with the phrase "In an apparent warning that hostilities are imminent . . ." Everyone did expect an attack of some sort. But like most White House staffers, Leslie could only guess what the president was planning.

"General, anything special I can do for you today?" she asked Dayton as he breezed past her desk mid-morning.

He stopped and smiled at her briefly, knowing the real question behind what she asked.

"Leslie, I wish I could tell you exactly what's going on, but it'll become clear soon enough. Yes, you can do something for me. Look over the daily incoming." He waved his hand at a five-inch pile of documents the courier had dropped off earlier this morning. These were the sensitive intragovernmental papers that Dayton usually sorted through himself. "Make sure there's nothing in there I absolutely have to deal with today." Leslie gave a disappointed nod, but Dayton didn't notice. He'd already started down the hall to the Cabinet Room.

Leslie did not leap to the job. She finished her croissant and coffee before placing the stack in the middle of her empty blotter.

As she flipped through it, the stuff looked routine—weekly intelligence summaries that were already out of date, foreign military assessments, copies of State Department foreign mission cables.

Near the bottom she picked out a government-brown envelope with the Defense Department seal and "Office of Inspector General" in the upper left corner. Stapled to the envelope's top was a red-edged sheet giving the distribution list: a munitions supply office at the Defense Department, the chairmen of a few relevant House and Senate committees and subcommittees. And here, the NSC.

Rubber-stamped in red on top of that was the security designation: Secret, a relatively low-level classification in the several-tiered hierarchy: Confidential, Secret, Top Secret, Sensitive Compartmented Information, and beyond—intelligence so sensitive the classification name was secret. She slit the envelope open and pulled out a twenty-page inspector general's report.

Every federal agency had an inspector general, a semiautonomous ombudsman whose job was to search for "waste, fraud, and abuse," to use the government's favored phrase. These officials were grafted onto the agencies in the mid 1970s, the era of consumer awareness across the United States. In the years since, most IGs had broadened their mandates. Now many of them also investigated unusual incidents that didn't seem criminal. As an example, when the director of the United States Information Agency had been accused of secretly tape-recording all his telephone calls, the USIA inspector general investigated and recommended that the practice be stopped. When the CIA allowed a high-placed KGB defector to slip away during dinner at a Georgetown bar, the agency's inspector general recommended changes in the established regimen for handling defectors.

And last month, when the contras claimed that the Sandinistas had walked into their ordnance depot and made off with two dozen Redeye antiaircraft missiles, the inspector general carried out an investigation. This was his report, sent to Dayton's office among others because during the RIG meeting last month the general had asked for it—more to get the matter out of the way so the contras could be resupplied than out of any real interest in the incident.

The document wasn't long. SECRET was stamped in red at the top of each page. Like all such reports it began with a statement of authority, followed by a neutral narrative description of the incident and the IG's introduction into the case. Then it gave the investigative methodology, followed by the conclusions and recommendations.

Leslie read that last part, then slowly reread the bottom line:

"All our findings combined lead us to one conclusion: It seems highly unlikely that Sandinista forces stole the Redeye missiles. More likely, the missiles were taken by contra elements themselves for sale on the black market, a general practice we have documented before."

She took a deep breath and checked the date again. Yes, this report was completed and stuck into the interagency distribution pouch before the Chinook massacre. So the investigators didn't know the implications of what they were saying.

A few minutes later Dayton swept past her into his office.

Leslie stood up. "General, can I talk to you for a moment?"

"Yeah, for just a minute," he said, looking at his watch without turning around. "We've got to be getting back to the Oval Office right away." Dayton sat behind his desk and immediately began gobbling a tuna sandwich waiting for him on a tray.

Leslie stood in front of his desk holding the IG's report.

"General, you asked me to look at today's docs." He nodded briefly without looking up, his mouth full of food.

"Well, the IG's report on the theft of those Redeyes last month came in, and I thought you should know about it right away. It's the IG's conclusion that the Sandinistas couldn't have taken the missiles. They think the contras took them so they could resell them on the black market."

She started to explain the IG's reasoning, reading relevant passages she'd underlined in the table of summary conclusions: "The munitions depot door was always well guarded by at least five men, and the door was locked with two heavy padlocks. There was no sign of forced entry, and whoever went in padlocked the door again on the way out . . ."

But the general broke in: "Leslie, you know how I feel about those inspector generals. All of them ought to go work for Ralph Nader. Whatever this fellow found, whatever speculation he's strung together there, it doesn't change the one essential fact: No one had a motive to shoot down those helicopters but the Sandinistas."

He put down his half-eaten sandwich, got up, and headed for the door.

"Thanks for letting me know," he said over his shoulder. "That report—you can file it."

Leslie stood there in his office for a long moment after he left, staring down at the document in her hands. The United States was about to go to war. The report suggested something was askew. How could she just file it?

Congress wouldn't have the guts to do anything with this report now, even if anyone up there on the Hill took the time to read it, which seemed unlikely. The senators and representatives were already too busy crowding into the Capitol press galleries, lining up to tell the newspapers and television how instrumental they had been in pushing the government to avenge the massacre.

"And I advised the president that this great country should teach those Sandinista Communists a lesson," they'd say in deep, dead-earnest tones. Already a letter signed by 146 members of Congress had been hand-delivered to Dayton's office. It called for "a firm but measured military response."

What should she do? Leslie wished she could give the report to Eaton. Back at her desk she put it in her "to file" stack.

NATIONAL PRESS BUILDING, WASHINGTON

Eaton didn't have any sources in the National Security Agency, the office in charge of electronic spying. No one did; all of the NSA's work was classified far beyond Top Secret. But he had a friend, a midlevel political officer in the U.S. embassy in San José, Costa Rica, who read most of the relevant intelligence the NSA put out, though sometimes it seemed he didn't understand what it meant. While some embassy political officers actually worked for the CIA, Eaton doubted Roger Yost was one. He wasn't sharp enough. Or he was putting up a pretty good front.

Eaton called him at the embassy now and then, and they'd trade information. Yost liked to know the gossip in Washington, the sorts of things people in the White House, State Department, and Congress were saying that didn't make it into the newspapers or down to San José in the State Department cables. In exchange he'd answer Eaton's questions—sometimes even giving what appeared to be classified information, and if Eaton used it, his news story would attribute the material to "an administration official." Everyone would think it was someone in Washington. Eaton figured it was only marginally deceptive.

Like everyone else he had talked to today, Yost too professed to have no idea what was going on.

"They're keeping us in the dark down here," he said.

"Roger, let me ask you something," Chris said, moving quickly to what he wanted to know. He tried to keep these conversations short, partly because of the cost. But he also knew that NSA satellites occasionally picked up conversations to and from U.S. facilities in the region.

"We keep track of all artillery and missile firings inside Nicaragua, don't we?" he asked.

"Sure. We have to. We gotta know what weapons the Soviets are giving them and what they're doing with them."

"Okay, but have you seen anything showing any test firings of Redeye missiles inside Nicaragua the last few weeks?"

"No, can't say I have. We'd notice that for sure. But there haven't been any. What are you getting at?"

"I don't know for sure. But I'm wondering how the Sandinistas learned how to shoot them so fast."

"Well, I'm not a military man, but what's to learn?" Yost asked. "Don't you just aim and shoot?"

"I don't know either," Eaton said. Better not to lead Yost any further down this path. Eaton already had what he needed. It was time to try the inspector general's office. He leaned over toward Max Jacobson's desk. His beat was the Defense Department, and he'd written a feature about the DoD inspector general a few months earlier. Eaton asked him for a little help, but Jacobson snapped, "Eaton, I can't believe it. We've got unusual ship movements out in CincPac, a carrier battle group going down to Nicaragua. We've got the Delta Force apparently activating down at Fort Bragg. We've got the United States about to go to war, and you want me to chase down some IG report for you? Give me a break!"

"Max, it's important."

"Sure, sure. All that contra stuff is important to you. I haven't got time now." He pulled a card out of his Rolodex and handed it to Eaton. "Call the guy yourself. He's just an investigator, but he's good. Tell him I suggested you call." With that, Jacobson turned away.

Eaton looked at the card. John Egart, deputy assistant inspector general, it said. Jacobson certainly wasn't giving out his top sources, but in this case it was just as well. Anyone who was senior in the office might not be willing to talk about the report right now.

Egart was a classic bureaucrat who did his job well enough and paid little attention to anything else around him. Eaton recognized the type from the bored monotone that greeted his call.

"Hi, Mr. Egart, I'm Chris Eaton. I work with Max Jacobson over at New World News Service."

"Yeah, Chris. What's up?" With that Eaton employed one of the journalist's favorite tools: the bluff.

"Well, I just wanted to check something with you, make sure I don't misinterpret something you guys have done. Your office just finished your report on the Redeye theft down in Honduras, right?"

"Yeah, but that's classified."

"I know, and it's not a big deal, but somebody in the loop who's seen the report liked it a lot and told me a little about it. You guys did a good job."

"Thanks."

"I don't know what I'm going to do with it, but I'd hate to describe your work with somebody else's interpretations that might be wrong. We're on background here, okay?"

"Well, okay, but I don't know how much I can tell you."

"Well, as I understand it, you checked out the security arrangements and found the depot pretty well guarded, right?" Eaton remembered that from his own trip to El Cuartelón.

"Yeah, I guess that's right. You know, I've already gone through two other reports since then. I don't have that one right on the top of my head this minute, and I just did the field work for it. I didn't write it. But that part's right. In fact, you know what? I remember now. One of our officers, a lieutenant, went over to the depot as soon as the alarm went out. He told us there was no forced entry. Whoever went in locked the padlocks again on the way out." He chuckled. "Those contra guys musta really been asleep at the switch on this one."

"What would it take to carry two dozen Redeyes away, anyway?" Eaton asked.

"Well, a pretty big force; two dozen men at least, especially if all of them are carrying full battle gear. Or they'd need a truck, but there's no road going all the way up there."

"That's a lot of men sneaking in and out of there, isn't it?" Eaton asked.

"Troop deployment, that's not my field," Egart said.

"Okay, but let me ask this: Nobody's picked up any evidence of Redeye test fires inside Nicaragua, right?"

"Hey, where'd you get that? That kinda stuff isn't supposed to get out."

"I'm sorry," Eaton said. "I don't want to get you in trouble. Just let me ask you something else. Is there much of a market for Redeyes? Could somebody make money with them on the black market?"

"Sure, of course. Hey, you've got a copy of our report, don't you? How'd you get this stuff?"

"No, no, I don't really, I—"

"Listen, I shouldn't be talking about this. I'm under the gun for another report anyway. I gotta get back to work. I gotta go."

Eaton didn't care. He had what he wanted. "Thanks," he said and hung up.

He was grinning and clapped his hands once as he walked over to Walter Abel's little glass-walled office.

"Hey, Walter. I think I'm onto a hell of a story. I'm not sure what all of it means, but—"

"You been able to find out what we're going to do in Nicaragua? Are we going to invade?"

"Well, I don't know for sure, but I'm starting to get some information that I think I better look into. I don't think the Sandinistas stole those Redeye rockets like the White House is saying. There's a DoD inspector general's report out that I've heard about. I don't have it yet but I've learned some things." He described what he'd found: A force large enough to carry off all the missiles couldn't sneak in and out unnoticed. There'd been no forced entry into the weapons depot; whoever went in unlocked the padlocks and locked them again on the way out. There were no Redeye test firings inside Nicaragua, making it unlikely that the Sandinistas could use the stolen missiles so accurately.

"I'm beginning to think maybe some contras took those Redeyes and sold them on the black market. That could mean it wasn't really the Sandinistas who shot down those helicopters."

Abel was shaking his head. "Chris, this is all speculation. It raises far more questions than it answers. Maybe you've got something there, but it's hard to tell. It would be irresponsible to run a story like that right now."

"Walter, I'm not suggesting we run a story. I don't have it yet. Just let me keep looking into it." He was brushing at his forelock. "I'm sure there's something there."

But Abel was shaking his head.

"Suppose the contras took the rockets and sold them on the black market? So? Who's to say Sandinista agents didn't buy them? Who's to say the Sandis didn't get their Redeyes from Cuba and practice with them there? I'd say work on this some more, but what you've got now is mush, and this isn't what you should be doing right now anyway. We're about to go to war, and you're the White House reporter. I want you working on that. We'll be sending the Marines into Managua, and you'll be off working on another one of your conspiracy theories."

"But Walter—" Eaton complained, throwing up his hands.

Abel cut him off, clearly exasperated now. "That's enough. You've been chasing conspiracies for the last two months, and an awful lot of your stories are getting denials from the White House."

"What's that mean?" Eaton asked, his voice defensive. "What are you saying exactly?"

"I'm saying we've probably got an invasion coming up, and we aren't going to do any irresponsible fanning of the flames. Get with the program!"

CHAPTER TWENTY

MANAGUA, NICARAGUA, APRIL 7

THE SANDINISTAS HAD ONLY A SMATTERING OF FIXED-position antiaircraft weaponry, most of it well-used hand-me-down Soviet equipment. After eight years of Black-bird flights, KH-11 spy satellite passes, and direct on-the-ground intelligence gathering, the Pentagon had collected a vast library of photographs, recorded radar images, maps, and charts pinpointing the location, type, and radar signature of every last AA placement.

Some were on the coast, but most were positioned around Managua. In fact, Gustafson's first brush with the Sandinista military had been the time he'd wandered up a public street to a high-fenced military area down by the lake and stood there peering through the chain link at a front-line AA station.

"Antique crap," he had been muttering to himself when a military jeep roared up and hauled him off to a damp basement jail cell. They'd kept him locked up for an hour or so, until Major Chamorro let him go. Then back at the embassy he'd prepared a report on the sorry state of Managua's antiaircraft defenses—"enough maybe to shoot down a Piper Cub," he'd written—another addition to Washington's growing collection of data.

The AA capabilities had improved somewhat since then; the Soviets had delivered some newer early-warning equipment. In addition the Army now had several hundred SA-7 portable surface-to-air missiles, similar to the American Redeyes, and even a few improved SA-14s.

But two days after the embassy evacuation, when the first squadron of FA-18 Hornet attack fighters took off from the *Enterprise* just before dawn, the pilots had exact coordinates for their targets—two dozen coastal AA positions armed with 20-millimeter and 40-millimeter guns, KS-19 57-millimeter radar-controlled cannons, and an assortment of other antiaircraft weaponry.

The Nicaraguans were as ready as they could be. The Casa Grande evacuation two nights before was as sharp a warning as they could have expected. But then the next morning they got the word directly from Moscow, and then from Havana.

The Soviet Union kept several hundred military "advisors" and technicians in Nicaragua. Cuba had almost a thousand there. As a courtesy—really it was a requirement, unless the United States had wanted to risk a larger war—right after the embassy evacuation Washington had advised the proper people in Moscow that they would be wise to remove their personnel from Nicaragua right away. Moscow in turn advised Havana. Years earlier, both Cuba and the Soviet Union had made it patently clear to the Sandinistas that they would not offer direct military help if the time ever came that the United States invaded. The Soviet Union acknowledged that Nicaragua, being less than a thousand miles south of the American mainland, lay within the United States' legitimate sphere of influence. Years earlier the United States had viewed the Soviet presence in Afghanistan the same way. Both countries had felt free to offer military and economic aid, but that's all.

As for Cuba, after the Grenada fiasco years earlier, Castro had told the Sandinistas point-blank that they shouldn't count on him for help fighting the Americans. So throughout the day after the embassy evacuation, Soviet and Cuban military transport planes took off and landed from military airfields all over Nicaragua. Several other East bloc embassies put their own people on the same planes.

As the foreigners withdrew, the Sandinistas were getting ready for the worst. Throughout the day troops were on the move. Two armored infantry divisions, twenty-four thousand men, were being deployed up north where, the comandantes believed, the main American assault force would roll down the Inter-American Highway. Another division was readying itself along the roads leading from the Pacific Coast beaches about forty miles west of Managua, and one more was positioned in and around the capital.

All day long and throughout the night, antiaircraft positions were fully armed and manned, their radars on. But at first nothing happened.

It wasn't until the next morning, as the black of night began melting into gray, that radar operators along the coast began to realize something was coming. They knew because their radar signals suddenly turned to fuzz.

Ahead of the attack planes were three EA-6B Prowlers, carrier-launched fighters specially equipped for ECM—electronic countermeasures. They were immediately distinguishable from conventional A-6E Intruder fighters by the bulbous electronics blisters grafted onto their tails and the other ECM pods that hung under the wings where missiles and bombs would normally be mounted. Each pod held high-power magnetron jammers already programmed for the Sandinistas' antiaircraft radar frequencies. And when the pilots turned them on just off the Nicaraguan coast, powerful bursts of electromagnetic energy directed ahead made the Sandinistas' early-warning, target-acquisition, and missile-guidance radars useless.

Right behind, roaring in at near supersonic speed, came a squadron of FA-18s, a dozen attack fighters armed with Shrike and HARM air-to-ground antiradar missiles specifically designed to destroy antiaircraft installations by homing in on their radar emissions. The planes launched their missiles from several miles off shore and then immediately turned around before they came within the shore batteries' range. Two dozen six-foot-long pencil-shaped rockets were fired, and the fixed ground positions were virtually helpless against the incoming missiles. Some ground sites managed to shoot off chaff rockets that exploded, dispersing thousands of shiny film fragments that fluttered through air to confuse the rockets' guidance systems. But they were too late. Most of the missile-targeting computers had already locked on.

Some of the missiles were armed with radar-proximity fuses and exploded twenty or thirty feet out, spewing fire and metal fragments across a sixty-degree arc. Others slammed through radar antennae, exploding on the way as they tore into the cannons or control buildings just behind. So many missiles were fired that most of the scattered placements along the coast were at least damaged. The early-warning/ground-control-intercept facility the Soviets had built at Masaya, fifteen miles inland, was utterly destroyed. That accomplished, two more squadrons of fighters flew on to take out the main AA emplacements around Managua.

At Casa Grande, Gustafson had climbed out onto a balcony looking over the city below, binoculars around his neck, a mug of coffee in hand. He'd been up before dawn, though he and the others had not been able to get much sleep the last two nights.

The first night, about thirty minutes after the evacuation, the phone had rung, and Ambassador Blanchard answered. It was Minister Zelaya. Their conversation had been brief.

"Mr. Ambassador," Zelaya had asked, his shrill, nasal voice dripping with contempt, "how many of you are left there on the residence grounds?"

"Minister, I needn't remind you that this is a United States diplomatic mission, and you have no right to enter here."

"Mr. Ambassador, I am not asking about entrance. I am simply asking how many people remain on the grounds."

"Well, Minister, I am here along with my deputy chief of mission, my political officer, and my military attaché. We have two support-staff assistants, six United States Marine guards, and several Nicaraguan nationals who work on the house staff."

"Mr. Ambassador," Zelaya had said, "I wish to advise you that I have my forces deployed at the entrance. The Nicaraguan citizens are free to leave, but you and the other Americans are restricted to the premises. Is that understood?"

"Are you telling us, Minister, that we are prisoners?"

"I am saying that you and the other imperialists are restricted to the premises. Please do not try to leave. Good night, Mr. Ambassador." Then he'd hung up.

Zelaya's Interior Ministry troops had been out in force the next morning. All through the day and the next night, sirens had wailed and aircraft had roared just overhead. Gustafson knew Casa Grande wasn't on the direct flight path between any two important points; it was just harassment. For all of them, the aircraft noise and the tension had made it difficult to sleep. But now, Gustafson was thinking, as he stood on the roof with a grin on his face, now we're gonna cause a little noise of our own.

The troops at Casa Grande's gate had leapt up at dawn, suddenly alert with weapons drawn as they began to hear the dull thud of explosions out on the coast. Gustafson could just make out the soldiers through the early-morning mist. At about the same moment the city's military-alert sirens opened up with a mournful wail.

The second wave of carrier-based planes didn't fly all the way into Managua. Their job was simply to take out the city's antiaircraft placements and, like the first squadron off the coast, they could do that by firing their missiles from several miles out.

Standing here near the top of one of Managua's highest hills, through his binoculars Gustafson could see the planes coming in from the distance. A couple of them were trailing black smoke, and one turned back west even as the colonel watched.

No air strike is ever totally effective. But even if all the radar-controlled AA placements on the coast had been destroyed, manually aimed antiaircraft cannons would still be intact because Shrike and HARM antiradar missiles have no way to recognize them. For years those obsolete World War II–era guns had been all the Soviets had been willing to give the Sandinistas. In addition, the hand-held SA-7 and SA-14 missiles used heat-seeking infrared targeting systems, not radar, so they too would not have been affected by the antiradar missile attack.

Firing from several miles off the coast, the first squadron had been almost invulnerable. But the second squadron had to fly over the coastal defenses to get to Managua, and apparently a couple of gunners had got lucky. As Gustafson watched, the trail of smoke behind the retreating plane grew thicker and darker. It was losing altitude as it flew out of Gustafson's sight.

Just then, Alec Kiernan, the deputy chief of mission, climbed out beside him.

"Is it safe to be up here?" he asked, eyes darting around.

"Oh, sure. Our boys know where we are. There aren't any targets near here."

"It's really starting, isn't it. I can't believe it. What's happened so far?"

"I think they nicked a couple of our carrier planes. I saw one of 'em heading back trailing some smoke."

"They said this was going to be a limited, no-loss operation," Kiernan muttered, shaking his head. "They had to know that couldn't happen."

"No-loss . . ." Gustafson spit the words. "I think this whole proportionate-response business is bullshit. We oughta just take these bastards out."

"Oh, come on Eric, you really want us to invade this godforsaken place?"

"Damn right," he insisted, rising to his full height, stepping right up to Kiernan, staring down at him with an impudent smile. But Kiernan stepped back, ignoring him. He was used to Gustafson by now.

"You're not really beginning to believe your own propaganda, that the Nicaraguan people would welcome U.S. Marines as liberators?" he asked, his voice filled with scorn on the last word.

"You know it," the colonel said. "And tell me what this little 'diplomatic air strike' is going to accomplish?"

"Chasten 'em. Make them think twice about doing something like shooting down our helicopters again. And maybe keep us out of another Vietnam."

"Oh, bullshit," Gustafson snapped. "They've just been waiting for something like this. You just wait and see if they're 'chastened.' Send the Marines in here and we'd roll them up flat in a day."

Just then Managua's AA batteries opened fire, loosing their missiles and radar-guided shells. But as the two of them watched, most of the rockets veered off course, then out of control, confused by the radar jammers. Some self-detonated in midair, onboard computers having decided that the chance of reaching a target had declined to zero. A moment later, the second fighter squadron's Shrike and HARM missiles began hitting their targets, and Gustafson and Kiernan saw and heard explosions all around the city. A second volley of American missiles struck about thirty seconds later. And then through his binoculars Gustafson saw the distant wave of planes turn back west toward the *Enterprise.* None of them had come closer than five or six miles from the city.

HARM missiles have a range of twenty miles or more, and the older Shrikes just less than half that. But the best of the Sandinistas' AA guns, the 57-millimeter automatic cannon, cannot reach a target more than about three miles away, and the other guns have ranges of only about a mile and a half.

An SA-7 hand-held missile has a reach of about two miles, and an SA-14 only about a quarter mile more than that. So Managua's main AA batteries were useless. The skies over Managua were riddled with yellow tracer lines rising from the cannons. Still, the gunners hadn't hit a single target before the U.S. missiles struck, and many of the installations were damaged or destroyed.

After the firing quieted and the aircraft noise faded into the distance, for just a moment the city was deathly still. The sun was up now, the day bright. But the birds, crickets, and other insects that normally provided Managua's daytime background noise were silenced momentarily by the clamor of war. Just then, Ambassador Blanchard stepped out onto the terrace. He didn't say anything at first, just nodded at the other two. Smoke columns were pouring up from attack sites all over town. In a moment, sirens started wailing, and outside Casa Grande's front gates somebody began blowing a whistle and shouting orders.

"God, I hate to see it come to this," Blanchard whispered, shaking his head. "Eric, you think we're safe up here?"

"Yes, sir, I think we'll be okay as long as we keep our heads low."

Blanchard looked around. "Can anybody see us up here? I'm not sure it's a good idea for us to be seen up here watching the destruction of the city."

Turning the other way, Gustafson rolled his eyes. "Nobody can see us up here," he said, trying without complete success to hide his disgust. "I think the Sandis have other things on their minds right now."

The sound of planes was gone, and now they heard fire engine bells mixing in with the alert sirens and the horns and screeching tires of military vehicles hurrying through the streets. About a minute later, the alert sirens gave a last wail as someone decided, wrongly, as it turned out, that the attack was over.

Just a few minutes later the roar of jet aircraft engines began to fill the air again, and on went the sirens. Blanchard and Kiernan went back inside, but Gustafson didn't move. He panned his binoculars and smiled when, from the southwest and the northwest, he spotted two waves of FB-111 swept-wing medium-range fighter-bombers roaring in fast and low, just over the treetops—eighteen of them, trailing long columns of thick black smoke from the single engines in their tails.

As soon as they got close to the city, the planes began firing off infrared jamming flares every few seconds. From the ground it looked as if the planes were spitting little fireballs behind them. They were to confuse the SA-7 AA rockets being fired up at them even now. But the FB-111's greatest defense was its speed. The heads-up display projected onto the cockpit windows—a moving map-image giving location, altitude, speed, and other facts—showed that the planes were heading straight for their designated targets at more than five hundred miles an hour, almost the cruising speed of a commercial jetliner. Short of an extraordinary stroke of luck, AA gunners weren't likely to hit a low-flying target whipping by that fast.

Each of the planes had been assigned primary and secondary targets, all of them military installations, and the weapons officers' orders were clear—better to come back with a full load of bombs than to loose them without being certain they would hit their objectives and not adjacent civilian areas. The other bomber groups over Corinto and León had identical rules of engagement.

As the city came into view, one by one the planes began peeling off left and right, lining up for their bombing runs. Some targeted military barracks, empty now. Two went after the large low building that was the Sandinista Defense Ministry, a primary target. Three headed for Sandino Airport northwest of the city, where reconnaissance photos taken last night showed four Hind helicopters parked in concrete-and-earthen blast revetments. Others plotted attack angles for military training centers, fuel bunkers, communications-intercept headquarters, battle-tank maintenance facilities, airfields—any in the myriad of military sites that the United States had been photographing, cataloguing, and targeting on a contingency basis for months or years.

On the ground, frustrated Sandinista soldiers shot their AK-47 rifles straight up as the planes roared past five hundred feet overhead. AA gunners wheeled around in their seats spitting off bursts of fire; others launched SA-7 missiles in furious volleys. But the bombers never slowed down. Most of these planes also carried infrared countermeasure jammers that fired off light pulses specially coded to confuse the SA-7s. The newer SA-7s could beat the jammers, but the Soviets hadn't given the Sandinistas any of those. So the Nicaraguans quickly found they were wasting their fire.

As the La Quebradita military barracks and tank maintenance headquarters a few miles south of the city came into view, Lieutenant Clarence Janeway, FB-111 weapons officer, turned to his targeting computer and radioed back to the attack command center: *"Enterprise, this is Blue Eagle Four-Zero-Four, we have the target visual. Starting target run."*

"Roger, Four-Zero-Four. Good luck."

Janeway and the pilot, Captain Michael Rising, had been strapped into their seats for more than three hours now. They'd lifted off from Edwards Air Force Base in Southern California just after three in the morning, refueled in flight over the coast, and now Janeway felt his adrenaline beginning to rush as the bomber bucked left and right from AA fire exploding in the air around them.

Near the city, the plane's enemy-attack radar-indicator light had been popping on and off as the plane was "painted" by several ground-radar stations that had somehow survived the first attack. Once, the missile-targeting buzzer had blared, warning that a ground-based missile had locked on to the plane's tail.

"Evading," Rising had barked as he jerked the stick left, but just then the buzzer went off. The missile must have gone after an infrared flare or been confused by the ultrasound cacophony of ECM signals filling the air over Managua.

As they settled into their attack run, Janeway's training took over; he was working by rote as he focused on the electronic tactical map that moved across his targeting scope in pace with the plane's position. A couple of miles out, infrared sensors in the plane's nose began picking up heat emissions from the sprawling barracks complex, and a three-dimensional holographic image of the target formed on Janeway's screen. With the flip of a switch, a targeting laser also under the plane's nose fired and locked on to the barracks complex, marking it at a spot that had been chosen using Blackbird aerial photographs.

"Target illuminated," Janeway told Rising.

They were only about twenty seconds from release, ten miles out of town, and out here the AA fire was light. Behind them, they could hear the first of the explosions as other planes dropped their bombs.

Behind their seats, a computer calculated the plane's speed and direction and the distance the bombs would fall to target. Using all that information, the computer released four two-thousand-pound Paveway II laser-guided bombs from under the wings at what it calculated to be just the right moment.

"Bombs away," Janeway said. Rising jerked the stick as the plane bucked, suddenly eight thousand pounds lighter. As the bombs fell, sensor pods in their noses locked on to the laser mark reflecting back from the target. Tiny fins and aerofoils on the bombs' tails flipped left and right to keep the fall straight down the laser path.

The four bombs struck the row of buildings one after another, setting off a quarter-mile trail of explosions down the center of the barracks. As the buildings erupted into flame, a video camera in the bomber's nose recorded the scene for verification. After a moment Rising pulled up and turned the plane back around for a Maverick TV-missile run on the way out.

Janeway pointed the nose-mounted TV camera at the low building that Intelligence had told him was the maintenance center for tanks and armored personnel carriers. Several BTR-60 APCs apparently awaiting repair were parked in a row right out front, and by all rights the underground fuel depot should have been just under the concrete apron. Janeway flipped on the missile target seeker. Looking at the crosshairs on his video monitor, he designated the spot he wanted to hit. When the computer gave him its target-lock signal, he launched.

A short, stubby white missile dropped from under the wings and fell about fifty feet before igniting and roaring down to the target. This was not a proximity warhead; the Maverick was armed with three hundred pounds of penetrating blast explosives. A little TV camera mounted behind a plastic window in the nose focused on the spot Janeway had designated and homed in at a speed approaching Mach 2. Janeway watched as the Maverick slammed through the forward edge of the roof, engulfing the front half of the building in flames, effectively taking out the vehicles parked outside. Not surprising; TV Mavericks had a combat kill record of 87 percent. The explosions rattled the plane, but as Janeway looked back he shook his head. Apparently they hadn't hit the fuel tank. A couple of miles out, Rising banked back around to get the scene on tape. But just then the whole complex seemed to explode. Flame and black smoke poured straight up in a fiery jet through the missile hole in the concrete apron. The force of the explosion shook the plane.

"Bingo, buddy," Janeway said, turning to Rising, thumbs up.

"Good work," Rising told him. Janeway flipped on the camera recorder right away. They didn't want to get much closer, in case the fuel tanks were compartmented and another one exploded.

Rising switched on the radio. "*Enterprise*, Blue Eagle Four-Zero-Four. Mission completed. Coming back your way."

"That's a roger, Blue Eagle Four-Zero-Four. Good work."

"Roger, *Enterprise*."

Three of the eighteen planes over Managua returned to base with full loads of bombs. In two, attack computers malfunctioned, and the other plane encountered such heavy AA fire that it couldn't get close enough to make an assured no-risk, no-collateral-damage bomb run.

Another rule of engagement for a "diplomatic air strike" was that pilots were to abandon their attacks if they faced what they judged to be significant risk of being shot down. After all, this attack had two audiences, one in Managua, the other in the United States. The Pentagon was well aware that the American public would not approve of this venture if they had to watch the president on television, wet-eyed as he walked between flag-draped coffins lined up in a hangar at Edwards Air Force Base.

As it was, only one FB-111 was missing; no one knew what had happened. Search teams over the water found no signs of wreckage and picked up no rescue beeper signals. It must have been shot down over Managua, and undoubtedly the Sandinistas would show off the wreckage when all was done.

A damaged FA-18 fighter, the one Gustafson saw turning back toward the Pacific, had ditched in the water on approach back to the *Enterprise*, but the pilot was rescued unhurt, except for a broken arm.

All day and in some spots through the next morning, dark columns of smoke poured into the skies over Managua, León, and Corinto. Satellite and Blackbird reconnaissance photos along with on-the-scene reports by journalists and others indicated that the planes had done significant damage to almost 70 percent of their targets. The Defense Ministry building appeared to be totally destroyed. Out at the airport, nothing but twisted metal was left of three Hind attack helicopters. And when thousands of Sandinista troops returned to their barracks the next day, many of them found their living quarters burned to the ground. Midafternoon, a few hours after the planes returned to Edwards, the Defense Department held its daily briefing at the Pentagon and declared the air raid "a complete success."

But even in high-tech modern warfare, no bombing raid is ever quite as precise as planned. By late afternoon the day of the raid, Managua television crews were out filming rescue efforts at a civilian hospital that had been struck by bombs. Viewers were shown a long row of bodies lying uncovered on the sidewalk. State television also showed part of the Intercontinental Hotel's south wing, damaged in the attack, but the tape didn't show any rescue efforts there. The rooms must have been unoccupied.

The Nicaraguan government claimed that "hundreds of innocent civilians" were killed, though they offered no particular evidence to support that. They also claimed to have shot down eight American planes. But the ambassador and others at Casa Grande knew that wasn't true. By midday they had already received a coded cable with the first after-action report saying two planes had been downed.

Blanchard, Kiernan, Gustafson, and the others were clustered around the TV watching CNN when in Washington the president stepped into the White House briefing room and read a short statement explaining that "the limited raid this morning was a carefully determined proportionate response to the unprovoked massacre in Honduras." And in answer to the first question, he declared, "No, we are not planning any further military action at this time."

Ambassador Blanchard turned to Gustafson, Kiernan, and the others, saying, "All in all, I guess it could have been worse." But later, when President Ortega came on Nicaraguan TV, red-faced, shaking with rage, Gustafson looked at Kiernan.

"Doesn't look like he's been 'chastened,' does it ol' buddy?" he said. Kiernan didn't answer.

Watching Ortega inveigh against the imperialists and promise revenge, Kiernan began to turn pale. He and the others at Casa Grande began to realize that they were the only "imperialists" within easy reach. Gustafson sat stiff-backed, teeth clenched— a Marine, ready for a fight.

Interior Ministry troops were still stationed outside Casa Grande's gate, but by late afternoon nobody had come by or called. About four Kiernan telephoned the embassy building downtown. Only a few loyal Nicaraguan security employees had been left there, but the man who answered the phone said, "Lieutenant Orozco speaking."

Carefully, Kiernan hung up the phone and muttered, "Oh, shit." He found the ambassador right away, out on the sunporch. Gustafson was at the window, his back to them as he looked down at the city.

"Don, they've taken over the embassy building."

Blanchard frowned. "I knew this would happen. The whole idea of leaving us here as a demonstration of good intentions while we're also killing people was *stupid*." That last word came out with a vehemence uncharacteristic of a career diplomat. "I told them, I told them," he said. But after a moment the anger passed, and he added, "At least there's nothing of value in there for them to see anymore. Go tell Washington."

As Kiernan walked off toward the cable transmitter in the basement, he looked back over his shoulder and asked, "We're in for it now, aren't we?" Blanchard didn't answer. But Gustafson had turned to face him. Standing straight, hands on hips, he gave Kiernan a steely smile.

The next morning, all six of them—Blanchard, Kiernan, Gustafson, Marlin Hershey, the political officer, and two staff assistants, Chris Imhoff and Larry Barnard—were at the dining-room table eating breakfast in silence when the Marine security guard monitoring the front gate came in and bent to the ambassador's ear. "Sir, Minister Zelaya is outside the gate requesting permission to come in and speak to you."

Blanchard glanced around the table. The other men laid down their forks and looked at each other.

"Let him in," Blanchard sighed.

"I guess this is it," Hershey said after the Marine had left the room.

"Marlin, they aren't stupid," the ambassador told him. "They know that if they harm us, they'll have the entire weight of the United States armed forces to worry about."

"Maybe they'll just deport us," Imhoff suggested.

But Hershey shook his head. "It's too late for that."

"Why don't all of you stay here," Blanchard said as he got up and headed for the study.

The study was bright with early-morning light filtering through slatted wooden shutters. Holding himself as erect as he was able, Zelaya limped in, with an aide a few steps behind. He stopped in the middle of the room, standing on the central pattern of the room's huge oriental rug. He glared for a moment, his beady eyes now just angry red slits. Behind a massive mahogany desk Ambassador Blanchard stood up and nodded to him.

"Mr. Ambassador," Zelaya snarled through clenched teeth, "the atrocities your country committed against mine have so enraged the Nicaraguan people that we can no longer protect you here. As a result, we are forced to move all of you to a more secure location."

"Minister, we believe we are most secure right here. We do not wish to leave."

"Mr. Ambassador, in this matter there is no room for discussion. After the genocide your country has committed, you should feel fortunate that we are concerned for your welfare at all. You have ten minutes to collect a few things."

"Minister Zelaya, may I remind you, this is the United States embassy. You have no right . . ." But Zelaya had already turned to leave.

"Ten minutes," he repeated over his shoulder as he limped through the door. Blanchard returned to the dining room immediately.

"Gentlemen, I'm afraid Zelaya is going to take us away from here. We have ten minutes to pack a bag. Larry, go down and send a quick cable telling State what's happening, then use the acid and destroy the equipment before you leave the communications room. The rest of you, if you have anything you want to say to Washington, tell Larry. Then get your bags and meet me in the front hall."

"What's this mean?" Chris Imhoff asked, not even trying to hide his apprehension.

"Well, buddy boy," Gustafson said, eyebrows raised, voice affecting a hard, matter-of-fact composure, "it looks like we're gonna be invasion hostages."

CHAPTER
TWENTY-ONE

WASHINGTON, APRIL 9

BY CHRISTOPHER EATON
NEW WORLD NEWS SERVICE

WASHINGTON—Within hours of the United States air strike on Nicaragua Thursday, the Sandinista government seized the United States embassy in Managua and then took Ambassador Donald E. Blanchard and his skeleton staff captive, the White House announced yesterday.

The administration denounced "the taking of American hostages" and demanded that they be released immediately.

The president and his senior advisors were meeting late into the night, and White House officials said privately that further military actions were being discussed. The United States military remained on full alert.

"The president is furious," a senior White House official said. "I don't know what he's going to do exactly, but the way he's talking right now, I'd sure hate to be the Sandinistas."

Intelligence officials said the ambassador and five aides stayed behind after the emergency evacuation of most of the embassy staff Wednesday night "as a show of good faith." One of them added that the Americans are now being held in several secret locations around Managua, "probably as protection against an invasion."

The Sandinista government said they were removed from Casa Grande, an embassy residence building, "for their own protection," but would not say where they had been taken.

In Central America, Honduran and Salvadoran armed forces were being mobilized on full war footing yesterday. Any United States invasion of Nicaragua is unlikely to occur without at least token participation by other Central American armies, in an effort to legitimize the action under the 1947 Rio Accords, a military cooperation treaty between the United States and the nations of Latin America.

Pentagon sources said the aircraft carrier *Theodore Roosevelt* and its accompanying battle group, recalled last week from leave at Barcelona, Spain, were due to reach Nicaragua's Caribbean coast on Saturday. The carrier *Enterprise* and its accompanying battle group, used in the air raid two days ago, remain off the Pacific coast, the sources said.

Meanwhile, an overnight ABC News/*Washington Post* opinion poll showed that 76 percent of the American people approved of the air strike on Nicaragua while only 14 percent disapproved.

Witness for Peace and several other religious and pacifist groups held vigils and hunger strikes outside the White House and in cities across the United States yesterday. Otherwise, however, protest was limited. The White House said its phone calls and telegrams were running ten to one in favor of the attack. And on Capitol Hill, leading Republicans and Democrats alike said they fully approved of the raid.

A few members of Congress, including Senator Robert Kelly of Ohio, the president's likely opponent in the elections next fall, said they wanted a White House briefing on justifications for the attack before they offered an opinion. But as of last night the White House had offered no briefing, and only a handful of congressmen were openly criticizing the attack. . . .

"I miss you," Leslie whispered into the phone, looking around the office to make sure no one could hear. Even though it was Saturday, everyone was there. She hadn't seen Eaton in several days; her husband had been in town for the last week.

"I miss you too," Eaton said from his own office. "When's he leaving?"

"I don't know. With everything that's going on, the president needs polling data every day. Hey, nice story this morning. You made it into *Current News* again."

"Oh, yeah?" Eaton said, delighted. "So how's the mood over there?"

"Grim. As you already know, the president's pissed. He's been holding Pre-Crisis Planning Group meetings all morning. The Chiefs went in an hour ago. The gossip is we're going back in with the Marines. But it's just gossip. I don't know. All I really know is the president's really steamed. General Dayton's pissed too."

"Any word on where they've got the ambassador and the others?"

"Just what's already out. They're spread all over Managua. They did pick up information that Sandinistas took the embassy Marine guards over to the El Chipote prison in Managua. That's already out; maybe you heard it on the radio."

"You're kidding! I hadn't heard that. That's the torture prison. They lock you up totally naked in pitch-black cells only about a yard high and half a yard long and wide so you can't really stand up or sit down. Are you sure of that?"

"Well, nothing's sure, but that's the report. That's what General Dayton was going to tell the president."

"He'll invade for sure when he hears that. Anybody said anything about what they're doing with the contras all this time?" Eaton knew that under invasion contingency plans drawn up long ago the contras were supposed to take over the Highlands and make sure the Sandinistas couldn't take refuge up there and then start their own guerrilla war.

"I don't think anybody's worrying much about the contras right now," Leslie said. "The RIG is totally cut out of the picture. That guy Terry Ascher keeps calling over here sounding kind of pathetic, and Dayton won't even answer his calls."

"Oh, yeah?"

"I don't think anybody trusts those guys anymore. Too many questions about that dinner-party massacre. People keep saying if it hadn't been for that, we wouldn't be in this mess now. And everybody thinks Terry Ascher's the one who planted the idea for that in the contras' minds."

OLD EXECUTIVE OFFICE BUILDING, WASHINGTON

Ascher looked dreadful. Linda and everyone else in his office, even other people who knew Ascher only from passing in the hall, all were whispering about how sickly he seemed. It wasn't just the Valium. Ascher had been taking at least thirty milligrams a day for so long now that most people had stopped noticing the dull droopy-eyed look.

No, it was his pallor. Ascher was so drugged, so disconsolate over the turn of events, that after years of devoted daily use he was no longer bothering with his sunlamp. He didn't care anymore, and people who'd never seen Ascher without that deep sienna tan were alarmed by his natural skin color. That plus the way he seemed to drag himself through the day convinced people he must be deathly ill.

After a few days of seeing him like that, Linda had poked her head into his office to ask if he was all right. She found him sitting up in his desk chair gazing vacantly out the window. She had to speak his name several times before he even realized she was there.

"Terry, what's wrong?" she asked. But he just stared at her for a moment before shaking his head and waving her back out the door.

Ascher had nothing to do. The contra RIG had not been formally disbanded, but it might as well have been. The RIG had about as much functional purpose now as the United States trade envoy to Japan the day after Pearl Harbor. His office still hummed along; Linda and the others had to pay the contras' bills and keep the supply lines flowing. But all the decisions were now being made over in the West Wing. Ascher figured Christopher and the others had taken over not just because of the extraordinary turn of events. He knew they blamed him in part for what was happening; he was no longer trusted. If it hadn't been for the dinner-party massacre . . .

When Ascher called Christopher, Dayton, or others to find out what was going on and how he might help, they didn't even bother to call back.

Yesterday his father had called; he was home from the hospital now. Ascher had been down the hall, and when he got back the message lay on his desk blotter. Even the name on the phone slip seemed to sneer up at him. Ascher couldn't bear the idea of speaking to him right now, so he waited until after four, when he knew his father would have gone to the hospital for his daily physical therapy appointment. Then he called and left a message on the answering machine.

"Father, I'm sorry I missed you. I'll try again, but we're very busy here, you know."

Actually for the last few days Ascher had come in to work late, after ten, and gone home early, by four. Nobody noticed, nobody cared, except maybe Linda.

At home each night, maybe he'd warm a Stouffer's frozen dinner in the microwave before going downstairs to watch one of his video war movies. It didn't matter that he'd seen every one of them several times before. By the time he turned it on he was so drugged and drunk that he could barely focus his eyes. Sometimes he'd fall asleep even before all the credits had finished running, then wake up early the next morning with the movie still blaring. His VCR's normal setting, unattended, was endless repeat. That was Ascher's life.

Under his administration, the contras had helped drag the United States into a war. No, he kept thinking, it wasn't his fault directly. After all, it was the Sandinistas who had shot down the Chinooks. But only because of the dinner-party massacre, and he'd been the one who proposed urban guerrilla raids. Even if no one knew anything about the disastrous "black" operation he'd cooked up with Mendoza and Gustafson, everyone probably believed he'd been the one who planted the idea of hostage-taking operations in the contras' minds. He'd also been the one who suggested moving the contra camp north into Honduras. If it hadn't been for that . . .

Someone had to take the fall, and he was the logical choice. His career was ruined. He hadn't heard from Mendoza either. Rafael must be just as disconsolate.

SOUTHERN HONDURAS

Over the weekend, the contras moved their camp again, back down to El Cuartelón. Most of the Sandinistas had gone back to Managua, and in the Highlands they'd left behind just one eight-hundred-man light infantry unit, the Simón Bolívar Battalion. The contras were the last thing the Sandinistas worried about now.

The move was extraordinarily easy. No mule trains, no long hikes. This time they got a United States Army airlift, and back down at the border a contingent of National Guard engineers from Arizona helped them rebuild their camp. In just under forty-eight hours they had better facilities than they'd had at any time during the long war.

Sunday afternoon the Directorate was meeting in their new command hut. It came complete with electric lights and an air conditioner, unaccustomed luxuries, and the latter especially welcome since the temperature outside was well over ninety degrees. A U.S. Army generator hummed out back.

Jorge Paladino couldn't remember the last time all of the directors had been in country at the same time, much less down here at the front. But events were moving fast. They had spent days shocked and angry over the dinner-party massacre; most of them thought it would spell the end of the contra movement. But with the air strike and then the hostage-taking, now everyone was gleeful. Certainly an invasion was coming at last. They'd be back in Managua soon.

No one seemed happier than Rafael Mendoza, who walked in as the meeting was getting under way, his grin even broader than usual. But as soon as Mendoza closed the door, the group grew silent. All of them had tried to ignore Mendoza the last two weeks he'd been in camp, since the day after the dinner-party killings. The old sycophancy had vanished in an instant. Only Francesca had seemed to spend time with him, and that was still a source of resentment for most on the Directorate.

"My friends, things are picking up, are they not?" Mendoza asked, standing behind Chairman Coronel at the head of the table, his hand on Coronel's shoulder. Coronel twisted around and glared at Mendoza's hand, but Mendoza acted as if he didn't notice.

No one smiled, no one responded to Mendoza's banter. Instead, in English, Jorge asked him, "Have you found Major Paz?"

"I am afraid not," Mendoza answered in Spanish, still smiling. "He's still missing."

"And how about Comandante Venganza?"

"He has not returned either."

"So two weeks have passed, and you still cannot give us any answers on what happened to cause the dinner-party killings?"

Jorge had lost all reluctance to ask questions like these. Even the Directorate knew that Mendoza's standing with the U.S. government had dropped. The directors could tell by the brusque, dismissive way the other American officials treated him. Mendoza certainly was no longer a subject of esteem among the contras' leaders either. He had been Paz's de facto commander, after all; the directors blamed him for the dinner-party raid.

None of this bothered Mendoza. True, in Washington's view the contras had dragged the United States into a war while he was running the program. The biting tone of the cables he'd been getting from Langley left no doubt where he stood. But Mendoza didn't care. His smile was genuine. He was achieving his goal, and he had been prepared to pay the price. The cold stares from around the table didn't touch him.

As Mendoza's star fell, Paladino's was rising. After years of warning the others about Mendoza and the agency, now he had become one of the most influential men on the Directorate.

"We will find out what happened in time," Mendoza assured them. "But now we have more pressing matters. I am leaving you for now, back to Tegucigalpa in the morning. Coming here in a little while is Colonel Robert Teeley, U.S. Army Military Group commander at Palmerola. He brings you new instructions, and from now on direction and advice will be coming from our military, not my agency." Several men around the table smiled.

"It's been a pleasure, my friends, and I hope I will see you in Managua." Despite themselves, several applauded at that.

CHAPTER
TWENTY-TWO

As MONDAY DAWNED BRIGHT AND CLEAR OVER THE Pacific, more than sixty American warships were steaming on station fifteen miles off the Nicaraguan coast. Even at daybreak, sunlight at this longitude could be withering. But out here on the water a steady breeze gave the morning a chill. On board many vessels, sailors wore sweaters under their life jackets.

The last of the dock landing ships, the *Whidbey Island,* was dropping her stern gate into the water, and inside the docking well, LCAC landing-craft pilots were starting their engines, adding the loud roar of high-speed propellers to the varied sounds of a Navy/Marine amphibious assault force readying itself for attack.

A moment later the *Whidbey* looked as if she were giving birth. One after another, four air-cushion landing craft popped out of the tail and flopped into the water. Pushed by two gas turbine propellers mounted over the stern, and lifted by two more under the crafts' wide rubber skirts, the LCACs maneuvered like water bugs as they skimmed off to the southeast and joined up with their squadrons. Over several square miles of ocean, thirty LCACs holding almost a thousand men from the Fifth Marine Amphibious Brigade skimmed in circles, waiting.

Aboard the *Enterprise* meanwhile, two squadrons of FA-18 fighters were fueled, armed, and lined up on deck, pilots in cockpits, canopies up. Not far away, aboard the amphibious assault ships *Tripoli* and *New Orleans*, pilots and Marines were strapped into their seats aboard two dozen Sea Stallion troop-transport helicopters. Lift cables were strung between a dozen more Super Stallion heavy-lift choppers and the Piranha Light Armored Vehicles they would ferry to shore.

A little closer in, the battleship *Missouri* was in firing position, all nine of her sixteen-inch guns turned, raised, and trained at the coast. Everyone was on station, everything ready: fighters, troops, tanks, helicopters, a battleship, an aircraft carrier, and dozens of other support ships, all poised for a massive coordinated assault. With all that, a Marine squad leader standing on the bridge of LCAC-18, looking for the first signal that the invasion was about to begin, trained his twenty-power binoculars on the *Missouri* about a mile away and waited for the launch of a little model plane.

After a couple of minutes he saw what looked like two tiny flares jump from the aft deck. A few yards out, miniature rocket boosters extinguished, propellers took over, and two small Pioneer remotely piloted vehicles buzzed off toward the shore at about sixty miles an hour. As soon as these target-spotting drones were on station three thousand feet over the resort beach at Masachapa, and their on-board television cameras were transmitting in focus, the *Missouri* would open fire with her sixteen-inch Mk-7 guns—the most powerful naval artillery pieces in the world. The invasion would begin.

A full two weeks earlier, the president had ordered the military to start preparing for a possible invasion—just in case. The directive went out as soon as the United States first learned that Nicaragua was massing its tanks on the Honduran border.

At the time, no one believed the United States would actually have to attack, but the military had to be ready anyway. If nothing happened, it would be a good exercise. But as always, the Joint Chiefs had said they'd need a month, maybe more, to get ready. And if they did have to invade, "we'll need three divisions, maybe four," General Stark had told the president. "And that'll draw down our NATO readiness."

In truth, the Pentagon didn't want to do it. Never had. Despite public rhetoric to the contrary, the generals worried that Nicaragua would indeed be another Vietnam. Once trapped there, the military would become pariahs again. Congress would start paring down their budgets; once again, only high school dropouts would volunteer to serve.

But the president spat back the commander in chief's normal retort: "I give you $370 billion a year, a 630-ship navy—whatever you ask for—and you can't handle a backward little country like Nicaragua?"

Though he was certain the Joint Chiefs already knew it, General Dayton recited the intelligence about Nicaragua's military capabilities: obsolete weapons, demoralized conscripts, antiquated antiaircraft, and nothing even resembling an air force. "And our Air Force has already taken out a good chunk of their defenses. You mean to tell me you need four divisions, more than sixty thousand men, to defeat that?" Dayton asked, eyebrows raised.

"Three divisions, that's all," the president ordered. "A fourth on ready reserve if you want, but in the States or at South-Com"—Southern Command in Panama—"not down in Honduras unless I approve first."

The Chiefs grumbled but were mollified a bit when told they could have an all-service invasion, using Army air-mobile and tank battalions, Navy surface-ship and airborne weapons, plus Air Force fighters and bombers.

Elements of two Marine amphibious brigades would get to carry out the first full-scale amphibious landing under fire since the assault on Inchon, Korea, in 1950—demonstrating, as the Marines had wanted to do for years, that their primary mission was still important in the modern world.

Even a couple of submarines would be used, to sneak Navy Seals in for reconnaissance the night before. And out of all that, young officers from every field of service would get combat experience, not to mention medals—important badges for advancement.

The attack strategy had been drafted years ago but was revised several times as new information came in. The Sandinistas had an odd habit of describing their defense plans to visiting American reporters. And in the latest interview, printed just a few months earlier, they'd said: "Nicaraguan defense officials say they believe an American invasion would be staged from Choluteca in Honduras into Chinandega Province in northwestern Nicaragua" while "the United States Marines mounted an amphibious assault on the Pacific Coast." To stop this, the newspaper story had said, "the Sandinistas have plans to fall back along successive lines of defense to keep their army between the invaders and the capital."

Well, reconnaissance photos were showing that the Nicaraguan army had deployed for just the defense described. And the United States was planning to play its part too, just the way the Sandinistas had predicted.

When the president finally gave the invasion order Saturday evening, thirty-six hours after the hostages were taken in Managua, the military had been preparing for two weeks. Though the Chiefs had complained that they would need a month, Monday morning the forces were ready.

At 6:26 A.M. aboard the command ship *Coronado*, a converted dock-landing vessel, Vice Admiral William J. Conners gave the order to open fire. And aboard the *Missouri*, one after another the Mk-7 guns opened up, firing 1,900-pound projectiles in a 45-degree arc toward shore.

Before now, Mk-7s had been used in battle only one time since the *Missouri* and the other three *Iowa*-class battleships were recommissioned during the 1980s. In 1983 and early 1984, the battleship *New Jersey* had fired at Druse militiamen in the mountains over Beirut, to no good effect. Back then, the Navy didn't use Pioneer RPV targeting drones that showed where the shells were landing so gunners could adjust the aim. The shells had scattered over an area of several miles.

Truth be told, even though the Mk-7s now used drones, the *Missouri*'s thirty-two Tomahawk cruise missiles were much more effective. With on-board radar guidance, they could hit targets almost every time. Whatever the Tomahawks and other missiles failed to destroy, the FA-18 attack fighters could take out. But the old battleship's monster guns had a larger purpose. Firing them caused a thunderous crack that could be heard, even felt, fifty miles away, and as the projectiles tore through the air, closing on their targets, people on the receiving end began to hear a shrill descending whistle that could stop hearts. And when the shells detonated—well, Navy wags liked to say that firing the 1,900-pound shells "is kinda like shooting a Volkswagen into the air, and when it lands, it makes a parking lot." All in all, the Navy hoped the guns would terrify the enemy. They did.

The targets this morning were two dozen T-55 tanks dug into shallow protective pits on either side of the highway leading back from the beach. Arrayed behind them were a dozen 152-

millimeter howitzers. The tanks and guns were carefully camouflaged, but between the Navy Seals who'd snuck ashore the night before and the air-reconnaissance photos, nearly all of the enemy positions had been located and plotted on the attack map in the *Coronado*'s combat information center.

The first rounds scattered all over the Masachapa-Montelimar area, blasting craters fifty yards wide, sending dirt and chunks of debris sailing half a mile. From three thousand feet up, the RPV drones transmitted TV pictures with superimposed targeting grids back to the *Missouri*, and the gunners adjusted their aim. But on shore, even rounds exploding a mile away shook the tanks and sent rattling vibrations up through the treads. As the nine guns kept firing—eighteen shells a minute that fell closer and closer to the targets—the fourteen-ton tanks started bouncing off the ground. Inside, the crews' ears were ringing, and anything loose rattled or crashed to the floor. Gunners grew dizzy and deaf. Then as the shells homed in closer and closer, tank drivers radioed back and forth to each other. Their voices grew more and more panicky as one tank after another dropped off the air with each new shelling.

In one tank, a gunner who'd strapped himself into his seat so as not to hit his head on the ceiling while the tank bounced around watched helplessly as an explosion jarred one of his 100-millimeter cannon shells out of its rack. It fell nose-first onto the floor. The shell didn't detonate, but no matter. The gunner unbuckled himself, threw open the hatch, jumped out and ran down the road toward Managua, picking himself up and running even faster each time a new shell detonated, knocking him into the dirt.

The naval gunfire lasted about twenty-five minutes, and toward the end the LCACs started dashing toward shore at about forty miles an hour. Slower, conventional landing craft trailed behind, and the *Missouri* stopped firing only when the LCACs approached the surf. Overhead, meanwhile, a squadron of FA-18 fighters roared past and strafed the beach with their 20-millimeter multibarrel cannons. Sandinistas fell sprawling into the sand all along the beach. But almost right away others fired off SA-7 antiaircraft missiles, and one FA-18 exploded just five hundred feet over the beach. The rest turned back.

When the air-cushion craft reached shore, they powered right up the white sand, stopping at the road. And when the Marines poured out, the Sandinista forces waiting for them had been thinned considerably, not because most were wounded or killed.

No, to many of the Nicaraguan soldiers—involuntary draftees to begin with—the odds seemed so long, death so certain, that they just dropped their weapons and ran away, ignoring their officers' shouted curses. Some of the others seemed to be in shock—rattled and deafened by the *Missouri's* withering gunfire, stricken to see wounded and dead comrades lying beside them—casualties of cannon fire from the FA-18 jets that had screamed by just overhead.

Yes, these were battle-hardened Sandinista troops. But years of fighting the contras—ducking M-16 rounds and, occasionally, grenades or mortars—were no preparation for repelling a full-scale invasion by the United States armed forces. When Sandinista infantrymen did open fire, the opposition seemed lackluster at first. Even as they tried to shoot, the Nicaraguans were still trying to shake their heads clear.

Marines were fanning out across the beach, ducking behind trash cans and tourist concession stands as they fired rifles, rocket-propelled grenades, known as light antitank weapons, and mortars at the scattered enemy positions in buildings on the other side of the highway.

"Too easy," some of them were muttering as they fired LAWs into open windows. But then, from behind a beachfront hotel, an MI-24 Hind attack helicopter rose into the air and started spitting cannon fire and unguided missiles all over the beach. Rifle shots bounced off the chopper's heavy armored skin, and the Hind dodged and weaved to avoid lucky RPG hits.

The Marines weren't carrying Stinger AA missiles, and none of the fighter planes overhead were armed with Sidewinders or other air-to-air missiles either. The Sandinistas had no air force, but somebody had forgotten about their Hind "flying tanks"— a deadly oversight.

The Marines dug in, but several were hit as the Hind bobbed up and down, its nose-mounted Gatling gun spitting 23-millimeter rounds at a rate of fifty per second. Wing-mounted rocket-launcher pods were firing unguided fragmentation missiles one after another, and one of them hit an LCAC still unloading; the fuel tank exploded, and sixteen Marines were immolated.

Dug into the sand behind an oil-barrel trash can, only scant protection, a Marine radioed back to his ship for help. Right away, the pilot in an A-6 fighter orbiting the *Enterprise* battle group fifteen miles out fired his laser targeting designator at the Hind, plotted the chopper's position in his attack computer, and transmitted a digital burst down to the guided-missile cruiser *Vincennes* just below. The cruiser hadn't been expecting an air battle either. Long-range air defenses weren't properly armed. But immediately an order went out to the gunners: Use a Deadeye instead.

The crew inside the ship's aft 54-caliber gun quickly loaded a Deadeye five-inch guided projectile. Using the A-6's targeting information, they adjusted the gun and fired—all within ninety seconds of the radio call. Once it was in the air, the long, thin missile's fins unfolded, and its own rocket engine fired. The targeting computer in the Deadeye's nose locked on to the A-6's laser marker, and six seconds later the projectile detonated on the ground just under the Hind, sending up a fireball that seemed to consume the chopper. It exploded in a roaring burst of flame.

The Marines had the beach secured in under thirty minutes. The Sandinistas, true to their word, had pulled back and dug in about five miles up the highway at their next line of defense, joining more than one thousand troops already there.

With the beach under control, troop and equipment transport helicopters lifted off from the *Tripoli* and the *New Orleans*. And then the tank-landing ships *Frederick* and *Tuscaloosa* made for a nearby concrete dock. There, each ship's bow doors folded open, a ramp was laid out, and the cargo—almost fifty M1 Abrams main battle tanks—began rolling ashore.

CHOLUTECA GAP, HONDURAN-NICARAGUAN BORDER

To the north as this was going on, a U.S. Army tank division was rolling down the Inter-American Highway and the plains to the east and the west. As soon as the Americans crossed the border, they fired more than a dozen camouflage artillery rounds that exploded and filled the air ahead with clouds of crimson smoke to hide their advance. But minutes later, when the U.S. forces emerged from the smoke, Nicaraguan tanks, multiple rocket launchers, heavy artillery, and a full division of men opened fire. This, more than anything else, was the assault the Sandinistas had been preparing for since 1979.

Right away, twelve Cobra attack helicopters swept in from the west. Gunners fired cannons at the tanks to neutralize machine gunners who shot at them from above the turrets. At the same time every one of the choppers aimed and fired their Hell-fire antitank missiles. They took out almost every Nicaraguan tank they targeted. The thin-skinned T-55s were built before anyone had conceived of shaped-charge, armor-piercing, laser-guided antitank missiles, and one after another the Nicaraguan tanks burst into flame. Some rolled over onto their sides. Few crew members managed to get out.

Even with that, the Nicaraguans were putting up a good fight. Their SA-7 AA missiles managed to explode a couple of the Cobras. And up here the Americans couldn't call up naval gun support. No Mk-7s, no Deadeyes.

But with one quick radio request, the Army ordered the next best thing. An entire tactical fighter wing of F-16 Fighting Falcons, seventy-two fighter planes, was now stationed at the "temporary" Palmerola air base in Honduras. Within a few minutes, two dozen of them flew in from the northeast. Right away they proved the military maxim that air superiority wins the war.

The fighters dropped twenty-four time-delayed area denial cluster bombs right on top of the Sandinista troops. The bombs blew open about fifty feet above ground, scattering thousands of baseball-sized armor-piercing bomblets. They fell over a wide area among the Sandinista forces and began detonating in sequence over a ninety-second period. As they went off, Nicaraguan ground forces began running in all directions, some of them dropping their weapons along the way. A soldier would see a bomblet explode to his left and tear off to the right, only to run into another time-delay bomblet that went off as he passed. From the air, the American pilots watched as soldiers fell everywhere and others scattered, routed and out of control, time-delay bomblets continuing to take them down even as they fled.

On their way out, the F-16s made another pass, spraying the surviving Sandinistas with fire from their twenty-millimeter automatic cannons. Meanwhile the surviving Sandinista tank drivers turned their vehicles around and sped south toward the next defensive position as American tanks rushed after them, gunners aiming and firing TOW missiles at the T-55s' tails. As the TOWs flew, they unraveled long thin guidance wires that led back to the launcher. Gunners continually adjusted the missiles' aim, sending the new targeting information through the trailed wires. The TOWs followed the fleeing tanks and struck them in the tail, one by one.

The opening assaults were going as well as any of the American commanders could have hoped. The Nicaraguans were running. Still, the Americans knew they would need two full days of bloody fighting, maybe three, to push the Sandinistas all the way back to Managua.

Once in the capital, they'd probably have to fight from house to house. Air superiority wouldn't be much help there; simply bombing or strafing the capital was out of the question. Too many civilian casualties. So taking Managua would cost a lot of men. Even using controlled fire and restraint, hundreds of unarmed civilians would probably be killed as well.

Though victory was certain, the American commanders knew this would end up being a costly, bloody little war.

SANDINISTA ARMY GENERAL HEADQUARTERS, MANAGUA, NICARAGUA

The Sandinista comandantes realized they couldn't win. But they were more than ready to fight to the painful end. They continued exhorting their troops and kept supplies flowing to the front. And even though the Sandinista lines were falling backward faster than expected, in Managua the comandantes felt a strange optimism. They believed they were really giving the Americans a fight.

By late afternoon, the fighting was beginning to die down for the day. The American forces were still a safe distance from Managua. So, on a whim, the generals decided to visit the wounded over at the military hospital. The army's three senior comandantes climbed out of the underground concrete command bunker that had been built in secret beneath the Defense Ministry building and walked over to the hospital just down the street.

The Defense Ministry had been destroyed in the American air raid a week before, but the concrete bunker under the basement was not damaged at all. Though the building hiding it was gone, the bunker roof was covered with piles of half-burned rubble and debris. The comandantes liked it that way. Only the entrance to one side had been dug out. The bunker was still secure. Or so it seemed.

Since the first air raid, SR-71 Blackbirds had been crisscrossing the skies over Managua, taking damage-assessment photographs for the U.S. Air Force. The photos were of immediate tactical value, but the Pentagon also wanted to see exactly how their bombs and missiles had worked. Some weapons used in the air raid had never been fired in combat before.

In Washington, analysts had pored over the photos, paying

special attention to the Defense Ministry building, one of the primary targets. In several photos analysts had noticed unusual activity near one corner of the rubble. In one picture, a uniformed general seemed to be climbing up from under the debris. So Washington had sent up another Blackbird, this one loaded with infrared film, and when the IR photos came back they'd shown a large rectangular bright spot under the Defense Ministry debris. With additional concentrated surveillance photos and a little help from a Nicaraguan "intelligence asset" on the ground, the Pentagon figured it had found the Sandinistas' new command bunker, relocated from the old bunker next to the El Chipote prison. The Americans were delighted, and they came up with a plan.

Just before five P.M. the comandantes were walking back from the hospital along Avenida Bolívar, the city's wide ceremonial avenue. Managua seemed strangely quiet, despite the scattered booms of artillery many miles away. Hardly any vehicles were on the streets; most people were staying indoors. The capital was eerily peaceful.

"It's kind of spooky," one general murmured. The other two nodded.

Under the orange light and long shadows of late afternoon, the city seemed warm and beautiful. The temperature was dropping; above them as they walked, palm fronds rustled in a slight breeze. Managua was their home, and with the low rumble of fighting in the distance, the generals looked at each other, bittersweet smiles on their faces. Soon, each of them knew, they would have to leave.

The Sandinistas' political leaders had already left in secret for Cuba, carrying out contingency plans made long ago. Even now, they were setting up a government in exile. These comandantes here in Managua wouldn't acknowledge it to one another, but every one of them had already packed his bags and set them by the front door at home. They'd transferred their money to foreign bank accounts, in Panama or Venezuela. When the time came, probably a few days from now, they'd be ready to go.

They walked up the street in silence, lost in personal reflections about times past, lives to come. Then behind them they heard jet noise approaching from the distance.

"Another air raid," one muttered, cursing as they turned and looked into the sky for the planes. But there were no planes. Instead, in the distance over the lake they saw a tiny dot in the sky, bobbing up and down ever so slightly as it grew gradually larger. It flew directly toward them, only about thirty feet over the water. Within a few seconds it passed over land, heading straight for the Rubén Darío Theater, the roar of its engine growing louder. Over the lake it had left a long white trail.

A few feet from the theater building it jigged up a few feet, roared over the roof, and then jerked back down on the other side, flying in a straight line up Avenida Bolívar. As it approached the comandantes, it suddenly slowed down. Still only about thirty feet up, it passed over the generals at more than one hundred miles per hour, and they just had time to read the bold black lettering above the stubby wings: UNITED STATES NAVY.

It was a jet-powered Tomahawk cruise missile, fired from the *Missouri*'s deck seventy miles away less than three minutes earlier. General Dynamics technicians had spent all morning setting the missile's on-board terrain-contour-matching inertial navigation system. Using reconnaissance photos, they'd programmed the locations and characteristics of every piece of ground between point of launch and point of impact. And now the Tomahawk was heading unerringly for its target, looking for landmarks, feeding each new bit of information into its on-board computer, which adjusted the missile's course all along the way, almost as if a live pilot were inside.

Standing still, the comandantes watched helplessly as the twenty-foot cream-colored missile flew up the street two more blocks, turned its nose up all of a sudden and then plunged straight down, slamming through the rubble into the center of their command bunker, where, but for a whim, the three of them would have been right now. The Tomahawk's hardened steel warhead lanced into the ten-inch concrete roof and exploded only after it had broken through the other side. Even though they were three blocks away, the noise and concussion knocked the generals off their feet. Smoke and flame poured into the sky; concrete chunks and debris fell to the ground all around them. Slowly they got up and brushed themselves off. For almost a minute they stood dead still and stared at the conflagration up the street. Then they looked at one another in stunned silence.

Within half an hour they had gone home and grabbed their suitcases. Without speaking they rode together out to Sandino Airport, where they climbed aboard a Cubana de Aviación AN-26 military transport. The plane flew east at treetop level, trying to keep out of sight of American fighters. But in fact, American AWACS radar planes high over Nicaragua tracked the AN-26 from the moment it left Sandino field. No fighters were sent up because, in truth, these generals were no threat anymore. In flight, they were an asset.

Word that the comandantes had fled got to the troops at the front by nightfall. Before dawn more than half had deserted. When the Americans started their engines at dawn Tuesday morning, fired off their camouflage smoke rounds, and rolled their assault forces forward, they found almost nobody to fight.

The Marines were in Managua by dusk, about thirty-six hours after the first assault. The Army arrived two hours later. The Sandinistas were gone.

SUBURBAN MANAGUA, NICARAGUA

Gustafson enjoyed watching his guards grow demoralized. When they brought him his food Monday evening they were no longer glaring at him, expressions cocky. Instead he was grinning back at them with his own insolent look, and they declined to meet his eyes.

Since he and the others had been taken from Casa Grande in separate jeeps, blindfolded, he had been held in the bare cinderblock basement of a private home he judged to be southeast of the city. There were no windows, and only one bug-stained low-wattage bulb hung from its cord. His captors had dragged down a single foam mattress and a ragged blanket. The only other fixtures were an oil-stained work table stripped of all its tools and a couple of empty aluminum trash cans. The entrance was up the wood-frame steps, through a locked door that led into a kitchen. And when two guards brought him meals twice a day—black beans, a piece of hard bread, and water—one of them stood at the top of the steps, an AK pointed at Gustafson's chest, as the other set the plastic plate on the concrete floor at the bottom of the stairs. He taunted them, but they ignored him.

"You boys ready to get blown away?" he asked the first day. "Think your buddies in Havana are gonna come save you?"

Sunday morning he looked at the soldier standing at the top of the steps and gestured at his rifle, saying, "What do you think you're going to do with that little peashooter when a whole squadron of F-16s comes tearing down after you?" The soldier stared back, expressionless.

Through the weekend Gustafson did push-ups, ran in place. But he got so little food that by Monday he was tiring easily. Besides, he wanted to listen.

Monday morning, Gustafson heard the unmistakable sound of big naval guns off in the distance. On Tuesday he heard scattered artillery and mortar fire, some of it Sandinista but most American. Then in the evening he began to hear the crackle of individual rifle fire not too far off. By nightfall he was smiling to himself; he recognized the chop of U.S. Army Blackhawk helicopters and the crack of M-16s. And then just past dawn this morning he'd heard the familiar reassuring drone of Air Force C-130 troop transports flying past almost overhead, probably coming in from Dyess Air Force Base in Texas. We must have secured Sandino Airport, he thought. After he'd counted five or six C-130s flying past, he realized it was late and no one had brought him breakfast. So he bounded up the wooden steps and beat his fist against the door.

"Who's out there? Whoever's out there, we need to talk, now! You hear me?" He pounded some more, then put his ear to the wooden door. Silence.

"Anybody out there, you better come over here, right now," he shouted. Still nothing. So with one hand on the railing, the other braced against the stairwell wall, he reared back and slammed his foot into the door. That hurt. He was wearing light Reebok track shoes. But after three or four hard kicks, the deadbolt smashed through the thin pine frame, and the door swung open. Gustafson shook his head; these Nics can't make anything worth a damn.

He stood quietly for a minute, listening. Then, crouching, he stuck his head around the corner into the kitchen. Nobody there. Creeping into the kitchen, he opened the refrigerator and grabbed a hard roll and a can of beer—there wasn't much else—downed the roll in two bites, and swigged half the beer in a couple of quick gulps. Then he opened some drawers until he found a long carving knife.

He peered around the corner into the empty living room, knife in hand, then quietly moved to the front door and opened it a crack. Outside just a few feet away on the front walk, a little man in blue jeans and a T-shirt stood with his back to him, a military backpack at his feet. The man was obviously nervous as he waited, apparently for someone to come pick him up. Gustafson recognized him; this was the little soldier who'd stood at the top of the steps with the AK-47. Now he had changed into civilian clothes, just as Somoza's National Guardsmen had done when the Sandinistas were approaching Managua in 1979.

Quietly Gustafson opened the door, then leapt out and grabbed the little man around the neck, knife in his face.

"You heard me shouting, didn't you? You were gonna leave me down there without anything to eat, weren't you, you little Commie son of a bitch!"

The soldier couldn't answer; he was gasping for breath. Gustafson's arm was strangling him.

"All right, you little prick. Gimme your gun." Gustafson kicked the pack at their feet. "I know you got one in there." He loosened his grip slightly, and the soldier's hands desperately scrabbled for the pack. He pulled out an automatic pistol and held it up for Gustafson, butt first, his arm shaking.

"Clips. Gimme your clips too," the colonel barked, tightening his grip again, but then said, "Oh, never mind."

Gustafson dropped the knife, picked up the pack with his free hand and shook the contents onto the walk. Two clips rattled onto the concrete, along with some shirts, underwear, a canteen, and a Sandinista military web belt.

"There, you see?" Gustafson said, reaching for the clips.

"Señor, señor, take them, señor."

"Of course I'm gonna take 'em, you little Commie shit." Gustafson let the soldier go, then backed up a foot or two and gave him a sharp kick in the rear end. The soldier fell sprawling onto the walk.

"Get the fuck out of here," Gustafson growled, already turning away. The soldier scrambled to his feet, and leaving his few possessions scattered over the sidewalk, he ran off down the road, looking back several times, eyes round with fear.

By now the sun had risen above treetop level. There were no clouds; it was already so hot that even the small exertion with the little Nicaraguan had caused Gustafson to break into a sweat.

As he set off down the street, sun to his back, the city was alive with the sounds of aircraft—helicopters near and far, jet fighters lifting off, and over to the right, another C-130 making its landing approach. The plane pulled into view over the trees, wheels just dropping as the fat, ungainly four-engine prop lumbered past. There'd be almost one hundred troops on board.

Save for occasional single-shot rifle fire, he couldn't hear much fighting. Gustafson smiled to himself as he walked along. Just two days, and the United States seemed to have Managua under control. It really had been like "falling off a fucking log," as he'd been saying for years. He thought of Kiernan, wondered if he was free, looked forward to taunting him.

"Another Vietnam, huh?"

Looking around at the hills, he knew where he was, about two miles southeast of the city in an upper-middle-class neighborhood, home to mid-level Sandinista party officers and their friends. Pistol in hand hanging at his side, finger on the trigger, extra clips in his pockets, he walked down the sidewalk toward town.

The streets were deserted. In most homes the curtains were closed. After a couple of blocks Gustafson heard a vehicle coming his way from around a corner. He pulled behind a telephone pole and pointed his pistol toward the intersection. Just then a military jeep, one of those funny-looking Soviet models that looked like a fifties Nash Rambler without the roof, came screeching fast around the turn, heading in the direction from which Gustafson had come. Three men were aboard, all in civilian clothes. Maybe they were on their way to pick up the soldier he'd just booted in the ass.

They had already started up the street when they noticed Gustafson. The colonel stepped from behind the pole and spotted an AK lying in the front passenger's lap. He pointed his pistol right at them, and they all stared back at him as the driver stepped on the gas, pulling the jeep as far away as he could, halfway up onto the opposite sidewalk. The man with the rifle didn't reach for it. But Gustafson took aim, pistol out at arm's length, and peeled off five rounds as the jeep pulled away up the street. He saw the windshield cloud up and then shatter but couldn't tell if he'd hit anyone before the jeep rolled out of sight over the crest of a hill. Gustafson reached in his pocket, changed clips, and walked on.

After a couple of blocks, he left the neighborhood, turned onto Avenida Isidro Centono Lopez, and headed down toward the Manolo Morales hospital. Still more than a mile from the city, this avenue was no busier than the neighborhood streets he'd just left, but soon he saw another jeep coming toward him. This time he stood in the middle of the sidewalk, pistol raised in front of him, until the jeep got close enough to be recognized.

"Hey, Marines! Marines!" he started shouting even before they could possibly hear him. The jeep stopped thirty yards away. Two Marines jumped out and crouched behind it, training their M-16s on Gustafson from either side of the TOW antitank missile launcher mounted on the vehicle's tail.

"Throw down your weapon and identify yourself!" one of them shouted.

"Colonel Eric Gustafson, USMC. Chief military attaché, United States embassy, Managua." He tossed the pistol into the grass.

"Hey, he's one of the hostages," one of the Marines said to the other.

"Coming forward," a soldier shouted, stepping from behind the jeep with his weapon still at his shoulder. "Show me some ID," he said when he got a few yards away. Gustafson pulled out his wallet and flipped it open, photo-ID card showing.

The soldier lowered his weapon and saluted.

"Damn happy to find you, sir. Sergeant Tom Clarity, 5th MAB, Camp Pendelton. Lots of people been looking for you guys. How'd you get away?"

"The little Commie cowards just ran off, Sergeant. Any word on the ambassador and the others?"

"We got the Marines outta that god-awful jail right away. They were okay. They found Ambassador Blanchard and two other guys too, last I heard. They were all fine. We've been on patrol, and maybe they've found everybody by now."

"Sounds good. Now, where's the GHQ?"

"Over at the embassy."

"Take me there," Gustafson said walking to the jeep. "So how'd it go?" he asked, climbing in.

"They fought pretty good at first, but they got no air, you know," Sergeant Clarity said. "We pounded them hard the first day, took out all their command and control. They just fell apart and started running away."

"Casualties?" Gustafson asked.

"They say we lost a couple hundred-some dead and more wounded. Don't know for sure."

"Sandis?"

"Jeez, sir, we creamed 'em pretty bad. It almost wasn't fair. I'd say we took out a couple thousand, but I haven't heard any official counts."

Pulling into the city, they saw a few people walking along the streets. To Gustafson they didn't look either happy or sad to see the jeep and the other U.S. military vehicles that began to crowd the streets as they got closer in. Many of the Nicaraguans just looked weary, resigned.

"Stop the jeep," Gustafson ordered as they pulled alongside someone Gustafson recognized. It was the street vendor he'd interviewed while sipping an orange drink a few months earlier. The colonel remembered the old man telling him his grandfather had fought with Sandino, but he'd be happy if U.S. troops came in. Now they were here.

"Señor," Gustafson shouted, climbing out of the jeep, smiling, stepping right up to him. "You remember me? We talked at your stand? Remember?"

The old man stepped back a foot or two and looked the colonel up and down. Then he slowly nodded. Who could forget this tall blond gringo.

"So?" Gustafson asked, smiling, arms outstretched, palms up. The old man looked back, puzzled.

"We fixed it for you. Took care of the Sandinista Communists." The man nodded again. "So what do you think?"

The man squinted and looked up at Gustafson, head cocked. Then he sighed.

"You Americans, you think it is so easy," he said at last as he started to walk away. "You think you can just shoot the trouble away."

"Huh?" Gustafson dropped his arms and walked with him a few steps. "What's that supposed to mean?"

"It means maybe you Yanquis ended one war. But just like the last time, you probably started another one."

Gustafson stared after the man, then shook his head and walked back to the jeep.

"Crazy son of a bitch," he muttered as they pulled off.

CHAPTER
TWENTY-THREE

NUEVA SEGOVIA PROVINCE, NORTHERN NICARAGUA, APRIL 14

I F ONLY THE LAST DOZEN YEARS COULD HAVE BEEN LIKE
this.

Sandinista troops were pouring into the Highlands by the
thousands, fleeing for their lives, and the contras lay in wait.
Under normal circumstances that would have been trouble for
the contras because the government troops were trailing their
mobile howitzers and truck-mounted multiple rocket launchers
into exile with them. When contra fighters ambushed, the
Sandinistas simply wheeled the weapons around and opened fire.
After all these years of war, the guerrillas still had not found
an effective antidote to the Soviet heavy artillery, even though
most of it was of World War II vintage. In some Eastern European countries the BM-21 forty-tube mobile rocket launcher was
still known by the nickname Stalin's Organ.

But now to all of that, in heavily accented English, contra
comandantes were saying, "No problem," repeating a phrase
they'd picked up from their American handlers. Every time the
Sandinistas opened fire, the guerrillas just hunkered down while
radiomen called in the United States Air Force. And a few minutes later two or three F-16s would roar overhead, shoot their
automatic cannons or fire off a couple of missiles, and that would
be that. No need to get bloody.

In fact, while the Sandinistas were furiously fighting for survival, none of the contras seemed much interested in taking any risks. They had already won. The only thing left was the victory celebration. No one wanted to take the chance of dying *now*.

Up at the border, the Directorate met every day in the little hut the Arizona National Guard had built for them, and Theodore Maloney, the one-star general the Americans had sent down, kept exhorting them to fight.

"We'll keep offering you all the air support you want," he told them, standing over the table Thursday afternoon. "But for God's sake, don't let them establish a position up here."

The Americans estimated that three quarters of the roughly 75,000-man Sandinista Army was no longer fighting—between 5,000 and 7,000 men had been wounded or killed, and more than 50,000 soldiers, most of them conscripts, had deserted. That left about 20,000 hardcore regulars, a force as large as the contras' at its height, still fighting up in the hills, where they planned to emulate their martyred namesake, General Sandino.

For years the Sandinista generals had been telling whoever would listen that they'd retreat to the hills and fight a protracted guerrilla war when the Americans finally came. Sure, the gringos could take Managua, but they'd never pacify the country. The Sandinistas, guerrillas again, would pick off Marines one by one until Americans tired of seeing the body bags on TV. Just like Sandino. Just like Vietnam. Domestic and international pressure would force the Americans to leave, and then the Sandinistas would march back into Managua—now truly invincible.

That had been the Sandinista plan, and from their plush new homes in Havana, Minister Zelaya and the other members of the Sandinista "government in exile" were saying the same things even now.

Well, the one inviolable proscription the president had given the U.S. military was that no American ground forces were to do any fighting up in the Nicaraguan Highlands. "In and out, fast as you can," he'd told the Joint Chiefs several times. "Use the resistance."

The contras, after all, were masters of the Highlands. They'd been fighting up there all these years, and now they were supposed to deprive the Sandinistas of a mountain sanctuary.

Later, when the Americans pulled out, the new government's military would be in charge of dealing with any small pockets of resistance that might remain. The United States would offer whatever aid was needed, but Nicaraguans would carry on any fighting left to be done. That was the American plan—the deal Colonel Teeley had laid out to the contra Directorate the previous weekend, after Rafael Mendoza had left. And now General Maloney was urging them not to back down in the breach.

"If you fight hard now, while our Air Force is still here to help you out," the general said, "you can keep them from establishing themselves up here in the first place, and your new government will inherit a nation at peace."

"General, we'll do our best," Chairman Coronel told him. But around the table the resolve was thin.

As soon as the general left, Directorate member Joaquín Murillo spoke right up. "So who's going to set up the new government in Managua while we're up here getting shot at?" Murillo had been an opposition member of the National Assembly before he moved to Miami two years ago and opened a video arcade in a Key Biscayne shopping center. Like all the others, the CIA had recruited Murillo at a secret salary of about $4,500 a month, and now he had ambitions.

"We've been up here fighting for our people for seven years," he said, waving a hand over his head. "We stay up here now, and the Americans are going to put in a coalition government and leave us out in the cold."

"We cannot let that happen," Coronel said, nodding.

"But what about our promise?" Paladino asked. "How can we deal with that?" Coronel gave him a hard look. The question was sticky, rising from an incident in the contra movement's early days.

Back in the early 1980s, when the CIA had picked the second in what would become a long succession of new contra Directorates, the agency had brought all of the new directors together in a Miami hotel conference room. After the preliminaries, the Americans took Adolfo Calero aside and told him he was going to be the new chairman. Calero, former head of the Coca-Cola bottling plant in Managua and a "friend" of the the United States even before the revolution, had all the attributes Congress demanded in a Nicaraguan leader. He'd never been a Somocista. He spoke English. And he was white.

As soon as the newly anointed chairman stepped back into the meeting room, it was said, an agency officer started clapping.

"Why don't all of you give a hand to the next president of Nicaragua," he'd said as everyone stood up. That's the way a former Directorate member described the scene, and even if it didn't happen just that way, his description had been replayed in the press time and time again over the years.

Well, a year ago the agency had picked Coronel as chairman of contra Directorate number seven or eight (by now most people had lost count). But before Congress had renewed aid this time, the Democrats had finally decided to extract a pledge. If the contras were to get any more money, Coronel and the others had to promise that they would not take power themselves, if somehow they ever did manage to kick the Sandinistas out of Managua. This time the Nicaraguan people would pick their new government—not the CIA.

Coronel had given the promise, and in public. All the American papers had reported it. Over the last week, needless to say, he'd given this little problem quite a lot of thought.

"Jorge, my friend," he said with a smile as he laid his elbows on the table and slowly clasped his hands together. "We did indeed promise we would not step in to help our people recover from the Communist reign of terror—if *we* were successful in removing the Sandinistas from power. Well, it was not *we* who removed them from Managua. The *Americans* did it."

The room was silent, but after a moment a thin smile spread across Paladino's face. "That is true," he said, nodding. He leaned back in his chair and crossed his legs, considering for a moment as he wagged a tasseled loafer.

"That is true," he said again. "Yes, Alfonse, I think you have it."

The previous night, over a whiskey in Coronel's hut, the chairman had promised Paladino he could be the new foreign minister. Coronel had given the others promises of their own, and around the table they all started to nod and murmur approval. It was done.

"Monday," Coronel pronounced.

"Monday it is," Paladino agreed. And with that, all of them shook hands and patted one another on the back.

First thing Friday morning, the Sandinistas launched attacks all over Jinotega Province, trying to drive the contras out so they could establish a foothold. The contra forces scattered; radiomen called for air strikes even as they galloped down the trail looking over their shoulders. By midday the Americans began to realize that the contras weren't fighting anymore. The Air Force was doing it all.

In the evening the Directorate sent a runner to find General

Maloney. He came over right away and took a seat at the far end of the table, facing Chairman Coronel.

"Good evening, General," Coronel said looking over at him, his slicked-backed hair glistening under the bare light bulb hanging just overhead.

"We have come to a decision. Monday morning, the Directorate is going to relocate to Managua. We think it will help restore morale among our troops."

Maloney didn't even try to hide his alarm.

"You can't do that!" he nearly shouted, standing up. "You know you can't." The chairman didn't answer.

"It's impossible. You know your men won't stay up here fighting if their leaders are eating steaks in Managua."

"Oh, I think they will, General," Coronel told him in a patronizing manner. "I think they will fight even harder if they see their comandantes leading them from the capital."

"But the new provisional government hasn't even been set up yet."

"Oh, I think we can be helpful with that."

"Chairman Coronel, you can't do this." Maloney was pleading. "Please. You'll ruin everything!"

"General, we have already decided."

Word spread to the fighters quickly. Actually it didn't have to spread very far. By Friday night most of them were back in the camp anyway. Radiomen had been calling for the F-16s every time they heard a rifle shot somewhere in the distance, and when the planes stopped coming for every radio call, most of the contras ran back across the border. After they learned that the Directorate was actually going to make its formal arrival in Managua Monday morning, by the thousands they started streaming south for the victory celebration, engaging Sandinista troops on the way for only as long as it took to run past them.

The State Department sent Ambassador Blanchard up by helicopter Sunday afternoon. He made a last plea, but the Directorate was intransigent. When he returned to Managua, Blanchard sent a cable back to Washington saying it was "probably unrealistic to have expected them to stay up there in the jungle for very long. We have at least agreed to a reasonable transition of power."

First thing Monday morning the Directorate members loaded themselves aboard the two old Huey helicopters the CIA had given them years earlier and took off for Managua. Thousands of their men were already there, and right after breakfast everyone started streaming over to Plaza 19 de Julio, named for the Sandinistas' day of victory. The Ortegas, Zelaya, Pastora, and all the rest had held their own victory rally there on July 19, 1979, and a year later, on July 19, 1980, Fidel Castro had addressed more than one hundred thousand Nicaraguans in the same park for the first anniversary.

Coronel had told his men he wanted the celebration right there, and by the time the helicopters landed, a flag-draped podium had already been set up at one end of the plaza. Tens of thousands of Nicaraguans were waiting, half or more still in their contra camouflage fatigues.

The sun was just rising above the treeline and cool shadows were pulling back across the field as hundreds of contras crowded around the helicopters and embraced the Directorate members stepping off. Thousands of other Managuans just watched, curious. Here in the city, unlike in some parts of the countryside, few people had shown much love for the contras over the years. They'd had no direct experience with them, except that every once in a while their power was cut off or their phones went dead. They didn't really know much about the Directorate, or its chairman, either.

As the owner of a well-known men's clothing store in Managua before—and after—the revolution, Coronel had been a prominent member of the business federation until he left the country. He was in his early fifties now and still dressed impeccably, though without his own store he'd had trouble finding clothes that fit his five-foot-two frame.

Before the Sandinista revolution he'd been chairman of the business federation's Guardia committee, the group that tried to monitor abuses committed by Somoza's National Guard. He'd been in the papers occasionally back then, shown as he met with President Somoza to give committee reports on documented Guardia abuses. Somoza would always listen with concern, promise to correct the problems, and then send Coronel out on Guardia maneuvers. He'd let Coronel dress up in a military uniform and ride around in one of the Sherman tanks. Then El Presidente would stop by Coronel's store and buy half a dozen suits. Somehow Coronel never really pressed the complaints.

Today most Nicaraguans remembered Coronel only vaguely, if at all. So when eager fighters lifted the chairman onto their shoulders and carried him to the dais while other contras cheered and fired their rifles into the air, most of the Managuans just stood back, arms folded, watching.

On the platform, Coronel smiled and waved. The rest of the Directorate was lined up on either side. Just to the left, contras were piling up a large stack of Sandinista memorabilia—red-and-black Sandinista National Liberation Front party flags, Sandino-the-determined-fighter posters, portraits of the martyr Carlos Fonseca, even a few plywood hammer-and-sickles. When they lit the pile, even many of the Managuans burst into cheers as it erupted into flames.

As the ovation began to fade, Coronel stepped to the microphone, climbed up on an empty ammunition crate someone had thoughtfully put there for him, and shouted, "Welcome to Free Nicaragua!" He waved his hands over his head to the thunderous applause and celebratory rifle fire.

"By order of the provisional government," he said after a minute, "I hereby rename this park Plaza of the Counterrevolution." The contras erupted into even greater cheers, and Alec Kiernan, standing off to one side with Gustafson, leaned over and muttered, "Plaza of the Counterrevolution. Has a euphonious ring to it, wouldn't you say?"

"Sounds okay to me," Gustafson said.

Kiernan shook his head. "Well let's see how they play out this provisional government business. See if they keep to the bargain."

Coronel went on to announce other streets and places that were, by decree, being returned to their old names.

"No more Sandino Airport," he declared, fist raised above his head as his troops cheered. "No more Pista de la Solidaridad." The cheering was growing fainter as he reeled off more Sandinista place-names.

"I think he's about run out his string on that one," Kiernan said.

Coronel must have realized that too. So when the crowd quieted, he said, "All right, to any of you here who may not know me, I am Alfonso Coronel, chairman of the Directorate of the Democratic Resistance. To my left and right is the rest of your Directorate," and then he introduced the others one by one.

"For all of us, this is the happiest day of our lives, being back here in Managua again, in Free Nicaragua. And we have the following announcements to make. We are establishing a provisional government which will remain in office until we can draft a new constitution and hold new elections." He paused a moment and then quickly said, "Six months."

"Son of a bitch," Kiernan moaned, stamping his foot. "They promised it would be only three."

"And as provisional president, by official decree I hereby declare that the state of emergency is lifted—forever. Right now, our country has freedom of the press. *La Prensa* and Radio Católica can reopen tomorrow!" More cheers.

"As of now, Free Nicaraguans also have complete freedom of speech, freedom of assembly, freedom of worship . . ."

"Well, so far, so good, I guess," Kiernan said.

Most of the American television networks carried at least parts of the victory celebration live. In Washington the president showed up in the White House pressroom a couple of hours later and welcomed " 'Free Nicaragua' into the family of democratic nations." The United States would provide one hundred million dollars in immediate emergency aid, he announced, and the Agency for International Development was "even now sending teams of experts to help the new government rebuild their proud nation."

By early afternoon, Gustafson was back in his old office at the embassy. The military command had moved out; the generals hadn't much liked working out of the cardboard building, so they'd commandeered their own building down the road, a grander facility: the former Cuban embassy.

Over the weekend, the State Department had sent most of the embassy staff back, and new officers were flying in from Washington to help with the burgeoning workload. In the afternoon, a State Department architect walked around asking questions and taking notes. Already Washington was starting to plan construction of a big new embassy building.

Everyone stopped by Gustafson's office to ask about his ordeal as a hostage, how he'd escaped, what the invasion had been like. He clapped his friends on the back, told a few anecdotes. But happy as he was, Gustafson felt drained.

"Been a hell of a couple of weeks," he kept saying to people, who nodded their heads knowingly, though of course they knew only about one-tenth of the story.

As soon as he could, he shut his office door, leaned back in the chair, closed his eyes, and sat for a minute or two. After a while he got up, pulled his KL-43 out from under some old newspapers in the back of a locked file drawer—apparently the Sandinistas had not discovered it—and plugged it into the telephone. He looked at the little computer for a few minutes, thinking about what he was going to say, wanting to get it just right. Finally he nodded to himself and called Rafael up in Tegucigalpa.

"It is done," he typed when Rafael came on the line. "We have solved the problem once and for all. As in all wars, there were casualties. We had our own. Some good men suffered and died for our cause, and we mourn for them. And you, I know, are paying a price of your own. But for both of us, the most important thing is that we are victorious."

"Well said, my friend," Rafael typed back. "Seldom in history have two men done such good for the world."

CHAPTER
TWENTY-FOUR

FOREIGN MINISTRY, MANAGUA, NICARAGUA, MAY 3

MINISTER ZELAYA HAD A LARGE CORNER OFFICE, JUST down the hall from the Foreign Ministry's formal dining room, best known as the site of the dinner-party massacre. The day after the victory rally, Jorge Paladino moved right in, boxed up all of Zelaya's ornaments, speeches, and five-year plans, then sent them off to Havana, and brought in a few belongings of his own. The room's furnishings weren't grand—a large Danish-modern desk and built-in bookshelves, filled now with his own library of American political books, mostly. A black vinyl sofa sat under the window.

Paladino had been in office about three weeks now, a troubling chaotic time, and one afternoon he was sitting at his desk, in a sour mood as he read still another U.S. Agency for International Development reconstruction proposal. In this one, the United States was offering to build a modern new electrical substation for Managua. The old Los Mártires station had never been repaired properly after the sabotage last year; even now Managua was subject to occasional brownouts. Better to replace it, the AID was saying. Fine, give us a new one, Paladino was thinking. But what's the real price going to be? Just then Mrs. Reyes, his secretary, stuck her head in the door. Someone was here to see him, a young man named Gonzalez.

"He doesn't have an appointment," she said. "But he says he remembers you from Honduras. He looks harmless."

Paladino shrugged. He didn't have many nonofficial visitors these days, and the official ones always managed to upset him somehow.

"Sure," he told her. "Send him in."

The little man shuffled in, head bowed, eyes leaping around the room. He looked instantly familiar. He was young, maybe twenty, and he wasn't just nervous. The little man was shuddering.

Paladino walked around his desk.

"Hello. I'm Jorge Paladino," he said, smiling reassuringly as he offered his hand. Paladino had already grown accustomed to intimidating people inadvertently, now that he was a powerful government officer.

The little man wouldn't look up from Paladino's tasseled loafers and stuck his hand out tentatively, just a few inches from his chest. The man shook hands quickly and pulled his hand right back to his side. He couldn't stand still; his feet shifted, his shoulders twisted left and right.

"I'm Alfonse Gonzalez, sir," he mumbled, voice tremulous.

"Alfonse, you look very familiar. Where do I know you from?"

The little man turned his face up sheepishly and looked into Paladino's eyes for only a second before turning away again.

"At El Cuartelón," he said. "I am Balita."

Paladino's mouth dropped open. He stepped back a couple of feet.

"Balita, Balita. Of course! I remember you," he said, looking down in wonder. Balita, "the child-fighter"—nursed, weaned, and raised as a contra. Paz's "son." He was a contra legend.

"You were one of Paz's men, weren't you?" Paladino asked. "My God. Please come sit down."

Balita sat at the far end of the sofa and pressed his back against the arm as if he wanted to be farther away still.

"How have you been doing since the war, Alfonse? Or do you prefer Balita?"

Balita didn't answer. He was squirming in his seat and in a rush of words blurted out, "Sir, I have to talk to you."

"Please, please do."

But Balita didn't need encouragement; he was hurrying on.

"We didn't like you in El Cuartelón, Mr. Paladino. The major said you worked against the Americans. He said you didn't like the CIA. He said you were the enemy."

"Well, I didn't like some of the things the CIA was doing, but I wasn't—" Balita cut him off, so Paladino decided to let him speak.

"The Americans helped us a lot. They saved our country. I always wanted to be an American, a Marine. The major promised. But now it can't be." He looked up at Paladino then. Tears were beginning to form.

"We were going to be Marines. But now, because of things the CIA ordered us to do, it can't be. I don't know what to do now. I didn't know who else to talk to."

Paladino pulled the linen handkerchief from the breast pocket of his blazer, walked over, and handed it to Balita. He sat down beside the boy and, as soothingly as he could, said, "My young friend, please tell me how I can help you."

Quickly Balita stood up, reached into his right pants pocket, and brought out a little piece of plastic. He thrust it at Paladino, who turned it over in his hand. It was a laminated identification card. A color picture of a man looked out with a broad, uniquely American grin. *B. J. Robertson. Sergeant, United States Army,* the card said. *Abilene, Texas.*

Balita had stopped crying. He was looking down at his hands folded in his lap, quiet now.

Gently, Paladino asked him, "Balita, tell me, what's this all about?"

Recently, Paladino had been feeling restless, anxious, and over the last few days his distress had bordered on despair. His new nation, "Free Nicaragua," was changing, deforming, turning into a misshapen mutant right under his nose. Already, it seemed, Nicaragua was being governed from Washington.

Early on he'd spoken up when he could. In the new government—really just the contra Directorate, plus or minus a few faces—he'd already slipped back into the old antagonist role he'd held before. And to make matters worse, he was now the foreign minister, the position traditionally given to the liberal agitator in most Central American governments.

While the other officers ran the country, the foreign minister was expected to deal with the gringos. And in fact, from his first day in office most of his energies had gone into bargaining with an unending train of American officials, all of them suggesting more and better ideas for his country, offered up in tones that made it clear he really had no choice. Paladino's job was to accept what he had to, then ask for more aid in exchange. After all, he kept saying, the United States had provided $240 million for fifteen thousand contras. Why just $100 million for an entire nation of more than three million people?

The problem was Congress, the foreign service officers would explain. Congress had to approve before anything more could be given.

"Boy, have I heard that line before," Paladino would say.

The American president hadn't specified how the $100 million in emergency money was to be spent, but within a week or two it became clear that Free Nicaragua would need significant military aid. At least fifteen thousand Sandinistas were still up in the hills, and in Managua there'd been several "terrorist incidents," as the provisional president called them—shootings of government soldiers and even a couple of American servicemen. In Havana, leaders of the Sandinista "government in exile" were claiming responsibility, spouting bombast, and warning that there'd be more.

So the new government rounded up a few "Communist perpetrators" and hauled them off to El Chipote.

American intelligence said the Sandinista troops up in the Highlands were hard at work reorganizing, trying to change their force structure from that of a standing national army with relatively reliable lines of supply into a free-form guerrilla force that lived with whatever supplies they were able to get. The Americans were also reporting that the Sandinistas had started getting supplies from the Marxist rebels over the border in El Salvador—an old debt being repaid. But for the moment at least, the Sandinistas weren't doing much fighting. They were waiting, the newspapers speculated, for the United States Air Force to leave.

Already the U.S. military was beginning to pull out, but not before the Defense Department had set up one of the largest programs ever established for the training of a foreign military force. The next Sunday, *The New York Times* Week in Review section published a photo of United States officers leading "New Army" soldiers through exercises, and right next to it an old picture of Marine leathernecks training the brand-new National Guard back in 1933.

Many of the former contras joined the New Army, but others said they'd had enough fighting. So President Coronel reinstituted the draft. Free Nicaragua needs a fifty-thousand-man standing army, he said.

La Prensa criticized him, saying it was an "inappropriate signal for a nation so eager to return to peace." But President Coronel paid no attention. "The draft is necessary to keep us free," he said. And he took to wearing a military uniform on occasion, a three-star general's outfit, explaining that it was to "assure our recruitees that the government is behind them."

Last week he'd had his picture taken, grinning as he rode around a field in one of the shiny new M1 tanks the United States was providing. The photo was fuzzy. Paladino couldn't tell for sure, but it kind of looked as if President Coronel was carrying a riding crop.

Then early this week, Paladino had been strolling over to Los Ranchos for lunch when he looked ahead and stopped dead in his tracks. Walking toward him was a little mulatto man with bright orange hair. The man was wearing camouflage fatigues, and his 9-millimeter Beretta was strapped into a holster at his belt. He wore what looked like a new pair of aviator sunglasses. On these, "Ray Ban" was stenciled in tiny white letters at the upper right corner of one lens.

"Paz," Paladino gasped. Major Paz stopped and looked at Paladino without expression for a moment before giving a curt nod.

"Minister Paladino" was all he said.

"Paz, Paz, I am so surprised to see you. Where have you been? What have you been doing?"

Matter-of-factly, Paz told him, "I have been serving my country. And now I am joining our New Army."

"What?" Paladino cried out, staring at him. "You're not serious, are you? Joining the New Army? You have to be kidding!"

But Paz didn't kid. "I am a colonel now," he announced. "Colonel Paz." Then the corners of his mouth twitched ever so slightly.

Paladino stared at Paz, speechless. After a moment Paz stepped around him and walked on, leaving Paladino staring at the sidewalk. Eventually, Paladino turned around. The colonel was already about twenty yards away.

"Paz, Paz, wait a minute," he yelled after him. Paz turned and looked back.

"The dinner-party shootings," Paladino shouted. "What happened? Tell me. Please."

But Paz didn't speak, didn't move, and for several seconds

Paladino stared back into his Ray Bans. Then Colonel Paz turned around again and walked away.

Lost in confused thought, Paladino went back to his office. Walking down the Foreign Ministry's long center hall, on impulse he stopped outside the state dining room. He'd had no reason to go in there the last few weeks, though sometimes he had winced as he passed by the doors. This time he opened a door, stepped in, and turned on the lights.

The room looked ordinary enough. The same long dining table he'd seen in all the newspaper pictures sat in the middle of the floor, chairs neatly spaced around it. He looked at the back wall. It was clean, freshly painted. But there was something . . .

He walked over and ran his hands over the surface, looked at it from the side. Then he shook his head.

"Son of a bitch," he muttered to himself, and suddenly he felt a rush of sorrow for his sad little country.

As was always the way here, lazy carpenters had done a sloppy job. They hadn't bothered to pull down the plasterboards and replace them with new sheets. Instead they'd just spackled over all the bullet holes, sanded everything down as best they could, and then called in the painters. The spackle was already beginning to shrink. And now under the shiny new paint dozens of bulletholes were beginning to pop back up in brutal relief.

Paladino marched out of the room. Back in his office, right away he told his secretary to call the carpenters and order them to replace the whole wall.

"Tell them to do it tomorrow!" he barked at Mrs. Reyes, who didn't understand what had made her normally placid boss so angry all of a sudden.

The next evening he went to an official state reception over at President Coronel's house. The Americans, concerned for Coronel's safety "in these troubled times," had given him Casa Grande to use for a while, "until things settle down." Without a moment's hesitation, Coronel had shipped all his belongings down from the big house the Americans had bought him in Tegucigalpa and moved right into Casa Grande. He'd taken to calling it President's House.

The reception was to welcome Air Force Major General Norbert Langston, who had just arrived from Washington. When Paladino walked over to meet him, the general's colonel introduced him as "the new chief of United States forces in Nicaragua."

Langston leaned over and winked as he whispered in

Paladino's ear, "Soon, of course, that's just going to be our military trainers." But everybody knew that the Pentagon wanted to open a big new American air base here, around the ten-thousand-foot runway the Cubans had built over at Punta Huete.

President Coronel was wearing his three-star general's outfit tonight. The jacket sleeves reached halfway down his thumb. Every time they passed, General Langston saluted him. When Paladino walked over to say hello to the president, he stopped short a few feet away, startled to see that under his arm Coronel was cradling one of those shiny chrome-plated steel-pot helmets. Every once in a while he'd reach over and polish it with his sleeve.

Paladino leaned down and whispered into Coronel's ear, "Alfonse, I've got to talk to you. It's important."

"Excuse me a moment," Coronel said to the retinue of smiling American officers clustered around him. Both of them backed away a few feet.

"What is it?" he asked, a little irritated.

"Alfonse, I ran into Major Paz yesterday." Coronel nodded. "He says he's in the New Army. He says he's a colonel now." Coronel kept nodding for a moment, but when Paladino didn't say anything more he looked up with an expression that said: So get to the point.

Paladino waved his hands in front of him. "Alfonse, how can you let that man in our New Army, after—"

Coronel cut him off. "I can't think of a better man to help us deal with the Communist enemies of the counterrevolution. He and his men have more experience with this kind of thing than anybody we have."

"His Pena de Muertes, too? You can't mean that!" Paladino's voice was despairing. "With his background, after all that man has done, the message that sends. What about the dinner-party massacre? What about that?"

Coronel looked up at Paladino, his eyes angry slits. "That's history," he spat. "I don't even want to hear about it anymore. That was war, remember. Things happen in war. I don't . . ." But then suddenly Coronel turned away, distracted. On the other side, someone had taken his arm.

Paladino recognized the earthy fragrance, the shiny black hair falling down her shoulders in exotic tangles, the sheer silk blouse unbuttoned to just below the tiny gold cross that dangled right in front of Coronel's nose.

"Jorge, you remember Francesca, don't you," Coronel said,

oozing self-satisfaction. Francesca squeezed Coronel's arm tighter as she looked over the president's oily head and gave Paladino a thin, triumphant smile.

That was only two nights ago, and Paladino had been gloomy, despairing ever since. Now, as he sat on the black vinyl sofa under his office window and listened to Balita's story, Paladino's eyes grew moist. Balita had no proof, just the ID card. But Paladino didn't think this ingenuous "child-fighter" could have made up something like this. Besides, the more he thought about what Balita told him, the more everything seemed to fit. Paladino dabbed his eyes with his handkerchief.

"Holy Mother, please save us," he whispered almost to himself.

Balita sat quietly, hands folded in his lap as Paladino blew his nose and straightened up.

After a minute, he asked, "And the man who came down to Cascabeles, you say he was from the White House?"

"Yes, sir, he was the representative of the president of the United States. We never could have done what we did unless he . . . I mean, the Americans, they know how to do these things, don't they?"

Paladino didn't answer. "Do you remember this man's name?"

"No, sir, I cannot remember. He was a tall man. His hair was all curly. He had on this funny suit. Tigrillo—you know his brother went to Catholic school up in Shreveport—he called it a safari suit."

"And he was with Rafael Mendoza?"

"Yes, sir. The CIA man was the one who told us what to do."

Thinking of Mendoza, still up there in Honduras as station chief, Paladino clenched his teeth. If only the Directorate had listened to him.

Paladino was quiet for a minute. Then softly he said, "Balita, you have done the right thing by telling me this. I promise I will protect your confidence. I want to think about this, figure out what is the best thing to do for our country. Please, would you come back here at this time tomorrow? Is that possible?"

"Yes, sir," Balita said.

The easiest thing, of course, was to forget it.

"That's history," Coronel had said. "Things happen in war."

The Americans had been manipulating his country for more

than 150 years, ever since independence. In a back hall of the Foreign Ministry building, he'd noticed, a tintype of William Walker's final defeat still hung. Maybe it was just Nicaragua's lot, a function of geography and bad luck, always to live under the heel of the giant to the north. Paladino had made the mistake of holding out hope for Free Nicaragua. But slowly, as he had been seeing over the last two weeks, the big Norte Americano heel was coming down. Sometimes he almost believed that if he looked up into the sky he could actually see it. Already his friends were turning into caricatures of the classic American puppet.

At home that night he stood in his den looking over his small collection of American books on Central America, just unpacked: *Inevitable Revolutions: The United States in Central America; Condemned to Repetition: The United States and Nicaragua.* There were others, too.

He didn't sleep much that night. By morning, though, he had decided what he ought to do. His feelings fell far short of unshakable conviction, but at the same time he was beginning to believe that a rude shock might be just the thing to alter his young nation's disturbing course. Still, as the day wore on he began to hope Balita wouldn't show up.

But if nothing else, the boy was a soldier. At three-fifteen, right on time, Mrs. Reyes stuck her head in the door saying, "Mr. Gonzalez is here to see you again."

Slowly Paladino laid down his pen and sighed.

"Send him in."

NATIONAL PRESS BUILDING, WASHINGTON

Eaton had spoken to Paladino several times in the three weeks since the invasion. His friend was ebullient at first, but even before today Eaton had begun to notice that Paladino's manner was turning dark.

The first time Eaton called, just two days after the victory rally in Managua, he was half afraid Paladino wouldn't come to the phone. After all, now he was the foreign minister. But Paladino's secretary had put Eaton through right away.

"Congratulations, congratulations," Eaton had said, his manner bubbly. "It's so exciting."

"You will have to come down and let me show you what we are doing with our new country," Paladino had told him. Eaton promised he would, though he'd been so busy since the invasion that he barely had time to go home, much less travel. Not only was there all the political/military news to report, but Eaton had been called upon to cover the big peace march up Pennsylvania Avenue—a sad affair, since few Americans were paying any attention. Far more numerous than the protesters were the Americans calling Eaton and other reporters asking for help with their food and clothing drives "for our new Nicaraguan neighbors." Out of all this, Eaton was writing at least one Nicaragua news story every single day.

The next time Eaton called Paladino, the foreign minister was not quite so buoyant. He told about the plans for the big new American air base at Punta Huete. That had made a big story.

Then on the third call, just a few days ago, Eaton had discussed his suspicions about the Redeye missiles and the inspector general's report he still hadn't seen. He'd been ruminating about it since the day of the invasion. Once he'd even discussed the whole business with Leslie. Usually when he talked about his work she nodded and smiled, saying something innocuous like "Sounds interesting." She didn't want to risk trouble again. But when Eaton told her what he'd found out about the missile theft, she looked up at him, suddenly serious.

"Chris, I'm saying more than I should. But you should keep going with that." She said nothing more, but that had startled him. In the last two weeks the pace of events had slowed down just enough so that Eaton had been able to dabble in the story again. But he hadn't gotten very far.

In the call earlier in the week, he and Paladino had puzzled over the matter for a few minutes.

"It's interesting, suggestive," Paladino had said, "but I am afraid I don't know anything more." He had sounded despondent.

"Anything wrong?" Eaton had asked.

"Oh, no. Just a lot of work."

That was only a few days ago. Now the receptionist was telling Eaton that the Nicaraguan foreign minister's office was on the line again.

"Jorge, it's good to hear from you," Eaton said. "Is everything okay?" There was a long pause, the time it took for Eaton's greeting to be shot up to a satellite and bounced down to the microwave receiver in Managua, and then for Paladino's response to make the several-thousand-mile return trip. The delays were always disconcerting. But then Paladino's crackly voice came back.

"Chris, I need your help."

Eaton sat up in his chair. "Of course. Anything, Jorge. Anything. What is it?"

"I don't want to say too much on the phone. But I have a young man here in my office who you must talk to."

"Well put him on."

"No. These things we cannot talk about on the phone. You should come down here and see him. It's very important."

Eaton looked to his right, through the glass partition into his editor's officer. Abel sat hunched over his Atex computer terminal, intently editing a story. His chin was raised, his eyes looked down through half-glasses, which had slipped partway down his nose.

"Jorge, I wish I could come down there. But I can't see any way they'll let me leave here now. It's too hectic. You know how it is." There was a longer than normal pause. Eaton spoke again, just as Paladino's response finally reached him.

"Tell me what it's about if you can."

"Chris, my friend, it's very, very important," Paladino was saying.

Eaton repeated his question. "Tell me what you can, and I will try to convince my editor."

"I can't tell you much here. But you remember what we were talking about the other day? Your inspector general and that report about the missiles? This young man can answer all those questions and much, much more. He was there. He knows it all. He was one of Major Paz's fighters. You can believe him. It's a tragedy for my country, Chris, and maybe for yours. But it needs to come out."

"Jesus, Jorge." Eaton looked at Abel again and sighed. But then he got an idea. He reached for his wallet.

"Jorge, will this man come up here to see me? We will pay for it." On the other end, Eaton heard mumbling in Spanish.

"Chris, he will do whatever I ask him. But he has never been out of the region. He speaks only a little English. I think he will come up there if that's the only way. But you must promise to take good care of him."

"I promise, Jorge. I promise." He read Paladino the number of his company International Air Travel credit card, and Paladino said his secretary would book the reservation then call back later with the arrival time.

As soon as Eaton hung up he walked over to Abel's office and raised his hand to knock on the door frame. Abel's back was to him; he was still at the computer terminal. Eaton looked at him for a second, hand poised in the air, but then he brushed nervously at his forelock a couple of times and walked away. Better to talk to this Nicaraguan, then tell Abel. If worse came to worst, Eaton could pay the company back for the ticket.

That evening, Mrs. Reyes called back from Paladino's office.

"The young man's name is Mr. Gonzalez," she said. "But he goes by 'Balita.'" He was arriving on an Eastern flight from Miami at nine-thirty the next morning. Eaton thanked her, hung up, and sat for a minute, thinking. One of Major Paz's fighters knew all about the Redeye theft. "He was there," Paladino had said. The implications . . . Eaton shook his head. He didn't want to draw any tentative conclusions now. It was just too big.

He considered for a moment but then decided. He called Leslie.

"Listen, something's going on," he told her. "I don't know what exactly. But it could be bigger than both of us. I need your help."

"What is it?" she asked, frightened by Eaton's manner.

"It's that business with the Redeyes we talked about once." His voice was low, somber. "There's a contra coming up from Central America to tell me about it. Jorge's sending him. Jorge's very upset. Leslie, the implications here . . . I don't want you to tell me anything. Just be with me, be a second pair of ears for me. It's too big for one person."

Leslie had never stopped thinking about that report she'd read, and about Dayton's blithe dismissal of it. The document still sat in the pile on her desk.

She thought a moment. "Okay," she said at last.

After they'd hung up, she waited an hour until everyone else had gone home. Then she pulled the inspector general's report from under the stack of papers on her desk. Along with some other papers, she took it across the hall to the photocopy room and made a single copy. Back in her office, she filed the original, carefully folded the copy, and stuck it deep in her purse.

Her husband was traveling again, so Leslie was spending most nights at Eaton's apartment. Over dinner, he'd told her all that Paladino had told him about Balita. But she hadn't said anything. Clearly she was uncomfortable, and Eaton wondered if he'd made a mistake involving her.

The next morning, though, she didn't hesitate to drive with him to the airport. Washington's spring was coming to an end.

The city was still in bloom, but the summer humidity had already begun, and they rode with the windows closed, the air conditioner turned on low. They didn't say much on the way. But at National, Leslie marched ahead of him to the departure gate and picked out the Nicaraguan right away.

"That must be him," she said, pointing.

He was standing alone just outside the arrival-gate security area, hands clasped tightly in front of him. He was glancing around in awe at the drab Eastern terminal, shifting from foot to foot, almost as if he were dancing in place.

Eaton walked up to him. "Are you Balita?" he asked in Spanish.

"Yes, sir."

"I'm Chris Eaton, and this is my friend Leslie Decker." For the time being they decided it was best not to give Leslie's real name.

"Hello, Señor Eaton, Señora Decker," he said in carefully enunciated English, a proud smile on his face. Balita picked up his bag, a canvas number that looked brand-new, and followed them out. To Eaton, this contra looked as if he was wearing someone else's clothes, though they seemed to fit well enough—blue blazer with gold buttons, striped web belt, button-down shirt, and cuffed chinos. The tasseled loafers gave it away. Paladino must have taken him shopping.

During the drive over the river from National Airport, Balita was riveted as he looked out the window at the monuments and other sights. Eaton played tour guide and translated Balita's reactions for Leslie, sitting in the back.

"And this is the Lincoln Memorial," he said in Spanish, pointing straight ahead as they crossed Memorial Bridge.

"I know Lincoln," Balita responded eagerly. "We had a Lincoln Brigade in the force. Lincoln was for freedom."

"That's right," Eaton said. "Lincoln freed the slaves." Balita looked away. Apparently he didn't know about that.

They took him to the Mayflower, a grand, expensive hotel on Connecticut Avenue. Some rooms could cost more than two hundred dollars a night. Paladino had warned that "there might be some security problems" once Balita's information got out. He hadn't said any more, but Eaton had decided not to put Balita in the Marriott next door to his office. It was the first place anyone would think to check. The Mayflower was only one Metro stop away, and since Eaton would have to leave Balita alone, he wanted to get him a nice room.

When they filled out the registration form Eaton gave a false name, one he thought Balita would remember.

"Alfonso Lincoln. Managua, Nicaragua," Eaton wrote, and then gave the clerk his American Express card. Balita was given Room 324, and Eaton wrote the fake name and the room number in his pocket reporters' pad.

A grand hall ran the full length of the hotel, from the front entrance on Connecticut Avenue to the back door on Seventeenth Street. When Eaton and Leslie finished at the front desk, Balita was standing stock-still, staring in wonder down the marble promenade with its glittering chandeliers, oriental rugs, gilt-framed mirrors, and silk-covered Chippendale settees. Leslie stood beside him, and Balita whispered in English, "This is America."

"Well, not all of America is like this," Leslie said with a smile.

"Come on, we'd better get to the room," Eaton said, and they headed for the elevators.

They were given a standard room with a king-size bed, a television with pay movies, a small refrigerator, and a minibar. Balita walked all around, eagerly trying the television, peering into the refrigerator, and opening every drawer—even turning the bathroom faucets on and off. Eaton and Leslie watched, bemused. After a minute or two Leslie looked at her watch.

"Chris, they think I've got a doctor's appointment, but I've got to get back before lunch. We better get started."

"Yeah, I do too. I've already missed the briefing." The daily White House press briefing was at ten, and Eaton seldom missed it. But the Federal News Service, a private company, taped it every day, and a couple of hours later sent verbatim transcripts to printers in clients' offices all over town. New World subscribed, so Eaton could read it later.

"Balita, why don't you come sit down," he said. "Could you tell us what you told Mr. Paladino?"

"Okay," he said. He walked over to the sofa, reached into his pants pocket, pulled out the identification card, and gave it to Eaton.

B. J. Robertson. Sergeant, United States Army.

Eaton looked up, puzzled.

Serious now, Balita told him, "I killed that man. He's American, I know. I killed him, and your CIA told us to do it." He looked away and then sat down in the far armchair. "Major Paz and I were going to be Marines," he said in a low, childlike whine. "Now we can't."

Leslie and Eaton looked at each other, puzzled. Eaton pulled out his microcassette-recorder and laid it on the table, though he didn't turn it on right away, not wanting to make Balita nervous.

"Balita, why don't you start at the beginning." And that's just what he did. Eaton translated for Leslie as they spoke.

"We had a special elite squad," Balita explained. "We were the Pena de Muerte commandos," and he gave the name with obvious pride. "We fought hard, very hard, for our country—and for America.

"My comandante, Major Paz, his grandfather was a United States Marine. The major was going to take me with him when he went to America to be a Marine.

"The Americans, they gave us our special camp, Camp Cascabeles. They treated us well. We did only special missions for them. Very important missions."

"Who is 'they'?" Eaton asked.

"The CIA. Rafael Mendoza."

Eaton turned to Leslie, eyebrows raised.

"Jesus," he whispered. "That's the station chief in Tegucigalpa." He reached over and turned on the tape recorder.

"So you worked directly for Mendoza?"

"Yes, sir."

"Starting when?"

Balita had gotten only through the Los Mártires electrical substation raid when Eaton turned to Leslie and asked, "Lunch?" She nodded without looking away from Balita.

"Please go on," Eaton said as he picked up the phone to call room service.

"When we were training at Cascabeles, a big American came down to see us," Balita was saying a few minutes later. "He said he was from the White House." When he described the man—"curly hair and a funny suit, Tigrillo said it was a safari suit"—Eaton and Leslie glanced at each other quickly. The name came out at almost the same moment:

"Ascher."

Balita was halfway through the story of the dinner-party massacre—"our comandante had gotten us some special rifles with silencing devices and special sights that let us see in the dark. They were bought with money the White House man gave us."

His audience was transfixed. Then there was a knock on the door.

Eaton turned off the tape recorder and covered it with the hotel magazine. He turned to Leslie.

"Can you believe this?" he whispered. "Incredible." She nodded, but as Eaton went to the door, she spoke up.

"Chris, I really don't think anybody in the West Wing knew about any of this. I really don't."

Eaton opened the door and let the waiter in. The man slid the lunch tray onto the coffee table and asked "Anything else, sir?" His accent was Spanish, and right away Balita looked up and asked, "*Hombre*, where are you from?"

"Salvador," the waiter said quietly.

"Nicaragua," Balita announced, beaming.

Standing behind the waiter, Eaton looked at Balita, finger to his mouth. Balita looked away. Eaton signed the check, gave the waiter a couple of dollars, and sent him away.

After the waiter was gone he told Balita, "I'm sorry, but I think it is best if we try to keep you a secret for now. It's for your own safety."

Balita nodded and started eating. Eaton took a couple of bites, and said, "Please go on."

Balita talked as he ate, speaking even when his mouth was full, so that sometimes it was hard to understand. Eaton and Leslie laid down their sandwiches when Balita started describing the shootings in the Foreign Ministry dining room.

"They were all Communists; we didn't mind killing them. We like killing Communists," he was saying. "But we didn't like doing it to Comandante Venganza. He was a good fighter. But the major, he said the CIA told him Venganza was a spy, sent by the anti-American cowards on the Directorate."

"Major Paz shot him?"

"Yes, sir. Comandante Venganza was trying to stop us from our mission. We put his body in the lake."

It was past one-thirty when Balita got to the Redeyes.

"This is it, this is it," Eaton whispered to Leslie under his breath.

"And then the major gave the guards at the door a lot of dollars. It looked like it was already arranged, because they smiled and let us in. We carried the rockets out and put them in the back of our truck and covered them up with blankets."

"Damn," Eaton said, looking at Leslie. She was nodding.

It was getting late, but neither of them cared. As Balita started into the Chinooks story, Eaton and Leslie said not a word. But when Eaton stopped him briefly to change tapes, Leslie spoke up again. This time she was insistent.

"Chris, if this is really true, the West Wing didn't know about any of this. They didn't. I'm sure of it. I can't believe anybody in there would do anything like this. I just can't."

Until this point, Balita had been telling his story with enthusiasm, even pride, arms waving. But now he looked down at the hands folded in his lap.

"The major told us that there were Honduran soldiers on these helicopters. He said they were corrupt *piricuacos.*"

"Literally, it means beggar dogs," Eaton whispered to Leslie. "It's the worst kind of insult."

"The major said they were going down to help the Sandinista Communists, for money. So we had to stop them."

Balita's voice dropped. "I would never kill Americans," he murmured. His voice was quivering now. "You have to believe me." He looked up at Leslie, and he was crying. "I wanted to be a Marine. I would never kill Americans. The CIA, why did they make us do it? The major, how could he? We were going to be Marines."

Eaton wanted to take the Army ID card with him, but Balita wouldn't let it go. So they told him to take good care of it. With Eaton translating, Leslie showed Balita how to order from room service, and both of them made him promise not to leave the room.

"It's for your own safety," Leslie told him.

Eaton wrote his home phone number on the back of a business card and put it next to the telephone.

"We'll be back no later than the morning," he said as they left.

They didn't speak or even look at each other as they rode down the elevator and walked through the lobby. But waiting for the light at K Street, Eaton turned to Leslie.

"Do you think it's true?"

She didn't answer right away. But then softly she said, "If it is, this could bring down the government."

"Ours or theirs?"

"Both of them."

Eaton took a deep breath.

Walking across Farragut Square, he was looking down at his shoes, whispering as he said, "I've got to make some calls. There are things I can check. What he says fits together, and Jorge wouldn't have sent him up here if he didn't believe him. But I've got to make some checks, see if it's really true."

Leslie didn't say anything. A minute later they were approaching Pennsylvania Avenue. The White House was in sight a block and a half away. From here they could see the lines of protestors marching back and forth in front of the fence.

WHY CAN'T WE LEAVE NICARAGUA IN PEACE? one demonstrator's placard read. REMEMBER THE LAST WAR! CAN'T WE EVER LEARN? said another, and NICARAGUA: ANOTHER VIETNAM. BRING THE BOYS HOME! said a third.

There were perhaps two hundred of them—Quakers, other religious pacifists, and a few aging sixties liberals who took vacation time from Common Cause or their public-interest law offices to come out here and feel again the righteous anger of their youth. But no one was paying attention. To say this war was popular understated the matter considerably. Leslie and Eaton no longer even noticed them.

They always parted here, on the other side of Lafayette Park, just far enough away so that no one could see them from West Wing office windows. Eaton's office was just across the park and around the corner. He squeezed Leslie's arm, saying, "Thanks for being with me. I'll see you later."

Still Leslie was quiet. But after Eaton had turned away, she stared at his back a moment and finally she called after him.

"Chris, wait a minute."

When he looked back at her, she was reaching into her purse, pulling out a carefully folded set of sheets.

"Here" was all she said, handing it to him. Immediately she walked off toward the White House.

Eaton unfolded the papers and glanced at the title, then looked quickly around to make sure nobody else had seen. Hastily, he folded the papers again.

"Office of the Inspector General," the photocopy of the title page said. "Report on Theft of Redeye Missiles from the Nicaraguan Resistance."

Back at the office, the news editor shouted at Eaton as soon as he walked through the door.

"What're we doing about the new aid request for Nicaragua the White House put out today?"

"Use wires," Eaton said without even looking at him as he walked past. "I'm on something more important."

"You sure?"

"I'm sure."

He went straight to Abel's office, but he wasn't there.

"He's over at the Pentagon, for one of those bureau chiefs' meetings about combat press pools," his secretary said. "Won't be back till late this afternoon."

So Eaton sat at his desk and read the inspector general's report.

"Holy shit," he muttered to himself as he ran through the conclusions. Then he pursed his lips and started flipping through his notes, trying to write down key points. But he couldn't sit still. His head was spinning. Suddenly he was full of energy.

He got up and walked down the hall to the men's room, went in, and immediately turned around and returned to his desk. Calm down, calm down, he was telling himself. He had to start trying to confirm some of this. So he called Salazar, the former contra spokesman who was now working out of the Nicaraguan embassy on New Hampshire Avenue.

Salazar had been especially helpful the last few weeks. Eaton figured he wanted to stay in Washington with the new government and was trying to keep his reputation in good standing. Salazar had been a friendly, helpful source from the beginning, though no one could ever replace Paladino.

"If anyone asks me, I'll give you a good recommendation," Eaton had told him a couple of weeks ago.

Though he'd grown to like Salazar, he didn't want to give too much away today.

"I'll bet you're calling about the new military aid request," Salazar said as soon as he got on the line. "We really do need it, you know. The Communists are beginning to pick up their fighting."

"Yes, I know, Augustín. But that's not what I'm calling about today."

"Oh?"

"Yes, I wondered if you could tell me if you've ever figured anything out about those Redeyes that got stolen."

"You still on that? Why? It is obvious that the Sandinistas stole them."

"Okay, now about Comandante Venganza. Did he ever come back?"

"No, we have not heard from him."

Eaton asked about Paz's camp, Cascabeles. Salazar confirmed that it was there.

"Has Paz been seen lately?"

Salazar sounded vague. "I don't know," he said.

Then Eaton asked, "You remember that guy from the White House, Ascher, the one we saw Francesca with when I was down at El Cuartelón last fall?"

"Yes, I remember."

"Did Ascher come down there again, maybe to Cascabeles?"

"Possibly. I don't know. I can check."

"Would you? Call me back?"

"Okay," Salazar said, but it was clear these questions were making him nervous.

"Another thing. Who was trained to use Redeyes?"

"Well, most front-line people. It was standard."

"So, as an example, Major Paz and his men would get Redeye training?"

"Of course. They were commandos."

Eaton needed to ask one more question. It was risky, he realized, but he had to know.

"Augustín, you ever heard of a fighter named Balita?"

"Yeah, sure, everybody knew of Balita—the child-fighter they called him. Been with us since he was in diapers. He was one of Paz's men at the end. A Pena de Muerte. But tell me, Chris, what's this all about?"

"Oh, just some threads I'm working on."

By four-thirty, he had called sources at State, Defense, the Senate Intelligence Committee, and elsewhere. Eaton hadn't confirmed every fact and knew he never would. But he'd found out enough to convince him that Balita was telling the truth. When readers saw that important elements of what Balita said were confirmed by other people, they'd be inclined to believe the rest of his story, as Eaton did.

A friend of his over on the Honduras desk at State told him that he'd seen Colonel Eric Gustafson having drinks with Rafael Mendoza in the hotel bar during a Central America regional officers' meeting in Miami last fall. "They looked pretty chummy," he said, and the two of them had hung around together at several meetings after that. Eaton already knew Gustafson's name; he had been one of the hostages, and a couple of weeks ago somebody at Defense had told him about the colonel's monthly "mood of Managua" reports saying that Americans would be welcomed as liberators.

"Gustafson was real gung ho," this source had told him. Now it fit.

A Senate Intelligence Committee staff member told him the committee had started to investigate the dinner-party massacre last month, and they'd had George Basham, head of the CIA's Central America Task Force, in for secret questioning. Basham had said he considered Rafael Mendoza something of a renegade, and the agency was investigating the massacre, too. But with the invasion, this staff member said, all the investigations had dried up. It didn't seem to matter anymore.

Then just a little while ago Leslie had called. All reserve seemed to be gone now, because in a determined, almost officious voice she told him she'd checked the White House travel records. Yes, Terry Ascher had been down in Honduras at the time Balita said he had come to Cascabeles to give a pep talk.

"On his voucher, he called it a fact-finding trip," she said.

"Bingo!" Eaton was jubilant as she finished. With all that and the Defense Department inspector general's report, he had the story.

On the other end of the line there was a pause. Finally Leslie asked, "What are you going to do with all this?"

"I'm going to write it, of course."

There was a long pause. Then in a soft voice she said, "Please be careful, Chris."

A little while later he was hard at work at his computer, headphones on his ears as he transcribed his Balita tapes. He sensed someone over his shoulder and looked up, startled. Abel was standing over him, teeth clenched, arms folded over his chest. Eaton took off his headphones.

"Hey, Walter. I'm glad you're back. I—"

But Abel cut him off. "Just what the hell do you mean 'use wires' when the White House is making a $650 million emergency military aid request for Nicaragua—more money in all than we give any country but Israel? You expect us to run a wire service story for that?"

"They're asking for $650 million?" Eaton asked. He looked down at the Federal News Service transcript on his desk. He'd forgotten to read it.

"You mean you didn't even know?" Now Abel was really mad. "What the hell have you been doing all day?"

"Walter, I have the most amazing story. You're not going to believe it."

"Damn right I'm not. Just where have you been all day?"

"Well, over at the Mayflower interviewing a former contra. Let me tell you."

"What's a contra doing at the Mayflower?"

"Well, I put him there." Abel started to open his mouth, but Eaton held up his hand.

"Wait a minute, Walt, you'll understand when you let me tell you what's going on. It's incredible. You won't believe it. This guy says he was involved in shooting down the helicopters, and—"

"Goddamnit, Chris, I am sick and tired of you chasing after all these conspiracies. Now you're ignoring a real honest-to-God news story that's going to lead every newspaper in the country. And you're spending our money to put contras up at five-star hotels? I just can't believe it!"

Eaton had never seen Abel this mad, and he hadn't even mentioned the airfare yet. Around the room other reporters looked up but turned back to their work after a minute, pretending not to listen anymore.

"Wait a minute, Walt." Eaton tried to stop him. "Let me explain."

But Abel wasn't listening. "I've had it, Chris. Write the foreign aid story right now! And be in my office at nine o'clock tomorrow morning." With that he spun around, marched off, and stormed into his office, slamming the door. Eaton sighed and slumped in his chair. There was no sense trying to talk to him now. The way Abel sounded, he might really be in trouble this time. But Abel would understand when he saw the story.

After Eaton finished the foreign aid piece, an easy story, he checked out one of the office's Tandy Model 200 lap-top computers and took it home, along with all his notes. He'd write the story tonight and have it ready for Abel at nine A.M.

Leslie was waiting for him. When he told her what happened, she made him a sandwich and some soup, then left him alone in the living room to work while she watched TV upstairs.

About eleven, she came back downstairs and set up the coffee-maker for the morning. Eaton was tapping away at the little computer keyboard at his desk in the corner.

"How's it going?" she asked softly.

"Fine, fine," he said without looking up. She stroked his hair for a second. Then she stood behind him and watched. He was so absorbed in his work that he didn't seem to be aware she was there. After a minute or two she went back upstairs to bed.

Eaton finished just after two A.M. and read it over one last time.

"Damn," he whispered to himself, shaking his head. "Hell of a story. Hell of a story." He took a deep breath, folded the computer screen closed, leaned back in his chair and sat quietly for a minute. Then he straightened his notes, climbed the steps, undressed quietly, and slipped under the sheets.

Leslie came half awake, rolled over, and put her arms around him in the dark.

"I love you," she whispered in his ear. "These are dangerous men you're writing about. Please be careful."

"I will, Leslie. I will."

After Salazar hung up with Eaton that afternoon, he sat with his hand resting on the telephone receiver for almost a full minute, puzzling over the odd conversation. Then he picked up the phone again and called Tegucigalpa.

"Rafael, hello. It's Augustín. How are you?"

"Fine, my friend. Just fine. And how are you?"

"Well, I am all right."

"You sound troubled. What is wrong?"

"I just got an unusual call from that reporter, Christopher Eaton. Do you remember him?"

"Oh yes, of course," Rafael said with a tone of weary amusement. "What's this little fellow after now?"

"Well, he was asking lots of questions about you and about Paz and the Pena de Muertes. About whether Paz and his men were trained to shoot Redeyes, and about this man from the White House, Ascher, if he'd ever been down to Cascabeles."

"Oh?" Rafael no longer sounded so amused.

"Then out of the blue he asked me about little Balita, if I knew him."

"Balita? He asked you about Balita?" Now Mendoza's voice was hard. "What did you tell him?"

"Nothing, really, just that I knew him, that he was a Pena de Muerte, the child-fighter and all that. That is all. But if you ask me, I think this man Eaton has been talking to Balita."

With that there was an unnerving pause on the line. After a minute, Salazar whispered, "Rafael, did I do wrong?"

"No, my friend," Mendoza told him. Then in a cold voice, shorn of inflection, he said, "Don't worry. I will take care of it."

CHAPTER TWENTY-FIVE

A T FIRST CHRIS HAD LOVED HIS FANCY NEW ELEC-tronic coffeemaker. He'd bought it last fall, part of his apartment overhaul just before Leslie's first visit. It came complete with its own built-in automatic grinder and brewed fresh-ground coffee to be ready at the time set in its internal digital clock.

Great. But damn, it made a lot of noise. Every morning at seven Chris was jolted awake by a screeching whine that sounded as if a dentist were hard at work drilling a patient downstairs in the kitchen. Chris wanted to get up at seven, at least in theory. He'd been the one who set the timer, after all. But the damned coffeemaker was tyrannical. It removed any freedom of choice. He'd grown to hate the blasted thing.

This morning, as usual, at coffee launch hour Chris jerked straight up in the bed, eyes wide. Beside him Leslie rolled away, pulled a pillow over her head, and moaned in disgust before going back to sleep. She wasn't even a coffee drinker.

A minute later, Chris dragged himself out of bed with a long sigh and headed for the bathroom. He was still bleary-eyed as he stumbled downstairs. He hadn't gone to bed until late, and then he hadn't been able to fall asleep right away. Yesterday had been quite a day. Another big day coming up.

He stepped out the front door, grabbed the newspapers and

threw them on the sofa, then shuffled into the kitchen and poured a cup of coffee, growling at the brewer. A little blue light blinked back at him, telling him the coffee was brewed. As if he didn't already know.

Back in the living room, he glanced at his desk for a moment and shook his head. His notes were strewn all over the place. He thought he'd straightened them up last night.

Chris walked over, pulled the papers together, and was stuffing them in a file folder when suddenly he froze. Behind him he heard a rustling noise, then coat hangers clacking in the closet. And when he turned he felt an immediate high-voltage shock of fear. Across the room a man was stepping out of the coat closet, a pistol in his hand.

Son of a bitch, Chris thought. This guy was trying to rob me, and the damned coffeemaker scared him.

"Who the hell are . . ." But it was clear the man was not here to talk. Without even hesitating he started moving toward Chris, gun pointed at his chest. Chris was terrified but also amazed. This was one strange-looking little man.

He was a mulatto with frizzy orange hair. Large brown splotches were splattered across his cheeks. He wore dark aviator sunglasses, and as he got closer Chris could see Ray Ban stenciled in white on the right lens. In the man's left hand was Chris's reporter's pad, the one that had been on the desk. Balita's pseudonym and location were in there. And in his right hand the man held a 9-millimeter Beretta pistol with silencer, pointed at Chris's heart.

Six feet away the man stopped for a moment and stared at Chris, standing there in his bathrobe, mouth open, a steaming cup of coffee in his hand. Then he raised his pistol to arm's length, took careful aim at the spot between Chris's eyes, and in carefully enunciated Caribbean-accented English said, "I am Paz. Colonel of the Guardia."

With that Chris jerked alert. Now he knew what this was all about. Major Paz. They must have sent him after Balita, up from Managua on the redeye. This guy was a stone-cold killer, and he'd stumbled into his way by mistake.

Right away Chris threw his coffee at Paz and most of it splashed the colonel square in the face.

"*Ahhhgg!*" Paz howled, raising his gun hand to wipe off the scalding liquid, and in that moment Chris ran for the back stairs.

Even with the Ray Bans protecting his eyes, Paz didn't recover immediately. Still, before Chris could get down even three of the five short steps he heard a sharp pop behind him. A second later he was hurtling forward and landed sprawling, face down on the back hall's hard slate floor. First his nose hurt. Then his left shoulder stung, and when he reached up to touch it under his bathrobe, his hand was wet. Already there was a lot of blood.

Apparently the bullet had gone all the way through, but it hurt like hell. He managed to get back up on his feet right away, ran to the back door ten feet away, and was tearing at the dead-bolt knob. Paz must still have been wiping the coffee from his eyes. But just as Eaton got the door open and slipped halfway out, he heard another pop behind him and then another. Beside him a bullet slammed into the door frame with a thwack. A split second later Chris's right leg collapsed under him, and he screamed in pain as he fell to his knees just outside the door. It felt as if a hot spike had been jabbed all the way through his right thigh.

Whimpering in pain, tears forming in his eyes, Chris dragged himself up on his left leg and pulled the door shut, engaging the lock. Just to his right was the stockade wooden fence around the parking lot. He grabbed the fence and started dragging himself along, but with every motion he could feel the strength draining from his arms. His right foot was wet; already blood was streaming all the way down his leg, filling his bedroom slipper. He could feel his T-shirt growing wet and heavy too. God, he must be losing a lot of blood.

Chris couldn't tell how much time was passing. He was growing faint, beginning to see spots before his eyes. Each dragging motion was an effort greater than he thought he could complete. Every time he grabbed the fence with his left hand he sobbed out loud from the pain.

But a moment later he had pulled himself behind a row of plastic trash cans up against the fence twenty feet from the door. He let go of the fence and with a heavy grunt fell hard to the pavement, screaming again when his injured shoulder hit the ground. He stayed on his side; there was no room to lie flat back here, sandwiched tight between the fence and the trash cans. But by leaning back against the fence he took most of the weight off his shoulder and gave another groan, this time of relief.

Lying there, Chris wanted to go to sleep. But behind him he could hear Paz wrestling with the dead-bolt knob. A second or two later the door swung open, and Chris heard it slam hard against the back wall inside. Through a partial gap in the trash cans right in front of his nose he could see only Paz's legs, up to the waist. Paz had stepped outside and stopped, probably looking around.

Chris struggled to stay awake, biting his lower lip hard to keep from crying out from the pain; he figured Paz would not find him. A dozen cars were parked around this lot, and as far as Paz knew, Chris could be inside any of them. Or he could have left through the gate and headed down the street. The trash cans were almost flush against the fence. Paz wouldn't think anyone could fit back here. Maybe he'd just give up and go look for Balita, the man he'd come for anyway.

The spots before his eyes were getting bigger. He was growing sleepier. But through the cans he could still see Paz's legs as he stood there. Chris could also see the pistol in his hand, hanging at his side. Then suddenly he saw Paz's head; the colonel was bending down almost to his knees.

With two fingers Paz swiped at the pavement between his feet and then looked at his fingertips. They were dark with blood. He started following the blood trail. Slowly Paz was walking along the fence line toward the trash cans, toward Chris.

But Chris saw Paz take only the first couple of steps. Just then his eyes closed and he went to sleep.

DOWNTOWN WASHINGTON

It took Balita a good five minutes to realize that everybody was looking at him. He was standing in the middle of the sidewalk across the street from his hotel, staring entranced up at the second-story window just above. The sign painted on the glass said BODY WORKS, and behind the tinted picture window three dozen women wearing glittery body suits were bending up and down, straining back and forth, and waving their arms over their heads in some sort of rhythmic dance. Balita had never seen anything like it. You could see everything under those shiny suits. He couldn't bring himself to tear his eyes away until someone in the morning crowd bumped against him by accident, breaking the trance. And when Balita looked around, everyone was staring at him as if *he* was the strange one.

Then the same thing happened a few minutes later. Across the street he'd been walking along, looking at the sights, admiring all the wealthy, important people, when he passed a man standing in front of a machine that seemed to be grinding out twenty-dollar bills. Damn! He stopped to watch, and after the man had pulled out five crisp, fresh bills another man stepped right up, slipped a little plastic card into a slot, pushed some buttons, and the machine started printing twenty-dollar bills for him, too.

Balita couldn't believe it. When that man finished, he walked over and tried pushing the buttons himself. Nothing happened. He pushed harder, but after a minute he saw that people were giving him those funny looks again. Still, what a strange and wonderful place was America.

Balita was having a great time, though he'd had a start a few minutes earlier. He had been walking along, a block from the hotel, when he stopped in the middle of the sidewalk and stared down the street. There, a block away through the crowd—was that a head of orange hair he saw turning the corner? It looked like the major. No, it couldn't be. But what would he do if it was?

Balita had never brought himself to talk to Paz about killing the American. He wasn't sure about Paz anymore. Had he really known there was an American on the helicopter? What about their dream of becoming Marines? The war was over now, and the major hadn't said anything about going to the United States. Maybe it had all been a lie.

Then, before Balita left Managua, Mr. Paladino had said something funny.

"If you should happen to see Major Paz—I guess it's Colonel Paz now—don't tell him you've been talking to me. And for God's sake don't tell him you're going up to Washington."

"But why not?" Balita had asked.

"Balita, Paz is a part of this whole thing."

"No!" Balita had insisted, even as he realized it was true.

"I wish it wasn't so," Paladino had said. "I don't think it was the major's idea, but remember, he does follow orders."

That was true. Balita had thought a lot about all of this and didn't know what he would do if he actually ran into Paz. But that *couldn't* have been the major down the street. Maybe he should have stayed up in the room. Mr. Eaton and Mrs. Decker had made him promise he would until they got back, and he had tried.

All day Thursday he'd sat there watching the TV, playing the in-room movies, which came on one after another when he'd figured out how to press the buttons just the right way. After it got dark he'd ordered dinner from room service. Mrs. Decker had showed him how, and fortunately the man who answered the phone was from Mexico and helped him pick out some food. He got a steak as thick as a rifle stock.

The waiter who brought the tray was Hispanic too and showed Balita how to call downstairs and get somebody to come up and give him a massage. Great idea. So Balita called, and a little while later there was a knock at the door and a man came in, saying he would give Balita "a rubdown." A *man*. Of all things. Balita sent him away.

Later there was another knock at the door, and this time it was a pretty girl wearing black stockings, a very short skirt, and a little white hat. She smiled at him and asked if she could come in and "turn down the bed." Well, sure. Balita smiled back at her, amazed. But when he climbed into the bed and looked up at her, she gave him a funny look, put a little piece of chocolate on the bedside table, and walked quickly out of the room.

What a strange and wonderful place was America.

Growing up in León, Balita—he was Alfonse then—had been to Managua a couple of times, but this trip to Washington was his first visit to a big city. He'd gotten out of bed early, six-thirty or so, ordered breakfast, and waited for Mr. Eaton or Mrs. Decker. But nobody called. About eight-thirty there'd been a knock at the door, and when he opened it another woman was standing there in one of those funny short skirts, except this woman looked like somebody's evil grandmother.

"Housekeeping," she chirped, and walked right in, carrying a pail. Who knows what *she* wanted, so Balita took his key and left.

He'd loved wandering around in this wonderland. Everything was so *clean*. All the buildings were painted, none of the windows were broken, there were no holes in the streets. The cars were so quiet, and just about every one of them looked brand-new. America!

First thing, he had turned left and kept walking. After a couple of minutes, there in front of him was the White House. So he crossed the street and peered through the black iron bars at the great white building. But after only a minute or two he found himself on the verge of tears again. Why did the president ask them to shoot down those helicopters with an American on them? Why? He dabbed at his eyes and walked on.

After the business with the money machine, he'd looked in a few store windows, searching for something he could buy with the hundred dollars Mr. Paladino had given him. He couldn't seem to find anything, certainly not any of the clothes he saw in the windows. The jackets all had pieces of colored cloth hanging out of the upper pockets; it looked as if somebody had ripped out the lining. And every pair of shoes was black. Did they have funerals all the time up here?

Then he saw a watch he liked in a window next to the hotel. Tiny silver screws circled the face; it looked kind of military. But then he turned his head sideways to read the price tag. This must be a mistake. Maybe it wasn't really a wristwatch. Maybe it was a secret field radio or something. Who would pay $3,200 for a watch, especially one that was so thin?

Finally Balita saw something he liked in a store window. He bought four *GI Joe* comic books and started back to the room. Maybe the ugly woman with the bucket had moved out by now.

When he got close—there, again, off in the crowd. Was that orange hair? He wasn't sure.

Back in his room, a little red light was blinking on the telephone. He picked up the receiver, and when the operator came on she said she would find a man who spoke Spanish to read Balita the message.

"Colonel Paz came by to see you," the man said. "He will be back." Balita froze.

"Hello? Are you there?"

"Yes," Balita said, but his voice was unsteady.

"Are you all right?"

"Yes, I think so."

"Can I help somehow?"

"I need to call someone," Balita stammered. He wanted to call Mr. Paladino, ask what he should do. But he realized he was choking up on the phone. The man said he would come right up to help.

A moment later there was a knock, and Balita let the man in. He was wearing a gray uniform with black stripes down the legs.

"Mr. Lincoln, my name is José Fernando. I am the valet. Are you okay? Can I help?"

Balita was disoriented, trembling. He didn't know who his friends were anymore or who were his enemies.

"I need to call Mr. Paladino. I don't know how."

"Do you have the number?" José asked. He walked over and picked up the phone.

"He's in Managua. He's the new foreign minister."

José put the receiver back down. "We can't call Managua.

That's expensive." He picked up the business card on the table. "Do you want to call Mr. Christopher Eaton, here on this card?"

Balita nodded, and José called.

"Hello, this is the Mayflower Hotel calling for Mr. Alfonse Lincoln, from . . ." He put his hand over the receiver and looked at Balita. "Where are you from?"

"Managua. I flew up yesterday on the airplane to see Mr. Eaton. He said he would be back this morning."

"From Managua. We are trying to reach Mr. Christopher Eaton." A pause, and then the valet told Balita, "Mr. Eaton isn't there. Would you like to leave a message?"

"Please tell him Balita is calling."

"Hello? Yes. Could you please leave a message that Balita called. At the Mayflower. Thank you."

"Is there anything else I can do?" José asked after he hung up. Balita shook his head. Now he didn't know what to do.

"I have to go now," José said as he started for the door. "If you need me just call the front desk."

When Abel arrived at work this morning, a little after nine, two police officers were waiting for him.

"Oh, dear God," he groaned when they told him what had happened. Just last night he'd decided it was time to warn Chris he was in danger of losing his job. Now somebody had shot him. He must really have been on to something. Shaking his head, Abel thought, If only I'd had the patience to hear him out last night . . .

Looking up, he asked the officers, "Will he live?"

"They don't know yet for sure," one of them said. "He'd be dead already, but the neighbors scared the guy off. Somehow Eaton got out of the house with two bullets already in him. This guy was coming out after him, but he must have made some noise. Some neighbors opened the window to find out what all the racket was about. Musta scared the guy away before he could finish him off. They called us. We don't think Eaton was his primary target anyway.

"We got an ambulance over there right away, and you know Eaton doesn't live real far from George Washington Hospital. The docs say they got him just in time. Lost a lotta blood."

"God. Dear God," Abel murmured, bending over in his chair and looking at the floor as he shook his head.

"Didn't look like a robbery," the other officer said. "His lady friend said it probably had something to do with something he was working on at work. You got any ideas?"

"No," Abel told him, "but maybe I can find out. I want to go see him first. Okay?"

"Sure. Go ahead. We got some other things to do."

Abel knew Chris had a girlfriend, but he was surprised to see this mature, handsome woman staring through the window into the intensive care unit, her face puffy from crying. He introduced himself and she gave her name, but it seemed clear she wasn't pleased to meet him. Chris must have told her what happened in the office last night. Still, she told him what the doctor had said: One bullet had gone all the way through Chris's shoulder, and in surgery they had taken the other round out of his thigh. Chris had a collapsed lung and a shattered thigh bone. He'd lost a lot of blood but would probably recover. They'd certainly have to put a pin in his leg, but that would come later. For now, his condition was critical but stable.

"They think he's going to live," she said, looking directly at Abel for the first time. He almost recoiled from the pain radiating from those brown eyes.

"He's stable now," she went on. "They don't expect any change for a while."

"Miss DeSalles," he started, but her odd reaction made him stop and look down at her left hand. Seeing the ring he tried to hide his shock.

"May I call you Leslie?" he asked, his voice faltering a bit. She nodded.

"Leslie, I think I might have made the most monstrous misjudgment of my career yesterday afternoon. Can we talk? Maybe you can tell me what the hell is going on."

"Okay," Leslie said. "Can we go somewhere private?"

"Sure. Why don't you come over to my office. It's just a few blocks from here."

Leslie hesitated. Involuntarily Abel glanced down at the ring, the huge diamond.

"Oh, I'm sorry," he said. "We can go someplace less visible if you'd rather."

Leslie sighed. Her name was already all over the police reports. In fact it had been the police sirens that got her out of bed this morning. She hadn't heard a thing while the shooting was going on. Wearing only a bathrobe, she had let two officers in. They told her what had happened, and right away she fell apart, distraught not only because Chris had been shot, but because she had slept through the whole thing, when she might have been helping him. Well, she was in it all the way now.

"No," she said. "Your office is fine."

They didn't say anything on the short cab ride over to the National Press Building, both of them lost in thought. But as they stood alone in the elevator, Leslie turned to him.

"I didn't tell the police much," she whispered. "Until you understand what we're dealing with, I don't think you should tell them anything either. Chris was on to something so big that it could . . . well, it's a very important story. I know. I work at the White House."

Abel looked at her, eyebrows raised.

"Chris trusted you," she said, ignoring the look. "Well, most of the time. And now I'm going to have to trust you too."

"Please," was all Abel said. Then the doors opened onto the ninth floor. The office entrance was across the elevator lobby. Inside, Abel grabbed his phone messages at the receptionist's desk. As an afterthought, he picked up Chris's too and was flipping through them as they walked down the hall. He held one out to Leslie.

"Balita at the Mayflower," he read. "Is he the one who . . ."

"Oh, God," she burst out, stopping short. "Why didn't I . . . They're probably after Balita too!"

Balita was still in his room, sitting on the edge of the huge bed, head in his hands. The phone rang, and he picked up.

"Hola?"

"Is this Balita?"

"Yes."

"Balita, my name is Walter Abel. I am Chris Eaton's editor." The man's Spanish was poor, Balita thought. He sounded nervous, agitated.

"I am here with Ms. DeSalles." Balita heard her voice softly in the background. "I mean Miss Decker. Now, Balita, listen to me very carefully. Mr. Eaton is in the hospital. He has been shot. You may be in danger too. You should stay there. Don't let anybody into the room. I am sending the police over to help you. Just stay there in the room. Do you understand?"

"Yes, sir."

"This is very important, Balita." The man was excited, his voice was rising. "Don't let anybody in."

"Yes, sir."

"Okay, Balita. Just stay there."

He hung up but didn't move. Somebody shot Mr. Eaton? Did the major do that? He couldn't have. He just couldn't.

Balita had been off the phone just a couple of minutes when there was a soft knock at the door. He sat up straight and remained quiet. He wasn't going to answer. Whoever it was knocked again, and then he heard his name.

"Balita, Balita. It's me." It was the major, speaking with that soft voice he used sometimes when the two of them were alone. "I've come to take you back. Let me in."

Balita rushed to the door, pressed his mouth to the crack. Already he was crying.

"Major, Major. I shot an American. In the helicopter at Río Jalan. I shot an American. I am sorry, so sorry."

Through the crack Paz whispered, "I know, Balita. I know. It is okay."

"You knew? Why did they have us kill an American? What about being Marines?"

"It was the war, Balita. Let me in, and I will explain." But Balita leaned against the door frame sobbing. Suddenly the door shook. Paz was rattling the knob.

"Let me in," he commanded, and Balita stood up straight. Now there was a threatening edge to the major's voice. He recognized it right away. Balita stopped crying.

"Major, they told me not to let anybody in. Please, Major."

He went to the desk, dragged the chair over to the door, and climbed up on it so he could see out the peephole.

"Balita, come on. It's me, the major." His voice was warm and soft again. "Let me in. I want to help you. Let me help you." But when Balita bent down and looked through the peephole, the major's face didn't look warm and soft. His right hand was under his zip-up jacket, obviously holding the butt of his pistol.

Balita didn't answer this time. Mr. Paladino was right. He couldn't believe it. The major wanted to kill him. The *major*. He stood straight up on the chair now and leaned against the top of the door, sobbing quietly again. The next thing he knew he heard four quick popping noises, and the chair jerked out from under him, falling backward and sending Balita careening to the floor.

He hit with a loud thump. Dazed, he lifted his head and saw four bullet holes in the thin paneled door. If he hadn't been standing on the chair, the major would have hit him in the chest.

As it was, the slugs had gone between his legs, striking the back of the chair.

Now he was under fire. He felt the familiar surge of heat and energy. He was in battle. It didn't matter who he was fighting. He wanted to reach for his rifle, but of course it wasn't here. Before he could move, Paz fired again, this time pointing down to where he guessed Balita lay. But again the chair saved him. The bullets struck the underside of the seat.

Now Balita scrambled over to the left, behind the sofa. Even before he got all the way over, the door started shaking. Paz was trying to knock through it, and the thin center panel flexed a little more with every kick. After two or three kicks, Balita could see cracks starting to appear.

Desperately he looked around the room for a weapon. The little table at the end of the couch. The leg. He pushed the lamp and the ashtray onto the floor with a crash, turned the table upside down, and ripped off the leg. It made an okay club. It even had a sharp screw sticking out of the end.

The door panel was cracking now. A few more kicks, and Paz would break through. He'd reach in and turn the latch. Balita pressed his back against the wall behind the door. When the major's hand came through, he would swing at it, screw-end first. Maybe that would stop him.

Paz kicked. Again. And again. Another kick and the panel cracked open at last, and the sole of Paz's shoe popped through for just a second. But if he pushed his hand through there now, it would get stuck. Paz wouldn't be able to pull it back out. Still, Balita raised the club over his head, waiting, waiting, waiting . . . But the kicking stopped.

Now it was quiet outside the door. Maybe somebody had walked by, and Paz had ducked out of sight for a moment. Maybe he'd gone to look for something to batter down the door. Still Balita stood there, club high over his head. He couldn't tell how much time was passing. His ears buzzed with the excitement of battle.

Then suddenly, *crack!* The door popped open and swung around so hard that it hit Balita in the face, stunning him. He dropped to his knees and let go of the club to put his hands up to his bruised nose.

Now I am dead, he thought, just as he had in a dozen tight battles before.

When he looked up, the first thing he saw was the pistol

pointed right at his face. But the large hand holding it was black. So was the face behind it. The man wore a blue cap.

"D.C. police," he barked. "On your feet. Hands over your head!" Balita understood that much English at least, and did as he was told, smiling now. He wasn't going to die after all.

A second policeman frisked him, and then the first one asked, "You Mr. Lincoln?"

He nodded. "Balita," he said.

"Balita, I think we saw the perpetrator running down the stairs. He saw us coming. We went after him, but he got away. We've got a call out for him. Can you identify him for us, please? What's this all about?"

"I do not speak good English," he said. "I do not understand."

And in truth he didn't.

The two officers were still with Balita, one of them talking on the phone, when Abel and Leslie arrived a few minutes later. The door was open, and Abel stopped short when he saw all the bullet holes.

"Jesus," he said under his breath.

"Are you okay, Balita?" Leslie asked, her hand on his shoulder. He nodded. "This is Mr. Abel, Chris's editor."

Abel introduced himself in his high school Spanish, thinking, This is just a kid. Comic books on the coffee table. Then he turned to the two policemen. "I am a newspaper editor, and this man is here under the care of one of my reporters. We can take charge of him now."

"The detective still wants to talk to him," one of the policemen said. "Maybe he better come down to the station with us. We can watch over him there until the detective gets done with what he's doing. You know, the perpetrator's still out there. I wouldn't go walking around out there if I was him."

Abel handed them his business card. "We'll take care of him, and if the detective needs him, you can reach us through my office."

"Okay," the policeman said. "It's your choice." They left, and Balita started gathering his things.

Downstairs, Abel gagged when he paid the bill.

"Seven in-room movies?" he whispered to Leslie. Balita was standing a few feet away.

Leslie smiled briefly, saying, "I guess he was catching up."

They took a cab back to the New World office and called the

hospital. Chris's condition hadn't changed. Abel asked his secretary to get some coffee and sandwiches, and then the three of them locked themselves in the conference room.

"All right, Leslie, why don't you tell me what this is all about," Abel said. He put a legal pad down in front of him on the table and fiddled with it as if he didn't quite know what to do.

"I used to be a reporter," he offered with an embarrassed grin.

Leslie settled back in her chair. "This man"—she pointed to Balita, who sat off to the side looking at one of his comic books—"has told us a story that, I am sorry to say, could very well bring down his new government and do serious damage to our own."

Abel looked at her. "Go on."

"Well, we should let Balita tell his own story. But in essence it's this: A small group of people in our government manipulated events to draw us into the war. I am certain that the president didn't know about it. But at least one man in the White House did, and so did a CIA officer and somebody from DoD. Balita's squad—the Death Penalty commandos, they were called—was their agent."

"Jesus. Can you prove this?"

"I can't, but I think Chris did. Just listen to this man. Balita?" she asked, turning to him. He looked up from his *GI Joe* comic and glanced at them for a second. Then he stood up, reached into his pants pocket, and pulled out the Army identification card.

"What's this?" Abel asked, turning it over in his hands.

"I killed an American," Balita said, his voice tremulous again. "I didn't know it was an American. I didn't, Mr. Abel. I wanted to be a Marine."

Abel wasn't sure he believed the story. But as soon as Balita finished talking, Leslie told Abel exactly who she worked for, what she did, and some of the things she'd been able to find out at the White House, including the details of Ascher's travel records.

"Chris had much more. He did a lot of research yesterday. I don't know all of the work he did, but I think he proved it."

Abel was shaken. "General Dayton's office" he asked, looking down at the table.

"Yes."

"All those stories of Chris's that got knocked down, the ones

I've been yelling at him about, most of them were accurate?"
He still wasn't looking at her.

"Not just most of them. All of them. I didn't help him in any
serious way before this, but I read his work. He knew what he
was doing. Believe me."

Head still bowed, Abel sat quietly for a minute, then sat up
and looked directly at her.

"Well, we're going to do right by Chris now," he declared,
slapping the tabletop. "I can promise you that." Leslie didn't
say anything.

"That research he did yesterday, we can check for his notes
here, but do you think he took them home?"

"I don't know about his notes. But he's already written the
story."

"What?"

"He brought a computer home with him last night. He was
up till after two A.M. writing the story. He was going to show
it to you first thing this morning."

Abel bowed his head again and squeezed his eyes closed.

"I'll be right back." He got up and quickly left the room. Less
than five minutes later he returned.

"First thing," he said, in full control now, "the hospital has
upgraded Chris's condition from critical to serious. He's getting
better." Leslie sighed her relief, and Abel translated for Balita.

"Second, Balita, my secretary is going to take you to a suite
we have rented at the Four Seasons Hotel—with in-room movies." He smiled. "She is hiring a bodyguard, too."

"I don't want any bodyguard," Balita whined. "Just get me
my gun."

Abel smiled. "I'm afraid things don't work that way here. And
third, Leslie, why don't you and I go over to Chris's apartment
and get that computer so we can see about publishing this story."

A young policeman was standing guard outside Chris's front
door, and a strip of yellow plastic tape was strung across the
doorway. On it were the words POLICE LINE. DO NOT CROSS.

Abel introduced himself and explained that they just wanted
the computer that was inside, probably on the desk. It belonged
to the company.

"I'm sorry, but you can't take anything out of here. Not even
a pin. No way. It's all evidence."

"For how long?" Abel asked.

"Don't know. That's up to the detective."

"But usually how long, roughly?"

"Usually a few days, a week, unless it gets taken down to the property room. Then not till after the trial."

Abel and Leslie looked at each other.

"Officer, would you let me look at it for a minute? Mr. Eaton left some information in the computer that we need. I just want to look."

The officer glanced at Abel and asked, "Now tell me who you are again?"

"I am the Washington editor of New World News Service. I'm Mr. Eaton's boss." He handed the officer his business card. "Just go in and look at the computer on the desk. You'll find a New World card taped onto the lid."

They waited on the front step while the officer went inside. "If we get in, talk to him for a few minutes," Abel whispered to Leslie. "Keep him occupied while I'm at the computer."

The officer returned right away and said, "Well, they've dusted everything, and the photographers have already been here. I got orders not to let anything out of here, but I guess it's okay to look. You try to take anything, though, and you're going to jail."

"I won't," Abel promised, and all three of them went inside.

Abel went right to the desk and pulled up the chair. Leslie sat on the edge of the sofa, looked at the policeman's name tag, and said: "So, Officer Fowler. Suppose you were a detective. Suppose this was your case. How would you go about it from the evidence in here?"

Officer Fowler warmed to that right away.

"Well, ma'am, first thing, I'd inventory all the physical evidence."

"Uh-huh. Uh-huh," Leslie said. "And how would you do that?"

While they talked, Abel slipped the telephone Y-cable out of the computer case and plugged the computer into the desk phone. He flipped open the computer screen, turned it on and looked through the directory for the story dated today.

PREXY, it was called, the standing name for New World White House stories. This one, the Tandy computer said, was 16,843 bytes, or a little over 2,700 words—a long piece. Then he activated the "telcom" communications program.

Behind him, Officer Fowler was saying: "I'd look through recent correspondence, bills, checks . . ."

"Mind if I use the phone a second?" Abel asked.

"Sure, go ahead," the officer said, turning halfway toward him for only a second. "Lots of times, you'll find stuff on the phone bill, or maybe a letter . . ."

Abel called his office's incoming computer number. When the modem at the other end broadcast its tone, Abel pushed a function key on the Tandy and cleared his throat to cover the noise of the computer's confirmation tone. Then he hung up the phone, turning the line over to the two computers.

"Nobody there," he told the officer with a smile. But Fowler wasn't paying any attention. Now he was into interrogation techniques.

At a transmission speed of 300 baud, sending the story took several minutes. On the way, it scrolled quickly across the Tandy's little screen, and Abel stared with such intensity that his eyes began to burn. He wasn't blinking, for fear he'd miss a line. Halfway through the story he found he was growing short of breath.

"Dear Lord," he was murmuring under his breath toward the end. "Save us from ourselves."

"What's that?" Officer Fowler asked. "You say something?"

"Nothing, nothing," Abel said. "Almost done. Mind if I use the phone again?"

"No, but let's hurry up. I want you out of here before the detective gets back."

Abel called his communications room to make sure the story had arrived intact.

"Take good care of that, Earl," he whispered into the phone. "And don't let *anybody* see it."

He hung up; then he deleted the file from the Tandy. No trace of the story was left in the little computer.

"Okay," Abel said as he stood up. "Thanks, Officer. Got what I needed. We're ready to go now."

CHAPTER
TWENTY-SIX

WASHINGTON, MAY 8

[Editor's Note: A former Nicaraguan contra, presumed by police to be the man identified in the following article as "Major Paz," attempted to assassinate Christopher Eaton, the author of this article, in his home early yesterday morning. Mr. Eaton is in the intensive care unit at George Washington University Hospital, recovering from bullet wounds to his shoulder and his right thigh. Last night he was still unconscious, and his condition was reported to be serious but stable. District of Columbia police report that Major Paz also attempted to assassinate the man identified in this article as "Balita," in his room at the Mayflower Hotel later yesterday morning. Balita was not hurt and is now being kept in protective custody. Both attempted assassinations are assumed to be efforts to stop publication of this article.]

BY CHRISTOPHER EATON
NEW WORLD NEWS SERVICE

WASHINGTON—A select squad of contra assassins, under direct control of a Central Intelligence Agency officer and other American officials, shot down the United States Army helicopters in Honduras last month and allowed the Sandinista government to take the blame as part of a carefully conceived

367

plot to bring about a United States invasion of Nicaragua, according to U.S. and Nicaraguan officials as well as a contra fighter directly involved in the scheme.

Elements of the plot, at least, were carried out with the apparent knowledge and participation of a senior White House official, Terrence W. Ascher, director of the White House office that managed the contra program. But there is no evidence indicating that the president or others of his senior aides were aware of the scheme.

Instead, it now appears that a small cabal of American officials succeeded in carrying out a grand ruse, manipulating events so that the president and his aides were led along to invade Nicaragua and depose the leftist Sandinista government.

The plan was conceived and managed, according to most accounts, by Rafael Mendoza, the CIA station chief in Honduras, along with Marine Colonel Eric Gustafson, chief military attaché at the United States embassy in Managua.

A well-placed White House official said the president and his advisors "were deceived like everybody else. We had no idea this was a setup." Apparently the contra leadership was not aware of the scheme either.

Told of New World's findings last night, Fred Hillard, the president's spokesman, first said: "This is just plain ludicrous. Where'd you get this stuff? You're not going to print this junk, are you?" But Hillard called back a short time later and said, "This is a very serious matter, and we are looking into it right now."

In extensive interviews, a longtime contra fighter who goes by the nom de guerre "Balita" said Mendoza maintained the 22-man "Death Penalty" commando squad as his own elite unit in a private camp in Honduras. The CIA officer used the commandos for missions of his own design. Other former contra officers confirmed that.

In interviews over the last two days, Balita said Mendoza and Gustafson ordered them to carry out the dinner-party massacre in Managua that prompted the Sandinistas to send troops into Honduras.

Mendoza and Gustafson "told us to kill all the Communists," he said. The dinner-party killings, he added, were not a mistake, as had been widely assumed. "It was the plan," and "the man from the White House came down to camp to tell us to do it."

Ascher declined repeated requests for interviews.

On March 21, a few days before the dinner party raid, Ascher accompanied Gustafson and Mendoza to Major's Paz's camp "and told us we were going on a very important mission," Balita said. Ascher "told us we were carrying out the president's orders." White House travel records confirm that Ascher was in Honduras visiting Mendoza on that date. Defense Department records show that Gustafson was in Honduras then too.

Jorge Paladino, the former contra leader who is now Nicaragua's foreign minister, said the dinner-party massacre, if deliberate, "could only have been intended to incite the Sandinistas to go into Honduras after the resistance camp." That's precisely what happened. But by that time, the main contra camp had been moved deep into Honduras—at Ascher's suggestion.

As Sandinista troops crossed the border, the president ordered U.S. Army helicopters to airlift Honduran troops and equipment to the region in case of trouble. Balita said Mendoza and Gustafson then told the commando unit to shoot down the helicopters, though Balita says he did not know Americans would be on board. As far as Balita knew, Ascher was not directly involved in this part of the scheme.

Major Paz "told us Honduran soldiers, traitors working for the Sandinista Communists, were on those helicopters," he said. The commandos used Redeye antiaircraft missiles they had stolen from the contra supply depot. The White House, acting on Ascher's information, had blamed the theft on the Sandinistas. But a Defense Department inspector general's report published before the helicopters were shot down concluded that it was "highly unlikely" that the Sandinistas stole the missiles.

"More likely," the report added, "the missiles were taken by contra elements themselves." The report was classified Secret.

Balita said Mendoza ordered them to shoot any crash survivors. But Balita added that he was shocked and revolted when he learned that he and the others had shot Americans. That prompted him to come forward and tell his story.

"I didn't want to kill Americans," Balita said with tears in his eyes. "Why did they make us kill Americans?"

After Balita realized what he had done, he took the Army identification card from the wallet of an American Army sergeant, B. J. Robertson, who had been executed as he lay wounded on the ground. He provided the card to the New World News Service . . .

A photo of the ID card ran with the story, which was published under six-column headlines in every one of New World's newspapers. With it were photos of Balita in his room at the Mayflower, the bullet-riddled door in the foreground. A sidebar by another reporter recounted the police description of Chris's "desperate effort to get away from his assassin," and a small photo showed the blood trail along the parking-lot fence. A picture of Eaton from New World's files ran beside that.

The D.C. police had dug up a photo of Major Paz, taken years ago while he was still in the Guardia, and most of the papers published that, too. Paz's unusual appearance was not apparent in the black-and-white picture, but he was wearing his Ray Bans.

When the papers came off the press in Miami about ten-thirty Sunday night, a courier carried two copies over to the Associated Press office a few blocks away. That was routine. But this night, AP-Miami took one look at Chris's story and called AP's world desk in New York. The New York desk called the Washington bureau, and a night editor there called the White House duty officer, who had a statement ready.

"These are grave charges," it said. "While it is absolutely clear that neither the president nor his top advisors were aware of this alleged plot, the White House takes the charges seriously and has already initiated an investigation."

That statement was almost a confirmation; the AP decided what to do immediately. The service sent out a "Flash," the highest-priority wire story. "Flash" designations were usually reserved for assassinations and declarations of war.

In newsrooms across the United States and much of the world, bells and buzzers sounded as the AP printers interrupted the story they were in the midst of printing and instead spit out a short lead.

WASHINGTON (AP)—Contra assassins under the direct control of a small group of White House, CIA, and Defense Department officers shot down the Army helicopters in Honduras last month as part of a broad plot that drew the United States into the invasion of Nicaragua, the New World News Service reported tonight.

The White House issued a statement tonight saying the president and his advisors were not "aware of this alleged plot." But the statement also said the White House took the charges seriously and was investigating.

Friday morning a former contra killer who was involved in the plot tried to assassinate the reporter who wrote the story, Christopher Eaton, in an apparent attempt to prevent publication, according to District of Columbia police. Eaton is hospitalized in Washington with bullet wounds to the shoulder and thigh.

MORE

By shortly after eleven P.M., the AP had sent out a full-length story on its A wire, along with the full text of Chris's article. Across the country, TV stations interrupted the sports or weather segments of their eleven o'clock news shows to read the report. By dawn Monday, the television networks had confirmed parts of the story and reported on it throughout their early-morning news shows.

The daily White House briefing was at nine, earlier than usual, and the pressroom was as packed as a subway car at rush hour. Photographers stood on their ladders; all the klieg lights were on. The room was bright—and hot. In the back, network cameramen were preparing to broadcast live. The air seemed full of sparks; the room was hushed as everyone waited. Reporters tested and retested their tape recorders. Photographers continually focused their lenses.

Microphone in hand, the ABC reporter stood in front of his first-row seat, looking over the crowd to his cameramen at the back. Waiting for the briefing to begin, the network cut to him live for a minute, and the other reporters watched as he suddenly stood straight and alert, then intoned, "Yes, Ted, the White House takes the charges very seriously, as they said in their statement last night. They don't really have any choice. The evidence supporting the charges is compelling. I'm told that the president was awakened early and shown a copy of the New World story. He met with his top advisors starting at seven this morning. I am told that he ordered a full and immediate investigation."

The reporter was quiet for a minute. He put a finger to his earpiece, listening, and said, "Yes, all of us here know Chris Eaton. He was quiet. He didn't speak up much, but his specialty was the contras. The White House denied a lot of his stories. But I guess all of us ought to take a second look at them now."

Over the public address system, a White House press officer announced, "The briefing is about to begin." So the ABC reporter sat back down.

A moment later, camera shutters and motor-drives erupted in clacks and whirs as General Dayton, Fred Hillard, and their aides swept through the door. All of them looked somber.

General Dayton stepped to the podium and unfolded a sheet of paper, setting off another storm of camera noise.

"I have a short statement to read," he began, "and then Fred will take your questions." He put his hand to his mouth, cleared his throat, and read from his sheet.

"The president was grieved to learn of the shooting of Christopher Eaton. The president tried to call Mr. Eaton at the hospital this morning to express his hopes for a fast recovery but was told he has not regained consciousness. He sends his best wishes to Mr. Eaton and his family, with hopes for a speedy return to full health."

Dayton paused there and rearranged his papers, then started up again.

"The United States takes the charges in the New World News Service account with the utmost seriousness and intends to investigate them completely and thoroughly. We are pleased that New World has agreed to make the contra fighter known as Balita available to government investigators immediately, and we are determined to make the facts known as they become available in as full a manner as possible.

"Now, our preliminary look—and I emphasize that it is preliminary—suggests that certain elements of the charges may be accurate." At that, a rush of surprised murmurs and exclamations swept through the room.

"But let me emphasize"—Dayton spoke up, raising his hand—"please, let me emphasize that neither the president nor any of his aides were aware of any plot. They—we—acted on what we believed to be genuine information and what appeared to be grievous provocations. We are utterly convinced that any investigations will bear that out.

"The president will address the nation on national television tonight," Dayton said as he folded his sheet. "And now I will turn this over to Fred Hillard, who will try to answer your questions as best we can at this early stage."

"General, General," forty reporters screamed as Dayton

started to leave the room. Someone in the front row shouted, "Have you talked to this guy Ascher? Was the White House really involved?"

One foot out the door, Dayton stopped to answer. "We haven't been able to talk to Ascher yet," he said.

"You haven't? Why not?"

"We don't know where he is."

"You mean he's gone?"

Dayton paused for a second, but then said, "We just haven't been able to find him yet." With that he ducked from the room.

"Filing break!" the AP and UPI writers yelled almost in unison.

"Okay, the briefing will resume in ten minutes," Hillard shouted, but already thirty reporters were shoving their way back to their telephones so they could file the news already out.

As Dayton spoke, Ascher was on an Eastern jet somewhere over North Carolina, flying south. He was using the Airphone, calling his accountant.

"Arthur, it's Terry Ascher. Yes, yes, I know. It's a long story, and I can't explain now, but they're wrong. I didn't do any of that.

"Listen, you've got to do something for me right away. I want my liquid assets transferred to my Credit Suisse account in the Cayman Islands. You've got the account number, the one we used before?

"No, no, I can't explain now," he said after a pause. "You've got to take care of this right away. This morning. Okay? I'll be in touch." He hung up.

Ascher had gotten first word the night before. Linda was at the office working late as usual, though Ascher could never figure out what she did. He'd had nothing to do since the invasion.

"Terry, Rich Christopher is looking for you," she said. "I told him I'd find you and get you to call him back."

"What's he want," Ascher asked, not really caring. It was after eight o'clock, and as usual he was drugged and a bit drunk.

"He said the press office got a call about you. He didn't tell me what it was, so I called the duty officer myself. It was Karen Hayes. She said New World News has some wild story about you tomorrow." Ascher wasn't surprised. All day long he'd been given phone messages from someone at New World who had kept calling, even after Linda told him that Ascher gave no interviews.

"They're saying you were involved with some other people, Mendoza down in Honduras and somebody else from the embassy in Managua, in a secret plot that started the invasion."

"What?" Fear cleared Ascher's head quickly.

"Yeah, something about the Major Paz commando squad that did the dinner-party massacre also shooting down the Chinooks with stolen Redeye missiles. They said you were down there and ordered the dinner-party massacre. It's crazy, isn't it?"

Silence.

"Terry? Are you okay?"

"Yeah, yeah," he murmured. "Thanks, Linda. I'll take care of it." He hung up.

He was in the kitchen and sat down heavily on the stool, staring at the refrigerator through a cloud that seemed to be gathering before his eyes. Ever since the dinner-party massacre, he'd been afraid something like this might happen. Somebody, maybe Kutler, would discover his role and, because the raid had gone bad, misinterpret everything. Without Mendoza to help explain, to back him up, there seemed to be no good defense. There was no way out. He had to talk to Rafael.

He didn't know how long he'd been sitting there when the phone rang, startling him. He stood up and looked at it but didn't answer. After almost fifteen rings, it finally stopped. A minute later the ringing started again, and this time Ascher unplugged the kitchen phone and then every other phone in the house, even as they rang. Then he began to pack. Even before this latest problem arose, there had seemed little reason to stay. His career was destroyed. His life in Washington was over. He'd get away, talk to Mendoza, find out what really happened, and together they'd come back and straighten everything out. What a mess!

Ascher had two large suitcases filled with summer-weight clothes when the doorbell rang at about ten o'clock. He crossed the hall to a front bedroom but stopped before he got to the window. Red police lights were bouncing off the ceiling. Peering out a corner of the window he saw a Secret Service uniformed-police cruiser out front, and below he heard pounding on the door.

"Police, Mr. Ascher. We have to talk to you." They pounded on the door several more times, then walked back and climbed into the car. They turned off the lights but didn't leave, just sat out front. It didn't matter. Ascher had already decided he had to leave tonight. Tomorrow there'd be TV reporters out front waiting to shout questions at him as he left for work.

Ascher finished packing as quickly as he could. Then he went through the house room by room, skirting the windows and leaving the lights off. He looked around one last time, picking up a few things here and there: his favorite superhi-fi video tape, *Apocalypse Now*, a framed photo of his mother; his graduate-school diploma; the little *Washington Post* story about his White House appointment, which he'd had embedded in a Plexiglas paperweight. He didn't really think he'd be gone that long, but still . . .

With those and a few other last items packed, he closed the suitcases and started carrying them downstairs. It took two trips.

There was a basement entrance to the garage, which opened onto an alley. Without turning on the light, he walked around his car and looked out the little windows near the top of the garage door. He sagged with relief. The alley was dark and empty.

He started loading the suitcases into the BMW trunk. Only three fit. The fourth he put in the back seat. He reached up behind the car and pulled the lever disengaging the automatic garage-door opener. Its grinding would make a lot of noise. Opening the door manually was much quieter. Then, as quietly as he could, he started the car, pulled into the alley without lights, closed the garage door again, and crept out to the street, turning right, away from the police car.

When he got on Connecticut Avenue he settled back, reached into his shirt pocket, and took one of the Valiums he had put there before throwing the bottles into his suitcase.

He drove down to K Street, stopped at his bank's automatic-teller machine, and took out three hundred dollars, the maximum. He got four hundred dollars more from another machine that took his American Express card, and another four hundred dollars from a third machine that accepted his "Plus" system Visa Card. Then, after midnight, he crossed the bridge and headed west for the Dulles Airport Marriott.

At Dulles Airport before seven the next morning, he worried that federal agents might be looking for him, but the departure lounge looked clear. It would take a while for anyone to guess he was leaving.

The Eastern flight stopped in Miami, but Ascher was cleared all the way through to La Paz, Bolivia. At the departure gate the attendant glanced at his black diplomatic passport, comparing him with his picture. He was tan in the photo, pale now. But this morning he was wearing one of his linen pinstripe suits and a red silk tie. He looked official. She stamped his boarding pass "Docs OK."

After takeoff, he pushed his first-class seat back and stared up at the ceiling. No Valium this morning. He wanted his head clear so he could figure out what to do. But it was tough. He didn't know how long he could go without a pill.

Klaus Barbie had hid out in Bolivia well enough, at least for a while. Robert Vesco too, or so the story went. Ascher knew the country well. He'd been stationed there, and he liked La Paz, once he adjusted to the altitude. In any case, it was for just a short while. He didn't think it was wise to go to Honduras right now. But as soon as things cooled down a bit he'd fly up to Tegucigalpa and find Mendoza, wait for him outside his home. Together he and Rafael could figure out how to clear their names of these ridiculous charges. Then he'd look for Francesca. He closed his eyes and smiled as he imagined their torrid reunion at the Maya Hotel. Then maybe, with Francesca on his arm, he could go back home.

The *Washington Post* he'd bought as he left the Marriott was an early edition. The AP version of Christopher Eaton's story was on the front page. Ascher had read it sitting in the airport departure lounge. There was a picture of Balita on the front page and another of Paz, an old shot, on the inside. Ascher was relieved not to see his own picture; it would be hard to get one from the White House on short notice.

He remembered Balita from that Cascabeles visit, the trip that was getting him into all this trouble now. Major Paz had introduced Balita specially; it was clear he was Paz's favorite. How could Balita have gotten things so screwed up?

Yes, he'd been down there and told them they were carrying out the president's orders. But he hadn't known the hostage-taking raid was going to turn into a massacre. That part looked bad; Mendoza would have to help him straighten that out.

But this business about Mendoza ordering Paz and his men to shoot down the Chinooks? Where'd Balita get that? What nonsense! No wonder Paz wanted to kill him.

After the flight attendant cleared away the breakfast trays, Ascher pulled a copy of *Time* magazine out of the seat pouch in front of him. Nicaragua was on the cover again, of course. "Will Democracy Come at Last?" was the headline. *Time* was published on Sunday, before the Eaton story had come out. Ascher flipped quickly through the magazine, looking at the headlines, quote blocks, and color pictures. The story wouldn't say anything he didn't already know.

Look—there was that little oily-haired worm Coronel. Imagine, he's the president now, and in this picture he's at a party wearing a general's outfit. Five stars, no less, just catching the light from the photographer's flash. Ascher snorted.

Coronel. A men's clothing salesman. Chosen, Mendoza had told him once, for his demonstrated capacity to be manipulated.

Suddenly Ascher stiffened in his seat. After a second he leaned forward, eyes wide open as he stared at the half-page color picture. Who is that woman clutching Coronel's arm? The cascading black hair, tumbling over her slender shoulders. Ascher could feel his temples pounding. No, it couldn't be her.

He was having trouble focusing on the page now. The woman's face was turned away; mostly the photo just showed hair. Shiny black hair. Lots of Latin women had long black hair. It wasn't her. It wasn't. It couldn't be.

But then, looking down, Ascher sucked in his breath, and when he let it go, the air came out as a gasp.

Deep in the valley revealed by the woman's low-cut dress, caught in the light of the photographer's flash—shining, glinting, branding the page—was the little gold cross.

Ascher squeezed his eyes shut, and his hands lost their grip. The magazine slid to the floor.

"Miss," he whispered to a flight attendant after a minute. "Can I have a glass of orange juice, please?"

"Yes, sir," she said and brought it right away. Immediately he took two five-milligram Valiums.

Ascher rolled toward the window and closed his eyes again, waiting for the pills to take effect. He'd figured Francesca had been up in the hills with the fighters all this time, unable to call. But she was in Managua. And now she'd latched on to that little twerp Coronel, the clothing salesman, the man chosen because . . . because he could be manipulated.

Is that what she's doing with Coronel? he thought. Manipulating? Is that what she was doing with me too?

Ascher's eyes popped open. Tension was rising up from his belly. The newspaper story.

Balita said Major Paz and his men shot down the helicopters. Why would Balita make up something like that? And what about the B. J. Robertson ID card? Where'd he get that?

Balita said Mendoza had directed them to do it, and Paz never did anything without orders. Everybody agreed on that.

Paz and his men also shot everyone at the dinner party. That was clear. He, Ascher, had done what Mendoza had asked. He'd stood up there telling the Pena de Muertes that they were carrying out the president's orders, though of course the plan *he'd* agreed to didn't call for anyone to be killed. But again, Paz didn't do anything without orders.

That afternoon in the Miami safehouse apartment a few months ago, Mendoza and Gustafson had made a big deal about the Redeyes, asked him to explain the theft to the RIG. He'd done what they'd asked, but even then he had thought it was funny. Why didn't they just report the theft themselves? Now it looked as if the Pena de Muertes, Mendoza's own men, had stolen the missiles, again on orders from Mendoza. No wonder Rafael didn't want to request the new missiles himself.

They'd taken his money to buy "equipment for the raid." What equipment? Maybe the money was for bribes to get the Redeyes out from under the noses of their guards.

They'd taken away his KL-43 at the last minute, just before the moment came when he had wanted to start asking questions. Mendoza had set him up with Francesca when his services were important. After he'd done his part, Francesca had disappeared. Now, Ascher guessed, Mendoza had set her up with Coronel. All of it was beginning to fit.

The Valium was beginning to kick in. He closed his eyes again. It wasn't going to do much good to find Mendoza now. If all this was true, he'd probably vanished already anyway.

Maybe the thing to do was go back and tell the truth. Clear his name. Explain himself to his father . . .

He sighed. Bolivia could be a nice place. He liked La Paz. Or Santa Cruz, where the cocaine kingpins lived. They certainly had a BMW dealership there. And the drug barons would need places to buy fancy stereos and Dolby Surround Sound televisions. He could buy a little ranch the way the drug dealers did. With U.S. dollars, he could live like a king. He could start building his tan again.

Women would flock to him . . .

"Ladies and gentlemen," the flight attendant said, "we'll be on the ground shortly. For those of you leaving us here in Miami, thank you for flying Eastern, and have a pleasant stay. Through passengers to Guayaquil and La Paz, we'll be on the ground forty-five minutes. The United States Customs Service requests that everyone leave the plane during the stop. Please be sure to take your boarding passes with you."

As they stood in the aisle waiting for the door to open, the woman behind Ascher muttered to the man next to her, "What do we have to get off for?"

"Beats me," the man said.

Ascher had taken a third Valium. He was feeling pretty good now. Calm. He turned back to them and matter-of-factly said: "Routine. Customs checks the plane for drug smuggling. Bolivia's a drug-producing country." He remembered that from his last job. While they waited in the lounge, Customs would sweep through the plane.

But the woman gave Ascher a funny look and shook her head. Ascher turned back wondering what that was about. Sometimes the Valium slurred his voice. But he hadn't taken much so far this morning. Only fifteen milligrams. That was another good thing about Bolivia. Valium was sold over the counter. He was almost down to the last two bottles from Honduras, the ones Mendoza had given him.

They were walking down the ramp when he heard the woman muttering again. "Who's ever heard of smuggling drugs *to* a place like Bolivia?"

Through the drug haze it didn't register for a minute. He was already at the end of the ramp, stepping into the B concourse, when he stopped in place. The person behind bumped into his back.

Customs checks planes coming *into* Miami from drug-producing countries like Bolivia, not planes going out. How could he have gotten that confused? So, why were they getting off the plane now? But then he saw the answer. Ten feet away, two men in dark suits were scrutinizing the passengers getting off the plane and then looking down at a card or something each of them cradled in his hand. Photos?

One of the men looked right at Ascher, glanced back down at his hand, up at Ascher again, and then tapped the other man on the shoulder, nodding Ascher's way. A second later they were standing on either side of him. Each grabbed an elbow.

"Mr. Ascher?" Ascher didn't answer.

"FBI. Would you come with us, please?"

With a firm grip on his arms, they led him right across the bright lobby and immediately onto another Eastern jet leaving in ten minutes for National Airport in Washington. Since the FBI was buying, they sat in coach.

"Am I under arrest?" Ascher asked as soon as they sat down. He had the middle seat.

"We have the authority to arrest you, Mr. Ascher," one of them said. "There are charges prepared if necessary. But at this point you are wanted for questioning, and we are hoping you will cooperate with us."

Ascher didn't say anything. He folded his arms, leaned his seat back, and closed his eyes. It took him only a few minutes to make up his mind.

Mendoza had tricked him. Used him. Goddamnit, he wasn't going to be the one who took the fall. He was going to tell everything. He'd admit his small part right up front. That helped with credibility. Then he'd answer every question, even the embarrassing ones. It had worked for John Dean in Watergate. Dean had been a hero of sorts, a star. He made lots of money on the college lecture circuit. And he certainly had a beautiful wife.

Ascher could see himself on national television, testifying before a Senate committee. He'd open his green eyes wide and speak in earnest tones. Yes, he was pained by all that had happened, deeply troubled by even his own small role.

He'd be on the cover of *Time*. His photo, standing in the Senate hearing room, his right arm raised as he took the oath, would run at the top of the front page in *The New York Times*.

Publishers would start calling with book contracts. The *Today* show, *Nightline*. Maybe the president would ask him in to thank him for coming forward—an honest man who erred.

A little later one of the FBI agents looked down at Ascher. He seemed to be asleep. The agent reached over and tapped his partner on the shoulder, then pointed at their charge, mouthing, "Look at that." Ascher lay back, arms crossed, eyes closed. But across his face was a broad grin.

Reporters and cameramen were crowding the sidewalk outside Ascher's home. They pushed lenses and tape recorders at his face as he stepped out of the car, but an agent on each arm pushed him quickly up the sidewalk.

"Mr. Ascher, Mr. Ascher, did you really plot to start the war?"

"Where's your buddy Mendoza now?"

"Where were you going this morning?"

"What are you going to do now?"

Ascher had thought about how to handle this, and he didn't say anything. He raised his chin, looked straight ahead, and tried to appear concerned but confident. That was the right expression. And in just a few seconds they were through the front door.

The two agents pushed him inside and then stepped back out, closing the door behind them. Suddenly Ascher was standing alone in his front hall. The noise behind him was receding as the reporters moved back to the street. But then three men in dark suits stepped out of his living room. One of them walked up and offered his hand.

"Mr. Ascher, I'm Louis Sheehan, assistant attorney general in the Justice Department's Office of Legal Counsel. May we talk for a moment?"

They moved into the living room, and as soon as they sat down Sheehan started his pitch—possible leniency in exchange for full cooperation. But Ascher cut him off.

"Mr. Sheehan, I didn't do anything, and—"

"Mr. Ascher, I would have to advise you at this point not to make statements without speaking to an attorney first."

"I don't need a lawyer," Ascher said. "I've done nothing wrong. I was fooled just like you were, and I'm going to tell everything." Sheehan and his aides gave each other startled looks.

"I want to rest now. But come back tomorrow morning. We'll get started then."

Sheehan gave a surprised smile. "Well, okay, I am glad to hear it," he said as the three of them stood up. "You're doing the right thing."

"I have nothing to hide."

"We'll be back at nine o'clock tomorrow. Okay?"

"I look forward to it."

In the front hall Sheehan turned to Ascher and said, "You should get a lawyer now, you know. You have to."

"I will," Ascher said as he closed the front door.

He was excited. This was going to be great. About three in the afternoon the doorbell rang, and when he opened the door somebody slid his suitcases inside. Out on the street the photographers were in a frenzy, firing off as many shots as they could, expecting Ascher to close the door right away. But instead he stepped out on the porch, smiling and waving at them. The whirring and clacking of cameras sounded almost like an ovation. Then he went back inside and shut the door.

He wondered why nobody called, not even Linda, but remembered that he'd unplugged all the telephones the night before.

That was just as well for now. Still, he reconnected the phone in the kitchen long enough to call his old college friend Arnie Crowell, now a hot criminal lawyer with offices on K Street. Crowell wanted to come over right away, but Ascher didn't want to be bothered. He told Crowell the story in outline over the phone.

"Just come tomorrow at nine, and we'll talk a little bit before everything gets started," Ascher said. "It'll be okay."

When he unpacked the suitcases a little later, it was obvious somebody had gone through them. But everything was there, even his illegal bottles of Honduran Valium, still sealed. By dusk the photographers were gone, though he knew they'd be back in the morning. He was looking forward to watching the TV news to see how he was playing so far. Surely the idea that he was going to cooperate would have leaked out by now. And the shots of him smiling and waving on the front step would be a nice touch. He must be the talk of Washington by now.

He hadn't had any lunch, and a little after six he was in the kitchen eating a turkey sandwich, watching the clock inch toward six-thirty, when the first TV news show would be on. The doorbell rang again. He put the sandwich down and went to answer it. The FBI agent on the porch told him, "You've got a visitor."

"Who?" Ascher asked, but the agent just pointed down the sidewalk. It was beginning to grow dark, and at first Ascher didn't recognize the figure moving slowly, painfully, up the walk, leaning heavily on a walker.

"He says he's your father," the agent said, and Ascher sucked in his breath as if in pain.

"You okay?" the agent asked. But Ascher didn't answer. He barely heard. He stared at the head of white hair. Wallace was looking down at his feet as he struggled to push the walker a few inches at a time. A uniformed nurse stood at the curb, arms crossed as she leaned back against the car, looking on.

Ascher watched with dread. His body sagged, his shoulders slumped. The whole scene began to disappear behind a haze.

Finally Wallace made it to the front step and looked up for the first time—at the agent, not at Ascher. But Ascher stepped down to take his father's elbow. Instantly Wallace tore his arm out of Ascher's grip. Ascher pulled his hand back as if it had been burned. His father looked up at the agent, who immediately stepped down and helped Wallace up the stairs.

Walking almost like a robot, Ascher went into the living

room, plopped down on a sofa, and stared with unfocused eyes toward the dining room. When he heard his father's walker scraping across the marble front hall, he reached into his shirt pocket, pulled out the last two Valiums there, and swallowed both of them without water.

He didn't look as his father dragged himself across the room and with a heavy sigh fell into a chair across from him. Neither of them said anything, but after a moment Ascher turned slowly to his father and tried to focus on his face. He saw just what he expected; Wallace glared at him with his brutal, pursed-lip grimace.

"How could you do this?" he snapped, his voice hoarse with anger. "How could you do this to yourself, to your family?"

"Father, I didn't . . ." But Ascher couldn't finish. He slumped forward, looking at the floor. His arms were wrapped tight around his stomach, and he started to rock, up and down, up and down.

"Father . . ."

But Wallace wasn't saying anything now. Ascher's eyes were closed. His ears buzzed in the silence. Then, after a moment, he stopped rocking and froze, still bent over, his head between his legs. Across from him, Wallace Ascher was speaking in a hoarse whisper.

"A monster," he was saying, seeming to speak only to himself. "How could I have created such a monster? How could I have loosed this creature on the world?"

Sheehan showed up at nine the next morning, right on time. He brought along a retinue of agents, assistants, stenographers, and two court reporters with their portable machines. The agent on duty at the door rang the bell, and they all waited. No one answered. The agent rang two more times and then pounded the knocker. As they stood there, photographers out on the street fired away. After a minute the agent used his key and stepped inside.

"Mr. Ascher?" he shouted up the steps. No answer. He turned and gestured the group inside. A moment later there was another knock, and Arnie Crowell, Ascher's lawyer, stepped inside too. All of them stood awkwardly in the front hall.

"Must have overslept," Sheehan said.

"Who can blame him?" quipped one of his assistants.

The FBI agent started upstairs but stopped after only a few steps, turning his head to listen. He gestured for everyone to be quiet and then bent his head over the railing, turning his ear to the floor.

"Wait here, please," he told the group as he came back down and headed for the back steps. As he went down the stairs, he reached under his jacket and pulled out his revolver.

The sound was coming from the video room in the back, and the agent moved toward it cautiously, gun ready.

He turned the corner and relaxed when he looked down the hall into the room. It was a tape, playing on the big screen. A war movie, from the sound of it. No wonder Ascher couldn't hear the doorbell. He had it turned up loud.

The agent shook his head. Who'd want to watch a war movie at nine in the morning? But then obviously this Ascher guy was one weird character. This was probably the least of it.

He stepped to the doorway.

"Mr. Ascher?" No answer. "Mr. Ascher, you have company."

Except for the screen, the room was dark. He recognized the film, *Apocalypse Now*. It had just ended. As the credits flashed, napalm burst across the screen. The explosions reverberated through speakers circling the room. Just then the tape ended, the recorder started to rewind. The room was quiet and dark now.

"Mr. Ascher?" the agent whispered in the sudden silence. "It's the FBI. You have visitors upstairs. Mr. Ascher?"

After a minute, he reached over and flipped on the lights, took one look and froze. The back of the sofa faced him. On the table in front of the couch—little brown glass bottles, tops off, cotton packing swabs beside them. A half-empty brandy snifter sitting on a piece of note paper. The agent stared for a long time.

Then the video tape wound back to the beginning and automatically started playing again. Huey helicopter noises reverberated around the room. The agent looked down.

There, hanging off the end of the sofa. An arm. Limp. Dead.

Ascher's death was listed as a suicide. There was a note, and under District of Columbia law that made it official. But nobody ever really knew for sure.

First, there was the tone of the suicide note: "I have done nothing wrong. I will be vindicated in heaven. And eventually I will be proved innocent here on earth."

People determined to be proved innocent usually don't kill themselves, the FBI experts said.

Then there was the matter of the pills, two brown bottles of

Honduran Valium, "25 *comprimidos*" in each, according to the labels. Paper seals and cotton packing lay on the table beside them—apparently both bottles had been full before they were opened. But Ascher didn't take all fifty pills. No, he counted out exactly thirty-seven of them and then put the others back in the bottle.

Thirty-seven was a number that might stick in the mind of a regular Valium user. When a well-known government official had tried to commit suicide after he got in trouble a few years ago, he'd taken exactly thirty-seven pills. It had been in all the papers. He didn't die, and he got a lot of sympathy when it was all over. The public's attitude toward him seemed to improve right away.

But Ascher had been drinking brandy. No two people are the same; identical dosages have different effects on different people, especially when the wild card of alcohol is thrown in. With Valium it's chancy. You can never tell.

Most of the FBI agents on the case thought it was a sympathy attempt that backfired. But it wasn't the odd note or the carefully counted pills that made up their minds. If only those two facts had leaked to the newspapers, the final public opinion of Terrence Whitfield Ascher might have been somewhat more charitable.

No, it was the classified report from the FBI forensics lab that tipped the balance in most people's minds and formed Terrence Ascher's pathetic legacy.

"If Terrence Ascher had really wanted to kill himself by poison," the report said, "he didn't have to rely on the known unpredictable effects of Valium. He had an infallible means readily at hand."

When the FBI searched Ascher's effects, they found a little brown plastic capsule in his wallet. It was filled, the forensics report said, "with CIA-issue cyanide."

"It is our conclusion," the report said, "that Terry Ascher never intended to kill himself. He miscalculated. It was a sympathy manuever that backfired."

Rafael Mendoza's Valium may have taken his life. But it was the smiling Cuban's cyanide that destroyed him.

EPILOGUE

THE AMERICAN PEOPLE HAD ALMOST UNANIMOUSLY supported the invasion. In the first several days, approval ratings approached 90 percent. The only groups that came out as unequivocally opposed were the American Friends Service Committee and Witness for Peace. Even Senator Robert Kelly, who was running against the president, found he had little choice but to give it his grudging approval.

Then, a month later, the invasion conspiracy shook the country. Overnight the public approval rate fell by more than half. Within twenty-four hours, Kelly had picked up the scandal as a campaign issue. With this, he figured, victory in November was assured.

On national television the day the story broke, the president announced he was appointing a special investigative commission. He told it to "get all the facts out . . . leave no stone unturned." A respected former senator from Illinois was named chairman and promised that he and the others would be "tough, absolutely uncompromising."

Both the Senate and the House of Representatives formed investigative committees of their own. They hired New York lawyers, opened offices, requested classified White House documents and computer tapes, and said they would be subpoenaing witnesses until the end of the year. And of course a special prosecutor was named.

But somehow none of it quite seemed to take off.

Terrence Ascher was dead. The main player, Rafael Mendoza, had disappeared without a trace. The government was looking for him, of course, but everyone knew that a trained intelligence officer could remain missing just about as long as he chose. So the only member of the troika left was Marine Colonel Eric Gustafson, and he wasn't going to make the prosecutors' job any easier. Far from it.

The day after the New World story was published, without being asked, Gustafson flew up to Miami on his way to Washington. With his wife at his side, he walked right up to the reporters and cameramen waiting for him at the gate. The colonel was in uniform now, a Marine. He stood tall, short blond hair shining, battle ribbons glinting as he looked directly into the cameras.

"We made mistakes," he began in a deep, determined voice. "As in all wars there were casualties. I mourn for ours. But we did what no one else had the courage to do. We took risks, and we rid this great land of a Communist blight on our doorstep. And we gave our God-fearing neighbors in Nicaragua back their freedom. Of that, ladies and gentlemen, I stand here and tell you I am not ashamed."

Gustafson lifted his chin then, his jaw set firm, and looked around at the crowd. Beside him, his wife wiped her eyes. The reporters peppered him with questions; off-camera they sounded like a flock of crows up in a tree. Finally Gustafson gave a confident grin and told them, "Folks, I'd love to stay here and chat with you awhile. But me and the little lady have got to go catch another plane." Then he waved, wrapped his arm around his wife's shoulders, and strode off to another gate.

Of course that tape played on the news shows for weeks. It was electric. Gustafson was in Washington now, closeted with Connecticut Avenue lawyers who were coaching him on how to be an effective congressional witness. As if he needed coaching.

The colonel was the only firsthand witness left, but soon the story leaked out that the congressional committees were searching for legal reasons *not* to have him testify in public. Already they were beaten.

After only six weeks, the special White House commission cleared the president of any direct responsibility and offered several carefully worded recommendations. The president promised to act on all of them.

The Senate and House investigative committees never seemed to get around to putting on public hearings, with or without

Gustafson, and soon the congressional term was going to expire. With it the investigations would die.

Then, in November, the president won reelection. The vote was close; if a couple of big states had gone the other way, Senator Kelly would have been elected. But the invasion conspiracy had been at the center of Kelly's campaign strategy, and as it turned out, the public just didn't want to hear about it anymore. Analysts suggested that Americans had grown weary of government scandals. It wasn't that nobody cared exactly, but there'd been so many of them.

Long before the elections, surveys measuring the public's view of the invasion showed that the approval rate had started creeping back up little by little. It was not a new ground swell; certainly no one said he liked the idea of shooting down American helicopters and executing a dozen U.S. servicemen. But in many people's minds, all of that grew to be obscured somehow by the notion that, even if mistakes were made, the United States had brought freedom to a grateful neighbor.

Leslie never returned to her White House job. Her name had been mentioned in the news reports. Though she wasn't really notorious, she knew her government career was over, so she didn't even try to go back.

Right away she left her husband. Actually, Wyche kicked her out, furious about her affair with Eaton and afraid his wife's association with the scandal, even indirect, would ruin his career too. He paid her off, in essence. It was just as well. She was more than ready to leave, and with the settlement money she moved into an apartment a few blocks down the street from Eaton's.

Slowly Leslie stopped seeing her friends. The first week, her friend Stephanie had raised her eyebrows and chirped, "Honey, I never *knew* you had this other side to you." And as it turned out, most of her friends seemed to believe she'd led a double life, duping them for years.

In truth, she did feel different. Helping Eaton with that story—investigating, giving him critical information that made the story work—she had felt for the first time in her life that she was doing something important, instead of typing letters, filing papers, and nodding agreeably, even to requests she knew were bad ideas. For the first time, in her own way she'd been a policymaker of sorts.

But what had all the important work accomplished? The

country didn't seem to care. Worst of all was seeing what it had done to the man she'd grown to love.

Abel gave Eaton a full-pay medical leave for as long as he wanted, and he did not recover quickly. He was in the hospital more than a month, and the doctors warned that he would require a long convalescence, both physical and emotional. The day Leslie brought him home, a staff psychiatrist had taken her aside and advised, "Debilitating shooting injuries, especially in highly charged circumstances like this one, can lead to serious depression. He's going to need all your help, your affection."

That was fine with Leslie. She wasn't feeling her best either, and maybe helping Eaton come back to life would revive her own spirits.

When Eaton got home, his right leg was in a cast all the way up to the groin, and he was so weak he could barely move or speak. First it was the drugs and the pain. But when his physical condition slowly improved, his mental state did not.

The psychiatrist had advised Leslie not to tell Eaton what was going on in the outside world during his first few weeks at home. But by mid-June, Leslie decided it was time to start bringing him up-to-date. She'd been saving the newspaper clippings, and one afternoon she laid the file on his bed while he napped.

The stories talked about Gustafson's TV appearance, the failed investigations, and the growing American indifference toward the scandal. There were the surveys on America's view of the invasion, showing the dramatic drop in the approval rating after Eaton's story ran and the gradual climb back up, until it finally settled in at close to 60 percent.

When Leslie went back upstairs a couple of hours later the clippings lay in a pile on the floor. Eaton's eyes were closed. His face seemed locked in a grimace of grief. Leslie gazed at him for a moment, then quietly turned around and went back downstairs.

They didn't speak much in the normal course of a day. But one afternoon, when she brought him lunch on a tray, Eaton looked up at her and whispered, "Nothing we did matters. Nobody really cares, do they?" She just patted him on the arm and turned around to go back downstairs. But then she stopped and said, "Chris, life goes on. We've got to get our lives moving again."

A couple of weeks later a little story got into the papers saying Eaton was returning to full health. Doctors reported that they had removed the cast. Almost right away Eaton got letters from

The New York Times, The Washington Post, and others. They wanted to talk to him about jobs. *Nightline* and *Meet the Press* wrote to say they wanted him as a guest. But when Leslie read him the requests, Eaton whispered, "Maybe when I'm better." Frowning, she put the letters aside.

The next day she stood over his bed, hands on her hips, and told him, "You've got to get some help. We can't continue like this." But he just looked up at her with that hurt look of his. She felt guilty right away and went back downstairs.

Shortly after that, Leslie stopped coming over every day. Eaton had started using crutches and didn't need so much help. Besides, he didn't really seem to care if she was there or not. In fact, sometimes he seemed irritated by her presence. As softly as she could she kept trying to convince him that he had to start his life moving again, that he should get help if he needed it. But he'd just snap at her, "You don't understand. You can't." And with each new discussion, he seemed to grow more resentful.

One morning she came over to make him breakfast, but he was already up, leaning on his crutches before the stove. She walked up to him and tried to take the spatula from his hand, but he pulled his arm away.

"I don't need your help now," he growled. "Just leave me alone."

Leslie stepped back and looked at him; frowning, he kept his eyes on the frying pan. After a moment, she sighed.

"See you later," she said. Then she left.

When he thought about it in the following weeks, Eaton missed her. Every once in a while he picked up her telephone in the bedroom and felt reassured to hear the dial tone. But he didn't call her. One warm evening in August he did see her, across Connecticut Avenue, eating dinner at an outdoor café with a man who, as Eaton watched, reached over and touched Leslie on the hand. Eaton looked away.

Eaton returned to work on a cold, gray day in November, shortly after Election Day. He walked leaning on a cane, and on the way to his office the cane kept slipping on the wet leaves that covered the sidewalks. Doctors said his limp would improve in time, and at Eaton's request, Abel put him on the night copy desk, "until you're back to full strength."

The job was mindless. New World copy editors just wrote headlines, a mechanical task, and corrected spelling. Eaton showed up on time every day, and the other copy editors loved

having him on the desk. He didn't mind taking the weekend
hours and the holidays. At home he usually slept late, sometimes
until noon. He'd eat soup or something for lunch, and then it
would be almost time to go to work. He'd get home after one
in the morning, watch a late movie, then sleep until noon the
next day.

Abel tried talking to him sometimes.

"Chris, come on, get some help if you need to. We'll pay for
it. But you've just got to snap out of this."

Eaton would give a pale smile and say, "I will, Walt," then
limp back to his desk.

In the spring Eaton won a Pulitzer Prize, for Meritorious Public Service. The jury cited his "courage and willingness to bring
the American people the truth, whether or not they liked it, even
at the risk of his own life."

Eaton was still on the copy desk then. He no longer needed
his cane, though he still walked with a slight limp. Winning the
prize seemed to lift his spirits a bit. Again he got letters from
the *Times* and the *Post*. *Washingtonian* magazine said it would
like to do a profile. Eaton didn't answer the letters. But instead
of putting them upstairs in the desk drawer, this time he left
them out on the dining-room table.

Columbia University held a ceremony for the Pulitzer winners
in New York every year. Eaton sat at the head table with the
others. There were speeches through the luncheon; then the
moderator went down the table, introducing the winners one by
one, and each stood up and smiled. Just before it was Eaton's
turn, he nervously brushed his forelock back into place.

During the keynote speech, Eaton looked out at the crowd.
He knew a few of the people, but most were strangers. Then at
a table off to the far left he saw Leslie. She was looking at him
and smiled. He smiled back, but then they both looked away,
embarrassed. After the ceremony, he ran into her out by the elevators.

"It's good to see you, Chris. How are you?"

"Okay, I guess. Better. Thanks for coming up."

"I wouldn't miss it. I wanted to call when I read about it,
but . . ."

Eaton nodded. Almost involuntarily he glanced down at her
left hand. She wasn't wearing any rings. Then he looked up at
Leslie, and her brown eyes warmed him again.

"You going now?" he asked.

"Yeah."

"You want to go uptown and get a cup of coffee?"

"Sure," she said.

They got into the crowded elevator and then walked together out of the building, down the street to look for a taxi. Neither of them said anything. Eaton looked down at the sidewalk. But then as they walked along, Eaton found that he was smiling gently to himself. Through the corner of his eye he saw that Leslie was smiling ever so slightly too.

Without looking up, slowly Eaton reached over and took her hand.

If the preferred American view of the invasion was that the United States had brought freedom to a grateful neighbor, there was no question that Nicaragua was overflowing with gratitude.

American aid started pouring into Managua, and the standard of living began to improve for everyone, particularly for those in the new government. A few officers from the State Department and the U.S. Agency for International Development complained that some of the aid money seemed to be disappearing. But from the President's House up on the hill, Coronel explained that if there were any disparities, that was because of the military's growing needs. After all, up in the Highlands the Sandinista rebels were becoming more and more aggressive, while in Managua the number of "Communist terrorist acts," as President Coronel liked to call them, seemed to increase with each passing week.

The Sandinista government in exile was promising war in perpetuity, and from Havana, Minister Zelaya was spewing torrents of bile-laden venom. To one recent interviewer he'd said, "We are the ghosts of Sandino, and we will kill and kill and kill some more until we drive the harlequin fools and their bloodthirsty imperialist masters from our home."

A couple of weeks after Eaton's story broke, Jorge Paladino resigned from the government "for personal reasons" and moved to Miami. He gave no interviews, but word leaked out that he was unhappy with the way Free Nicaragua's new government was developing. An unnamed friend quoted in La Prensa said he had been complaining about "the increasing totalitarian tilt."

In Managua, President Coronel called that "part of a new disinformation campaign by enemies of the counterrevolution." Now, he announced, he was really going to get tough on the

Communists. Special government security troops rounded up several dozen people and hauled them off to El Chipote. Colonel Paz was in command of the operation. Among those arrested were two men who had said they planned to run against Coronel in the upcoming election.

When Balita finally finished his government interviews in Washington, he flew home to Free Nicaragua. Several Nicaraguan reporters tried to interview him at the airport, but Balita told them he wanted a few days of rest first. "I've been talking for two weeks," he complained. But several days later, when a *La Prensa* reporter tried to look him up, Balita was nowhere to be found. No one knew where he'd gone. The government hypothesized that he'd just melted into the countryside somewhere. But *La Prensa* wrote that he'd become "another disappeared." "Disappeared" had first been used as a noun in El Salvador and Guatemala, where it referred to people spirited away by rightwing death squads.

Coronel postponed the elections twice, saying "The growing Communist insurgency makes holding truly free elections impossible." But his opponents attacked him, and finally he set a date. The elections were held four months late, and to no one's surprise Coronel won by a wide margin. When losing candidates studied the electoral commission's records, they howled. The opposition claimed that the vote totals for Coronel exceeded the total number of registered voters in all of Nicaragua. One candidate found that his own mother had voted for Coronel three different times. She'd been dead since 1977.

There were muted whispers of criticism in the United States, but Americans figured that some voting irregularities were to be expected in Latin America. At least the Nicaraguans were holding elections now, and after everything America had done to bring democracy to Nicaragua, people were quick to forgive the "imperfections."

A few weeks after the election, Sandinista commandos snuck into Managua and blew up the newly rebuilt Los Mártires electrical substation, blacking out half of the city. It was their first successful urban raid. Analysts said it signaled a significant escalation in the insurgency.

The government was furious. From the President's House came word: Now we're really going to crack down. President Coronel imposed a new state of emergency and ordered more arrests. *La Prensa* attacked him, but the United States responded by approving more military aid. The insurgency had to be crushed. There was even talk of giving the New Army support from the F-16 Tactical Fighter Wing now stationed at the big American air base at Punta Huete.

Early one morning a couple of weeks after the raid, Mrs. Carrión, the editor of *La Prensa*, sat alone in her kitchen when the president—General Coronel, he liked to call himself now—stopped by unexpectedly. She offered him coffee, but he waved it away.

"Señora," he told her, "you have been publishing articles sympathetic to the enemies of the counterrevolution. I am afraid that, starting today, you are going to have to submit every article for official government review."

"No, no," Mrs. Carrión said, standing up. "You can't censor us. You just can't do this!"

"I'm afraid we must."

"How can you get away with this?" she shrieked, near panic now. "What about international public opinion? You just can't get away with this!"

"But señora," General Coronel said, his voice matter-of-fact. "We are at war."

NOTES

CHAPTER 1
The Los Mártires electrical substation is fictional, but in 1986 and 1987 the CIA did provide contra sabotage squads with old maps and blueprints of Nicaraguan dams, bridges, utilities, and other infrastructure built by the U.S. Agency for International Development and the Army Corp of Engineers during the Somoza regime.

CHAPTER 2
Minister Zelaya is a fictional character, but his line "The imperialist circus masters are telling us: Drop dead, or we'll shoot you" is a paraphrase of a quotation from Nicaragua's foreign minister, Miguel d'Escoto Brockman. When the Reagan administration offered a Nicaragua "peace plan" of sorts in April 1985, d'Escoto remarked, "What President Reagan has said is: 'Drop dead, or I will kill you.' "

For several years, military attachés at the United States embassy in Managua did interview citizens on the street and send optimistic reports back to Washington, suggesting that a military victory would be easy and that most Nicaraguans would welcome U.S. "liberators." On occasion, an attaché was brought to Washington to brief senior government officials. One of those attachés, whose views were shared with the National Security Council, told a reporter at the time that while attacking Nicaragua was not a good idea "from a propaganda point of view," an invasion would be easy, "like falling off a log."

CHAPTER 3
The United States spent years threatening and cajoling the Bahamas to sign a Mutual Legal Assistance Treaty. When the Bahamas finally agreed in 1987, the United States was reluctant to sign the treaty, saying the Bahamian regulations implementing it were inadequate.

On several occasions, United States Army Blackhawk helicopters ferrying Bahamian police to drug arrest sites were stoned and fired upon by angry Bahamians.

The contra program was managed in the broad sense by a Restricted Interagency Group, a RIG, with one or two members each from the State Department, the Defense Department, the National Security Council, and the CIA as well as other officers at various times. The RIG members were not congressional appointees, and some of them, including Lieutenant Colonel Oliver North, were in fact true ideologues. However, the RIG was not intended to direct specific military operations. That was left to the CIA.

CHAPTER 4
During President Reagan's vacations in Santa Barbara, members of the White House press corps from the major media did set up "tong" dinners that tended to exclude reporters from smaller news organizations. But in the final year of his presidency, the system fell apart because most of the new White House officials weren't much interested in being taken to dinner.

CHAPTER 5
Almost as a matter of routine, Sandinista military convoys driving in the Highlands waved strangers' cars ahead, hoping they'd be the first to hit any mines that had been laid on the road.

CHAPTER 6
The contras did seize a large tract of wilderness territory in north central Nicaragua, on the border about seven miles south of their main camp in Honduras. They named it El Cuartelón, "the Fortress," and managed to hold on to it for long periods, though at times the Sandinistas were able to take it back. Once, the Sandinistas flew American reporters up to the territory for a press tour.

CHAPTER 7
During the early years, at least, the contras often executed prisoners taken in ambushes and raids. (The Sandinistas undoubtedly executed prisoners too.) In later years, the United States provided special funds for "human rights" training of the contras, to end those and other abuses.

The United States delivered Redeye antiaircraft rockets to the contras beginning in 1986, and as a result, the guerrillas were successful in shooting down several Sandinista helicopters, including MI-24 Hind attack copters that had been effective in routing contra forces.

CHAPTER 8
The U. S. embassy in Tegucigalpa, Honduras, actually had two CIA stations. One handled the normal intelligence duties and the other managed the contra program. Most of the CIA officers maintained covers as embassy political officers, giving little Honduras one of the biggest U.S. embassy offices of political affairs in the world. But the chief of the CIA station managing the contras was believed to have been under deeper cover, perhaps as a businessman in Tegucigalpa.

Congress and the Defense Department frequently argued over the real purpose of the Palmerola "temporary" military base in Honduras. Members of Congress accused the Pentagon of trying to equip Palmerola as if it were a major foreign base, despite the huts and the tents. The suspicion was that the Defense Department wanted a forward base in case the day ever came when the United States launched an invasion.

CHAPTER 10

U.S. government officials often debated sending the contras on high-profile urban operations patterned in a rough sense on Edén Pastora's raid on the National Palace. CIA director William J. Casey was reported to have favored the idea. But the CIA officers running the program at the time didn't believe the contras were capable of carrying out that sort of operation successfully. Instead, the CIA hired Hispanic mercenaries to mine Nicaragua's harbors, among other actions, and tried to give credit (or blame) to the contras. Edgar Chamorro, a member of the second contra Directorate until he quit in 1984, recalled being awakened early one morning by a CIA officer who ordered him to read a radio script saying the contras had been the ones who mined Nicaragua's harbors.

CHAPTER 11

Under several administrations the White House has on occasion issued broad public denials of stories in the news media—"knockdowns"—while privately confirming to reporters that the stories were correct.

CHAPTER 13

La Prensa, Nicaragua's only independent newspaper, has played a major role in Nicaraguan history for more than a decade. The paper's difficulties have also influenced U.S. policy.

When the paper grew aggressively anti-Somoza in 1978, its editor, Pedro Joaquín Chamorro, was assassinated. General Somoza was widely assumed to have ordered the murder, though he denied any role in it. The public was outraged. Chamorro's murder and Edén Pastora's raid on the National Palace that same year were the two principal events galvanizing the Nicaraguan public to push for Somoza's downfall. The murder also helped turn the Carter administration against Somoza, who had been one of America's staunchest allies.

The Sandinistas have at times censored *La Prensa*, reduced its newsprint allotment, or closed it altogether. The government's repression of Nicaragua's free press, as much as any other single act, helped convince Congress to provide aid for the contras.

In the early 1980s, the United States did carry out what the government called a perception-management program to keep the Sandinistas afraid the United States might attack. At least once,

in November 1984, SR-71 Blackbird surveillance aircraft based
at Palmerola were sent over Managua to set off sonic booms.

In March 1986, the United States ordered the Honduran government to accept $20 million in "emergency" military aid after
Sandinista troops crossed the border briefly to attack the contras.
The Hondurans didn't want to take the money; accepting it was
a tacit admission that the contras were in fact based in Honduras. At that time the Hondurans liked to pretend that the contra
base was actually on Nicaraguan territory. But in the end they
did take the money.

CHAPTER 15
"Bright Lights" was an operation carried out near the border
of Libya and intended to intimidate Muammar Qaddafi, the Lib-
yan leader. No such operation was ever carried out in Central
America.

CHAPTER 18
When the Sandinistas crossed the Honduran border to attack
the contras in 1986, the U.S. Army airlifted Honduran troops
to the area of the fighting aboard Huey and Chinook helicopters.
But by the time the Honduran troops got there, the Sandinistas
had already crossed back into Nicaragua. U.S. forces airlifted
Hondurans to the border once again in the spring of 1988, to
deal with another Sandinista border incursion.

CHAPTER 19
If the United States ever did decide to attack Nicaragua without
warning, existing contingency plans call for helicopter-borne
Delta Force officers to fly in from the Pacific and evacuate embassy personnel more or less as described here. One plan did call
for gathering everyone together at a Casa Grande "party" so the
Delta Force helicopters would have to visit only one extraction
point. It's unlikely, however, that the ambassador and his senior
staff would be left behind, precisely because it is feared that they
would be taken hostage. Instead, if anyone remained, it would
be junior officers.

CHAPTER 20

United States policy in recent times has called for "proportionate" military responses to provocations. The bombing of Libya in 1986 and the shelling of an Iranian oil platform in the Persian Gulf the following year were examples. There were discussions, too, of "proportionate" attacks on Nicaragua in response to suspected or projected provocations. Once, the United States considered bombing a suspected "terrorist" training camp near Managua. But no such attacks were carried out.

CHAPTER 22

Should the United States ever invade Nicaragua, general plans drawn up long ago call for an armored assault through the Choluteca Gap in Honduras into northwestern Nicaragua with a fast injection of airborne troops behind enemy lines. Those troops would seize control of Sandino Airport or the 10,000-foot airstrip at Punta Huete so that C-130 troop airlifts could begin. While Sandinista troops were drawn to the fighting in the north, a Marine amphibious assault force assembled secretly at sea would land on the beaches west of Managua.

CHAPTER 23

Edgar Chamorro, the former contra Directorate member, first told the story of Adolfo Calero's selection as Directorate chairman and the CIA officer's quip: "Why don't all of you give a hand to the next president of Nicaragua."

Far from extracting pledges from contra leaders that they would not seize power if they defeated the Sandinistas, the CIA, when it picked that Directorate in 1983, told new officers they'd be in Managua governing Nicaragua within a year.

EPILOGUE

From the moment the Sandinista government took power in 1979, its leaders said they expected the United States to invade one day. And, as related here, the Sandinistas have promised to retreat to the hills, switching places with the contras, and to fight a guerrilla war for as long as necessary. American intelligence officials believe the Sandinistas have prepositioned significant quantities of military supplies in the Highlands for just that eventuality.

For the last five or six years, the White House has repeatedly warned that an invasion of Nicaragua would be the only option left if support for the contras is ended. Secretary of State George P. Shultz once warned that if Congress did not reapprove aid to the contras, "they are hastening the day when the threat will grow, and we will be faced with an agonizing choice about the use of U.S. combat troops." In a classified report to Congress, President Reagan once said that the use of military force in Nicaragua "must realistically be recognized as an eventual option in the region, if other policy alternatives fail."

Still, most analysts believe that the United States could be drawn into an invasion of Nicaragua only under an extraordinary set of circumstances—such, perhaps, as those related here.

About the Author

JOEL BRINKLEY began his journalistic career at the Charlotte, North Carolina, bureau of The Associated Press, after which he became a reporter at the Richmond *News Leader*. In 1978 he moved to the Louisville *Courier-Journal*, and in the following year he covered the Vietnamese invasion of Cambodia, an assignment that brought him a Pulitzer Prize for International Reporting. In 1983 he became a correspondent in the *New York Times*' Washington bureau and soon began covering Nicaragua and the contras. After traveling extensively in the region, Brinkley published a series of stories on U.S. military preparations for a possible invasion of Nicaragua. In April 1988 Brinkley became chief of the *New York Times*'s bureau in Jerusalem, Israel, where he now lives.

This is Joel Brinkley's first novel.